# The Handyman's Reality

by

Nick Poff

Bloomington, IN    Milton Keynes, UK
authorHOUSE®

AuthorHouse™
1663 Liberty Drive, Suite 200
Bloomington, IN 47403
www.authorhouse.com
Phone: 1-800-839-8640

AuthorHouse™ UK Ltd.
500 Avebury Boulevard
Central Milton Keynes, MK9 2BE
www.authorhouse.co.uk
Phone: 08001974150

© 2007 Nick Poff. All rights reserved.

No part of this book may be reproduced, stored in a retrieval system, or transmitted by any means without the written permission of the author.

First published by AuthorHouse 4/24/2007

ISBN: 978-1-4259-9746-5 (sc)
ISBN: 978-1-4259-9747-2 (hc)

Library of Congress Control Number: 2007902370

Printed in the United States of America
Bloomington, Indiana

This book is printed on acid-free paper.

Grateful acknowledgment is made to the following for permission to include copyrighted material:

**Kiss You All Over**
Written by: Michael Chapman/Nicholas Chinn
© 1979 **BMG Songs (ASCAP)**
All rights for the US administered by BMG Songs (ASCAP). Used by permission.
BMG Songs claims 100%

**Time**
Written by: Alan Parsons/Eric Woolfson
© 1981 **Careers-BMG Music Publishing (BMI) / Woolfsongs Ltd (PRS)**
All rights for the world on behalf of Woolfsongs Ltd (PRS) administered by Careers-BMG Music Publishing (BMI). Used by permission.
Careers-BMG Music Publishing claims 100%

ALSO BY NICK POFF:
*THE HANDYMAN'S DREAM*

# Acknowledgments

Here's a thank-you and a big hug to my wonderful friend, and promotional wingman, Blake Truex. Without your support, encouragement, and warm companionship, this book may not ever have been finished.

Once again it's my pleasure to say thanks to Edgar Huntington for his gentle suggestions, enthusiastic support, and general encouragement. Yeah, the boys are back, Edgarbear!

Many thanks go to friend and attorney Solomon L. Lowenstein, Jr., who shared his knowledge of the more obscure aspects of Indiana inheritance law, and to Beth Stevens as well, who not only sold me my dream house but also shared with me her real estate licensing experience.

With much gratitude I thank Paul and Mona Kioebge for the wonderful meals, the occasional peek into a master carpenter's workshop, and the kindness you both share with everyone you know.

Here's a shout-out to James Carson and Abel Law, my cohorts at www.writermen.com, and two of my favorite writing buddies. Your support and heartfelt encouragement have been a genuine blessing to this still wet-behind-the-ears novelist.

Many thanks go to Eileen Chetti for her wonderful editing work on the book's manuscript.

Thanks and the promise of more fresh catnip from "Auntie Cari" go to Ivan, who insisted on jumping into my lap during my moments of deepest concentration, lying on my desk when I was trying to type, and occasionally napping on the manuscript. I could have done it without you, but I'm glad I didn't have to.

The biggest thanks of all goes to the readers who embraced Ed and Rick and their story. Without your support and pleas for more of their saga, there would not have been a reason to send this book into the world.

# Dedication

In memory of Thomas M. Evans—childhood playmate and young adult guide into the labyrinth that is gay life. You are still deeply missed, my friend.

# THE HANDYMAN'S REALITY

## Chapter One

A bird was singing in his dream.

Ed Stephens's eyes slowly opened. Through the slits in his bedroom window blinds, he could see a cardinal sitting in the lilac bush outside the window. The red bird was cheerfully chirping his morning song.

Ed was getting over a nasty bout with the flu. He had to blink several times to make sure he really saw the cardinal, whom he'd nicknamed Mr. Redd, and to realize he was really in his own bed in his own bedroom. He'd had a few disorienting moments during the past week, and he wanted to be positive this was not a dream. Yes, that was Mr. Redd; yes, those were the same old blinds in the window; yes, that was his clock radio on the table next to the bed; and best of all, that hairy arm lying across his chest was really there, and it belonged to the man of his dreams, Rick Benton.

Ed heard, in addition to Mr. Redd's chirps, a soft snoring near his ear. He smiled. He recognized that snore, all right. It belonged to Rick as much as that hairy arm did. It was further evidence to support the fact that the man of his dreams was indeed real and was lying next to him.

Ed knew if he turned his head he'd see for himself that Rick was there, but there was one last thing he had to clarify in his mind. He thought back . . . let's see, according to the clock, about seven hours. Yes, that conversation with Rick had really occurred. It wasn't his flu fever talking. Rick had made the decision to move into Ed's house. They had made a serious commitment to each other. They were, for all intents and purposes, married.

Well, not really, of course, but they were married in Ed's mind. Let the heteros have their ceremonies, vows, blood tests, and cakes with plastic figurines. He'd never been overly impressed with those particular rituals. What mattered to Ed was the spoken commitment between two people to merge their lives into one. He didn't need a legal document and a clergyperson to marry him to Rick. He had Rick's word, and anyone who knew Rick Benton at all knew his word was more than good; it was genuinely golden.

So the man lying next to him wasn't his boyfriend anymore, right? He was . . . what? Ed frowned in thought, wondering whether it would be fair to steal the word *husband* from the heterosexuals. He remembered Rick once saying life wasn't fair, even, or equal, so he gleefully swiped the term. Okay, if he turned his head, he'd be looking at the man of his dreams who also happened to be his *husband*.

So Ed turned his head, and sure enough, there was the man with the hairy arm who was snoring in his ear. It was Rick. It was indeed his husband, the man he loved.

He studied Rick's face, wondering whether Rick was truly handsome, or whether his love for him only made him the handsomest man in the world in Ed's eyes. He carefully stroked Rick's thick, dark brown hair, noting that his equally dark brown beard seemed in need of a trim.

Rick sighed, and his very nearsighted brown eyes opened. His eyes blinked, attempting to focus. Once he seemed to realize he was looking at Ed, he smiled sleepily. "Hey, baby." The words came out as a rough whisper. "Whatcha doin'?"

Ed smiled back at him. "I was watching my husband, the handsomest man in the world, sleeping. That's all."

"Umm," Rick moaned, his eyes closing briefly as the arm across Ed's chest pulled Ed closer to him. "Why don't you hand me my glasses so I can get a good look at *my* husband, the other handsomest man in the world?"

"Ugh, the way I look? Still getting over the flu?" Ed reached for Rick's glasses on the bedside table. He reluctantly handed them over.

Rick fumbled his glasses onto his face and looked deeply into Ed's light brown eyes. He raised a finger to softly trace Ed's thick, sandy-colored mustache, as though in need of a reality test of his own. Ed's favorite smile, the one he privately referred to as "Rick's warm and tender special," spread over his face. "Sick or well, you look damn good to me." He pulled Ed to him for a sleepy, sweet kiss. "It's Sunday, isn't it? Thank God we don't have to get up until we want to."

Ed shifted so he could put his arms around Rick. "Yeah, it's Sunday. You married me about seven hours ago, just after midnight. Remember?"

"I sure do!" Rick kissed him again. "Sunday, April fifth, 1981 . . . hmmm. Seems to me I once got a fortune cookie that said I would marry the most wonderful man in the world on that day."

Ed snickered. "Did that cookie also tell you you'd have to move to Porterfield, Indiana, to find him?"

"Nope! They left that part out. Believe me, if I'd known I had to come here to find you, I would have been here a hell of a lot sooner."

"I'm just glad you got here." Ed brushed his fingers against Rick's slightly shaggy beard. "I mean, you are here, aren't you? I've always said you were the Dream Man, but I'm not dreaming this, am I?"

"If you are, so am I, and if that's the case, I don't ever want to wake up." Rick's smile broadened. He grabbed Ed's hand and squeezed it. "'Cause I've never been this happy before. You're my Dream Man, too. I don't know what I did to deserve you, but I'm sure glad I did it."

"Oh, I could list all your wonderful qualities, but I don't want you getting a swelled head." Ed returned the hand squeeze. "I almost can't believe it. We're really and truly together now." He looked around the room, then back at Rick. "So what do we do next?"

Rick was about to answer when the bedroom door, which had been left ajar, slowly opened. Their black cat, Jett, walked into the room. With one leap he was on the bed next to Rick. He stared at them with his yellow-green eyes for a moment and meowed to make sure they were aware of the fact he was in need of attention.

Rick pulled the cat to where they could both pet him. Jett began to purr and knead his claws on the comforter. "I guess the first thing we need to do is feed the cat." Rick tickled Jett's ears. "So much for the honeymoon."

"Well, after that, then," Ed persisted. "I've never been married before."

"Neither have I, really." Rick frowned. "That disaster with Jack doesn't count, in my opinion."

The mention of Rick's ex-lover reminded Ed of what had happened the night before. Jack had taken a bus from Indianapolis to Porterfield to see Rick on some apparently urgent matter. He had found his way to the home of Rick's sister, Claire Romanowski, where Rick had been living for the past nine months with Claire and her three children. Rick, though, had been at Ed's, as he had been for the past several days, looking after Ed while he had been sick. Rick had very reluctantly gone to see Jack, and all Ed knew from that point was that Rick had driven Jack back to Indianapolis, and on the drive home had made the decision to move in with Ed and make good on his earlier proposal of marriage.

Ed didn't really want to spoil the nice romantic moment they had in progress, but his curiosity got the better of him.

"You know, darlin'," Ed said to Rick, his eyes on Jett, "you never did tell me what happened with Jack last night."

Rick heaved a weary sigh. He rolled over and stared at the ceiling. " He just wanted what he always wants when things aren't going his way. He's alone and not happy about it, so he thought he could talk me into trying again."

He sighed again. "I s'pose it wasn't very nice of me, but I really rubbed it in about how much I loved you and what a good man you are. I told him I was prepared to spend the rest of my life doing my best to make you happy, and that as far as I was concerned, he was ancient history." Rick shrugged. "I think he got the message. I doubt he'll be bothering us again."

Ed saw that peculiar mix of emotion on Rick's face that always appeared when he talked about Jack. For the first time, though, it didn't bother or worry him. Ed knew Rick loved him and wanted their life together as much as he did. He realized Rick would probably spend the rest of his life regretting the time he felt he had wasted on Jack, even though Ed suspected those bad times had helped to shape the man he loved today.

"Enough about him," Rick said. He turned back to Ed, leaning over Jett to kiss him. "To answer your first question, I think now that we're married we're supposed to consummate it. I was just too damn tired from that long drive last night to do anything but sleep, and you haven't exactly been in the mood this week. However, someone needs to feed the cat, and frankly, I'm pretty hungry myself. How 'bout I give the cat some Tender Vittles, and then make my handyman husband some pancakes?"

"Deal." Ed threw the covers back, accidentally hitting Jett in the face. With one aggrieved meow, Jett jumped off the bed and stalked to the door. He gave them both a pointed look and marched off to the kitchen, obviously expecting them to follow him. "You know," said Ed, pulling on his tattered old bathrobe, "I spend most of my days doing odd jobs for cranky old people; then I come home to that cranky cat." He paused, and a look of wonder came to his face. "But now I get to come home to you. A part of me still can't believe it."

Rick reached for a pair of sweatpants and a sweatshirt he kept at Ed's house for Sunday morning breakfast preparation. "Well, now you've got a cranky husband to think about, too, but I'll do my best to keep the cranky part to a minimum."

"I'm not worried about it." Ed pulled Rick to him for another kiss. "I know how to de-crank a cranky husband—at least mine. Speaking of which, with my appetite for food coming back, I think my appetite for something else is coming back, too. I think I may be up to consummating our marriage before the day is over."

"Hmmm. Well, I'll add it to my schedule of activities for the day, along with telling you about forty times how much I love you." Rick's arms encircled Ed, and they stood together for a moment, grateful for each other and for the happy turn their lives had taken.

Jett let forth with an impatient meow from the kitchen. Rick sighed. "I love you, baby. Hell, I even love that cranky cat!"

After Jett had finished his breakfast, Ed shoved him out the back door for some fresh air. Ed himself ventured into the backyard, pleased to feel the spring sunshine on his face after being cooped up in the house for several days. The daffodils had begun to bloom while he'd been sick, and he picked a few for the breakfast table, noticing that the tulips were still a few weeks away from blooming. He remembered telling Jett a month ago that Rick would surely be living with them before the tulips bloomed. He shook his head with a grin. *It really happened! He's really here.* He looked at Rick's car in the driveway and listened to Rick making their breakfast in the kitchen.

Ed's eyes rolled heavenward. "Thanks," he whispered, doing some quick but thorough blessing counting.

While they wolfed down Rick's pancakes, they talked about the immediate future. "Isn't it great I have tomorrow off?" Rick said, pouring himself more coffee. Rick was a mail carrier for the Porterfield Post Office, and while he always had Sundays off, his other day off had a tendency to float around the rest of the week. "I mean, we can hang around here all day and take it easy; then, if you're up to it, we can move my things over here tomorrow, since Dr. Weisberg told you not to go back to work for awhile."

"I am definitely up to moving you in here." Ed dumped a generous amount of maple syrup on his stack of pancakes, pleased his appetite was indeed back. "I told Mrs. Heston I'd see her Tuesday morning as usual, but I'm free all day tomorrow." He looked up at Rick. " Does it bother you, us starting our marriage in my house?"

Rick dosed his own cakes with syrup. "Oh, not really. I've spent so much time here, I kinda feel like it's my house, too. You know, I meant what I said last week about sharing the expenses and all that. Yes, someday I'd like a bigger place for us, but for right now I'd like to think of this as our honeymoon cottage."

"You mean like Betty Jo and Steve had on *Petticoat Junction*?" Ed said with a smirk. Rick had once confessed to having a teenage crush on the guy who'd played Steve on that TV show.

Rick chuckled. "Yeah, except we won't have Uncle Joe barging in."

"No, just my mother," Ed sighed. His mother had done her best to accept the growing relationship between Ed and Rick, but he wondered how she would react to this latest development. Norma, his mother, had a tendency to be rather opinionated, and she wasn't at all shy about sharing her thoughts.

"You're not worried about that, are you? Norma's been great about all of this. In some ways I think she's been better than my parents, who are supposed to be the big, bleeding-heart liberals!" Rick frowned. He had been annoyed with his parents for several weeks, as they had recently voiced their doubts about the safety of two gay men pursuing a relationship in a small Indiana town.

"Well, speaking of them, do you want to go see them? I mean, since a lot of your stuff is in storage at their house, shouldn't we bring it up to Porterfield now that you'll have the room for it?" Ed wanted to do whatever was necessary for Rick to feel at home.

"No, I don't particularly want to see them, but yes, I want to get my stuff." Rick rolled his eyes. "I can just imagine what Mom will say when she hears I've moved in here. Shit!"

"Well, like you kinda said at some point, we'll just have to prove them wrong." Ed was more concerned about Rick's possessions. "How much do you have? Can we get it all up here in my truck?"

Rick laughed. "Oh, I think so. Like I said, I sold off most of my furniture before I moved here to be with Claire and the kids. I really don't have much in the way of worldly possessions." His warm and tender special spread across his face. "I think I was waiting to find a place to settle down, once and for all. I think I found it."

"I hope so." Ed smiled back at him. "Maybe we can go next weekend. I just want you to be as happy as possible here."

"I will be, as long as you're here." Rick reached for Ed's hand across the table. "I don't really care where we live, as long as we're together. I know we have a lot of dreams about the future, but for right now all I care about is us together, building a life together, first here, then wherever. Okay? Don't worry about it. It'll take awhile for us to get everything sorted out, but we're gonna be fine. I know it."

Rick cocked his head toward the music coming from the living room. Ed had stacked some of their favorite 45s on the stereo's turntable before sitting down to eat. "One Man Band" by Three Dog Night, "their song," was playing. "We're going to make some beautiful music together in this house, and I plan on tuning up for some right after breakfast. I'm gonna take my incredible new husband back to the bedroom, and I have every intention of creating a symphony or two while I show him and tell him how much I love him."

◈●◈

Monday morning Ed was back at the kitchen table, halfheartedly eating some breakfast and scrawling notes on a scratch pad while Rick picked up some empty cardboard boxes from the IGA. He had another stack of his old 45s playing on the stereo. He mentally sang along with one of his teenage favorites, "Heaven Knows" by the Grass Roots, thinking of Rick. *Geez, all this time I just wanted us to be together, and for him to move in.* He looked at the some of the fun-filled notes he had written: laundry chores, house cleaning, yard work. *I kept thinking about the romance, but not the reality.*

Ed and Rick had met the previous autumn when Rick began delivering mail on Ed's street. Once they were aware that the powerful attraction they had for each other was mutual, their relationship had developed quickly. Ed had known very early on how deeply he loved Rick and how much he wanted to share his life with him. To his amazement, Rick felt exactly the same way. Almost from their very first kiss, it seemed they had been heading toward this moment. Their five-month romance had been the happiest period of Ed's life so far, and he couldn't help but wonder whether marriage would cool the passion and excitement that had sustained them for so long.

"Aw, crud," he said to Jett, who was wiping milk from his whiskers. "We need a honeymoon! I'm not ready to take this seriously yet."

Jett paused in his morning washing, one paw in the air, to give Ed a disapproving look. The cat turned and strutted into the living room, leaping to his favorite sunny-day nap place in the east window. "Oh, what do you know about love anyway?" Ed called after him. "You just fuck and run!"

The record changer clicked, and another record fell onto the turntable. Petula Clark began to sing "Don't Sleep in the Subway" just as Ed heard a knock on the back door.

"Yoo-hoo," he heard his mother, Norma, call through the door. Not waiting for an answer, she barged up the steps to the kitchen, carrying a grocery bag. "Ed Stephens," she barked at the sight of him. "After nine in the morning, and you're still sitting around in that ratty bathrobe. Honestly!"

Ed gave her his most aggrieved look. "Well, *honestly*, Mom, I'm getting over being sick. Dr. Weisberg told me to take it easy. Considering that you never wait to be let in, would you prefer I was sitting here naked?"

"Humph," she snorted as usual, all five feet three inches of her managing to look indignant. Her hair had been newly dyed a sandy-brown shade similar to Ed's, and the Merle Norman makeup was perfectly applied. Norma did not approve of widows letting themselves go. "Sick or not, you could at least get dressed. And get a new bathrobe! I think you were wearing that mess when you were still living at home."

Ed looked at his list. BUY NEW BATHROBE TO MAKE MOM HAPPY, he added to it in big letters. "It's on my list, along with wondering why you're here."

Norma pulled a casserole dish out of the grocery bag. "I took pity on you. This is a chicken and vegetable casserole, so you don't have to worry about cooking for awhile." She pulled open the refrigerator door, scowling at the contents. "Honestly! If I didn't cook for you, you'd never eat right." She moved the milk and orange juice cartons to her satisfaction, making room for the casserole dish. She actually seemed to be humming along with the music from the living room. Ed couldn't believe it.

"Geez, Mom, getting soft?" he teased. "You haven't hollered at me to turn the stereo off yet."

She slammed the fridge door. "Oh, I'm just trying to spare your sick feelings," she snapped. "Actually, although I shouldn't admit it, I've always liked that Petula Clark. She always struck me as a nice girl, and she didn't dress like a hippie. And for once you have the volume at a respectable level. What's the occasion?"

Ed sighed. "I was thinking, making some notes. You might want to sit down, Mom. I have some news."

Norma looked at him with suspicion. She pulled the other chair out from the table. "What nonsense are you up to now?" she asked, sitting down.

Ed found himself grinning. "Well, Rick is living here now. He just moved in over the weekend."

Norma's eyebrows shot up. "For Pete's sake," she exclaimed. "What brought this on?"

Ed pondered a moment, debating how much to tell her about the past week or so—the discussion he and Rick had had during their weekend getaway to a secluded lake in Michigan that led to a mutual proposal of marriage; Rick's devoted care of Ed while he had been sick; Jack, Rick's ex-lover, suddenly appearing, prompting Rick to make the final decision to move into Ed's house. "We just decided it was time," he finally said, thinking she might not really enjoy hearing the details of her son's love life with another man.

Norma sighed. "Well, I knew it would happen sooner or later. I suppose it's for the best. If it were anyone other than Rick, I'd probably be horrified, but he's a good man, and better than you deserve." She looked at the table, tracing the place mat's pattern with her fingers. "Ed," she said in a very soft tone for her. "I am happy for you, in my own way. I just hope you know what you're doing."

Ed looked at her in surprise. "What do you mean?"

She frowned. "Any kind of marriage is serious business. There's a lot of give-and-take involved, and an awful lot of compromise. You've been alone here for a long time, and this is the first time you've ever been this serious about anyone. If your father was here, I know he'd sit you down for a talk about this. Since he's not, I guess it's up to me to make sure you realize what you're getting into."

"I think I do," Ed said with a confidence he wasn't feeling.

Norma snorted. "Oh, I'm sure you do! The two of you have been playing house here for months. This is different. Why, the fights your father and I had the first year. It takes awhile to adjust to another person, and don't think for a minute it doesn't."

"I can't imagine Dad fighting with you," Ed protested.

She glared at him. "No, because by the time you kids came along, we'd learned to accept each other, faults and all. I know I'm not the easiest person in the world to get along with, and your father learned to accept that. I learned to accept that he had ways of dealing with things and looking at the world that were a lot different than mine. Still, there were times that first year, despite how much I loved him, that I thought about moving back to the farm with Mom and Dad, shucking the whole thing. I'm just warning you, Edward. You will have times like that with Rick. Everybody does."

Ed shrugged.

"Sure," Norma sneered, "I know you think you're above all that, but you're not, and neither is he. As much as I like Rick, the man isn't perfect. He can be just as bossy as I am. There will come a day when you'll stop thinking that's cute, and you'll be ready to clobber him. Mark my words!"

Ed stirred uneasily. "Maybe you're right, Mom," he allowed, "but like you just said, it's a part of the game. I'll have to cross that bridge when I get to it. Right now I'd like to just enjoy it. Is there anything wrong with that?"

"No," she admitted. "But I want you to know, here and now, that when you're ready to walk out on him, don't think you can come running home to Mother. I'll just march you right back here, telling you to find a way to make it work. That's what my mother did. You've made a commitment to this, and I expect you to see it through."

Norma stood up and headed for the sink. She began rattling dirty dishes, reaching for the dish soap. "You don't have to do that, Mom," Ed said softly.

"I know I don't! I just need to keep busy. I may not understand, or entirely approve, of the idea of two men together, but I know it's no different from a man and a woman coming together. You may not have a marriage license, but that doesn't give you any right to bail out when the going gets tough. Don't feel you're special either," she added. "I said pretty much the same thing to your sister when Todd proposed. Your father had some words of his own for Laurie as well."

Ed felt the usual wistful sadness wash over him as he thought of his father, who had died almost three years earlier. "I wish Dad was here," he said. "I know you're right, Mom, that he'd be lecturing me the same way you are, but I know he'd be happy for me, too."

"I *am* happy for you," Norma insisted, running hot water into the sink. "Honestly! What do you want, a wedding present?"

Ed chuckled. "No. That's okay. The fact that you're dealing with this is present enough."

"I'm a good mother," she said, shutting off the faucet with a jerk. "I may not feel a hundred percent right about this, but I'll support you on it. I told you that the first time you brought Rick to the house. I will, too. I want you to remember this, though: You've taken on an adult responsibility, and it's your responsibility to behave like an adult. You owe it to Rick and to yourself. I would be just as angry with you for hurting him as I would with him for hurting you. Keep *that* in mind!"

"I will, Mom," he said humbly.

"See that you do." Norma turned her attention to scrubbing a dirty dish. The record changer clicked again, and the Supremes' "Come See About Me" began to play. "Oh, for Pete's sake," she moaned. "Diana Ross. What you hear in that woman's nasal screeching is beyond me. I don't suppose Rick's taste in music is any better than yours."

Ed was comforted by the return to her usual complaining. "No, it sure isn't," he said cheerfully.

"Well, your father loved the Andrews Sisters, and I never could understand that," she muttered, shaking her head. "At least you two have got one thing in common."

⟨∗•∗⟩

That afternoon Ed backed his old white Chevy pickup out of the driveway, followed by Rick in his battered but beloved burgundy Monte Carlo. They went around the corner, drove past the front of the little white house on Coleman Street, and headed for Claire's place on the west side of Porterfield.

Once there, Ed grabbed a few of the cardboard boxes Rick had collected earlier from the bed of his truck and followed Rick into the suburban-style ranch house. He glanced at the crayons and coloring book on the coffee table, five-year-old Jane's teddy bear parked on the sofa, some of Judy's records scattered near the stereo, and a Star Wars lunch box near the front door. Rick picked it up and shook it.

"Empty," he commented. "For a moment I was afraid Josh had forgotten his lunch. Must be pizza day in the cafeteria."

Although Ed had spent a lot of time in the house, it all looked different to him today. Seeing the children's possessions scattered around, he suddenly felt guilty at the idea of taking their uncle Rick away from them. Claire had told him they would be fine, but Ed had been so focused on getting Rick to move in, he hadn't given much thought to the change in the children's lives. In addition to the guilt, a wave of shame washed over him. He was fond of Claire and the kids and knew, despite Claire's reassurances, that Rick's move would create a noticeable void in the crowded house.

He looked at Rick, half tempted to say something about waiting longer.

Rick grinned at him. "So! Wanna help me pack up my shit?"

Ed grinned back at him. "Okay." *Oh, well. He doesn't seem to be worried about it, so I guess I shouldn't be either.*

Ed took one of the boxes into the tiny room Rick shared with his nephew, Josh. Toys and games were scattered about. A poster of Snoopy in his World War I flying ace outfit, flying his Sopwith Camel doghouse, was taped to the wall over one of the twin beds. A dog-eared library copy of *Paddington Helps Out* was lying on the other bed. Rick picked it up with a chuckle.

"He's been using my bed as a bookshelf. I have a feeling he'll be awfully happy to have his room to himself again." Rick sat down on the bed. "Even though I love the kid, I have to admit, bunking with an eight-year-old hasn't been the most fun experience of my life. I'm really looking forward to bunking with my twenty-eight-year-old handyman."

"Aren't you afraid he'll miss you?"

Rick shrugged. "Oh, I'll still be around, still hauling him to the library when he wants, but I don't think he'll miss that alarm clock going off at five every morning."

Ed could understand that. He wasn't much looking forward to hearing that five a.m. alarm every day himself. "Well, what do we need to pack?" Ed could see little evidence of Rick in the room.

"My clothes, for starters." Rick pulled a suitcase out from under the bed. "I have some books in the closet, and this nightstand is mine, and of course"—he gave Ed a wicked smile—"the alarm clock!"

He reached out for Ed's hand. "There's one thing I want to do first." He pulled Ed next to him on the bed. Arms around each other, they sprawled full-length upon it. "I had to see what this feels like," Rick said, giving Ed a quick kiss. "I spent so many nights in this bed wishing you were here."

Ed struggled to find a comfortable position on the narrow bed. "Well, I don't know how much sleep we would have gotten. I'm sure glad I've got a double bed."

"I know. I didn't care about sleep, though. I just wanted to be next to you." Rick kissed him again." I'm just so glad we found each other. I don't even want to think about what I'd be doing right now if I didn't have you."

"Well, wouldn't you be doing exactly what you were doing before we met? I mean, delivering mail, living here, helping Claire with the kids?"

Rick sighed. "Yeah, I s'pose." A faraway look came to his eyes. "I never told you what happened before I moved here, did I?"

"Huh?" Ed wasn't sure what Rick was talking about. "You mean with Jack? You told me all of that, I think."

"Oh, that was part of it, but there was more." After another kiss, Rick rolled off the bed and went to the closet. He pulled back one of the sliding doors, revealing a wardrobe about as limited as Ed's. Neither one of them could be called a clotheshorse. "There was some other stuff going on around that time. I didn't really want to talk about it, 'cause I was afraid it would worry you."

"So you're gonna tell me now?" Ed laughed. He rolled off the bed and joined Rick at the closet. "You were right about one thing, darlin'; you don't have much stuff." He hoisted a box full of books out of the closet. "I don't know why we even brought those cartons over here." He gave Rick a speculative look. "Does your not having a lot of stuff have something to do with what you didn't tell me?" His imagination immediately went to work, as all sorts of terrible possibilities went through his mind.

"Yeah." Rick pulled his postal uniforms out of the closet. "It's nothing awful, though." He chuckled, seeing the look on Ed's face. "You see! Already you're worrying. I just didn't want you to know how sorry for myself I was feeling."

"Okay, now I'm really confused." Ed sat down on the bed, arms crossed. "Confess."

Rick sat next to him. He put an arm around Ed and sighed. "I was very unhappy when I moved here. In a way, moving here was running away, and I guess I was a little ashamed, too. Who knew I'd meet you, and my life would change so much? I still can't believe it sometimes. Baby, do you really love me?"

Ed leaned his head against Rick's. "Yes. I love you more than I ever thought I could love someone."

"There. That's just it. I never thought that would happen to me, so I was planning for a different life when I moved to Porterfield. Okay," he said, seeing the puzzled look on Ed's face. "Here's the whole story.

"About the time Claire first hinted at the idea of me moving here, I was dating a guy named Dan. He was a nice guy, very stable. He was an accountant, and spending time with someone like that after Jack was pretty refreshing, to say the least."

Rick shrugged. "It wasn't fireworks. It wasn't anything like I feel for you, but as I said, he was nice, and I began to think about what it would be like to settle down with someone like that. I was willing to give up romance and passion and all that good stuff if it meant I could have a companion. You know, just someone to come home to, to do things with, build a life together."

He turned to Ed for a kiss. "I never, never thought, after Jack, that I'd find all of that in one person."

Ed kissed him back. "I know. You're not just my lover; I think you're my best friend, too."

He was surprised to see tears come to Rick's eyes. "I'm so glad, baby. That means the world to me, that you feel like that. I feel the same way.

"Anyway, about the time I starting thinking about a future with this guy, he disappeared. Long story short, his ex-lover came back into the picture, and they decided to try again, and poor old Rick was on his own again. Man, did I feel sorry for myself! I was so sick of going to the bars, meeting guys who just wanted to party and fuck around. I just wanted someone to share my life with, and there didn't seem to be anybody like that out there. Oh, occasionally I'd meet a decent guy, but there wasn't any connection between us. I began to think it was my destiny to be alone, that I was just too damned weird, or I just didn't fit in anywhere, or something."

"I know the feeling." Ed did. Being with someone like Rick was a dream he'd never honestly felt would come true.

"Yeah! So, in all my self-pity, I decided to map out a different life, and pretty much just gave up. When the job opening came at the post office here, it seemed like a sign. I decided to get rid of all the furniture and anything that reminded me of Jack or all those years I spent trying to find someone. What I didn't sell I threw away. I decided to move to Porterfield and give it a year. I'd been visiting Claire here for years, and I'd always liked this town. I don't know if you can see it, living here all your life, but it really is a pretty town, and I began to think living here wouldn't be so bad. I was tired of Indy, tired of the gay scene and everything that went with it.

"So I moved here last summer. My plan was, if things didn't work out in Porterfield, I'd find another town, someplace where I could maybe buy a house and settle down. I'd start all over again, building a life for myself . . . kind of accepting the fact that I was alone. I wanted a home that made me feel good, made me feel like I really was at home. Those apartments I had in Indy never felt like home. They felt like waiting rooms.

"So that was the plan. When the time came that Claire and the kids could get by without me, I'd start a new life for myself." He laughed, shaking his head. "How could I have known that when I finally gave up I'd meet the man of my dreams? *And* in Porterfield."

"Geez, I'm sorry I wrecked your plans," Ed teased.

"I'm not! I never told you any of that because I didn't want you to think I was still thinking that way. I didn't want you to think I was going to move on, or for you to worry about it. 'Cause the minute I met you, the plans *were* wrecked. I've never thought about any of that stuff since you came into my life. Every thought I've had about the future has included you."

Ed hugged Rick as tightly as he could. "Me, too. I'm sorry you were unhappy, darlin', but if it got you to move here so I could meet you, I'm not too sorry!"

"Funny how life works out." Rick locked his own arms around Ed. "I gave up on love and went out searching for a home, and somehow I managed to find both."

Rick kissed Ed one more time, and Ed could feel every bit of Rick's love in that kiss, along with a great deal of gratitude. "Oh, baby," Rick whispered, tears again in his eyes, "I'm so happy I've come home at last."

# Chapter Two

It didn't take long to transfer Rick's possessions from the house to his car and Ed's truck. Ed found himself rather fatigued by the first real physical activity he'd experienced in almost a week and ruefully realized that as one of the victims of Porterfield's influenza outbreak, he would probably need awhile to regain all of his usual strength.

The nervous feeling in his stomach, however, was not from the flu. He knew the reason for that was his anticipation of what was yet to come that afternoon: telling Judy, Josh, and Jane that Uncle Rick was moving across town.

Searching his mind for something else to think about, he suddenly remembered a phone call from earlier in the day.

"Hey, I forgot to tell you," he said to Rick as they were tidying Josh's room. "Mrs. Penfield called while you were out running errands. I told her about you moving in for good, and she just laughed, saying she knew it, that her female intuition told her it had happened."

Rick snickered. "Not only a wise old woman, but a witch. Maybe she worked some extra mojo on me over the weekend."

Mrs. Hilda Penfield, Ed's former teacher and current favorite handyman client, had become a good and trusted friend to both of them. Ed, sensing he could easily confide in her, had told her about his relationship with Rick in its early stages. Mrs. Penfield, indeed a wise and compassionate woman, had become a great source of comfort and inspiration to them.

"Well, I don't know about her mojo, but when you talked to her last week and told her you were staying at my house while I was sick, she had a feeling you wouldn't bother to leave."

Rick shook a dust rag out the window he had opened. "I repeat: a witch.

She knew that before I did. I'm sure glad she's on our side, though."

"Yeah, me, too. Oh, and she wants us to come over to dinner Wednesday evening to celebrate. I told her it was okay. It is, isn't it?"

"Of course!" Rick's warm and tender special spread across his face as he turned toward Ed. "Especially if Effie Maude's cooking," he said, referring to Mrs. Penfield's housekeeper. "We might even get leftovers out of it. Maybe we can even find out about this 'wedding present' business she keeps alluding to."

"Considering how much her support has helped us already, I think leftovers are enough of a present." Ed had already told the elderly woman she had done enough for the two of them, but she still seemed insistent on acknowledging their marriage in her own way.

"Baby, if she wants to do something else for us, we should let her. Graciously, too."

Rick slammed the window shut and once again flopped on his former bed. "I mean, her support and friendship have made us happy, right? If doing something nice for us will make *her* happy, who are we to get all modest about it?"

"Yeah, I guess you're right," Ed conceded. For a brief moment he allowed greed to enter his mind, wondering what kind of gift Mrs. Penfield was considering for them. It was no secret that her late husband, the town's most successful lawyer, had left her comfortably fixed.

Rick smirked at Ed, and he suspected Rick knew exactly what he was thinking. Ed shrugged away thoughts of avarice and kicked on Claire's old Electrolux.

Later that afternoon Ed and Rick were resting in the living room when Ed saw something yellow go by the window. He looked closer and saw a Porterfield Community Schools bus come to a stop at the corner. As the usual assortment of elementary school children piled off and headed for their homes, he was able to pick out the three he was concerned about: twelve-year-old Judy huddled with and whispering to her friend Angie, and skinny, lanky Josh, who was going on nine, obviously exasperated as he tried to lead his kindergarten sister, Jane, toward home. When he saw Ed's truck in the driveway, he grabbed Jane's hand and hurried her to the front door. All three of them were fond of Ed, and an unexpected visit from him was something to be excited about.

Josh and Jane burst into the house with loud greetings, Jane immediately heading for Ed's lap. Judy, who'd also spotted the truck, followed more slowly, reluctantly breaking off her conference with Angie. Hollering "I'll call you" as she entered the front door, she gave Ed a tight-lipped smile. She had recently acquired braces, and Ed knew she wasn't about to let anyone see them if she didn't have to. He understood. He'd been through the hell of braces himself at that age.

"Hi! What's going on?" Judy greeted the men. She flung her math book on the coffee table in disgust. "More stupid fractions."

"We'll look at it before supper," Rick said almost automatically. "Josh? Homework?"

"Spelling test tomorrow like always." He tossed his spelling workbook on the table next to Judy's math book.

"I don't have any homework," Jane crowed, bouncing on Ed's lap.

"Enjoy it while it lasts," Ed told her, wincing a bit. "You will soon enough."

"Look, kids, we'll get to the math and spelling in a little while," Rick said. "And we'll see what we've got in the house for a snack. First though, Ed, your mother, and I have something we'd like to talk to you about."

"Yeah," Judy said, flopping on the sofa. "What are you doing here in the afternoon, Uncle Ed?" She gave him a suspicious look. Of the three she was the only one who genuinely knew the truth about her uncle Rick's relationship with Ed, and he couldn't help but wonder whether she also knew the reason why he just happened to be there after school.

"We'll get to it when your mom shows up. She had a short day at work, and she'll be home soon," Rick told her.

At that moment, Claire's old station wagon pulled into the garage. A few moments later she appeared in the living room clad in the white uniform she wore as a dental hygienist. She worked for Dr. Wells, on the north side of town, and as Ed had discovered during a checkup over the winter, was a thorough but gentle teeth cleaner.

Claire, a few years older than her brother, was dark-haired like Rick, and her warm smile matched his as well. Ed was glad to see that smile directed toward him as she greeted her brother and answered the multitude of questions the children threw at her. Her approval of Ed, his relationship with Rick, and her belief that Rick belonged with Ed as opposed to staying with her and the children meant a lot to him.

Once Claire was settled in a worn recliner across from the sofa, Rick took a deep breath and let it out. "Well, kids, you know Ed here has become the best friend I've ever had."

Judy rolled her eyes but said nothing.

"And you know I spend a lot of time at his house. We've talked about this a lot, and we've decided it would be a good idea for me to move in there."

Three pairs of surprised eyes met his.

"I think this is the best thing for Uncle Rick," Claire said cheerfully but firmly. "He did us all a great favor when he moved here from Indianapolis, and his help has been a blessing, but I think it's time the four of us proved how capable we can be without him. I've had long talks with both Uncle Rick and Uncle Ed about this, and I think it's a wonderful opportunity for both of them."

"Since you're all doing so well now, there's no reason for me to be here all the time," Rick added. "I'll still come over after work and stay with you until your mom comes home from work, but then I'll go home, too. To my new home."

As none of the children appeared to have anything to say yet, he continued. "You all know exactly where Ed lives . . . well, where *we* live, and you know the phone number. You can call us anytime you need to. You can think of Ed as an uncle, too. I mean, I know you already do, but he really is now."

Claire, Rick, and Ed looked apprehensively at the children. Josh was the first to react.

"You mean I get to have my room to myself again?" His face, so much like Rick's, lit up. "And I can have my friend Eric over for sleepovers and stuff?"

"Yep," Rick said with a nod.

"Neat! No more snoring." Josh laughed.

"Unless Eric snores," Ed said, giving him a poke on the arm.

Josh rubbed his arm and grinned at Ed. "But you'll still come over sometimes, right? To play games?"

"Sure. And like Rick said, we're just across town, and you can always come visit us, too." Ed was relieved at Josh's reaction, but the rest of the jury was still out.

Jane put her arms around Ed's neck. "Why don't you just move in here?"

Judy snorted. "Like there's room for another person in this house."

Ed hugged Jane. "Judy's right. It makes more sense for Rick to move over to my place, but you'll still see him all the time, and you've still got me for Chutes and Ladders and Candy Land."

"Oh, okay." Jane grabbed her teddy bear and crawled off Ed's lap, heading for the TV. It was time for one of her favorite shows, *Gilligan's Island*, and even something as big as this news was not going to change that.

Ed glanced at Claire, who appeared unconcerned with Josh and Jane's easy acceptance of Rick's move. Claire shrugged and grinned at Ed, whispering, "I'm beginning to think kids are more adaptable than we realize."

Ed looked at Judy. "What do you think about this?"

She pulled herself upright on the sofa, crossing her arms. "So what happens when school's over with next month?"

Rick put his arm around her. "Your mom's already arranged to have Mrs. Busby come and stay every day while she's at work, like last summer. I won't need to be here, but you know where I am if you do need me."

"Her again?" Judy's eyebrows shot upward. "What do we need her here for? I'm twelve now. That's too old for a babysitter!"

"That may be," Rick told her sternly, "but considering you spent most of last summer down the street at Angie's house, someone needs to be here for the younger kids. Do you really want the responsibility of being here every single day, keeping an eye on them? Besides, the way you fight with them, neither your mother nor I feel you're mature enough to be in charge."

Judy looked at her mother, who nodded. "Rick's right, Judith Ann. You're going to have to grow up and show me you've learned a lot more about accepting responsibility as the oldest before I would feel comfortable leaving you with your brother and sister on a daily basis."

Judy stood up. With a venomous glare at the adults, she stormed down the hall to her room. The door slammed, followed soon by the sound of The Knack's "My Sharona" being played at full volume on her phonograph.

"Make her turn it down, Mommy," Jane commanded, turning away from the TV. "I can't hear Gilligan."

Josh looked up from his spelling book. "She always plays that record when she's mad," he told Ed confidentially. "It makes Mom mad 'cause she says it's a dirty song."

Ed looked at Claire, who sighed in disgust. Ed agreed with her. It *was* a dirty song, but he'd always liked it, and was reminded of how close Judy's taste in music was to his.

Ed put a hand on Rick's shoulder as he stood up. "Let me go to talk to her. Why don't you guys get started on those spelling words?"

Rick grabbed Ed's hand for a quick squeeze as he walked around the coffee table. "You're the best," he whispered with a smile.

Claire grabbed his other hand as he walked by the recliner. "I'll second that," she said under Gilligan's shouts for the Professor.

Ed knocked on Judy's door. "It's me, Ed," he called. "Can I come in?"

The volume of "My Sharona" lowered considerably. "Yeah. Come in," Judy muttered from the other side of the door.

Ed walked in and sat tentatively on Jane's bed. Judy had her back to him as she shuffled through her records on a table by the window.

"You mad at me?"

Judy shrugged. "No, I'm not mad at you." She turned the volume even lower.

"Well, so why are you mad? I know what your mom just said isn't anything she hasn't already said, so it's not really that, is it? Judy, you know what's really going on with Rick and me. We've talked about it. What's bugging you? I thought you'd be happy about this."

"I am happy," she said, turning to face him. "Anything you want to hear?"

"You got 'Morning Train' yet? I like that one." Ed grinned at her.

"Yeah, I bought it with my allowance last week." She pulled a 45 off the top of a pile and handed it to Ed.

"Cool," Ed said, studying the record sleeve. "I wondered what Sheena Easton looked like." He handed it back to Judy. "So if you're happy Rick and I are going to be together, what's wrong? I mean, are you really that ticked off about Mrs. Busby coming over again? I thought all you kids liked her."

Judy took the Knack off the turntable and replaced them with Sheena. "Oh, she's okay, I guess. And I really am happy about you and Uncle Rick. I think you should be together. I've thought that ever since New Year's, when I told you I knew what was going on. It's just . . ."

"Just what?"

She sat down on her bed, looking at the floor. "Well, things have been so much better since Uncle Rick moved in. Mom was having a hard time after Dad left. I know that. And it's like some kind of a fairy tale, you know, the way he met you and fell in love. And we get to have another uncle, which is cool and all, but . . . what if Dad comes back? I mean, I knew he wouldn't as long as Uncle Rick was here, 'cause he hated him, but now what?"

Ed looked at her. Braces or not, he had always suspected she'd be a beauty when she made it past the horrors of puberty, and he also suspected she'd be as popular as her mother had been in high school. However, Ed had to admit, Claire had not been the daughter of a deadbeat dad.

Hank Romanowski had abandoned his family one cold winter night the year before. Hank had never been the most stable of men, nor had he been held in particularly high regard in Porterfield, but he had somehow managed to become a decent husband and father during the early years of his marriage to Claire. At some point, though, his drinking had become excessive, and he had openly cheated on Claire. Rick had also discovered that Hank had lost his construction job for dealing marijuana and as a result had caught the attention of the Porterfield police. No one had seen or heard from him since the night he jumped into his Firebird and left town.

To Rick's knowledge, neither Claire nor the children knew of Hank's illegal activities, and he wanted to keep it that way. He felt both the family and its reputation had suffered enough. He had told Ed what he knew but had sworn him to secrecy.

Ed doubted, as Rick did, that Hank would be returning to Porterfield anytime soon, but he knew he couldn't tell Judy why. Rick was right, Ed thought. The kids had been through enough already, and adding to any shame they may have felt over their father wouldn't help.

He got up from Jane's bed and sat next to her. "Judy," he said softly, "please don't worry about that. I know your dad didn't like Rick, and he wouldn't like me either, for the same reason. But I don't think he'll be back anytime soon. Even if he is stupid enough to come back here and stir up trouble, you've got two uncles to protect you now. I feel as close to you and Josh and Jane as I do to my own niece and nephew. I'm not gonna let anybody hurt you, and as long as Rick and I are just across town, just a phone call away, nobody will."

"What makes you think he'll stay away?" Judy turned skeptical eyes to Ed.

He remembered Mrs. Penfield and her comment about female intuition and said, "Oh, just call it a homosexual's intuition."

Judy laughed, as he had hoped. "Like a woman's intuition?"

"Yeah. Only mine's stronger, 'cause of all the things I've had to think about, being different and all."

"Mom's gonna get a divorce. Did you know that?"

Ed nodded. Rick had recently told him that Claire had begun to talk with Robert Mason, the law partner of the late George Penfield. In addition to filing for divorce and petitioning to obtain full custody of the children, Claire was going to file a restraining order against Hank.

"With all that legal stuff, it'll make it harder for your dad to cause trouble," he said, not wanting to get into all of the details.

"Yeah, I know." Judy grimaced. "But Dad acted pretty stupid sometimes."

Ed nodded again. " I know. But Rick was in Indianapolis then, and I wasn't around. We are now. We'll be keeping an eye on things, even if we're not here all the time."

Judy studied Ed's face for a moment. Apparently she was satisfied with what she saw, as her own face broke into a smile. It was still a tight-lipped one, but Ed could see the relief behind it.

"Okay, I believe you. And I really am glad about you and Uncle Rick." She put her arms around Ed. "I hope someday I get as lucky as he did."

Ed laughed, feeling relieved himself. "Oh, you will. I know how much you hate those braces. I went through it, too, ya know. But when they come off . . ." He shook his head. "But you've heard that crap already, haven't you?"

"Yeah," she sighed.

"It's true, though." He grabbed for the record sleeve with Sheena Easton's picture. "You'll be even prettier than she is someday. I just hope you meet some guy as nice as your uncle. He's made me awfully happy."

Judy giggled. "You guys are so cute! I know, I know, I'm not supposed to tell anyone, and I won't, but I'm glad you're part of our family now. It's like you're getting married or something."

"So we're cool on all of this?"

"Yeah."

"Okay." Ed stood up. "I need to haul some of Rick's stuff back to the house. So you'll come back out and let him help you with those fractions, right?"

"Yeah, yeah," she sighed, reaching for a Pat Benatar album. "I promise I'll go back out after that stupid *Gilligan* is over." She rolled her eyes. "I've seen that one about the meteor at least three times."

She looked at the album cover, then back at Ed. "Do you think I'll be as pretty as Pat Benatar?"

"Well, I'm sure you'll look as good as she does, but I don't know if you'll be able to sing like she does. Practice 'Heartbreaker' a few times, and I'll get back to you on that."

Ed gently closed the bedroom door behind him. Claire was coming down the hall from her own bedroom. She had changed her clothes and was now wearing jeans and a faded blue T-shirt. She was running a hand through her shoulder-length hair when she spotted Ed.

"Is the royal princess over her snit?"

Ed nodded and smiled. "Yeah, everything's fine."

Claire chuckled softly. "Thanks, Ed, for calming her down, and for taking my goofy brother off my hands. I don't have to ask you to take good care of him, 'cause I already know you will."

"I will do my best, ma'am."

"I have a feeling your best is pretty good, but if he drives you too crazy, just threaten to send him back here, okay?"

He chuckled with her. "Okay."

Ed returned to the living room with a discreet thumbs-up sign for Rick, who grinned at him. Jane was still glued to the tube, and Josh was rattling off his spelling list. Ed squatted on his heels next to Josh.

"I'm sorry I'm stealing your roommate," Ed said to him after he successfully spelled the word *across*.

"It's okay." Josh gave Ed's arm a poke. "Now you get to listen to him get up at five o'clock every day."

"Yeah," Ed sighed. "How 'bout that." He glanced at Rick. "I'll head on home now, and I'll heat up the casserole my mom left for supper, okay?"

Rick's warm and tender special spread over his face. "Yeah," he said quietly, under Josh's spelling and the blaring TV. "I'll see you at home."

⋞⋟•⋞⋟

A terrible buzzing sound swarmed around Ed's ears. *Aw, crud! The killer bees are coming!* He felt Rick's hand brush his head as Rick rolled over. The buzzing stopped. It was just Rick's alarm clock. Ed usually set his own alarm clock to music, but Rick claimed only the shrill buzz of an alarm would wake him at five a.m.

Ed heard Rick sigh as he flopped back on the bed. Ed felt a twinge of sympathy. It was Tuesday morning, and time for Rick to go back to work. Waking up at five a.m., especially after two days away from it, had to be a bitch, all right. For a moment he wondered whether Rick was going to get up, but he heard the bed creak and Rick pulling himself up to a sitting position. He crawled out of bed with another sigh, and Ed could hear the bedroom door softly close behind him.

Ed rolled over, hogging the covers. He tried to will himself back to sleep, but that alarm kept playing in his brain. Rick had spent the night at Ed's place numerous times during the workweek, so his early rising wasn't a complete shock to Ed. Somehow, though, it felt different today. Ed sleepily realized he'd be hearing that five a.m. alarm five or sometimes six days a week for as long as Rick continued to carry mail for the Porterfield Post Office.

Over the past few weeks they had begun to talk of a future for Rick away from the postal service, but Ed knew it would not be happening anytime soon. He reminded himself that marriage was about compromise, and listening to that damn alarm clock every day was a small price to pay for what he was getting in return.

He had to admit, though, that Rick was extremely considerate about his early rising. He was obviously used to performing his morning routine in a house of sleeping people, and he went about his business as quietly as possible, keeping obtrusive light to a minimum. *Just another reason to love him*, Ed thought as he rolled over again.

Ed had almost returned to sleep when Rick crept into the room. Ed sensed his presence and opened his eyes. In the dim morning light he could just make out Rick, dressed for work, smiling down at him.

"I promise I won't make a habit of it," he whispered, "but do you suppose you could send your new husband off to work with a little kiss of good luck, this being his first day at work as a married man?"

Ed could see the eager, hopeful look in Rick's eyes. He found himself smiling as he pushed himself up, reaching for him. "How 'bout a *big* kiss for good luck, and a hug, too?"

Rick sat next to him on the bed, putting his arms tightly around him. Ed could taste Rick's usual morning breath, that peculiar combination of toothpaste and coffee. He hoped his own breath wasn't too sour.

"Have a good day," Ed whispered after a very long kiss.

"Thank you, baby. Thank you for loving me enough to marry me, and for putting up with a mailman's hours."

Ed kissed him again. "I do love you, darlin'. I just have to remind myself that if you weren't a mailman, we may have never met."

Rick regretfully let him go. "I don't even want to think about that. I love you, too, baby, and you have a good day with Mrs. Heston. Don't overdo it, okay?"

"I won't. She's my only appointment today. I'll come back here and rest this afternoon. I promise."

"Good." Rick grabbed his cap from the dresser. "Well, then I'll see you when I deliver your, no *our*, mail this afternoon."

He started to leave the room but paused. "Oh! I fed Jett and let him out, okay?"

"Okay," Ed murmured.

Rick left by the back door. As Ed heard his car pull out of the driveway, he lay back down, anticipating his own alarm at seven thirty. He toyed with the idea of just getting up and getting it over with, as his mind seemed wide-awake. He still couldn't believe how much and how quickly his life had changed, and the thought of going to Mrs. Heston's, as he had done almost every Tuesday morning for six years, comforted him. Changes, bad or good, take some getting used to, and Ed had a feeling the changes had only just begun.

Ed's truck rolled into the driveway behind Agnes Heston's home on East Clark Street promptly at nine o'clock. Their Tuesday ritual began. Ed met Mrs. Heston at her kitchen door and took her purse as she slowly made her way down the back steps with her walker. They went to the garage, where Ed helped her into the passenger seat of her old but trusty sedan. He stowed the walker in the backseat, got behind the wheel, and rolled backward out of the driveway, heading for the IGA on the south side of Porterfield.

Mrs. Heston had been Ed's first regular handyman client. He had been laid off from his job at the electric motor factory in town during a mid-seventies recession, and rather than return to a job he had begun to intensely dislike, he decided to take advantage of his talent with basic home repairs and begin his own handyman business.

Mrs. Heston heard about him through a friend and immediately hired him on a regular basis. She wasn't so much concerned with home repairs, she told him, but needed someone to help with the chores she could no longer manage herself because of myriad health problems. She did not, she commented, want to go to one of those awful nursing homes, and if having a strong young man helping her every week would delay that possibility, she'd happily pay whatever he charged.

Ed, being the practical and pragmatic person he was, immediately realized his business would grow a lot faster if he actively courted others like her. Porterfield was filled with older folks who needed an occasional helping hand, and with Mrs. Heston's enthusiastic praise of his work ringing through the senior set's grapevine, he soon had as many clients as he could handle on a regular basis. He was deeply grateful to the old woman for kick-starting his new career. As he often said, it was folks like Mrs. Heston who kept him out of that factory and kept a roof over his head.

Mrs. Heston fumbled through her purse as they headed south on Main Street. She was a short, ill-shaped woman, her sparse gray hair pulled back in an untidy bun. Her face, though, was kindly behind its maze of wrinkles, and her faded blue eyes still twinkled behind her trifocals with an almost wicked zest for life. With Ed's help she had put off the nursing home her children had suggested for six years and, at age eighty, planned to continue doing so for as long as possible.

"Who was that who answered the phone when I called last night?" Mrs. Heston asked as she frowned at a handful of coupons. She had telephoned to make sure Ed was feeling better and up to their usual Tuesday, and Rick had taken the call while Ed was washing the dinner dishes.

Ed glanced at her, wondering why it hadn't occurred to him that his clients might be curious about someone moving into his house. Most of them had Ed pegged as a solitary, small-town bachelor, so this latest development was sure to create some talk. He was glad Mrs. Heston was the first to ask. She loved a good story as much as the next person but generally kept judgment on other people's actions to a minimum.

"Oh, well, that was my new roommate," Ed said, trying to put a casual tone in his voice.

"Roommate?" She transferred a Tide detergent coupon into her wallet and stuffed the rest of them in her purse's side compartment. "What brought that on? You having money troubles, Ed?"

"Oh, no. Not at all." Ed wished he'd prepared an explanation, as he wasn't always the greatest at lying on the spot. "Rick is a good friend, and it . . . well, it occurred to me I might be able to save some money if someone else was there to share the expenses. You know, maybe save some money for . . . uh . . . the future."

"The future?" Mrs. Heston gave a wheezy chuckle. "You got big plans I don't know about?"

Ed shifted uncomfortably as he braked for the red light at Cedar Avenue. "Well, not really, but you never know."

"No, you don't, do you? If Wilbur hadn't've worked so hard all those years, I don't know how I'd be getting by now. You're a sensible man, Ed. Always have been. Well, good luck with this . . . what did you say? Mick? I hope it works out."

"Uh, Rick." Ed glanced at her again. She was studying her shopping list, and apparently her curiosity had been satisfied.

He turned his attention back to the traffic, both relieved and annoyed. He wasn't at all sure how Mrs. Heston, or any of his other clients, would react to the truth of his relationship with Rick. He hated to lie on principal and hated even more the idea of being secretive about something, and someone, that had made him so happy.

His troubled thoughts continued as he slowly followed Mrs. Heston through the supermarket aisles. He had an excellent rapport with his clients, and the name Ed Stephens was highly regarded among Porterfield's senior citizens. *What would they say if they knew Rick was my husband? Would they all get together and throw Bibles at me and fire me, or just overlook it 'cause they like me so much?*

He knew there had already been talk in town of his relationship with Rick, but it had been instigated over the winter by a loud-mouthed jerk who worked with Rick at the post office. What little trouble he had managed to stir up had died down quickly, and aside from Ed's brother-in-law, Todd, no one had ever mentioned it to him.

It was still troubling him later that day. He was doing his best to relax and recuperate but found himself pacing the living room floor with Sly and the Family Stone's "Everyday People" playing over and over again on the stereo. He had always loved the song's plea for acceptance of people who were different. Its message was as relevant in 1981 as it had been in 1969, but Ed bleakly felt little progress had been made regarding people like himself.

He lightly kicked a sofa leg, waking Jett up from a nap. The cat gave him an annoyed look and minced into the kitchen for an afternoon snack. Jett was occasionally cranky and bossy, but he was also warm and affectionate when he wanted to be, and he certainly didn't care that the two people who fed and petted him were two men who loved each other.

"Why the hell can't everyone else feel that way?" Ed shouted toward the kitchen.

Jett turned his head to look at Ed, and Ed would have sworn the cat shrugged, as if to say, *Don't ask me, bud.*

The bottom line behind Ed's current frustration was simple. He had been so eager to join his life with Rick's, so determined for them to be together, that he had confidently and somewhat blindly assumed they could overcome any obstacle or problem that might crop up as a result of pursuing their relationship in a small midwestern town.

Ed had, in his mind and in his heart, committed himself to Rick for the rest of his life. He wouldn't change that commitment for anything. He had felt that the deep and genuine love they had for each other would be enough to keep them safe and secure, and he was furious with himself for allowing doubt to creep into his mind now that their marriage was a reality.

"I don't want to lie about how much I love him," Ed shouted over the music, as Sly proclaimed people were all the same.

Ed felt tears in his eyes as he looked at a framed photograph his younger sister, Laurie, had given him. The picture had been taken at Laurie's house the previous Christmas. Ed and Rick were posed in front of the Christmas tree, arms around each other's shoulders, smiling happily at the camera. No, he didn't want to lie about his feelings for Rick; he never wanted to deny the couple in the photo, but he knew he probably would go on lying until he knew for sure he no longer had to lie to protect the two of them.

Ed turned away from the photograph just in time to see Rick hurrying up the walk, mailbag over his shoulder. Instead of knocking as he'd always done previously, he used the key Ed had given him to unlock the front door and step inside.

"How 'bout that," he exclaimed, dropping their mail on the end table near the door. "Delivering mail to my own home. I could get used to this," he added, sweeping Ed into his arms for a hug.

Ed pushed gloom aside in favor of the comfort he always felt being close to Rick. He glanced at the pile of mail on the table, noticing a book club announcement for Rick.

Rick's eyes followed Ed's. "I put in my official change of address this morning. It won't take effect right away, but when no one was looking I grabbed this from Dave Brown's route and snuck it into mine."

Ed had to laugh. Rick's eagerness to be "at home" in the house on East Coleman Street was a good thing for him to see. He thought back to that October afternoon when Rick had first walked into his house, still amazed that fate had sent his Dream Man right to his door.

His mind returned to his earlier thoughts, and he realized they were hugging in front of the open door. Was Mrs. Van Vleet from across the street watching? He didn't want to give a damn if she was and was still disgusted with himself for caring.

Rick put his hand under Ed's chin and gently raised his head. "Something bugging you?"

Ed shrugged. "Oh, not really," he fibbed. "I guess I'm still just run down from being sick."

Rick nodded. "I thought so. I know you didn't want to disappoint Mrs. Heston this morning, but after all that packing and hauling yesterday, I think you should have spent the day in bed. Plus," he said studying Ed's face, "the flu has a tendency to mess with your head a little bit, make you kind of depressed.

After all the excitement of the past few days, you're probably crashing. How 'bout a nap, huh?"

"Yeah, that's a good idea. I'll go lie down after you leave."

"Which I need to do right now," Rick said regretfully. "I'm running a little behind. I'll be home after Claire gets off work, and I'll heat up the rest of your mom's casserole for dinner. Oh, that reminds me: I took Gordy aside this morning and gave him the news." Gordy Smith, one of Rick's coworkers, was their only gay friend in Porterfield. "Of course he got all excited and insists on taking us out to celebrate. I told him I didn't think you'd be up for it tonight, and we've got Mrs. Penfield's tomorrow night, so he wants to go out Thursday for an early dinner. Is that okay? Think you can handle two nights in a row?"

Ed smiled. "I can definitely handle two nights of celebrating with people who are happy for us."

"Good." Rick gave Ed and extra squeeze and a quick kiss. "I love you, baby, and I'll see you in a few hours." And with that he was out the door and down the front walk, his easy mailman's stride propelling him confidently across Grant Street to the next house on his route.

Ed watched Rick until he disappeared from view on the next block as he had so many afternoons the past five months, feeling some additional comfort in the routine. Things would work out. Rick was probably right; he was still getting over the flu, and it was responsible for the apprehension he couldn't seem to shake.

He was surprised by a sudden yawn. He absently covered his mouth with his hand and turned away from the door. "Maybe a nap's not such a bad idea," he mumbled.

With one last glance at the framed photograph, he shut off the stereo and headed to the bedroom.

⊰•⊱

By the time they were in Rick's car, on their way to Mrs. Penfield's Wednesday evening, Ed was feeling somewhat better. His uneasiness was still in the back of his mind, but as he had told Rick the day before, he was definitely up to the outing and very eager to be in the company of someone who was genuinely pleased about their relationship.

Mrs. Penfield met them at the door of her huge, old Victorian home, a brick Second Empire built by her father-in-law in 1898, located just south of downtown Porterfield. Ed and Rick admired the house almost as much as they did Mrs. Penfield and as usual took special pleasure in being her guests in the dignified old place.

Mrs. Penfield warmly congratulated them on their decision to live together, and then led them—walking with the aid of her cane—to the large, high-ceilinged dining room. The table was set with heirloom china, and candles were lit.

"Oh, Mrs. Penfield," Rick said helplessly. "You've done it again! You spoil us more than our own parents would."

"That is my privilege and my pleasure," the elderly woman said, smiling fondly at him. "It's seldom I have a reason to celebrate anything these days, so please allow my indulgence."

Effie Maude Sanders, her longtime housekeeper, strode into the room, turkey platter in hand, a huge white apron covering her equally ample body. "Good china, candles, and a roast turkey," she commented with her raspy voice. "Here it is a weeknight, and not even a holiday. Land's sake, what's all this fuss anyway?"

"Ed and Rick are now living together," Mrs. Penfield said tactfully. "We're very happy for them, aren't we, Effie?"

Effie Maude's eyes grew big with surprise. "Is that so?" she marveled. "Why, that's downright modern of you two. I s'pose next they'll come up with a way for folks like you to have children." She shook her head, returning to the kitchen through the swinging door.

Rick, always amused at the sight of Effie Maude, giggled. Ed rolled his eyes at Mrs. Penfield.

"Well, I believe that is her way of saying she's happy for you," Mrs. Penfield said, chuckling.

"Oh, she's a grand old gal," Rick said, still giggling. "I wonder, though, why *she* never married?"

"Too much woman for the men in this county," Ed snorted.

"Effie Maude is a bit raw," Mrs. Penfield said in agreement, "but her heart is twenty-four-karat gold. I've never had a cross word with her in almost forty years. Now then. Tell me, how is it going for you the two of you?"

Over Effie Maude's excellent dinner, they both joyfully informed her of the progress they had made establishing a home together. "We've got a long way to go, but so far, so good," Rick concluded.

Mrs. Penfield turned to Ed with a twinkle in her eye. "And Norma? How is she taking the news?"

Ed grinned. "Oh, pretty good for Mom. She gave me a long lecture on marriage, then told me not to bother coming to her when I was ready to kill him."

"I can only imagine what my folks are going to say," Rick sighed. "We're going to Indy on Sunday to get some of my things out of storage. Considering my mother's concern for us, living in this evil, small town full of bigotry and prejudice, I'm sure she'll have some choice words on the matter."

"That's a mother's right, Rick," Mrs. Penfield gently reproved him. "I understand her concerns, and although I don't agree with her, I can see where she has not had my advantage, seeing the two of you together, day in and day out in this community. I've said it before, and I'll say it again: Porterfield needs you more than you need it. The town will realize that eventually."

"Laurie feels the same way," Ed said. "When I broke the news to her on the phone the other day, she said they should install a plaque on the courthouse square to us for being brave enough to stay here, and for putting up with any abuse we may get. She also said she's betting we single handedly lower the divorce rate around here."

"I suspect she may be right," Mrs. Penfield said with a smile. "Shall we adjourn to the parlor for coffee or tea? I'd like to hear more of your plans."

Once they were settled with after-dinner beverages, Mrs. Penfield asked them again about the future. "What do you plan to do once you've settled into your relationship? I can't imagine, from what I already know, that this is the end of your ambitions."

Rick looked at Ed. "You wanna go first?"

Ed shrugged. "Okay. Well, I know you and Rick have talked about it, but I've decided I'd like to investigate the idea of working with wood, maybe making some kind of furniture. I always said my dad was good enough at it to make a living, even though he didn't. I guess Rick nagged me about it enough that the idea began to appeal to me."

"I didn't nag," Rick said, looking at him fondly.

Ed smirked at him. "Well, you talked about it an awful lot. Anyway, I'd like to set up my dad's workshop again, but I don't know where. I don't think it would be a good idea to do it at Mom's, for a lot of reasons, and I don't have the room for it at our house. I'd also like to see if there is anyone in the area I could maybe study with, or watch, and learn something." He sighed. "Sounds like a pipe dream, doesn't it? I don't have the space or the teacher, not to mention this is my busy season with work. I'm going to spend the rest of this month painting everything from living rooms to garages, in addition to my regular chores."

"Hmmm," Mrs. Penfield said, gently stroking her coffee cup with her arthritis-ravaged fingers. "Rick? How do you feel about this?"

"I'm all for it," Rick told her. "Ed's more skillful with his hands than anyone I've ever known. He's right, though. The timing isn't quite right. But it will happen, if I have anything to say about it. I think the time has come for him to stop fixing and start creating."

"I see," Mrs. Penfield said with a thoughtful look at Rick. "I'm inclined to agree with you, Rick. I've often thought Ed had talent in those directions. What about you, though?"

"Oh," Rick said, looking down modestly. "I've been thinking about going into real estate. The postal service has been good to me, but I'd love to have a job where I could make my own hours, especially since I have Ed to consider now. You know me," he said, grinning at her. "I love to snoop through people's houses! Ed and I have even discussed buying an old house, fixing it up, and selling it, that sort of thing."

Rick shrugged. "I don't know. It sounds good, but again, like Ed, I certainly can't afford to quit my job and start blindly with something that may not pan out. We need the money too badly right now. I'm determined that we stay as debt free as possible, and I'm still helping Claire out as well."

"I see," Mrs. Penfield repeated. She frowned, considering them both. "Ambitious plans indeed," she murmured, more to herself than to them. "Well, I really didn't expect anything less from the two of you. I've no doubt you could succeed at anything you tried. You're young, strong, and intelligent. I'm pleased to note, Rick, that your sense of practicality matches Ed's. I would hate to see you in a position of overextending yourselves. It seems a shame, though, to hold off on your dreams."

Ed glanced at Rick. "There's a lot of things we'd like to do, Mrs. Penfield, but we've got our whole lives ahead of us. Rick's only thirty, and I'm twenty-eight. That's not exactly over-the-hill. The dream I had about Rick and me getting together came true, so I think the others will, in time."

"Oh, don't get me wrong, Ed," she said hastily. "As I said, I have no doubt you can accomplish all of your dreams. It's simply my wish to see you progress with them. You're both very special young men, you know. Yes, I'm rather prejudiced in that belief, considering my fondness for you both, but I approve of, and agree with, your ideas."

She slowly reached for the coffeepot. "More coffee, Rick?"

He shook his head. "No, thank you. Early day tomorrow, as usual."

"Ed? More tea for you?"

Ed shook his head, smiling. "I hear that five a.m. alarm myself now, you know."

"I believe earlier this spring I mentioned something about a wedding gift," she said, pouring more coffee for herself. "I've been giving the matter a good deal of thought, and what you've told me tonight increases my desire to do something for the two of you. However, I'm not quite ready to reveal what I have in mind yet."

Ed and Rick both looked at her curiously. "Oh, come on, Mrs. Penfield," Ed teased. "What's going on in that sneaky head of yours? Don't forget, I sat in your English class for two years. I know the surprises you can pull."

"I can assure you a pop quiz is not among my ideas," she said, laughing. "No, Ed, allow me some additional thinking time. It would very easy for me to buy you something, or even give you something of value from this house. I know you would deeply appreciate it, but I'd much rather do something for you with the potential to help you in the longer run."

She smiled mysteriously at both of them. "Would the two of you like to join me for Easter dinner next Sunday? I think by then I may have something to share with you."

Rick shrugged. "Okay by me. Ed?"

Ed nodded slowly. "Oh, I guess so. Mom might get a little bugged, but it won't kill her for me to be gone for one holiday. We usually don't make that big a deal out if it anyway. I think Laurie, Todd, and the kids will be with Todd's family, so Mom will probably go to Crestland and spend the day with Uncle Chester and Aunt Eleanor. So yeah, count me in."

"Wonderful," she said happily. "It may not be quite the feast we had tonight, as Effie Maude has the day off, but I think we'll be able to celebrate the season of rebirth properly."

"I've got an idea," Rick said enthusiastically. "Are you going to Easter services, Mrs. Penfield?"

She nodded. "I had planned to, if my old friend arthritis allows me the pleasure."

"Well then," Rick said, pleased. "Ed and I can come over in the morning and prepare dinner while you're at church. You've had us over so many times, I'd like to take the responsibility for a change."

"Not to mention messing around in her big kitchen," Ed smirked at him. "As long as *you* do most of the cooking. We like Mrs. Penfield, remember?"

"Oh, I know my way around a baked ham," Rick said confidently. "Mrs. Penfield? What do you think?"

"I think it's a splendid idea," she said, beaming at him. "It shows me, once again, that my instincts are correct where you're both concerned. I would be delighted to be your guest for Easter dinner, here in my own home."

"Maybe we'll even bring you an Easter basket," Rick said roguishly. "How do you feel about chocolate bunnies?"

She laughed outright. "Oh, I haven't eaten one in a good many years, but I think I would enjoy it. You needn't plan an egg roll for the back lawn, however. I don't quite think I'm up to that."

"No egg hunts; just some treats, then. It's a date!"

Later, as they were driving home in Rick's car, Ed took his hand. "That was so nice, your idea to make dinner for Mrs. Penfield. I would never have thought of it, but you're a much better cook than I am."

Rick squeezed his hand. "Well, I'd been thinking about having her to our place for dinner, but it occurred to me tonight that she'd be more comfortable at home. And you're not such a bad cook. Tell you what; I'll let you tear up lettuce for the salad, how 'bout that?"

Ed giggled. "That I can handle."

"What do you suppose the foxy old lady has up her sleeve where we're concerned?" Rick wondered, letting go of Ed's hand to pull into their driveway.

Ed shook his head, sighing. "I can't imagine. I'll bet, though, it'll be an Easter to remember."

# Chapter Three

Late Thursday afternoon Ed was putting his Rolling Stones *Hot Rocks* LP on the turntable when he saw Gordy Smith pull up in front of the house. Ed had pulled the Stones record out of his second-floor storage room in Gordy's honor. He had learned, during their recently begun friendship, that Mick Jagger and Keith Richards were musical heroes for Gordy more akin to gods.

Ed watched Gordy climb out of his year-old, shiny blue Grand Prix. He wondered wistfully when he and Rick could afford something as extravagant as a new car, even as he realized he'd never trade his marriage to Rick for any car, new or otherwise. Still, Ed was as naturally acquisitive as anyone, and he couldn't help but envy Gordy his car. He hoped Gordy planned on driving for their dinner date.

Gordy trotted up the front steps and knocked on the door. Ed noticed that Gordy was looking a bit trimmer these days. He had gone through with a vow he'd made to return to jogging and other regular exercise with the warmer weather. Gordy was a handsome man in his early thirties—big, tall, blond, and blue-eyed—but he'd allowed his high school football build to slide over the years he spent struggling with his sexual orientation. Ed was pleased to think that his support, along with Rick's, was helping Gordy to achieve a comfort and happiness with his life that had been lacking for many years.

"Hey, bud," Gordy exclaimed when Ed answered the door. "How's married life?"

"So far, so good." Ed grinned at him.

He settled Gordy in one of the easy chairs with a Budweiser, Gordy's favorite beer. "You know, I've been layin' off this shit," Gordy said, accepting the beer. "But in your honor, I'll happily drink it." He lit a cigarette. "These, however," he said ruefully, "are a little harder to give up."

Ed laughed. "Don't sweat it on my account. I'll get you an ashtray, since Rick isn't here to give you shit about smoking."

"Why isn't he home yet?" Gordy called to Ed, who'd gone into the kitchen.

"He's keeping an eye on the kids until Claire gets home from work. He does it every day. He'll be here pretty soon."

"Damn. Makes for a long workday, doesn't it?"

Ed returned to the living room, handing Gordy an ashtray. "Nah. It's no different than what he was doing before, except he has to get in the car and drive across town to come home." Ed smiled smugly.

Gordy snorted, exhaling smoke. "Man, just look at you! The cat that ate the fuckin' canary! Shit, you look like you ate the whole pet store."

Ed sat down, trying to look modest and humble. It was a pitiful attempt at best. "I can't help it, Gordy. I dreamed about this for so long, and for the most part, it's going okay. Oh," he continued guardedly, "I'm still kinda worried about us living together here in town and stuff, but as for just me and Rick, we're doing fine, adjusting to living together. I know it's been just a few days, but so far, so good."

Gordy petted Jett, who'd jumped into his lap. "Hell, I don't blame you. Enjoy it! I would. As for the other . . ." Gordy paused for a puff on his cigarette and slowly exhaled, a thoughtful look on his face. "Well, just take it as it comes. Short of moving away, there isn't much you can do, ya know? Besides, I'm betting on you guys to make it, 'cause if you can, I can."

"You're next, buddy."

Gordy shrugged. "We'll see." He sang under his breath with Mick Jagger as "Gimme Shelter" played. "Just a kiss away for me, right? Imagine kissing Mick Jagger. Those lips?" He snickered. "I use to think about that. Actually, he's not really my type, but yeah, I hope I stumble over some guy who can gimme some real shelter one of these days."

Ed had the usual reaction of a recently married person to a single friend. He wanted Gordy to be as happy as he was, but his pragmatism told him to stay out of Gordy's search for a mate. "Well, it's not all hearts and flowers, I'll admit. I mean, we used to spend weekends here, just making each other happy. Now it's all about who's going to do the laundry, and talking about chicken breasts being on sale at the IGA." He shrugged. "Already it's taken some getting used to, his being here all the time. I love it, but I realize my mom was right, that I lived alone for a long time." He shuddered. "Did I say that? Crud, don't tell my mom, or I'll never hear the end of it."

Gordy laughed. "Marriage is work, but you guys'll be fine."

The back door opened, and Rick bounced in, still wearing his postal uniform. "I am home. We can now celebrate."

Gordy turned his head to see Rick in the kitchen. "Not dressed like that, we aren't. I ain't takin' you to dinner wearin' that. Go change your damn clothes!"

Rick entered the room, plopping himself on the sofa next to Ed. "Fuck you! I'll change my clothes when you put out that goddamned cigarette."

"Oh, can it, you two," Ed said, kissing Rick.

"Umm," Rick moaned, returning the kiss with a tight hug. "Did you have a good day?" He let Ed go, grinning at Gordy. "How 'bout that? Company we can kiss in front of."

Gordy rolled his eyes, stubbing out his cigarette. "Yeah, yeah, rub it in. I'll remember that when I get a boyfriend."

"You can make out with him here all you want," Ed told him. He turned to Rick again. "My day was okay, but I'm starved. Why don't you change your clothes so Gordy can haul us somewhere in his car and feed us?"

"Where are we going?" Rick reluctantly stood up.

Gordy chuckled evilly. "Oh, I know you, Benton. You think I'm gonna drag you out to the P & J Root Beer Stand. You think we'll sit in the car and eat chili dogs. Ha! We're going to Fort Wayne, to a little Italian place I discovered. They've got the best lasagna I've ever eaten. Get ready to eat pasta till you bust."

Rick smiled happily. "Well, I suppose I should say you shouldn't spend the money on us, but it sounds great."

Gordy grabbed Rick's hand as he walked by. "Hell, the sky's the limit for my best buds. Maybe it'll give me good luck."

"And you're driving, Gordy, right?" Ed asked.

Gordy nodded.

"Shotgun!" Ed called.

"Aw, crud! Shotgun for the ride home, then," Rick hollered from the bedroom.

"Man," Gordy snorted, shaking his head at Ed. "He's even talking like you now. I hope when I get married I'm not as goofy as you guys are."

⋄•⋄

Ed crawled into bed that night while Rick was in the bathroom, removing his contact lenses. Rick was usually in bed by nine and asleep by ten. These days, Ed would join him, reading in bed until his own preferred bedtime of eleven. Rick was an easy, heavy sleeper, so he wasn't bothered by Ed's presence and was very pleased to have Ed next to him as he fell asleep. For that reason, Ed was glad he'd picked up his old reading habit, not to mention that there seemed to be little on television lately either one of them cared for, aside from the occasional old movie.

Rick walked into the room, wearing his own slightly shabby bathrobe. "It's a good thing Mom hasn't seen your bathrobe, darlin'," Ed teased. "Yours isn't much better than mine."

Rick took the bathrobe off and hung it on a hook located on the bedroom door. He slid into bed next to Ed. "Oh, well," he sighed. "At least we know what to get each other for Christmas this year."

"You know what's weird?" Ed shook his head, thinking of past gifts they'd given each other. "We're both so romantic, yet so damned practical."

Rick chuckled as he reached for his own book on his nightstand. "I know. Speaking of practical, since we're going to Mom and Dad's on Sunday, I want to go shopping for our groceries and that Easter dinner I promised Mrs. Penfield tomorrow night or Saturday, before the stores get too crazy next week. You wanna go with me?"

"Sure," Ed said, moving closer to him. "Did you talk to the kids about coloring Easter eggs next Saturday?"

"Yep. They're looking forward to it. I'll meet you at Claire's after work."

Ed laughed softly. "Easter hams and coloring eggs with three kids. Wouldn't my friend Glen laugh himself silly, saying we're turning into some hetero, suburban couple? I told Gordy there was a lot of that stuff going on with us. You know, the day-to-day stuff, instead of the fun stuff."

"Well, *I'm* still having fun," Rick said, kissing his cheek. "We're just weird, like you always say. Still," he said with another sigh, "with me having three days off in a row for Easter, I sure wish we could do something extra fun. I knew putting in all that overtime during the flu epidemic would pay off, but so what? I've got the time, and you don't."

It was Ed's turn to sigh. "I know. I wish I could go out and play with you after Easter, but I've got to finish painting the Grubers' garage. They were awfully nice about letting me put it off, first for our weekend in Michigan, and then when I was sick."

He closed his book, thinking. "Do you s'pose we can go away somewhere this summer? Just us? I know we shouldn't spend a lot of money, but I'd love to do something special, even if it's just a trip to Cedar Point to ride the roller coasters."

"Of course," Rick said definitely. "We'll do something, and I've never been to Cedar Point, so that sounds like fun. Don't worry. Maybe we're getting serious about life and the future, but we'll still have lots of fun. I promise."

Rick put his book aside, then pulled Ed to him, taking him in his arms. "Everything's gonna be fine. You know that, don't you?"

"Yes," Ed said, resting his head on Rick's chest. "I know it. I guess I'm just getting used to all of this. Really, I've never been happier, but it's—" The uneasy thoughts he'd been having all week returned, and determinedly he pushed them aside. "It's funny how it sometimes hits me that I'm really married. If someone would have told me a year ago this was gonna happen, I woulda just laughed."

"I know. Me, too. But if I was lying here next to someone else, I don't think I'd feel as confident about the future as I do now."

*Rick's right,* Ed told himself for the second time that week. *If he's not worried, why should I be?*

Rick kissed Ed deeply, and Ed finally felt something other than uneasiness stirring within. "Darlin, do ya s'pose . . ." he began.

"Oh, yes, baby. Please. Will you make love to me, your new husband, here on a Thursday night?"

"Yes," Ed whispered. "I can do that." He crawled on top of Rick. "Why don't you lose those glasses," he said, smiling into his face. "I don't want them getting broken."

<∋•∈>

Later, Rick resting in his arms, Ed sighed. "You okay?"

Rick moaned softly. "Oh, yes. I am most definitely okay."

Ed chuckled. "Damn. Married five whole days, and it's still good."

Rick smiled, his eyes closed. "I used to hear people talk about chemistry, but I never gave it much thought until I hooked up with you. We've got it. Let's just be glad."

"Oh, I am." Ed glanced at the clock. "It's past your bedtime, you know."

"That's okay. I'm about ready to drift off, lying here in my lover's arms. Can you hold me close, like this, until I fall asleep?"

"Even after that," Ed said, kissing him gently.

Ed closed his eyes, listening to Rick's even breathing, wondering when Rick's snoring would begin. Fortunately, he seemed to be getting used to it, as it wasn't terribly noisy, simply steady.

Ed carefully reached over to turn off the lamp. He was pretty tired himself; work had been more exhausting the past two days than he had been willing to admit. He settled against Rick, taking him back in his arms, thinking, *Marriage may be about laundry and chicken breasts on sale at the IGA, but it's about this, too. I need to remember this when the bad times come. Mom is right. We'll end up fighting about something someday. I think I can handle that, but what will happen when people really understand what's going on with us?*

He held his husband in his arms, relaxing in the soft darkness and quiet of the bedroom where he'd spent so many nights alone wishing for just such a man to be his companion, lover, and committed spouse.

*If only we could just stay here where it's safe, and not have to worry about what people think, or our jobs, or any of that shit.*

But Ed—always practical, always pragmatic—knew that outside the walls of the little house on Coleman Street lay the town of Porterfield, the state of Indiana, the rest of the world, and a good many people who wouldn't see the warmth and strength of their love for each other. No, they'd see only two perverts and instantly condemn them.

Ed remembered Mrs. Penfield telling him they would have to be strong to deal with the adversity that might come their way, and for months he had confidently felt he was strong enough, but now that his dream had come true, the stark reality of sharing his life with another man in a society that often disapproved of such a relationship continued to weigh upon his mind.

*Please just let it be the stupid flu that's making me feel weak,* he thought. *Please let me have the kind of strength I need, and the kind Rick deserves in a husband.*

Rick began to snore. Ed found himself smiling in the dark, immediately comforted once again by the reality of Rick, his Dream Man.

Only time would tell what kind of problems they might encounter, and as Gordy had counseled, Ed would have to just take it as it came.

❦

Ed spent the rest of the week mentally preparing himself for their road trip to Indianapolis to see Rick's parents and collect the rest of Rick's things. Considering the thoughts he had been having, he felt he needed all the self-encouragement he could muster.

John and Vera Benton, liberal big-city teachers that they were, had gracefully accepted their son's sexual orientation and were pleased at his choice of Ed as a life partner. Their concerns rested with the viability of Ed and Rick making a life together in Porterfield, and since their thoughts were similar to the ones Ed had been having himself, he wasn't overly excited about seeing them again.

Although Rick was still put out by the opinions they had expressed during a visit to Porterfield a month earlier, he was eager to claim the possessions they had been storing for him and told Ed he would listen to whatever they had to say, and do his best to withhold comment, if it meant he could move the rest of his things into what was now their home together.

"Shit! I can only imagine what little speech Mom has cooked up for us this time," Rick had snorted in disgust when they originally made plans for the journey.

By midmorning on Sunday, they were headed south on I-69 in Ed's truck, toward Indianapolis, and toward a possible confrontation.

Ed, preferring not to think about what Vera called "a mother's prerogative to worry," turned up the radio volume, singing in his extremely off-key voice to Juice Newton's "Angel of the Morning."

Rick smirked at him. "Baby, you know I love you, but you can't sing any better than I can."

Ed chose to ignore that remark. "I think I like Juice Newton's version of this song better than the original. What do you think?"

Rick shrugged.

Casey Kasem, the host of *American Top 40* and Ed's favorite disc jockey, followed Juice Newton, promising he wouldn't stop countin' 'em down until they reached number one.

"I wonder if 'Rapture' will be number one again this week." Ed turned the volume back down for the commercials. "You know, Judy likes Blondie, too. I should get her the album, or at least buy it for us and let her borrow it. What do you think?"

Rick gently put his hand on Ed's right leg. "Baby, it's not working."

"What?"

"Trying to distract me. Look, I know you're nervous about seeing them, and even more worried I'm gonna make a scene again. Hell, I'm worried I might not keep my mouth shut, but whatever happens, we'll get though it as gracefully as possible."

Ed glanced at him. "Yeah, I know. I just wish they could be as happy for us as everyone else seems to be." For the first time that week he allowed himself to say out loud what he'd been thinking. "I can't help it. Their worrying about us makes me worry. It makes me think we're in for more trouble than we think we are."

Rick's hand squeezed Ed's leg. "They are happy for us, in their own way, just like your mom. They just want us to move to a place they think is safer for us. And like I said that weekend at the lake, we're gonna show 'em they're wrong."

"Where do you get all of your confidence?" Ed didn't want to admit his own confidence had weakened recently, but he was curious as to why Rick didn't seem to be having the same thoughts.

Rick leaned across the seat and gave Ed a very quick kiss on the cheek. "My love for you is the only confidence I need. Well, that and knowing how much you love me. They say love conquers all, and I, for one, am gonna believe that until it's proven otherwise."

Amazed, Ed felt his own confidence begin to soar and his nervous anticipation fade. The road ahead of them was deserted, so he risked leaning across the seat for a cheek kiss of his own.

"I don't know how you do it, but you always manage to say something to make me feel better."

Rick squeezed his leg again. "That's what I'm here for, baby."

Ed drove the truck into the heavier traffic on Indianapolis's north side. Rick directed him to the northeast neighborhood where he had grown up and where his parents still lived in the same comfortable, two-story brick house on a shady street.

They both hopped out of the truck, glad to stretch their legs after the long drive. The front door opened and John and Vera walked onto the front steps, drawing them in with cheerful greetings.

As Ed and Rick, with some help from John, moved boxes of Rick's belongings from his old bedroom to the truck, Ed kept waiting for some sort of comment from Vera or John, but it appeared they either had nothing to say or were keeping their thoughts to themselves.

"You sure you really want all this junk in your house, Ed?" John grinned at him as he shoved a carton of books into the truck. Ed grinned back at John, feeling as he usually did that he was looking at an older, gray-haired version of Rick.

"If it'll make it home for Rick, I want every last bit of it."

Rick and John carefully loaded an old easy chair into the truck while Ed secured a floor lamp next to it. Ed was pleased to see several boxes of kitchen supplies go into the truck next. They would come in very handy in his sparsely appointed kitchen. He could tell that Rick, who was already assuming the lion's share of the cooking responsibilities, was pleased as well. Ed couldn't explain it, but seeing such basic, homey things in the truck bed seemed to make the house on Coleman Street have the potential to be more of a home for the two of them than it had already become.

Vera—tall, thin, and just as gray as her husband—insisted they stop for lunch. Over sandwiches and coffee—and tea for Ed, the non–coffee drinker—they discussed general matters: the weather, the recent assassination attempt on President Reagan, and John and Vera's plans for a trip across Canada that coming summer. It was relaxed and cozy, and again, Ed felt his pessimistic thoughts diminish.

When the truck was loaded and it was time for Ed and Rick to return to Porterfield, Vera beckoned them into the family room. Ed looked at Rick, assuming lecture time had finally come.

Vera stood in front of the fireplace, a solemn expression on her face. "Boys, before you go home, there's something I'd like to say."

Rick, obviously fearing the worst, put his hands on his hips. "Yeah, Mom?"

She opened her arms wide to both of them and smiled. "I just want to say I'm very happy for both of you." She hugged them, one arm around each man's waist. "And, Ed, welcome to the family."

Ed hugged his almost-mother-in-law tightly. The weak tears that had occasionally come to his eyes since his bout with the flu returned, but he knew this time they weren't tears of worry but tears of happiness and relief. Ed and Rick stood within the safety of Vera's welcoming embrace for a good long time, and Ed felt that maybe things would work out for them after all.

# Chapter Four

Ed, paint splattered from his work on the Grubers' garage, stopped by Laurie's house Good Friday afternoon with Easter candy for his nephew and niece. He had been spending so much time with Rick's nieces and nephew, he sometimes felt he was neglecting his own.

He found Laurie—as short as their mother was, but dark haired like their father—in the kitchen, knee deep in laundry.

"Little something extra for the kids' Easter baskets, from Uncle Ed," he said, showing her two hollow chocolate squirrels he'd purchased earlier that week while shopping with Mrs. Heston. He felt they were a fun change from the usual bunnies.

"Thanks," Laurie said, pulling a wad of towels out of the dryer. "Just set 'em down. The kids aren't around. Well, Lesley isn't. She's over at her friend Carrie's. Bobby, of course, you can hear in the backyard."

Ed stepped to the window. Seven-year-old Bobby was playing kickball with the boys next door. There seemed to be a dispute over whether one of the Schmidt boys had been legally tagged out.

"Todd," Laurie continued, "was dragged off to Good Friday services by his mother, who I'm sure wants all of Porterfield to notice how devout the Ameses are." She snorted. "I told Todd, as one of those awful heathen Stephenses, I'd stay home and do the laundry. It's gonna be a busy weekend."

"Bobby sure has grown this year," Ed remarked, watching him kick the ball solidly past third base. "Looks more like Todd every day. His birthday's coming up, isn't it? Eight already! Doesn't seem possible. Is there anything special he wants this year?"

"What doesn't he want?" Laurie groaned. "Oh, you might get him a Rubik's Cube. Trying to figure that out should keep him quiet for awhile."

"Oh, man." Ed laughed. "Rick wanted to get me one, but I'm afraid I'd waste too much time on it. He thinks I'd be good at it for some reason."

"I'm sure I'd end up throwing it across the room." Laurie giggled.

"Well, I'll get one for Bobby, but I'll tell him to keep it away from his mom," Ed said, sitting down. "Speaking of a busy weekend, did you hear Rick and I are going to Mrs. Penfield's for Easter dinner?"

"Yeah. Mom told me. She was remarkably calm about it, but then she's always liked old Hilda. I think she gives her credit for the two of us making it through high school with passing grades."

"By the way," she continued, looking at him over her laundry basket, "Mom plans on stopping by your place later today with chocolate chip cookies for you and Rick, her idea of an Easter treat. She knows how much you both like them."

"Good," Ed said gratefully. "We bought so much candy for the kids, and even some for Mrs. Penfield, that we didn't buy anything for ourselves." He picked up one of the chocolate squirrels, smiling. "Mrs. Penfield has been so good to Rick and me. She even wants to give us some kind of a wedding present. Can you believe it?"

"Well," Laurie said, folding towels. "I'm glad you've both got her for a friend. You couldn't have a better one. I always said she was my favorite teacher in school. You know, with her son dying so young like he did in Korea, I've thought for years she's kind of adopted you. I'm glad she likes Rick just as much." She grinned at her brother. "I'll say this much. Married life is agreeing with you. Honeymoon is going strong, huh?"

"Yeah," Ed sighed happily. "No problems at our place—at least not yet."

"That's good to hear. She rolled her eyes at the sound of another argument from the backyard. "Just don't screw it up by having kids. You'll never have a peaceful moment for the rest of your lives."

Ed laughed with her. "I don't think you need to worry about that. We decided, between your two and Claire's three, that we have more than enough."

"Good thinking." She flopped into a kitchen chair. "With Lesley in first grade next year, I'd really like to return to work full-time in the fall. Todd swears we don't need the money, but I think I need to get out of the house more." She sneered at the laundry waiting to be folded. "I am no Stepford wife."

"Funny, isn't it, how marriage changes things," Ed mused.

Laurie nodded. "Yeah. I wouldn't trade Todd or the kids for the world, but sometimes . . . oh, I think about other things I could have done with my life."

"Like what?" Ed asked, intrigued.

"Oh, maybe have moved to Fort Wayne after I finished secretarial school, maybe had my own apartment for awhile. I went from Mom and Dad's to Todd's. Sometimes I wonder what it would be like to live alone."

Ed snorted. "It ain't all it's cracked up to be, believe me."

"I know you had to wait a long time for Rick to come along," Laurie said wistfully. "Thing is, I think you appreciate it even more 'cause you had to wait. Be grateful for that." She sighed. "Be grateful you don't have Eunice Ames for a mother-in-law, too. How'd it go with Rick's folks last weekend?"

"Okay. Better than I thought, actually. Vera seemed to be really pleased about our moving in together, and if she's still worried about us living together here in Porterfield, she didn't say anything. She just welcomed me into the family. It was really nice, but Rick said on the way home she was just sparing our feelings. He's still p.o.'d about the stuff she said when they were here visiting."

"Well, she sounds like a better mother-in-law than Eunice."

Ed groaned. "Geez, are you beginning to take Mom's nonsense seriously?"

Norma and Eunice Ames didn't care for each other, and both Laurie and Ed had found themselves in the crossfire of their barbed comments over the years.

"Despite whatever Mom says about Eunice, and the stuff I've said out of family loyalty, she obviously adores you and the kids. Hell, Todd told me last winter she even likes me."

"I know, I know," she said. "Yeah, Eunice does like you." Laurie giggled. "She always says how polite and respectful you are, probably just her way of saying how rude Mom is. No, Eunice isn't all that bad. I just get tired of her I'm-the-first-lady-of-Porterfield-and-don't-you-forget-it routine."

"Yeah, she used to pull that with Mrs. Penfield when she was on the school board. Still, if that's all I had to bitch about, I'd be happy."

Laurie gave Ed a shrewd glance as she pulled some sheets out of the dryer. She opened her mouth to say something, obviously thought better of it, and playfully tossed a pillowcase on Ed's head, as she would have done when they were younger.

"Hey!" Ed yanked the pillowcase off his head and pushed his hair back into place. "Watch it, Shortshit. The Easter Bunny's coming, ya know."

Laurie laughed and purposely shook a sheet out of the dryer in Ed's face. "So is Rick getting settled in okay?"

Ed, batting the sheet away, debated whether to answer her question or find something to throw at her. He decided to act his age, for the moment anyway.

"He's settled in, for the most part. Seems like he's been there longer than two weeks, except for all of his books. They're sitting in boxes in the far corner of the living room. I sure wish I could make him the bookcase I told him I'd make when we were in Michigan."

"It'll happen," Laurie said confidently. "Give it all time. If you try to rush things, you'll just get crazy. Heck, you've got your whole lives for bookcases and whatever. Enjoy the ride while you can."

"I *am*."

"Seriously. Don't worry about stuff. One day you'll look back, twenty years from now, wondering where the time went."

"I guess. You know what, though? I sure wish I had some more pictures of Rick and me together. Do you realize neither one of us has a camera? Do you think I could borrow yours sometime?"

"Sure," she said. "Anytime. That's not a bad idea. You need to start your own family album."

She pulled another pillowcase out of the dryer, and Ed grabbed it before she could do any more damage. He held it threateningly over her head.

Laurie threw her hands up in front of her face. "I surrender! Really, I just got my hair done."

"Throw in some free film with the camera, and I'll consider your surrender," he said, shaking the pillowcase at her.

"Yes, I'll give you the film. Let it be my wedding present to you, okay? Mrs. Penfield's not the only one who can be generous. Now, put that damned thing down!"

<figure>⋘•⋙</figure>

Ed awoke early Easter morning. Mr. Redd was chirping happily, and Ed could feel the sunshine through the window. He turned over, surprised to find the other side of the bed empty. Then he smelled coffee from the kitchen and smiled. Rick sometimes had a hard time sleeping in on his days off.

He rolled over again, and his eyes widened. There was an Easter basket on his nightstand. "When did he sneak that in here?" Ed muttered, reaching for it. It was a small wooden basket, painted in Easter's pastel colors. Inside, on a bed of Easter grass, was a solid chocolate rabbit surrounded by jelly beans. "I'll be damned," he said, grinning, wondering when and how Rick had concocted this surprise for him.

He put on his bedraggled bathrobe and, grabbing the basket, stumbled bleary-eyed into the kitchen. Rick was at the table, coffee cup in hand, reading the Sunday paper.

"Looks like the Easter Bunny was here this morning," Ed said, bending over to kiss him.

Rick grinned at him. "Looks like," he said as he returned the kiss.

"Now I feel bad," Ed murmured, hugging him. "I didn't get you anything."

"Don't worry about it. I'll take your mom's cookies over Easter candy any day. So what all did you get there?"

Ed peered into the basket. "Well, a bunny and some jelly beans. Thanks, darlin'. I'm sure the Easter Bunny had some help with this."

Rick mock frowned at him. "Is that *all* you got?"

"Well, yeah." Ed fingered a few jelly beans. "Am I missing something?"

"Hmmm," Rick said thoughtfully. "It seems to me the Easter Bunny was supposed to put something else in that basket. Why don't you try digging around in the grass?"

Ed looked at him with suspicion. "What are you up to?"

Rick looked back at him with wide-eyed innocence. "Why, nothing! I just happen to know the Easter Bunny brought you more than candy, that's all."

Ed carefully pushed the jelly beans aside, digging into the green plastic grass. Yes, there was something else in the basket, something hard and square buried in the grass. A few strands of the plastic grass fell to the floor as he reached under it, putting his fingers around a small box. He lifted it out, gasping. It was a velvet-covered box, the sort used for jewelry.

"*What* is this?"

Rick's warm and tender special was glowing. "Open it and find out, baby."

With trembling fingers, Ed fumbled with the lid. His mouth fell open in surprise. Lying on the velvet inside was a ring, a plain gold band. "You . . . what . . . ," he sputtered.

"Something extra for Easter for my wonderful husband, something I'll hope he'll wear for the rest of his life," Rick said softly.

Ed pulled the ring from the box, putting it in the palm of his hand. It was a standard sort of men's wedding band, simple and beautiful. Ed studied it through blurry eyes. "Oh, darlin', I love it, but—"

"No buts," Rick said firmly. "I know, we're supposed to be saving our money, but I started saving for this months ago, right after Christmas. I knew we'd be together like this someday, and I knew I would want you to have this. I've never been much for rings myself, but something told me this would mean the world to you, and if the look on your face is any indication, I was right."

Rick *was* right. Ed tried to wipe the tears from his eyes without dropping the ring. He couldn't believe Rick would spend his hard-earned money on such a conventional yet incredibly perfect gift for him.

Rick stood up, putting his arms around Ed. "Cry all you want. I might join you. There's just one thing I have to do first."

He let Ed go, hurrying to the stereo in the living room. In a moment "Baby, I Love You," the song that was playing when Rick first told Ed he loved him, came through the speakers.

Rick returned to Ed, taking the ring from him. "Look inside of it. There's something else."

He held the ring up so Ed could see the engraving. He looked closer. In tiny letters it read: E BABY I LOVE YOU R. At the sight of it, Ed began to cry harder. He threw his arms around Rick, hugging him tightly. "Oh, I love you so much, too!"

Rick, tears rolling down his own face, hugged him back. "I know, baby," he whispered. "I just wanted you to always know how much I love you, right now in the spring of 1981, for the rest of your life, however long that might be. Will you wear it, for me?"

Ed nodded his head against Rick's shoulder, unable to speak. Rick held him close while the song played, stroking his back. "C'mon," he finally said. "Let me put it on. Which hand do you want it on?"

Ed, composure regained, held out his left hand. "What do you think? I might as well let the whole world know I'm a happily married man."

Rick grinned at him affectionately. "Okay." He slid the ring on Ed's finger. "With this ring, I thee wed," he intoned solemnly.

"Boy, do I do," Ed whispered, admiring the ring on his finger. He had never, in any of his dreams, imagined having such a token of a man's love for him. It may have been a heterosexual kind of tradition, but he didn't care. It was from Rick, and he loved it almost as much as he loved him.

He kissed Rick, wiping away a few tears from his face at the same time. "Thank you, Rick," he whispered. "I just wish I had one for you."

Rick shook his head. "No, don't let it worry you. As I said, I'm not much for rings. I've just never cared for the feeling of them on my fingers." He grinned his mischievous grin at Ed. "However, there is something you could do for me someday."

"What's that?" Ed kissed him again.

Rick put his arms tightly around him. "Well, the one piece of jewelry I've always admired, always thought I'd like to have for myself, is a gold chain for my neck. I'd love to have one from you someday, so I could wear your love close to my heart."

He gave Ed a small shake. "But! Don't you go running down to Wexler's Jewelers tomorrow and buy one. Someday, that's all I ask. Someday when it's something you really want to do for me, because you'll know deep in your heart the time is right, like this was for me. I wanted to give it to you when I moved in, but I didn't have enough money saved, so I decided Easter, the time of new beginnings, would do just as well."

Ed smiled, looking at the ring. "Do you mean to tell me you walked into Wexler's downtown, on Commerce Street, and ordered this man's ring with this inscription?"

Rick nodded smugly. "I did."

"Geez, I'll bet Old Man Wexler's eyes bugged out of his head."

Rick chuckled. "Oh, he might have been a little surprised, but he tried not to let it show. I'm sure he was just happy to make the sale." Rick brought Ed's hand to his lips for a kiss. "It fits right, which is a relief. I swiped your old class ring out of your dresser drawer one morning. I was a nervous wreck, worried you'd find it missing."

"I never noticed a thing," Ed admitted. "I'm just glad my fingers haven't gotten fatter since high school." He sighed in complete contentment. "Well, once again, you've managed to make me the happiest man in the world."

"How 'bout that?" Rick teased, his love for Ed sparkling in his eyes.

Ed shook his head. "What are you gonna do for an encore, anyway?"

"Oh, I'll think of something," Rick said confidently. "You know, I plan on spending the rest of my life telling you how much I love you. I'll get an even better idea sometime."

Ed put his arms around Rick, smiling into his eyes. "Thank you, darlin'. I love you." He laughed, embarrassed, feeling the words were inadequate for what he was feeling. "Happy Easter!"

Rick threw his head back and let go a whoop of joy. "Happy Easter to you, too, baby! Enough of this romantic shit. We've got a ham to bake."

✧•✧

A few hours later Ed and Rick were busily moving around Mrs. Penfield's huge, old-fashioned kitchen, preparing Easter dinner. The baking ham was sending a wonderful aroma through the old house on the corner of Spruce and Race streets. Rick was frowning into a scalloped potato casserole he was making.

"Well, I suppose this isn't the most imaginative Easter dinner ever. It was standard fare at the Benton house for years, though, cooked by my mother, who is not known for her imagination in the kitchen. Still, I wouldn't want to get too carried away with Mrs. Penfield. You never know about an older person's digestion."

Ed was chopping vegetables for the salad, pausing occasionally to admire his ring. "Oh, it'll be fine. Mrs. Penfield's one of us, just a typical Hoosier, with typical Hoosier tastes. I was a nervous wreck, though, setting the table. That china of hers; it puts my grandmother's wedding china to shame. Mom would love it."

"This whole house," Rick murmured, sliding the casserole in the oven.

"So many beautiful things. I tell you, I didn't know how queer I was until I first stepped in this place. It makes me really want a place like this for us someday."

"Me, too." Ed smiled at his left hand.

Rick smirked at him. "Will you forget about that ring for a moment and get that salad made? You're gonna be wearing it for a long time, if I have anything to say about it."

Rick was testing the ham when a sedan pulled into the driveway alongside Ed's white pickup truck. A friend of Mrs. Penfield's, also a former teacher, had chauffeured her to Easter services, as her arthritis no longer allowed her to drive. She alighted from the car, cane in hand. "I'm kinda busy here. Could you go help her up the back steps?"

"Sure." Ed walked through the butler's pantry to the back entrance. He hurried down the steps, meeting Mrs. Penfield halfway up the walk. Arm in arm, they entered the house. Ed saw her glance at his hand. She smiled and said nothing. He suspected she had known about the ring long before he did.

Dinner, despite Rick's misgivings, was a success. Mrs. Penfield was lavish in her praise, and her young friends glowed with pleasure.

After dessert, an apple pie from Patterson's Bakery, Mrs. Penfield sighed happily. "That was delicious, boys. I expect no apologies, either, for a store-bought pie. I was enjoying Patterson's pies long before either of you were born. Now, I insist you leave the cleanup for awhile. Let's adjourn to the garden for a nice, long talk. Ed, would you fetch my shawl from the parlor? It's still a bit chilly for me, but the tulips are too beautiful to waste."

Soon Mrs. Penfield was settled on the bench located in the small rose arbor. Ed and Rick were seated on old-fashioned metal lawn chairs, facing her. The tulips were indeed glorious, a riot of pastel color throughout the entire backyard. Ed remembered his wish that he and Rick would be living together before the tulips bloomed. He reached for Rick's hand, smiling. It was, without a doubt, the happiest Easter Sunday he could ever remember.

Mrs. Penfield, seeing their hands together, smiled. "Well, as you know, boys, I have wanted to talk to you seriously for some time, and I'm finally prepared to speak my piece. I do hope you'll bear with me, as I may become a bit windy."

"Go right ahead," Rick said, grinning. He settled back in his chair contentedly.

Mrs. Penfield fell silent a moment, her gaze covering the grounds between her large, solid, nineteenth-century brick home, and the carriage house, made of the same red brick, which stood parallel to the alley. "As I'm sure I mentioned at some point in time, I first came to this house as a bride, fifty years ago next month. It hardly seems possible so much time has passed. On that May day in 1931, I certainly could not have imagined I'd be living here alone one day, the last of the Penfields. Oh, I had high hopes for many things, and I've been blessed. I realized a great many of my dreams. I had a career that gave me enormous satisfaction, a husband I loved dearly, and a wonderful son. Yes, he was taken from us too soon, but his memory is very dear to me.

"I've traveled extensively, thanks to my teacher's schedule and my husband's income. I've seen the world, and every time I returned from a trip, I looked at this house with great affection, glad to be home. My background, growing up in Adams County, didn't prepare for me for such gracious living, but I've enjoyed this house and its contents as if I had been born to them."

"That seems hard to believe," Ed said. "I can't imagine you anywhere but here."

Mrs. Penfield sighed. "Oh, no, Ed. My life was very different then. My parents were not well off, and they both passed away in the influenza epidemic of 1918. I was just eleven years old. A very kind bachelor uncle took me in after that. It was through his kindness that I was able to graduate high school, then obtain my teaching degree."

Rick grinned at her. "This bachelor uncle, do you suppose . . ."

She nodded with a grin of her own. "Yes, Rick. I do suppose. He had a very dear friend for many years. Someday I must tell the two of you about my uncle William and his friend. As odd as it may seem, I don't think I truly understood their friendship until Ed told me of his relationship with you. I've also begun to think he would be thrilled to see the two of you living together so openly. Oh, things may still be difficult for you, but let me assure you, there has been some progress."

She kneaded her gnarled fingers. "As I said, I certainly never expected to be living out the end of my days here alone. I've made the best of it, but as time goes on, and my old friend arthritis makes himself more at home in my body, I can't help but wonder what will happen to this place after I'm gone.

"Ed," she said gently, "when you first came to work for me some five years ago, I was pleased to have a favorite former student in my employ. I must admit I have been rather surprised, as my fondness for you has grown over the years. As I've said before, you much remind me of George Junior. It has done my old heart good to have your cheerful presence in this rambling brick pile of a house.

"As I also told you, however, the day you first informed me of Rick's entrance into your life, I had suspected throughout those years you were carrying a burden. It troubled me, and I can't tell you how relieved I am to see that burden has been lifted. I can only imagine how the burden of being different has taken a toll on you—on both of you—over the years. I am very grateful that God, in His infinite wisdom, saw fit to bring you together. The joy the two of you have brought to each other's lives is an inspiration, or at least it would be to many who would see fit to condemn you both, if they only opened their eyes."

"We've been very lucky," Ed murmured, looking at Rick.

"Perhaps," Mrs. Penfield said thoughtfully. "As you know, I feel it will take a good deal more than luck for you both to succeed in this world."

She turned to Rick. "As happy as I was for Ed when he first told me about you, I wanted to make sure you would be worthy of him." She glanced at the ring on Ed's hand. "It hasn't take me long to determine that you are. I remember well that cold January night, when I sent Ed out to scrape the ice from the sidewalks, that you told me of your intentions to purchase that ring Ed is wearing. I knew then the two of you had great potential for a long-lasting relationship."

"Thank you, Mrs. Penfield," Rick said humbly. "I'd do anything for Ed. You know that."

"Yes, I do," she told him. "That is why I have reached a decision." She looked gravely at both of them. "At age seventy-three, struggling with this demon called arthritis, I doubt I'll be here on Spruce Street for many more years. I have spoken at length with my attorney, Mr. Mason. I will soon be changing my will. Aside from certain bequeathals to the Porterfield Public Library, the high school, and of course, Effie Maude, I intend to leave my entire estate, including this house, to the two of you."

Ed and Rick looked at her, stunned. "Mrs. Penfield!" Ed softly exclaimed, tears coming to his eyes for the second time that Easter Sunday. "Why . . . why, I don't know what to say!"

"Me either," Rick gasped.

"A simple thank-you will suffice." She chuckled, enjoying their reactions.

"But—but," Ed stammered as he always did when so surprised. "But us? Are you sure?"

"Very sure," she said definitely. "Ed, you've worked hard to maintain this house for me for years now. You, better than anyone, know its eccentricities. Oh, I'm aware that much work needs to be done to restore it to its former glory, but I've no doubt the two of you are capable of that task. I've also no doubt the two of you will be together when that day comes. If I had any doubt, I might not being doing this.

"There's more, if you're ready to hear it," she finished.

"I don't know if I am," Ed said in a daze.

"I think I need a moment," Rick said, clutching Ed's hand. "Thank you, Mrs. Penfield! I . . . well, I never, ever imagined such a thing. I'm in shock!"

"Well, perhaps when that shock wears off, you'll begin to see how this gift could be a burden."

"How?" they both asked together, then grinned sheepishly.

"The taxes will be a burden, especially at first. Indiana has a rather steep inheritance tax for nonblood inheritances. Mr. Mason and myself, however, have come up with a plan to avoid this, if you'd like to hear it."

Rick glanced at Ed. "We're all ears, believe me."

Mrs. Penfield sighed. "My more immediate concern, rather than the future of this property, is my own welfare. As time goes by, I find myself in need of more assistance. Effie Maude does her best, but she, too, is getting along in years. Her life is on her farm, and I've resisted the impulse to ask her to move into the house.

"Ed." Mrs. Penfield turned to him. "Have you ever explored the second floor of the carriage house?"

"Why, no," he said, puzzled. "I've never had any reason to."

Mrs. Penfield smiled mysteriously. "I think it's time you did. Will you both assist me to the carriage-house stairs? I'd like for you both to see it now."

Ed and Rick helped Mrs. Penfield to her feet. They walked with her, slowly, toward the carriage house. It was an imposing structure, with heavy sliding doors on the alley side designed for the horses and carriages it had been built for in 1898. A garage door had been added to the opposite, south side, in the age of automobiles, and a driveway led from Race Street, on the east side, to a parking area in front of the garage door.

A regular door was on this wall as well, near the east side, adjacent to the garage entrance. Mrs. Penfield opened the door, leading them inside. The lower floor, aside from its ample space for cars, held a jumble of garden tools and various cast-off items from the main house. A flight of stairs, partitioned off from the rest of area, led steeply up the east side. Ed had indeed been inside the building on many occasions but had never ascended the stairs.

Mrs. Penfield, with their assistance, climbed the stairs to a landing with a leaded glass window facing right, and to the left, a closed door. She opened it, gesturing for them to go inside.

"Well, who knew?" Ed mumbled, looking around. The second floor had been made over into living quarters, the floor space nearly equal to the first floor of Ed's little house on Coleman Street.

"From the time the house was built, until the Depression, this was the quarters for the carriage man, handyman, whatever you would want to call him," Mrs. Penfield told them. "My father-in-law purposely designed it this way when he had the house built. We did have live-in help, occasionally, after the war years, but after my father-in-law died, George and I saw no need for the extra assistance. Twentieth-century living being what it is, it was no longer necessary. I'm afraid these quarters have been rather neglected, but as you can see, it would make a marvelous first home for any couple."

Rick, investigating the dusty kitchen area, turned to her with a smile. "Okay. What do you have up your sleeve?"

"I would, at my own expense, of course, have these rooms modernized and turned into the charming apartment it easily can be for the two of you, if you would do me the honor of living here. I would rest easier knowing I had two strong young men on the property. You would have complete run of the grounds, and the main house as well, within reason. It would benefit you in the long run as well."

"How?" Ed asked, taking in the tall, narrow windows, each topped by a faded but still beautiful stained-glass pane.

"Ah, that is where Mr. Mason comes in. He has informed me of a curious loophole in our Indiana inheritance tax. If the two of you were to live here, caring for the house and property—and to some extent myself—from now until the time of my death, you would be able to charge the fee of your services to me, so much per year, against the inheritance tax. By that time, you would owe nothing, or next to it. You also would have the benefit of living here, rent free, making any plans you see fit for the property when it becomes your own.

"Oh, we would have to sign a document to this effect. It would, in addition to erasing your tax burden, create an official agreement between us."

She gave them both a knowing look. "I'm sure the idea of caring for an old woman isn't too attractive, but I don't want that to weigh on your decision. Effie Maude will be here for the bulk of that responsibility, and if need be, I'll hire a nurse. In your case, I'm more concerned with the property's upkeep, and your future with it."

Rick was shaking his head. "I'm overwhelmed. I don't know what to think, or say."

"Why don't you both investigate the rest of the apartment," she suggested, leaning heavily on her cane.

Ed and Rick did just that. The main portion, inside the stairway door, was divided into a kitchen and dining area, facing toward the alley. The rest of it was an ample living area, with the two stained-glass-topped windows overlooking the garden. A hallway, midway on the wall opposite the stairs, cut through the western section. Ed and Rick walked the length of the hall, noting the cozy bedroom with windows facing the garden. On the other side of the hall were a large closet and a bathroom. Though in serious need of modernizing, it was bigger than the bathroom they currently shared on Coleman Street. A window at the end of the hall looked into the line of tall pines screening the property from the house next door.

Their footfalls echoed through the empty rooms. They looked down at the worn, faded linoleum on the floor and poked their noses into the hall closet and an equally spacious one in the bedroom.

"The help around here lived well," Rick remarked.

"I can't believe it," Ed murmured. "It's almost as big as our house. You'd never guess from the outside. Still, I'm sure it'd look a lot different full of furniture."

"You know a lot more about this stuff than I do," Rick said, noting the high ceilings. "What do you think?"

Ed's handyman frown came over his face as he stroked his chin. "Well, let's see. There's a good gas furnace downstairs for the whole building. I always wondered why that was there. Now I know! It would be easy enough to have that checked out, but at least we know we'd be comfortable in the winter.

"I worry about these high ceilings, though. I'm thinking there can't be much space between the ceiling and the roof. It could get pretty hot in the summertime, but I think two window AC units would take care of that, one here in the bedroom, and one in the living room. This part will be easier to cool, with all the shade from the pines as well. They would go a long way toward keeping the afternoon sun from heating the bedroom."

Ed sighed. "I know I couldn't do the work it needs, though. I've got so many jobs lined up, I'd never get it done. Still, Mrs. Penfield said she'd pay for the work, and I'd really prefer that. If we were going to live here for any length of time, I'd want this to be the best home possible for us." He shrugged. "I don't know, darlin'. I'm still in shock. What do you think?"

Rick smiled, a look of excitement in his eyes. "I can see it. I can really see us here! Do you realize we're only four blocks from the post office? Shit, I could walk to work. I don't know, though. It would be a big change for both of us, and a commitment as well, right when we've just made a commitment to each other. The idea sounds great, but we need to really think about it before we make a decision."

Ed nodded. "I need time to take this in. I'm still trying to get used to the idea of this whole place being ours when she's gone. Rick," he exclaimed, "can you believe she's doing this? It's like she's handing us our dream house!"

"I know," Rick said, hugging him. "It's like another dream coming true. A part of me thinks we should turn her down, say we don't want it—but why? It's what she wants; she wants us to have it. Besides, I can't imagine she's going to be gone anytime soon. We have plenty of time to decide what to do about the place when it's ours."

"Well, one good thing," Ed said, leading Rick to one of the bedroom windows, "even if we did decide to move here, it will take awhile before it's ready. That gives us lots of time to prepare."

Ed pushed at one of the long-shut windows. It groaned in protest but opened. "We'd need screens for these for the summer," he commented. He stuck his head out, looking down at the tulips in full bloom and the back of the main house. "It's incredible! You're right. It's a dream come true. But I don't know; I just don't know."

Rick stuck his head out the window as well. "We don't have to decide today. I'm sure she doesn't expect it. It's going to take some time for this to sink in—all of it. Shall we tell her, though, we'll consider it?"

Ed smiled at him. "Yes. Definitely. Let's go back. I'm sure she'd like to sit down, and there's no place to do it up here."

They joined Mrs. Penfield near the stairway door and carefully led her back to her seat in the rose arbor. "Well," she said, relieved to be off her feet, "what do you think?"

They looked at each other. Ed nodded to Rick to speak for them.

"We are . . . deeply moved you want to do this for us," Rick began. "We accept the conditions of your will. I don't want to even think about your leaving us, but since you've done us this honor, we'll do our best to make you proud of us, after you're gone.

"As for the other part," Rick said, sighing, "I'm sure you understand we need time to think. This is a lot to take in, and considering I've lived in Ed's house for an entire two weeks, the idea of another move is . . . well, unexpected at best."

Mrs. Penfield nodded. "I understand, and I would expect you to both think it over. There's no rush, no real sense of urgency. It will take some time to make the apartment livable by current standards. Take your time. If you decide to move onto the property, I want it to be a well-thought-through, confident decision from both of you."

"We thank you from the bottom of our hearts, too," Ed said, shaking his head. "To have you on our side is like, well, it's like a suit of armor. I feel so much stronger, knowing you're looking out for us and wanting to help us. I've often wondered what it would be like to live here. I can't believe it may actually happen someday, sooner or later."

Mrs. Penfield chuckled. "I've long suspected that, Ed. I've seen you admiring this house on numerous occasions. It gives me great pleasure to think of it owned by someone who loves it as much as I, after I'm gone."

Rick took Ed's hand, applying pressure to the finger wearing the ring he had only given him that morning. "We promise to consider your offer carefully. You know what, though? Right now I'm thinking about your dining room, and your kitchen, full of dirty dishes. Mrs. Penfield, why don't you rest while Ed and I clean up? It would give us some time to adjust to all of this."

"Gladly." Mrs. Penfield painfully rose to her feet. "I could use a bit of rest, and I think you two have had enough excitement for one day."

⋘●⋙

They sat in their own living room that evening, still trying to digest the news of Mrs. Penfield's decision regarding her will and the possibility of moving into the carriage house.

"I wonder what your mom will say?" Rick mused, relaxing in an easy chair.

Ed snorted. "Who knows? But whatever it is, I'm sure it'll be loud."

"And my folks," Rick said, grinning. "So convinced I was messing up my life moving here. Not only did I find you, but this wonderful woman is offering us insurance for a great future together."

"I still can't believe it. It's like she's our fairy godmother or something."

"Yeah, she's our godmother and we're fairies." Rick laughed.

Ed chuckled, looking around the room. He'd lived in this house for three years. He had taken a great deal of pride in buying and maintaining it on his own. The thought of leaving made him sadder than he would have thought. "I guess I've gotten attached to this place," he said, continuing his thoughts out loud. "I knew we'd be leaving someday, but never this soon."

They heard Jett bang against the front door. Ed got up to let him in. "Letting Jett in and out would be a bitch there, though. Up and down those stairs all the time."

"More exercise," Rick remarked.

"You get enough exercise, walking your route."

"I know. I'm just thinking." Rick got up from his chair and began to pace. "I just can't help thinking it would be a wonderful opportunity for us. Ed, you don't have to sell this place. We could rent it out, in case things don't work out over there."

"You're right. I hadn't thought of that."

"Well, that's just it. There's a lot to think about, probably lots of things we haven't come to yet."

"All I know," Ed said, looking at the ring on his hand, "is this is an Easter I'll never forget. Did I say that already today? I think I did. This whole day hasn't soaked in yet."

Jett stood in front of Ed, meowing. "Don't you have any food in your dish?" he muttered. He walked to the kitchen, the cat on his heels. He poured Meow Mix into Jett's bowl, unable to settle his thoughts. He loved the idea; he hated it. He just didn't know.

Once Jett was happily crunching away, Ed walked slowly to the living room. Rick was now sitting on the sofa, a faraway look in his eyes. Ed knew without being told that Rick was already seeing them cozily living together, Jett included, in the carriage-house apartment.

"You really want this, don't you," he said bluntly.

Rick looked at him. The warm and tender special slowly spread over his face. "Baby," he said softly, patting the sofa cushion next to him, "come sit with me, okay?"

Ed sat down. Rick's arm went around him, pulling him closer. "Mrs. Penfield's not the only one with a speech to make today. Can I say some things?"

"Sure."

"Okay." Rick sighed. "Well. Seeing as how you've been staring at the hunk of gold on your hand all day, you know how much I love you and how committed I am to us, right?"

Ed nodded. "I know that."

Rick looked fondly around the room. "I fell in love with you in this room, I think. The first time I ever saw you was right inside that front door. Oh, I still remember that day, last fall. How I stood there, trying to be cool, thinking that a man I was so immediately attracted to couldn't be gay, couldn't be someone for me.

Rick pointed into the kitchen. "I kissed you for the first time right there, beside that table. That's when I knew for sure I was going to fall in love with you."

"Me, too," Ed whispered.

"We made love for the first time in that bedroom," Rick said, pointing again. "I couldn't even begin to tell you how many times we've since made love in there, in that bed."

He looked into Ed's eyes, smiling. As always, Ed saw his own love for Rick reflected in Rick's eyes. "I love this house. My life with you began here. A part of me never wants to leave this place. I became the happiest man in the world in this house.

"Thing is, though, the house doesn't really matter. I'd still be the happiest man in the world, living in a bomb shelter, a bus station, or a cardboard box, as long as I was with you. You know that, don't you?"

"Yes," Ed said, feeling the need to kiss him, and doing just that.

"Baby, I can't help but think this is what we should do. I can't help but believe the Fates that threw us together are still being kind, being generous. I think we've been handed a golden opportunity, an amazing opportunity to realize our dreams. They say things happen for a reason. I have to believe there's a reason for all of this happening, even if it's happening sooner than I ever expected."

Ed sighed. "So you really want this?"

Rick shrugged. "I know I need to think about it some more. I will. I promise. But, yes, I think we should take Mrs. Penfield up on her offer, move into the carriage house, and continue our life together there."

"Oh, Rick," Ed whispered, burying his head in Rick's neck. "I just don't know. I need time to think. I'm just not as confident as you."

Rick pulled Ed's head away. He looked again into Ed's eyes. "If you don't want to do this, we won't. Period. If this isn't a one hundred percent unanimous decision, we stay right here. I would never, ever be able to live with myself if this in any way made you unhappy. You believe me, don't you?"

Ed nodded, feeling tears come to his eyes for the third time that Easter Sunday. *Damn*, he thought. *I am turning into one hell of a crybaby.* "I believe you."

"Oh, baby." Rick held him tight. "In the end, I don't care. All I care about is your happiness and our happiness together. I love you so much I don't care if we ever achieve any of those dumb dreams. I just want to be with you, no matter what."

Ed knew Rick meant every word he said, but Ed also knew how much those dreams and the goals they had set for themselves meant to Rick. He suspected that Rick was, for the moment, trying to ease his mind and take the burden of making this decision away from him. He appreciated that, but he realized that once Rick was taken with an idea, he would pursue it. Ed had begun to see that Rick was a good deal bolder than him and more likely to act on impulse than Ed as well. It was, Ed thought, something he was going to have to get used to, but he hadn't counted on dealing with it so soon.

Practical and pragmatic Ed clung to the occasionally impulsive man he knew he loved, and hoped he loved without restriction or reservation. No matter what Rick might say to reassure him, he knew this decision—the biggest decision they had yet to make as a couple—rested solely with him.

# Chapter Five

Little Anthony and the Imperials were playing softly on the stereo as Ed gulped a hasty breakfast. Little Anthony was moaning that he was goin' out of his head. Ed felt he was goin' out of his head, too, but for vastly different reasons than poor, tortured Little Anthony.

It was the day after Easter. After a night's sleep, Ed was still very undecided about the potential move into the carriage house. He had decided, privately, to give himself at least a few days of thought before he brought the subject up with Rick again.

It was on his mind, though. He was viewing the prospect from every angle he could think of, positive and negative. His main concern was easy enough: He simply wanted to do what was best for Rick and himself in regard to their future together.

The part of the song that still moved Ed after so many years, and so many repeated plays, poured out of the stereo. Ed listened as Little Anthony gently sang that his being shy shouldn't keep him apart from the one he so desired. Ed knew his own shyness could have cost him the life he was now living with Rick. If he hadn't taken the initiative to find out more about the new mailman the autumn before, he might still be alone. Fate had stepped in, given Ed a nudge, and brought them together, despite Ed's shyness and uncertainty. Was fate, as Rick said, still paving the way for them? Was his current uncertainty a stumbling block in realizing their dreams?

Ed chugged his orange juice, then sighed, thinking such a heavy, emotional song had been a poor choice for breakfast music this morning. He was relieved when the Surfaris replaced Little Anthony, drumming their way madly through "Wipeout." Instrumentals seemed a good deal safer, considering his mood.

He went to the bedroom to pull on his painting clothes. Rick was sitting in bed, coffee mug in hand, reading the morning paper, and obviously enjoying a rare Monday away from work.

"This is weird," he commented, "watching you get ready for work for a change."

"Yeah," Ed said, buttoning his shirt.

"You're hitting the road kind of early."

"Yeah," Ed repeated. "I'm going to stop at Mom's before I go to the Grubers'." He shoved his wallet in a back pocket. "What are you going to do today?"

Rick set his coffee mug on the nightstand, then stretched lazily. "Oh, get some chores done around here, I guess. I might walk to the library this afternoon."

"Walk?" Ed teased. "On your day off?"

Rick shrugged. "It's a nice day. I was thinking," he said, and then stopped.

"Yes?"

"Well, I was thinking I might stop by Mrs. Penfield's on the way back, look at the carriage house again." He gave Ed a timid look. "I told myself I wouldn't talk about it, but I really do want to see it again."

Ed smiled at him. He leaned over the bed for a kiss and a hug good-bye. "It's okay, darlin'. I love you, and hopefully I'll see you at lunch. Okay?"

Rick hugged him back. "Okay. Paint up a storm. I love you, too."

Ed hurried into the garage, then stopped suddenly, a thought occurring to him as his hand reached for the button to open the garage door. He paused for a moment.

No matter how many times he referred to this house as "ours," it was still "his." The house was in his name, as were the mortgage and the utility bills. Most of the furnishings were his, and even the bed he and Rick slept in together so happily belonged to him. He could tell himself, repeatedly, that anything he owned was as much Rick's as his, but the fact remained: Almost all of it was his, and had been long before Rick moved in.

He reversed it in his mind, putting himself in Rick's position. *What if*, he thought, *it were me, moving into his house? How would I feel?* He knew, without thinking too hard, that he would be uncomfortable. He now understood Rick's eagerness for the carriage house. Rick simply wanted a home that was truly "ours," not "his," and Ed didn't blame him a bit.

Those thoughts in mind, he drove to his mother's house on East Walnut Street. Norma had called late the night before, insisting she smelled gas coming from her stove and demanding Ed look at it as soon as possible.

After a brisk knock, he let himself in the back door. Norma was at the kitchen table, making a grocery list. She frowned at the Pepsi can in his hand. "Ed Stephens, honestly! Pop first thing in the morning?"

Ed pointedly looked at the coffee mug by her grocery list and said nothing. He set the can on the table, and then approached the stove, hands on hips.

Eagle-eyed Norma spotted the ring on his left hand. "Where on earth did that come from?"

Ed glanced at his hand, smiling. "Little Easter present from Rick," he said softly.

"Humph," she snorted. "Well, I'll say one thing for the man: He has good taste."

Ed began to carefully pull the stove away from the wall.

"I know it's none of my business," Norma said, "but do you think it's such a good idea to wear that on your left hand?"

Ed, his back to her, wasn't about to admit he'd been having second thoughts about that particular decision. After the excitement of receiving the ring had cooled, he wondered himself whether it was such a good idea. Not wanting to give Norma any ammunition for a discussion about his choice of a life partner, he muttered, "I don't care anymore. I spent the last ten years worrying what people in this town were thinking about me. If they don't like it, they can go to hell."

He braced himself for a heated retort but heard, to his surprise, a chuckle from her. "Well, that's probably what your father would say."

Ed grinned in relief. He studied the gas line, checking the connections, then the pilot light. He even went to the basement, poking around the furnace and the gas lines into the house.

He trotted upstairs to the kitchen. "I'm sorry, Mom, I can't find a thing."

"I know I smelled gas last night." Norma was adamant.

Ed shrugged. "Well, it's a mystery to me. Everything looks fine. If it happens again, call me, and I'll take another look. If worse comes to worst, we'll have to call the gas company."

"Wouldn't that just be my luck," she muttered. "Have those robbers come over and charge me an arm and leg for something that's probably all their fault."

Ed sighed impatiently. "Don't sweat it, Mom. I don't think the house is gonna blow up."

Norma looked at him closely. "What's bothering you?" she asked abruptly.

Ed, having avoided one early-morning battle, debated a moment whether to tell her about Mrs. Penfield's Easter surprise. Finally deciding she'd find out sooner or later, he sat at the table and told her the whole story.

Norma's eyes grew larger as he revealed the details of Mrs. Penfield's will and her wish for Ed and Rick to move into the carriage house. "For Pete's sake," she mumbled.

"I'm not sure how I feel about it," Ed confessed.

"Well, I know! You go tell that woman you appreciate what she's doing for you; then tell her no, you are not moving onto her property."

Ed looked at her curiously. "Why?"

"Ed Stephens," she hissed. "Think this through. Now, I have nothing but respect for Hilda Penfield. I think it's wonderful she wants to leave her house to you, although why you'd want to live in that mausoleum is beyond me. This other thing, though; you don't want to make a commitment like that. Why, you could be stuck there for years, chained to that woman and that house. She may not be in the best of health, but she could linger. Year after year, there you'd be, watching her, wondering when it would end. By the time she's gone, you probably won't even care anymore. You'll be pushing forty, wondering why you wasted your time."

Ed shifted uncomfortably. Norma was simply giving voice to thoughts he already had but was unwilling to say aloud.

"Remember your grandma Stephens?" she continued. "Oh, those last years were awful, for your father and everyone else. She went senile, and it was a blessing when she finally died. Do you want to go through something like that?"

"Mrs. Penfield's pretty sharp," he said uncertainly.

"Humph! So was your grandmother. Then one day she put the Windex in the refrigerator and the milk under the sink, and it was all downhill from there."

"I haven't made a decision, Mom," he said. "I'm just thinking about it. I know everything you say is true, but you have to admit, it could be a wonderful opportunity for Rick and me."

"If," she stressed, "*if* things work to your advantage. You don't know they will. Old women can be demanding and clingy. My aunt Marjorie was like that. Once I'd settled in with her when I moved to town, she never wanted me to leave. She even thought your father and I should move in with her when we got married. Do you want to give up your life to look after a lonely old woman, just for a tax break? And an apartment, when you already have your own house! I don't care how nice that carriage barn is, or could be. You'd be under her thumb. It would be just as bad as living with your in-laws."

"Okay, okay!" He sighed. "I get your point. I'll think about everything you've said. Geez, I already am thinking about that stuff."

"Keep thinking," she grumbled. "You think hard, Ed Stephens, before you move one stick of furniture or sign anything. And for what it's worth," she added, looking at him sternly, "your father would say that, too."

Ed left shortly after that. He got into his truck and slowly drove around the block. His mother's house—the house he grew up in—was only two blocks from Mrs. Penfield's. He drove onto Race Street and slipped the truck into neutral, staring at the carriage house.

How many times during his boyhood, he wondered, had he ridden his bicycle past that house, dreaming about living in such a grand home? He had admired the house, the carriage house, and the grounds for as long as he could remember.

He also remembered his excitement when Mrs. Penfield had first called him, asking him to add her to his list of handyman clients. He remembered his first time inside the house, looking in awe through the dignified rooms, hesitantly touching the beautifully crafted oak woodwork, imagining himself descending the elegant stairway.

Once Mrs. Penfield's will was changed, it was almost inevitable the house would belong to Rick and himself some day. He shook his head, still unable to truly comprehend it.

He thought of the rest of Mrs. Penfield's offer. He had no way of knowing how long she would live, how much responsibility might become his own if they chose to move into the carriage house. His eyes swept the backyard, seeing the tulips, imagining the rose arbor in full bloom.

He knew Mrs. Penfield would do what was necessary to make the carriage-house apartment a home Ed and Rick would love. She believed in them and wanted them to be happy. Yes, it was a serious commitment, one with potential hardship and unknown possibilities, but it also was a chance for the two of them to begin their life together on equal footing, in a home that belonged to both of them.

He shifted into drive, and the truck slowly approached the intersection with Spruce Street. Turning the corner, heading west to Main Street, he glanced at the house in his rearview mirror. Yes, his heart was already packing, but his mind stubbornly refused to follow it.

⁂

Ed was high on a ladder, painting the Grubers' garage, when he spied Laurie on the alley behind, walking toward him. He wasn't surprised. The Grubers lived only a short block from her house on West Elm Street, and obviously Norma had called Laurie the moment Ed had left her house that morning, telling Laurie the latest news and her own opinion on the matter.

"Hey, you!" she called, waving.

"Hey."

Laurie paused at the bottom of the ladder, looking up at him. "Okay. You have to know Mom called me. Like there was any way she was going to keep news like this to herself. I have come to throw my two cents in, whether you want to hear it or not."

Ed sighed. "Like I could stop you."

"Right. You can't," she said grinning.

"Lay it on me, Shortshit."

"Don't listen to Mom," she said flatly. "Do it! This is a golden opportunity. Clean off that damn paintbrush, go home, and start packing."

Ed rolled his eyes, tempted to splatter paint on her. "Why are you so hot for this?"

She snorted. "Who wouldn't be? Yes, I understand it could be difficult, being tied to Mrs. Penfield. So what? Every opportunity has pitfalls. But this, Ed! It's like you just found a winning lottery ticket in the street. You and Rick could be set for life. Imagine that!

"I called Todd at the bank," she said. Todd was a loan officer at Porterfield First National. "He said despite the lousy economy, there's probably going to be a real estate boom before the end of the eighties. You and Rick could be right on top of it. And did you think? After Mrs. Penfield is gone, you could move into the main house, and then rent that apartment. You know I don't wish her dead, but you're a fool if you let this go by."

She moved closer to the garage, inspecting his paint job. "Do you want to spend the rest of your life painting garages? Living in that dinky house on Coleman Street? I know how much you love Mrs. Penfield's house and how living there, even in the servants' quarters, would be a dream come true for you. I'm guessing, too," she added shrewdly, "that Rick wants to do it."

"How do you know that?"

She shrugged. "Because he's smarter than you," she said bluntly. "I'm sure he's seen the possibilities for the future. Sure, you may have to do some hard work, and you may have to put up with having an old woman under your nose, but it will be worth it in the long run. I'm sure of it."

Ed carefully laid his paintbrush on the top of the ladder. "I just don't want to . . . want to do something . . . that would—could—end up . . ." He paused, unable to say what was on his mind.

"Breaking you and Rick up?" Laurie finished for him.

"Yeah," he mumbled, not looking at her.

She sighed heavily, tapping a finger against the ladder. "Ed," she said, "from the moment Todd and I said 'I do,' I've lived with the possibility that something could break us up. Every couple does. So what do you do? Hide away, stay afraid to move forward? Shoot, just loving someone is a risk. I mean, what if you fall off that ladder and break your neck? What would Rick do? What would you do if he was killed, crossing the street, delivering mail?"

She looked at the ring on his hand. He had wanted to keep it in his pocket, afraid of getting paint on it, but couldn't bear to remove it from his finger. "That ring you're wearing may seem like a guarantee for a perfect marriage and a lifetime of happiness, but it isn't. You don't know what's gonna happen. Nobody does. Those marriage vows people take? They're just words. I don't care what anybody says. You say them, then hope for the best."

Ed rubbed his eyes tiredly. "Yeah, I know. I just wish this had come later. I'm still getting used to the whole idea of Rick and me being together."

"Remember when I was pregnant with Lesley? There I was, out to here with her, and the chance came up to buy our house. Oh, the price was right, but we couldn't really afford it. We knew I wouldn't be working for a while, and the thought of moving in my condition made me feel even worse. We did it anyway. Remember all the stuff you hauled into that house because I couldn't lift anything? I was terrified, wondering if we were making a mistake."

She shrugged, grinning. "It worked out. It will for you, too. Even if doesn't, you'll live. Both of you. Take this chance, Ed. I believe in you and Rick as much as Mrs. Penfield does. It would take an awful lot to break you two up. I think you owe it to yourselves to take this adventure. So what if it's too soon? Who knows when the next one will come along?"

"How come," Ed said, looking down at her, "you're younger than me, but wiser? That's not right."

"I've had to make decisions you haven't, and I've lived to tell," she responded. "You will, too. I promise."

"Okay. I still want some time to think it through, though."

"So think! Think all you want. But if I don't hear the right answer out of you soon, I'm coming over to your house and boxing up your shit and moving it for you."

<figure>※</figure>

The week progressed with Ed still undecided. Rick carefully avoided the subject. He spent his time off getting ahead on the household chores, even doing some spring yard work. Ed wondered whether Rick was trying to butter him up, then was ashamed of himself for thinking such a thing. Rick was simply doing his part to maintain their home, whether his name was on the deed or not.

Ed was pondering the situation Thursday afternoon while driving from the lumberyard to the home of one of his clients, Mrs. West. He drove onto East Clark Street by the post office and noticed Gordy outside taking a smoke break. Impulsively he slammed on the brakes, pulling into the parking lot.

Gordy looked up, grinning cheerfully as usual. "Hey, bud! What's up?"

Ed slammed the truck door. "Just wanted to say hi," he said, walking toward Gordy.

Since no one was around, Ed parked himself on the back stairs next to Gordy. "So what's new with you?"

Gordy snorted. "Nothing! Least nothing as exciting as what you've got goin' on."

Ed sighed. "Rick told you, huh?"

"Hell yes. I think it's great."

Ed looked at his friend. "Why do you think it's great, Gord? My mom is ready to kill me for even thinking about it, and Laurie practically has us moved. You might as well tell me what you think."

"Shit, opinions are like assholes, you know. Everybody's got one. Why add mine to the mix?"

"Well, humor me, and tell what your asshole has to say about this."

Gordy took a long drag from his cigarette, exhaling thoughtfully. "Well, I'll tell you what this asshole thinks, all right. And you know what? It's something your mom won't tell you, or your sister. This is something you'll only hear from me, 'cause I know stuff about you they don't."

Ed looked at him curiously. "What stuff?"

Gordy snickered. "I know stuff that only another gay man would know."

"What's that got to do with anything?"

"Plenty! You ready for this?"

"I don't know, but tell me anyway."

Gordy took another drag. "Ed," he said, exhaling, "you've got something most gay men would kill for. You've got a good man and a great relationship. You know I pick on Rick sometimes, but that's just 'cause I like him so much. He's crazy about you, you know."

"I know that," Ed said, looking down.

"Do you? Sometimes I wonder. Do you realize what you have with him? Oh, hell, the guy ain't perfect. No one is. But he's totally committed to making a life with you. Do you know how many gay men there are like that? Not a whole hell of a lot!"

Gordy flipped his cigarette away. He looked at the back door of the post office, then his watch. "Well, shit, guess I got time for one more," he said, lighting up another. "Anyway, I don't know about your sex life, and I don't really want to. Probably make me sick with envy. I can guess it's pretty good, though. I can also guess you don't have to worry about your guy messing around behind your back, bringing a case of clap home or something. That's pretty rare, too.

"Course all this shit about Rick goes for you, too. He's just as lucky as you are. I can't help but think you guys will make it, no matter how hard it may be living here instead of in a big city. Funny thing is, it might even be easier in the long run. Doesn't really matter what happens; you'll find a way to deal with it."

Gordy shook his head. "I know Rick thinks this is a good idea for the two of you. It doesn't matter whether I agree with him or not. I do know this much, though. That man would walk through fire for you. Hell, if he thought it would make you happy, he'd lead a parade, buck naked, down Main Street."

Gordy turned to Ed, blowing smoke at him. "He wants a home the two of you can share together. That would make him really happy. He'd do anything to make you happy. Can't you do this to make *him* happy?"

Ed looked at Gordy in surprise. *How simple*, he thought. *So simple I never thought of it.* "Geez."

"Whatever! Just think about it, okay?"

"I will," Ed said humbly. "Thanks, Gordy."

Gordy, cigarette clenched between his lips, put an arm around Ed and gave him a squeeze. "No sweat, buddy. When you need some help moving into that place, you give me a call, you hear?"

Ed laughed, shaking his head. "I'll save the heaviest lifting for you."

⋘•⋙

Ed finished his chores with Mrs. West, and then drove slowly home, thinking. He thought of Norma's words earlier that month about compromise in a marriage. He thought about Laurie's words regarding risks and chances. Mostly, he thought of Gordy's words, the ones that had penetrated his doubts and made up his mind.

It *was* simple. He loved Rick with all of his heart, and Rick's well-being had become one of the most important things in his life. If this was something Rick felt was right for them, felt would create a more secure life for them, then Ed, as Rick's husband, needed to trust his judgment, take his hand, and take a chance. Oh, he still had his misgivings, but he was willing to put them aside for now, willing to put his trust in the man he loved, the man he had entrusted with his own future.

He sighed. Maybe it wouldn't work out. What would he do then, blame Rick? Take it out on him? Maybe he would. Ed wasn't perfect either. He was just as capable of pettiness and resentment as the next person. But since Rick had made Ed's dream come true, maybe it was time to see what he could do to help Rick realize the dreams he had for both of them.

Rick's car was in the driveway. Ed pulled in next to it, thinking perhaps they should take turns with the garage while they still lived there. He laughed, thinking of the carriage house. *Hell,* he thought, *there's room for both vehicles, right under our bedroom!*

He jumped out of the truck, feeling lighter than he had all week. He glanced at the tulips blooming by the garage. They were starting to fade, but a few were still presentable. He bent over, selecting the nicest ones. Bouquet in hand, he went into the house.

Rick was on the sofa, reading. He looked up at Ed's entrance. "Hi. I didn't start dinner yet. I was thinking maybe we'd go out for a change. What do you think?"

Ed didn't answer him. He put the tulips on the table and walked to the stereo. Rick watched him curiously. Ed shuffled through a stack of 45s in the record cabinet, placing one on the turntable.

As Three Dog Night's "One Man Band" began to play, Ed retrieved the tulips from the table, holding them out to Rick. "Remember the night we got married, how you said you were looking forward to hearing the music from me, your one-man band, for the rest of your life? Well, how do you suppose the acoustics are in that carriage house?"

Rick's warm and tender special spread across his face. He stood up, taking the tulips from Ed. Carefully holding them in one hand, he put his other arm around Ed, squeezing him tightly. "Oh, baby," he whispered. "I think the acoustics are gonna be great."

Ed laughed, a wonderfully liberating laugh. For the first time since the reality of his marriage to Rick, he genuinely wasn't worried about them. "So much for the honeymoon cottage," he said, glancing affectionately around the room.

"Ah, well. Maybe this honeymoon's gone on long enough. Now it's time to get cracking on building a life together, you think?"

"I think. Best of all, we *both* think."

# Chapter Six

Ed's truck rolled into the driveway next to the carriage house at Mrs. Penfield's. Instead of stopping by the back walk as he done for years, Ed made a sharp right turn, pulling up in front of one of the garage doors. He hopped out, slammed the door, and frowned at the closed door, mentally figuring the cost of not one but two new automatic garage door openers. He had become thoroughly spoiled by the convenience of the automatic door he had installed several years ago in his garage at the Coleman Street house and pondered going without one of the few luxuries he had allowed himself for so long.

As he bent over to reach the door handle, he thought of the budget he and Rick had painstakingly drafted for their moving expenses and sighed. He gave the door a hard yank and it rattled upward on its track.

*This is all getting to be more expensive than I thought it would be. There's so many things we didn't think about.*

It was a Wednesday afternoon in mid-May. Almost a month had passed since Ed and Rick's mutual decision to accept Mrs. Penfield's offer. Although the months of his relationship with Rick had moved quickly for Ed, this last had seemed to disappear in the blink of an eye.

Ed moved away from the carriage house to a row of lilac bushes that stood between the parking area and the back garden. He shook his head, amazed that their yearly May blooming had come and gone with him barely noticing. He took a deep sniff, but the withering blossoms refused to yield any of the sweet fragrance that to him always signaled spring's triumph over winter.

With another sigh he walked back to the garage and stepped inside, his eyes blinking as they adjusted to the dim light after the bright May sunshine. Despite his financial concerns, he found himself smiling. Their decision to move had brought about a bonus he hadn't even thought of until after the fact. Not only was the lower floor of the carriage house big enough for his truck and Rick's car, but there would be ample space leftover for Ed to re-create his father's workshop.

"Why, of course," Mrs. Penfield had exclaimed when he asked her permission to clear away the odds and ends stored in the section between the garage area and the apartment stairway. "When you told me you wanted to set up your father's tools and do some woodworking, I immediately thought of the carriage house. In fact, I suspect that's when I first started to think of the two of you living there."

Ed was excited about the prospect but knew it wouldn't happen for a while. There were plenty of things that needed to be done even before Ed and Rick could think of moving into the second floor. The sound of banging over his head brought that reality back to Ed. Porterfield's most reliable plumber, Gene Woeber, was hard at work updating the bathroom. Shaking thoughts of the future workshop from his head, Ed went upstairs to check on Gene's progress.

When Ed had told Rick he believed accepting Mrs. Penfield's offer was the right thing for them to do, they had spent several days discussing what all would need to be done and the possible ramifications of the legal agreement with Mrs. Penfield. Once they felt comfortable enough to move forward, they had called her to set up a meeting.

"I just got one change of address filed, and now I'm going to have to do it again," Rick had mused. "How 'bout that?"

"I wouldn't worry about it just yet," Ed had cautioned him. "No one's lived in that apartment for close to thirty years. It's gonna take some work to make it livable."

Ed had not counted on Mrs. Penfield's enthusiasm for the project, however. Once they told her of their decision, she responded with the alacrity of a fireman to an alarm bell. Arthritis or not, Ed soon discovered Hilda Penfield could move quickly when she wanted to. Before Ed had completely adjusted to the idea of moving, she had hired Gene Woeber, had the carriage house's heating system inspected, and had stacks of carpet, paint, and wallpaper samples available for Ed and Rick's perusal. When both Ed and Rick worried that she was overextending herself, she easily brushed off their concerns.

"Nonsense! This is the most fun I've had in years," she said as she eagerly flipped through the carpet sample book. "I've always enjoyed interior decoration as much as gardening and landscaping. I'm thrilled I finally have an excuse to spend the time and money."

Reassured, Ed and Rick let her charge forward with her plans, while they concentrated on their own financial contributions to the project and the chores they needed to do.

Ed found Gene standing in the bathroom's claw-foot tub installing a showerhead in the wall behind the head of the tub. Gene had ripped a good deal of plaster from the wall, and the dust had coated every available surface. Ed's work boots crunched through the debris on the floor as he peered into the opening Gene had created for the shower.

"Looks good," he said with a nod.

Gene, who'd gone through school with Ed's father, Tim, ruefully shook his head. "Took me awhile, but yeah, you're gonna have a nice setup here when I'm done. I'm glad Mrs. Penfield decided to spend the money to have this done right. Course I should've known. She never did let anyone get away with half-assed work."

Ed chuckled. "Is there anyone in this town who didn't learn about doing things right in her class?"

"Only if they didn't graduate from Porterfield High," Gene said, brushing the plaster dust from his thinning gray hair. "Back in our day, we used to say that the only thing that stood between you and a diploma was Hilda Penfield's English class. We bitched about it, but it was a good lesson. If your dad was still here, he'd tell you the same."

"He did, at the beginning of my sophomore year. 'That woman's one of the best teachers you'll ever have, Eddie,' he told me when I was complaining about the homework. It makes me wonder how the English department has survived since her retirement."

"On a wing and a prayer, I imagine," Gene snorted. "All those newfangled educational methods they have? Hilda got out when the gettin' was good. Anyway, this took longer than I thought it would," he said, knocking the wall behind the tub. "Been a while since I had to deal with walls this solid and well built. They don't make 'em like this anymore. It'd take a tornado like the ones back in seventy-four to knock this place down. I'll be done by tomorrow morning at the latest, though. You're getting a really good deal here, Ed. I think your dad would be happy about it."

"Tell that to my mom," Ed groaned. Norma was still voicing her disapproval of the agreement with Mrs. Penfield whenever he spoke with her these days.

Gene smiled. "I tell you, I wondered why a quiet guy like Tim would team up with a hellcat like Norma Beale, but it sure worked out. Good marriage, two good kids; it's just a shame he went so soon."

"Yeah," Ed sighed. "I wish he was here to tell Mom to lay off about this. She's convinced I'm making the biggest mistake of my life."

"Well, Norma was a country girl. She didn't go to Porterfield High. If she had, she'd know you can't go wrong with Hilda Penfield. Don't worry about it, Ed. You and your friend are doing Hilda a good turn by living here, and she's doing you a good turn by fixing this place up for you. Everybody wins."

"I hope so." Ed still privately shared some of Norma's reservations but knew only time would tell if the decision to accept Mrs. Penfield's offer was a good one or not.

Ed thought he heard a car pull into the driveway. He walked across the hall and looked out one of the bedroom windows. Sure enough, Rick's Monte Carlo was parked next to his truck. He ran downstairs to meet him.

Rick was standing by the car, sorting through a pile of paint swatches. "Gene'll be done tomorrow morning," Ed greeted him.

"Oh, good," Rick said absently. He moved forward to kiss Ed, thought better of it, and settled for brushing some plaster dust off his T-shirt. "So who gets to clean up the mess he made in both the bathroom and the kitchen?" he asked with a grin.

"That would be us," Ed said, grinning back at him. "And we'd better get it done this weekend, 'cause Dick Elliott is scheduled to start fixing all the plaster Monday."

Rick shook his head in wonder. "How does Mrs. P. do it?" he marveled. Rick had recently adopted Effie Maude's habit of referring to Mrs. Penfield as "Mrs. P." "I still say she's a witch. She was supposedly the toughest English teacher ever at Porterfield High, but all her former students love her. Look at the way they're jumping to do all this work!"

"Well, she may have been tough, but she knew how to turn on the charm when she wanted. She always had a way to get us to do things we didn't want to do in class."

"Discipline, charm, and good solid teaching. I think my dad once said that was part of the recipe for a good teacher."

Rick tucked the paint swatches in the pocket of his postal uniform and started up the back walk toward the house with Ed. "Of course, Dad also says that in his day kids were taught to respect their teachers as they would their parents. That's changed, he says. He has more discipline problems in his history classes now than he ever did in the old days."

"Well, let's just be glad Mrs. Penfield was part of those respectful years. She's managing to get the work here done a lot faster than I ever thought it would be."

They entered the kitchen, where Effie Maude was putting several big pieces of freshly frosted spice cake on a paper plate. "These here are for Gene," she told them. "Don't worry, though. I'll make sure you have some to take home, too."

Rick laughed. "Mrs. P.'s charm and Effie Maude's baking! Yeah, I think that apartment will end up being done by Memorial Day with this kind of influence going on."

"Aw, pshaw," Effie Maude muttered, obviously pleased. "Mrs. P.'s in the study. Get out of my kitchen before I change my mind."

Mrs. Penfield was hanging up the telephone when they found her in her late husband's study. "I am happy to report," she said victoriously, "that the new kitchen appliances will be installed as soon as the plastering and painting are done. I just spoke with Peter Ripley at Ripley Appliance. He's giving us a wonderful discount, *and* free delivery and installation."

Ed and Rick gave each other a high five. "The great Hilda Penfield strikes again," Ed said smugly.

"Well, I certainly would be happy to take the credit for this miracle," Mrs. Penfield said with a mischievous grin much like the one Rick had on occasion. "However, I believe we can thank Ed for this one."

"Why?" Rick asked as he plopped himself in one of the wing chairs by the fireplace.

"Ed, do you recall all of that work you did for Sally Ripley several years ago?"

Ed nodded. He did indeed remember. Sally Ripley's mother had died in a terrible car crash shortly after his father had died from an undiagnosed heart ailment. Sally had been devastated at the sudden loss and had been unable to make her herself attend to the chores of cleaning out her mother's house, a rambling old place overflowing with stuff both precious and useless. She had hired Ed to go through it for her. Ed, his own loss fresh in his mind, had rearranged his schedule and devoted his spare time to the job, doing his best to make the process as painless as possible for Sally.

Mrs. Penfield, with some details from Ed, told Rick the story. "Sally and Peter were very grateful for Ed's help at a hard time, and I believe this is Peter's way of showing his gratitude."

"Well," Ed said modestly, "Mr. Ripley's always been so good about me buying parts from his repair department at cost for my clients, it was the least I could do."

"You would have done it anyway," Rick said, his warm and tender special glowing. "Not only are you the cutest handyman in Porterfield, Indiana; you've got the biggest heart of any handyman I've ever met. I knew I had found me the best there was when I found you."

"Don't make me blush," Ed whined as his fair cheeks quickly went crimson.

Mrs. Penfield and Rick laughed with great affection and tactfully changed the subject to paint colors for the apartment walls. The three of them studied and debated the various paint swatches and soon agreed on the proper shades for the walls in the kitchen, bathroom, and hall. Ed and Rick agreed with Mrs. Penfield's suggestion to paper the walls in the living room and bedroom and were pleased when she insisted on hiring a professional to do the work.

"Married couples have no business hanging wallpaper together," she said adamantly. "It's a guidebook for disaster. George and I tried it once, and we didn't speak to each other for a week. I've already spoken to Jinny Corning, and she has assured me she has time to do the job at the end of the month."

"Another former student?" Rick teased.

Mrs. Penfield nodded. "But of course."

"Well, if that's the case, Rick and I can spend Memorial Day weekend painting, or the next one, depending on when the carpet arrives," Ed said. "I mean, here I am, the town handyman, letting everyone else do the work on my new home. I can't handle that plastering job, and I've never really tackled wallpaper, but at least I know how to use a paintbrush."

"Ed, you said yourself that if you had taken on all of the projects, you'd never get it finished unless you abandoned your regular jobs and clients." Rick gave Ed a mock slap upside his head. "I don't think anyone in town, or any of your customers, is going to think any less of you for letting Mrs. Penfield hire other people to get this done. Why, do you realize? It's moving so quickly we may be able to move in next month, when originally we were thinking July or August."

"Geez, you're right." Ed mentally sorted through the jobs that had been done and the ones that were scheduled. "We're going to have to start thinking about packing already."

"Well, aside from my own selfish wishes to have the two of you here, it gives me great pleasure to do this for you." Mrs. Penfield beamed at both of them.

Her gaze drifted past them, and a faraway look came into her eyes. "I've been thinking of Uncle William lately, and how his kindness greatly affected my life. Perhaps helping the two of you realize your goals the way he did for me is my way of . . . oh, not so much paying him back, but rather acknowledging who he really was, taking advantage of the changing attitudes to give you both what he could never have."

"It's funny how you've spent so much time with Rick and me, but you never mentioned him until recently," Ed said, idly playing with the paint swatches.

"As I believe I said, it took some time for me to make the connection, and Uncle William has been gone a very long time as well."

"So what was the story with Uncle William?" Rick wanted to know. "I've been hoping you'd tell us what happened to him, and why you thought he was gay."

Mrs. Penfield sighed. "Rick, that is a term I would have never associated with Uncle William for several reasons. First and foremost, 'gay' was not a word used for homosexual men in Uncle William's era, and even the word 'homosexual' would have been whispered in polite company. It simply wasn't a topic for discussion in those years. In all of the years I lived with Uncle William, I never suspected he was different, and after he died, I still would have been hesitant to apply that designation to him. Secondly, my strongest memories of Uncle William are not gay at all, but rather sad."

"Why?" Ed asked as Rick said, "Okay, but what made you think he was different in the first place?"

"Well, let me tell the story from the beginning," she said, settling into her chair, absentmindedly kneading her gnarled fingers. "As I believe I told you, I came to live with Uncle William after my parents died. You don't hear much of it now, but there was an awful, almost incredible, influenza epidemic in 1918. It engulfed the entire world. It was at the end of the First World War, and I've always wondered if our victory in Europe helped overshadowed the horror of it."

"That's what my dad says." Rick nodded. "He says we actually won the war because of it and doesn't understand why the high school history textbooks never seem to discuss it in any detail. He always makes a point of telling about 'Spanish flu' when he's discussing WWI with his classes."

Mrs. Penfield nodded as well. "He may very well be right about the war, but for those of us who lost so many loved ones in the epidemic, there seemed to be an unspoken agreement to refrain from talking of it. The loss and despair went very deep. I have only vague memories of my parents' funerals and of Uncle William bringing a shabby suitcase and me from the only home I had ever known in rural Adams County to his little house in Decatur, the county seat. I believe I was in shock, and I remained in that state for quite some time.

"I had always been fond of my mother's brother, though, and after the grief and shock began to fade, I began to enjoy being his permanent houseguest. Over time I learned to keep house properly, and to prepare the kind of meals a hardworking man appreciated."

"What kind of work did he do?" Ed asked.

"Well," Mrs. Penfield said with a wry smile, "it may seem very typical by today's standards, but he was a florist. He had a small flower shop on the edge of town. He worked very hard, and the store did quite well. He had, as so many homosexual men do, an innate flair for color and design, and his flower arrangements were quite beautiful and original. His work was highly praised and desired by the more well-to-do women in town."

"A gay florist in a small town," Rick said, rolling his eyes. "I s'pose people whispered behind his back all the time."

"Not to my knowledge. Uncle William had none of the feminine mannerisms commonly associated with men thought to be 'queer' or 'funny.'

No, he was respected for his work, and if anyone saw fit to discuss his bachelor status, the talk never reached my ears. I do remember, however, that several of the neighbors thought Uncle William would marry after he assumed custody of me, feeling of course that a young girl needed a mother, but there were those who also assumed he refrained from marriage because of his responsibility to me.

"At any rate," she continued, "our life together fell into a pattern, and as I grew accustomed to life without my parents, I became more outgoing. I had a good many friends and became active in school activities. Uncle William encouraged this, as he spent so much time at his shop that he sometimes worried about neglecting me.

"Sunday was his one day off. We attended church each and every Sunday, and every other Sunday, without fail, we would climb aboard the interurban train and journey north to Fort Wayne to visit Uncle William's friend Benjamin.

"Benjamin was the manager of an exclusive menswear store in downtown Fort Wayne. Unlike Uncle William, Benjamin did have some of the more feminine mannerisms associated with what we now call gay men. I don't recall giving any thought to it at the time. I was very fond of the man I began to refer to as 'Uncle Ben.' He was wickedly funny and an excellent cook. He lived in an exquisitely decorated apartment above the store he managed, and it was great fun for me as a young girl to wander through the empty shop and its storerooms on those Sundays.

"In fact," she chuckled, "Uncle William would usually suggest it. 'Ben and I need to have some time for man-talk,' he'd say. That was my cue to go downstairs, or perhaps take a long walk through the quiet streets if the weather was nice. At this point in time I have no doubt of what they were doing, but of course back then I didn't have a clue. I just knew, the way children sometimes do, that they needed to be alone together for a time, and when I returned after an hour or so, they'd be smoking in the parlor, looking a good deal more relaxed than they had when I left."

"Those naughty boys," Rick said, giggling.

Mrs. Penfield allowed herself a giggle as well. "In retrospect, I'm certainly glad they had that brief time together. I'm sure they felt even those Sunday moments together were a risk. You must understand: They never showed each other any sort of attention or affection that could have been interpreted as odd. To any observer, including me, there was nothing between them but ordinary male friendship. However, as I look back, I realize they loved each other deeply and in their minds probably longed for the sort of marriage the two of you are creating."

"I need to remember that the next time I think Rick and I have it bad,"

Ed murmured.

"Yes. My heart aches now to think of how lonely they must have been. Instead of being together as they would have wished, they both staunchly maintained a facade of respectable bachelorhood. Imagine for a moment, Ed, that you felt the need to restrict your visits with Rick to once every two weeks to avoid suspicion, and even then cloak them with as much secrecy as possible."

Ed shuddered. "I don't want to imagine it."

"Me either," Rick added, reaching for Ed's hand.

"Times have changed a bit," Mrs. Penfield said with a wistful glance at their clasped hands. "I'm sure more than either Uncle William or Benjamin would have imagined.

"Those visits had begun long before my parents died and continued for many years after," she said, returning to her story. "When I was well into my teen years I begged off making the trip with Uncle William. By that time I had activities of my own, and I'm sure Uncle William was relieved to have uninterrupted time with Ben. When I graduated high school and began teachers college, thanks to funds Uncle William saved from his hard work and good money management with the floral shop, he still continued to visit Benjamin every other Sunday. By this time we were well into what we now refer to as 'the Roaring Twenties,' and perhaps the more permissive atmosphere eased their minds some. I do know that while I was away at school Uncle William began to spend more time with Benjamin in Fort Wayne.

"One Christmas I was prepared to make the journey home to Decatur for the holidays when I received a letter from Uncle William. Uncle Ben was very sick, he wrote, and we were going to spend the Christmas holidays with him in Fort Wayne. I was surprised at the change of plans, and I spent the train trip worrying about Uncle Ben.

"When I arrived in Fort Wayne, Uncle William wasn't at the Baker Street station to meet my train. Fearing the worst, I hurried to Ben's apartment, only to find that he had died the night before."

"What happened?" Ed whispered, holding Rick's hand tighter.

"Cancer. Apparently he had been sick for quite some time, and withheld it from Uncle William, who was as grief stricken as I had been when my parents died.

"It was the saddest, most somber Christmas I've ever experienced; in some ways more terrible than that first lonely Christmas after George Junior died. Uncle William, when he was able to talk, cursed Benjamin for not telling him sooner about his illness, and how he would have done anything to help ease his suffering. Even close to death, Ben refused to do anything that might expose their relationship.

"The funeral, held the day after Christmas, was sparsely attended. Uncle William and I were the only mourners who could be considered family. I asked Uncle William about Ben's family, and all he would say was that there were relatives in Pennsylvania, and Uncle Ben had lost contact with them. Now I can guess the reason why, but at the time I was puzzled by it.

"Uncle William maintained his composure until we returned to his home in Decatur. I vividly remember, despite Prohibition, him obtaining a bottle of whiskey and draining it that night. He continued to curse Ben when he wasn't weeping over his loss. I had never seen him act in such a way, and frankly I had no idea how to react or what to do. At last it seemed best to just let him be and express his grief in whatever way he needed.

"After the grim holidays I returned to school and shortly thereafter met a handsome young law student named George Penfield. In the excitement of falling in love for the first time, I quite forgot Uncle William and his grief. My visits home became fewer and fewer as I spent more time with George and his family in Porterfield.

"The last time I ever saw Uncle William was on my wedding day. The Depression was raging, and Uncle William's business was struggling to survive, but he managed to see to it that I had the most beautiful wedding flowers any bride could wish for. He was genuinely happy for me that day, but when I looked outside of my own happiness I realized how much he had aged since Benjamin's death.

"Times being what they were, and money so scarce, George and I had made no plans for a honeymoon trip, but Uncle William's gift to us was a brief vacation at Niagara Falls. I had never been outside of Indiana, and we were very excited. I remember hugging Uncle William at the train station, and both George and me overwhelming him with thanks. Uncle William was laughing, waving away our gratitude, but when I looked closely I could see the sadness that had worn its way into his face over the past few years. I remember waving as the train pulled out and his wistful expression. I now believe he depleted what was left of his savings to give us the trip he and Ben had probably always wanted but were afraid to pursue."

Mrs. Penfield looked down at her lap and twisted the rings on her left hand. "Uncle William died two weeks later," she said in a low voice. "The coroner said it was heart failure, and he was right, to a point. I've no doubt Uncle William's heart failed. His heart had broken beyond repair when Ben died; with me safely married into a good family, I'm sure he felt he had nothing left."

Ed sniffed, as Rick wiped hard at his eyes. "That's so sad," Ed mumbled.

"Yes, it is," Mrs. Penfield agreed, her voice still low. "Again, it wasn't until

I began to observe the two of you together that I started to realize the depth of the relationship between Uncle William and Ben. My hope, now that I see it for what it really was, is to honor them by helping you. By sharing my good fortune, and hopefully my own experience-based wisdom, it's my wish that you both achieve the things they were afraid to even contemplate for themselves."

"We'll do our best," Rick said quietly, squeezing Ed's hand. "We'll try to be worthy of your belief in us, and do what we can to make William and Ben proud."

"I know you will," Mrs. Penfield said, smiling fondly at her young friends. "Now, why don't we see about sampling some of Effie Maude's spice cake? The past is past, and the two of you have a wonderful future ahead. Now that I've shared Uncle William's story with you, I've no doubt he'll be watching out for you as well."

⊰•⊱

Uncle William was still on Ed's mind the next morning. He was working his way through a list of odd jobs for Herb and Gwen Hauser, and as he hauled their patio furniture out of the garage for the season, he found himself thinking of William and Ben and their Sundays together.

The story had saddened him, but for some reason it also encouraged him as well. The knowledge that gay men had found ways to be together in times even less tolerant than his own gave Ed a feeling of hope. Oh, it had been more than tough for those two men, but somehow they had met and fallen in love, and their relationship had endured. They weren't the only ones either, Ed thought, as he hosed down the Hausers' deck chairs. The past was full of such of men; he'd just never heard about any of them until the day before. He had a strong desire to sit down and talk with William and Ben and ask questions Mrs. Penfield couldn't answer. He felt as though he'd walked into the last ten minutes of a heavily censored movie. In his frustration, he slammed a chaise longue into place with a good deal more force than necessary.

It occurred to him that Memorial Day was coming up, and perhaps Mrs. Penfield would tell him where Uncle William and Ben were buried. The idea of laying flowers on their graves satisfied something within him. William and Ben had been undercover agents in the same war Ed and Rick were fighting today as foot soldiers, and it seemed appropriate to honor the veterans who had come before them.

Thoughts of William and Ben were still with him that afternoon as he drove to the new elementary school on the south side of Porterfield. He had agreed to take Judy to Fort Wayne for an orthodontist appointment and was scheduled to pick her up shortly before school let out for the day.

Ed's chauffeuring duties had been Rick's idea. Although Judy dreaded the regular orthodontist checkups and routinely returned from them with aching teeth and a bad mood, the younger children seemed to think the trip to Fort Wayne was a special treat for her that was denied them. So, in an effort to ward off any potential sibling squabbling, Rick had asked Ed to accompany Judy while he took Josh and Jane to the library, followed by an early supper at the P & J Root Beer Stand.

"Judy will enjoy having you all to herself, and the other two will finally think they're getting something she doesn't," Rick had said.

Ed had agreed, even though it wasn't how he had planned to spend the first free afternoon he'd had in some time. He had wanted to start sorting through the storage areas of the house to decide what to take on the move and what to throw away. However, with thoughts of Mrs. Penfield's Uncle William in mind, he cheerfully waved to Judy, who was waiting for him inside the school's big double doors.

*What if something happened to Claire, and Rick and I had to actually raise these kids? How would we handle it? There's a big difference between being a part-time uncle and being a full-time dad.*

Judy threw her schoolbooks on the floor of the truck and jumped into the passenger seat. "Cool, Loverboy," she exclaimed as she reached for the radio and jacked up the volume on "Turn Me Loose." "Sure beats Mr. Hopkins talking and talking about Mesopotamia. That's the only good thing about these stupid braces: missing some school."

Ed laughed. "Yeah, I remember."

He drove through Porterfield to Highway 401 and headed north.

"So how are things at your house now that Rick's been gone awhile?"

Judy, lost in the music on WFWQ and her own thoughts, shrugged. "Okay."

"Really?"

"Yeah, really. He's still there after school every day, and whenever Mom calls him, he shows up. No big deal. Well," she conceded with a brief glance at Ed, "I think Josh misses him more than he says. He thought it would be great to have that room to himself again, but I think he misses having Uncle Rick there."

"Oh," Ed muttered, feeling a little guilty.

"Don't worry about it. He'll get over it," Judy said with a big sister's typical lack of empathy.

She reached for the radio volume again as "Bette Davis Eyes" began to play. Ed tapped out the beat on the steering wheel as he thought about Josh. He decided that when the time finally came to do some junk sorting, he'd invite Josh to help him and maybe even spend the night. Maybe some "guy time" would reassure Josh that Ed and Rick were still there when he needed them.

"I love this song," Judy said, turning the volume even louder. "I need to get this record."

"Yeah, it's different," Ed shouted over Kim Carnes's raspy vocals. "I really like 'Sweetheart,' too."

"Franke and the Knockouts?" Judy shrugged. "They're okay."

"Well, I think they're kinda cute."

"Loverboy's cooler."

Ed rolled his eyes. "If you say so."

"I wish I could get some new records," Judy sighed. "I wish Mom would raise my allowance."

Something about that sounded familiar to Ed. He searched his memory and smiled. He had often said much the same thing to his dad when he was Judy's age. When they took care of the Saturday errands together, Ed and Tim usually ended up in the record department of the Porterfield Woolworth's, and Tim would slip Ed the money for the records he wanted.

"Well, you know, the Ayr-Way store is just down the road from your orthodontist's office. They have pretty good prices on their 45s. Maybe we can stop there after your appointment."

"I don't have any money."

"Yeah, but I have a few extra bucks on me."

Judy's eyes lit up. She smiled broadly, forgetting for a moment to hide her braces. "Really?"

"Why not? We'll call it . . . we'll call it a school's-almost-out present."

"Cool! I can get Kim Carnes, and maybe 'Stars on 45,' and—"

"Hey! I want to get some, too. I don't care what you say about Franke; I wanna get 'Sweetheart.' Maybe I should get the Kim Carnes record for myself. And *then*," Ed said, waving an imaginary cigarette and doing a very bad Bette Davis imitation, "and then, we can *all* have Miss Davis's eyes."

Judy laughed and shook her head. "Oh, Uncle Ed, you're funny. But thanks. Really. It'll make up for having these dumb wires tightened."

Ed, still waving his imaginary cigarette, grinned at her. "Yeah? Well, that's what we funny uncles are for."

⁂

Once Judy had been ushered into the torture chamber by a dental assistant, Ed settled back in a waiting-room chair, the latest issue of *Time* on his lap. He glanced at the cover story on Israel and halfheartedly flipped through the rest of the magazine, his attention finally caught by an article about high interest rates, followed by another on how to beat high mortgage rates.

Scanning through the articles, he realized anew how lucky he and Rick were. As Ed still owed money on the Coleman Street house mortgage, there was no way they could afford to buy a bigger home in the current market. The carriage-house apartment might be smaller than their present home, but it came essentially rent free, and with the promise of a beautiful, stately Victorian home someday—mortgage free. If Ed found a good tenant for the Coleman Street house, the rent would easily cover those mortgage payments. He and Rick could potentially come out of the whole deal financially years ahead of where they were now, and certainly farther than most couples in their income bracket.

He closed the magazine and leaned his head against the wall behind him, his eyes closing. His thoughts bounced from finances to nieces and nephews, and then to carpet laying and wallpapering. He thought about just how much stuff he had stored away on the second floor of his house and wondered how much money he had in his pocket for records. He thought about Rick going to the library and whether Rick had remembered to take a book Ed needed to return. From there he thought about the ring on his finger and why, as of yet, none of his clients had commented on it.

*Geez, I hate packing and moving, but maybe when we're settled in the new place things will calm down. Maybe Mom will stop bitching about it, and maybe Rick and I can finally settle into a routine; get used to the idea of being married. Maybe we can figure out the best way to spend time with the kids so Rick's not living with them anymore really isn't a big deal, like Judy said, and maybe everything else will fall into place, too. Maybe, if someone does ask about this ring, I can tell the truth, or at least tell them something that doesn't make me feel like an asshole.*

He frowned, eyes still closed. *I wonder what I was doing a year ago today.* He thought back, trying to remember what was going on last May, but nothing came to mind. *I was probably hauling the Hausers' patio furniture out of their garage. Then I probably had dinner at Mom's since there probably wasn't anything decent to eat at my place. Then I probably hung around her house, watching TV, 'cause I didn't have anything better to do.*

Ed thought about going back to where he had been, that state of suspended animation he had seemed to inhabit before Rick came into his life. His head shook, almost involuntarily. No, he didn't want to go back. The warmth and joy of Rick's companionship, and their mutual desires to make good on the promises they had made to one another, were the best things that had ever happened to him, and, he knew, something very rare among men like them. Even if it all came with occasional disruption and a little bit of uncertainty, they were worth it. Actually, worth a lot more, Ed thought.

He opened his eyes and watched the fingers on his right hand play with the ring on his left. He realized the ring symbolized everything he had ever wanted in a commitment from another man. He had dreamed and fantasized about it, and now he was living it. William and Ben most likely had a similar dream, but what had been just a dream for them had become reality for Ed, and for their sake as well as his own, he didn't want to blow it.

Judy, scowling, walked into the waiting room, a reminder card for her next appointment clutched in her fist.

"Can we go look at records now?" she mumbled.

"Yeah, yeah," Ed groaned as he pulled himself to his feet.

"That ring Uncle Rick gave you is beautiful," Judy commented as they walked across the parking lot.

"It is, isn't it?"

"I hope a guy loves me enough to buy me something like that someday."

"It'll happen, kid. When you get those dumb braces off, and you finish school, and you grow up, and . . ."

Ed stopped by the passenger-side door, keys in hand, and snickered, shaking his head.

"And what?" Judy asked, looking at him curiously.

He unlocked the door, grabbed Judy by the hips, and boosted her into the passenger seat, making her laugh as well.

"And when," he said, slapping the roof of the truck for emphasis, his words for himself as much as for Judy, "you finally understand what being an adult is all about."

# Chapter Seven

Ed sat on the floor and put his elbows on the bedroom windowsill of their new home in the carriage house. He missed his neighbors in the lilac bush, Mr. and Mrs. Redd, but he had to admit, the view from this window surpassed the one from the bedroom on Coleman Street.

Mrs. Penfield's garden was in early June glory. The peonies were at their peak, their heavy-headed blossoms every color from light pink to mellow wine. The deep red roses were coming on in the arbor, and the iris bed was a blaze of purple and yellow.

Ed sighed happily. If the way he felt right now was any indication, things were going to work out well for them here in the carriage house.

The rapid pace set early in the remodeling project had continued through May and into June. Mrs. Penfield's organizational skills combined with Ed and Rick's eagerness to settle into the new home pulled the originally anticipated finish date from midsummer to late spring. When it had become apparent that they could indeed move in earlier than they had originally thought, Ed and Rick had devoted every spare moment to packing. Aside from customary graveside decorating, including visits to the graves of William and Ben, they spent Memorial Day weekend in a nonstop painting spree, which had left them exhausted and paint stained from head to toe, but very satisfied with their accomplishments.

After the carpet had been laid, the process of moving could begin. Now, on the second weekend in June, it was almost complete, and Ed and Rick, along with Jett, would be spending their first night in their new home.

Ed felt a hand on his shoulder. "Beautiful, isn't it?" Rick murmured.

Rick sat on the floor next to Ed, observing the garden below. He, too, sighed, putting an arm around Ed's shoulders. "I can't tell you how happy I am today. It would be as hard as trying to explain how much I love you."

Ed leaned over and kissed him. "I know. Me, too. I almost can't believe this is really happening." He fingered the ring on his left hand. "It seems like Easter was just a moment ago, and we were talking about living in a place like this someday. And now we are." He shook his head in amazement.

"The fact that this all came together so quickly and smoothly just reassures me that this is meant to be. Somebody up there likes us, baby, so let's enjoy it." Rick hugged him, smiling out the window.

"I know what I'm going to enjoy tonight," Ed said, looking behind him.

Rick turned his head, looking in the same direction. "Oh, yes."

They both stared fondly at their new bed. They hadn't allowed themselves to splurge much for their new home, but both had agreed upon a new, bigger bed. "Queen-size bed for a couple of queens," Rick had snickered when they picked it out. As much as Ed loved sleeping close to Rick, he was looking forward to the additional stretching space for his six-foot, broad-shouldered body next to Rick's six-foot-two, equally broad-shouldered body.

"Maybe we should give it a trial run," Rick said with his mischievous grin.

"Darlin', we don't even have the sheets on it yet."

"So? Who needs sheets?"

Footsteps on the stairs were followed by the sound of a heavy carton being dropped on the living room floor. "Are you forgetting?" Ed stroked Rick's beard. "We're not alone."

Gordy appeared in the bedroom doorway. "Aw, shit! Are you guys making out again? Hell, I do all the work, and you have all the fun." He made a face at them. "The last of your books are here, Benton. Happy reading."

"I am going to be much too busy for any reading," Rick said, kissing Ed.

Gordy groaned. "Gawd. It's like being in a porno movie. So, what's my reward for hauling all of your shit over here and watching you two slobber over each other? A box of Girl Scout cookies?"

"Will you settle for a beer?" Rick asked, grabbing Ed's crotch to further irritate Gordy. "There are some cold ones in the fridge."

"Yeah, I guess I can live with that." Gordy shook his head at them in disgust and stomped down the hall to the kitchen.

"And don't smoke in my new house," Rick hollered after him.

"Fuck you, Benton!"

"Oh, can it, you two," Ed said, getting up. "C'mon." He pulled Rick to his feet. "I want one of those beers. I don't care what he says. We've been working hard, too. I'm thirsty."

The three of them settled in the living room, resting and admiring the space. The midday sun shone through the newly washed stained-glass panes above the regular windows, and Ed marveled at the rainbow of colors the light threw against the opposite wall. "A room with stained-glass windows," he whispered.

"In the bedroom, too," Rick said, smiling. "We won't see those colors in the morning, with those windows facing south, but it sure is great this time of day."

"What's that song they sing on *The Jeffersons*?" Ed commented. "We are movin' on up."

"Yeah, I'll remind you of that the first time you have to haul groceries up those stairs," Gordy said, knocking back his beer. "I used to live on the second floor, and it sucked."

"You're not gonna spoil my good mood today, so don't even try." Ed smirked at him.

Ed set his own beer on the floor near some cartons. He walked over to the stereo, anxious to get it hooked up and plugged in. Although his records, along with Rick's stash, were still in boxes, he could at least get the radio going.

While Rick and Gordy traded insults, Ed connected the speakers. The radio came on, loudly blaring "Stars on 45."

"Man, they are playing this one to death," Gordy grumbled.

Rick shrugged. "I actually like it. I mean, who ever thought a medley of Beatles songs would be a hit in the eighties?"

"Even Judy likes it," Ed put in, settling the stereo speakers in the room's corners. "Although the beginning of it always makes me want to hear 'Venus' all the way through. Maybe since this is so popular, they'll start playing old songs on the radio again, instead of just new stuff."

"Yeah, and give your worn out 45s a rest," Rick teased.

All three heads turned toward the echo of heavy footsteps on the stairs. Effie Maude appeared at the open door. Gordy's eyes grew big at the sight of her. "'Lo, boys. Thought I'd come see how this all turned out. I wager I haven't even been up here in nigh on twenty years at least."

"Come on in," Ed said, getting to his feet.

Ed showed her around the place, Effie Maude exclaiming over the changes. "Can't believe it's the same place. You done good. It's nice and homey."

She walked to the door, then paused, arms across her substantial chest. "Oh, I've got a message from Mrs. P. She said she figures you don't want to be bothered tonight, but she'd like you to stop in for Sunday dinner tomorrow. Don't worry. I'll whip it up 'fore I leave today, and it'll just need to be heated up."

"Tell her we'll be there," said Rick, amused as always by Effie Maude, and with Gordy's reaction to her.

Effie Maude took one last look around, nodding with satisfaction. "Well, welcome to the place, boys. I think you'll do just fine here. Takes a load offa my mind, knowin' I don't have to worry 'bout Mrs. P. at night anymore. Good luck."

She turned to leave, then hesitated. "See that you keep it lookin' good. I ain't cleanin' it." On that note, she headed downward, the stairs creaking in protest under her feet.

Ed and Rick, as usual, giggled. Gordy blinked a few times and shook his head. "What the hell was that, the watchdog?"

"Well, I wouldn't want to tangle with her," Rick said, still chortling.

"Imagine meeting that in a dark alley," Gordy roared. "Hell, it's a good thing I'm already queer. That woulda made up my mind if I wasn't."

"Don't pick on her," Ed scolded them. "I have a feeling we may be on the receiving end of her good cooking sooner or later."

"You should come to dinner tomorrow, too, Gordy," Rick said, giving him a shove. "I'd like to know if Mrs. P. enjoyed you in school as much as she did Ed."

"Oh, man." Gordy rolled his eyes. "I can just hear her. 'Gordon,'" he said, trying to imitate Mrs. Penfield's voice, "'you have an A-plus mind. Why are you doing C-minus work?' Shit! She'd probably spend the whole meal correcting my grammar."

"She doesn't do that anymore," Ed told him, grinning. "She's retired, remember?"

"Once an English teacher, always an English teacher," Gordy said flatly. "No thanks! I'm glad she's crazy about you two, but when she finds out we're all buds, she may throw you out."

Gordy stood up. "Now I am going down to the yard for a smoke, so I don't contaminate Rick's precious little house."

"Be careful Mrs. Penfield doesn't see you out the window," Ed teased.

"Hell, I can still run faster than she can." Gordy walked out, pulling his cigarettes out of his pocket.

"After all the work he did for us today, the least you could do is let him smoke up here," Ed said to Rick. "The windows are open."

Rick sat on the floor next to Ed, pawing through a box of records. "Oh, he can smoke up here. I just like giving him shit. You know that. He knows it, too. I think that was just his way of letting us be alone for awhile."

"Alone? You want to be alone with me?" Ed asked him in mock surprise. "We still don't have any sheets on that bed, remember?"

"Baby, we don't need sheets, and we don't need a bed. I have every intention of christening every room in this place with you at one time or another." Rick leaned over for a kiss, a very long, very satisfying one, in Ed's opinion.

"But that will have to wait," Rick said pulling away and shuffling through Ed's 45s. "There is one song I want to hear, right now, with you, in our new home."

Rick pulled "One Man Band" out of the box. Ed shook his head. "I may have to get a new copy of that. We're gonna wear it out."

"Get three or four, baby. I plan on playing this song every time we have a big day like this in our life."

Rick put the record on the turntable. He pulled Ed to his feet, putting his arms around him. As the song began to play, Rick sighed with contentment, his face against Ed's.

Ed pulled Rick closer to him. "I love you, darlin'," he whispered.

"My wonderful, wonderful, one-man band," Rick murmured, swaying to the beat. "I love you, too. Oh, baby, I think we are going to make some very beautiful music here."

◈◆◈

Gordy took off shortly after his smoke break, saying he had his own chores to worry about for the rest of the day. He waved off any thanks other than a big hug from each of them, and the rest of the six-pack from the fridge.

"When the day comes that I need to move, you know who I'm calling," he told them, heading down the stairs.

Ed and Rick proceeded with unpacking boxes, Ed happily putting away records in the cabinet his father had made for him years before, while Rick sorted through kitchen utensils.

"We should get a microwave oven," Rick commented. "We've got the counter space for it."

"You think so?" Ed had never given the matter much thought.

"Why not? So many people have them now, I'm sure the price has come down. It might come in handy when we get busy with stuff around here, you know, maintaining our jobs and maintaining the property."

"Yeah, I s'pose you're right," Ed mused. "Geez, we just got used to sharing the work on Coleman Street; now we have to figure it out all over again. Remind me to ask Mrs. Penfield when would be the best day for us to do our laundry. I'm sure Effie Maude won't do it for us."

Rick laughed. "Yeah, she may be glad we're here, but not that glad. She sounded like Benson on *Soap* earlier. Well, when we sit down for supper, let's make a list to discuss with Mrs. P. tomorrow. We've been so busy getting moved in, we haven't really talked about it. I want to make sure we're all on the same page with this stuff."

Ed was about to reply when the doorbell he had recently installed rang, followed by the sound of someone climbing the stairs. Those footsteps sounded awfully familiar to Ed. Sure enough, his mother appeared at the open door.

"Yoo-hoo," she hollered, barging in as usual.

"Geez, Mom, we're up a flight of stairs, behind two doors, and you still just walk in, bold as you please."

Norma narrowed her eyes at Ed. "Do you have something to hide from your mother?"

"Yeah," he retorted. "We're growing marijuana up here!"

Rick laughed as Norma gasped. "Ed Stephens! We aren't more than five blocks from the police station. Watch your mouth."

"Don't worry, Norma," Rick said, still laughing. "We've got 'em bribed to look the other way."

"Honestly," she huffed. "You've just moved into this fancy place, and already you're getting too big for your britches. I should've known."

Norma had not been in the least shy about voicing her disapproval of their decision to move into the carriage house. She had argued the matter until the day Ed and Rick had signed the legal agreement with Mrs. Penfield. Norma had then declared she was washing her hands of the whole thing, and they'd better not come running to her when it all blew up in their faces. Still, her curiosity about their new home had obviously gotten the better of her.

Norma deposited a grocery bag on the kitchen table with a clank. "Chili soup," she announced. "People who have spent the day moving have no business cooking. Well, are you going to give your mother a tour of this place, or are you going to send me away wondering?"

Ed got to his feet with a smothered sigh. He took her through the rooms, waiting for her to find something to fuss about, but she was politely complimentary. She paused in the bedroom, looking out the window at the garden.

"Well, it's all very nice. I understand why you wanted to do this, although I still think it's a mistake. You just make sure that woman is absolutely clear on what you will do and what you won't."

"We're going to talk about it tomorrow," Ed told her. "Don't worry about it, Mom. Rick and I would've never agreed to this if we thought for even a second that Mrs. Penfield would cause any problems."

"Humph! I certainly hope so."

Much to Ed's surprise, Norma sighed, looking wistful. "I remember when your father and I bought the house on Walnut Street. I was still working for Patterson's Bakery, and I'd walk to work by some of these big houses, wondering if we'd ever be able to afford something like this."

She turned to Ed. "I know this wouldn't be happening if it weren't for all of the hard work you've done for folks like Mrs. Penfield. I do understand,

Ed, even if I don't approve. I hope you and Rick will be happy here, and that it all works out. Just be careful!"

"We will," he said smiling at her. "Look at it this way, Mom. We're only two blocks away from you now. The next time you smell gas, I won't even have to drive."

"I won't hold my breath," she grumbled. "You'll probably be so busy trying to keep this place going, I'll have to take a number."

"Mom, you're still number one on my client list. That hasn't changed, and I'm guessing Mrs. Penfield wouldn't have it any other way."

"We'll see," she snorted, walking back to the living room. She glared at Jett, who was waking up from a nap in his favorite chair. "Couldn't you at least have left that beast behind?"

"Just think of him as a grandson with an attitude problem," Rick teased.

"Honestly! It's bad enough my son is with another man. Now I have to think of the cat as a grandchild? When is this going to end?" She walked to the door. "Speaking of grandchildren, your sister talked me into babysitting again, so I'll just be on my way."

Rick, unwrapping newspaper from a stack of plates, grinned at her. "Thanks for the chili, Norma. Left to our own devices, we probably would have just called Gino's for pizza."

"I thought as much," she said smugly. "Somebody's got to make sure you're still eating right. Behave yourselves, and you might get cookies this week," she promised.

"Thanks, Mom," Ed said gratefully. "Call me if you need anything."

"Oh, you can be sure of that," she said as she headed down the stairs. "Honestly. These stairs! You'll get tired of this soon enough. I'll see you all later."

Ed and Rick called their good-byes. Jett, once the coast was clear, jumped down from his chair, curious, as most cats would be, about the open boxes. He investigated the one nearest him, crawling inside to settle down for an afternoon wash.

"He's taking this all well," Ed said, putting Norma's soup pot in the refrigerator.

Rick shrugged. "Well, he still has his favorite chair, and he knows where his food dish is. I'm guessing, too, he's too young yet to be really set in his ways. Still," he concluded thoughtfully, "I'll bet he's getting close to a year old. We may have to think about getting him fixed, for his sake and ours."

Ed hugged Rick from behind. "That's okay, as long as the vet stays away from *your* equipment."

Rick snickered. "We still don't have sheets on that bed, remember?"

Ed gave him a squeeze. "That just may be my next chore."

◆

Ed and Rick joined Mrs. Penfield in the dining room of the main house the next day. Effie Maude had prepared an egg-and-sausage casserole, and they hungrily dug in, Rick making a note to ask Effie Maude for the recipe.

"Something to add to my breakfast menus," he said, smiling fondly at Mrs. Penfield.

The old woman beamed at her new tenants. "I can't tell you how delighted I am with how things are going. Already it's a joy to have you both here. I had grown very tired of living alone, so again, for my own selfish reasons, I'm very pleased this has worked out so well. Is everything satisfactory in the carriage house? I apologize for not stopping in yesterday, but I simply wasn't up to those stairs."

"We're fine," Ed assured her. "We have a little unpacking to do, but that's it."

"I noticed Gordon Smith helping you yesterday," she said rather wickedly. "I can only assume he was avoiding me on purpose."

Ed and Rick laughed. "I think he's afraid you're gonna quiz him on *Hamlet* or something," Ed said.

"Oh, Gordy and I had our disagreements about his abilities," Mrs. Penfield chuckled. "However, I was always fond of him. Please make sure he knows the witch of English 11 has retired her broomstick."

"He's become a wonderful friend to both of us," Rick commented.

"I'm glad to see that," said Mrs. Penfield. "And again, please make sure he knows he is welcome here, along with all your friends and family. This is your home now," she stressed. "You mustn't stand on ceremony."

"I'm glad to hear that," Rick said with a grin. "Claire and the kids are coming over this afternoon, and I know Claire would love to see the big house."

"Of course, of course," Mrs. Penfield said, nodding. "I'm anxious to meet her, and the children, too. My, it's been too long since the sounds of children's voices were heard in this house. I know I was correct in one assumption. Your presence here will turn this museum back into a home."

It was another warm, sunny day, so after brunch they retired to the garden for a more serious discussion about Ed and Rick's responsibilities. Happily, they all were, as Rick would say, on the same page. In addition to routine chores, Mrs. Penfield also outlined some future projects for the main house. "These are not things I'm overly concerned about in the short run," she emphasized. "I'm thinking more of your future, when the house will belong to you," she added, mentioning the age of the roof, some plumbing concerns, and a basement damp spot."

Ed nodded, making notes. "Yeah, I've thought about some of that stuff, too. Once we're really settled, and I get my house rented, I'll take a closer look. Unless anything needs attention right away, I'll probably put it off 'til next year."

"Oh, you've definitely decided to rent your house on Coleman Street?"

"Uh-huh," Ed said, with a look at Rick. "We decided the rental income would cover the mortgage payments. Depending on how things go, we might use it as a fix-up-and-sell project in a year or two." What Ed did not say was that they felt it was in their best interest to hold on to it, in case things did not work out with the carriage-house arrangement.

Mrs. Penfield nodded. "That sounds wise. Well, I wouldn't expect much less from you two."

Claire's station wagon pulled into the driveway. Rick rose to meet them. Judy, Josh, and Jane tumbled out, eager to explore the grounds and Uncle Rick's new home.

Introductions were made, and soon Claire was seated next to Mrs. Penfield on the rose arbor bench, as Rick led the children to the carriage house. "I'm so glad to finally meet you, Mrs. Penfield," Claire said warmly. "I'm really excited for Rick and Ed, having this chance. Our parents are pretty curious about it as well, so I have a feeling they'll be making a visit when they return from their trip to Canada."

Mrs. Penfield smiled at her. "I am excited about it as well," she assured her. "I was telling Ed and your brother earlier how nice it is to have a little noise about the place. I noticed yesterday," she said with a teasing glance at Ed, "that Ed's taste in music hasn't changed since high school."

"Aw, crud," Ed said, embarrassed. "Did I have the stereo going too loud? I'll turn it down from now on."

"It didn't bother me at all," Mrs. Penfield said, chuckling. "I would have never admitted it during my teaching years, but I've always found rock and roll to be a rather joyful noise. My late husband, however, detested it. I'm sure he would be horrified to hear it on this property."

"I just hope he doesn't decide to haunt the carriage house in protest," Ed said sheepishly.

"I'm sorry to disappoint you, but the Penfield house seems to be ghost free," Mrs. Penfield chuckled.

"Shoot," Claire said with a chuckle of her own. "There go my plans for a séance, like they used to have on *Dark Shadows.*"

"I loved that show," Ed smiled at her. "You, too?"

Ed and Claire were soon deep into a debate on the history of Barnabas Collins. Mrs. Penfield listened, a pleased smile on her face. It had never really occurred to Ed that Mrs. Penfield had been lonely, living in such a large place alone. He relaxed, realizing that a little noise and confusion probably meant more to her than any home and garden chores they might perform.

Rick and the children joined them. "Can we see inside the other house?" Judy asked eagerly. She was so excited she forgot to smile with her mouth closed.

"Let's all go," Mrs. Penfield said, slowly rising. "I'm actually feeling spry enough to lead the tour myself today."

"Ed's our new uncle," five-year-old Jane said to her. "Does that make you our new grandma?"

"Jane," Claire protested, embarrassed.

Mrs. Penfield, however, laughed outright. "Why, if you wish to think so, I'd be delighted." She smiled fondly at Jane. "I never had any grandchildren of my own, so if you want to adopt me, I would be honored."

"Do you like Candy Land and Chutes and Ladders?" Jane asked, taking her hand.

Josh, the lone boy eternally stuck between two sisters, groaned. "Those are baby games," he said in disgust.

Mrs. Penfield, with a wink at Josh, regarded Jane seriously. "I'm afraid I've never played those games, but if you think you can teach an old woman how to play, perhaps we could give it a try sometime."

As they all entered the house, Rick gave Ed's hand a squeeze. "Now I see why she was your favorite teacher," he murmured.

"She knows her way around kids all right," Ed murmured in response.

Mrs. Penfield led the party through the downstairs rooms, from kitchen to front parlor. Upstairs, Josh's attention was drawn to a small flight of stairs. "What's up there?"

"An attic filled with a great deal of junk of interest to boys such as you," Mrs. Penfield told him. "Some rainy day you'll have to do some exploring."

"Neat," Josh whispered, peering up the stairs.

Mrs. Penfield paused in front of the bedroom she had converted into a library years before. She turned to address Rick. "I keep forgetting to ask if you would like to store some of your books in this room. I know it's not terribly convenient, but with space limited in your quarters, I thought it might be practical."

"I'd like that very much," he replied with a grin. "You may see me up here emptying boxes before the day is out."

Tour complete, Mrs. Penfield and the children returned to the garden to enjoy a pitcher of lemonade Effie Maude had prepared, while Ed and Rick showed Claire through the carriage house.

"You guys are really lucky," she said, admiring the stained-glass windows and the freshly painted and papered rooms. "And Mrs. Penfield is a dream. I have a feeling this is going to work out for you; I really do."

"I still can't get over it," Ed said. "It's like a fairy tale with a happy ending."

"Oh, this is no ending," Rick said confidently. "It's just the beginning."

"I have to admit I was little worried about the whole arrangement," Claire confessed. "But Ed's right. There doesn't seem to be a big, bad wolf in this one. Well," she said, hugging her brother. "I hope you'll be very happy here. We miss you at home, but it looks like I just found an extra babysitter."

They looked out the living room window at Mrs. Penfield, who seemed to be telling the children a story. "Gordy was right about one thing," Ed remarked. "Once a teacher, always a teacher."

"She's an amazing woman," Rick said softly. "Since our grandparents died so many years ago, I have a tendency to think of her as a grandmother myself."

"Hopefully she'll adopt me, too," Claire said with a giggle.

"I think she already has," Rick said. "There seems to be a lot of room in that big heart."

Claire descended the stairs to rejoin the others. Ed and Rick lagged behind, gazing contentedly around their new home.

"Maybe it is a fairy tale for us two fairies," Rick said, hugging Ed. "Right now I can sure see us living here happily ever after."

He led Ed back to the windows. "I can see us in that garden, old and gray, debating what to plant every spring. I can also see Judy, or maybe even Claire, if she finds the right man, getting married in that rose arbor."

Ed smiled at him. "We may not be legally married, and not have any kids of our own, but we've got one hell of a family, don't we?"

"Yep," Rick said with a kiss. "We've got each other, a family, and a place to build our future. Meeting you made me the luckiest guy in the world, and the luck's still holding out. Oh, I still wonder about this town, and how people will react to two guys taking over a place like this, but we'll worry about that when we need to."

"I've already decided," Ed said, returning the kiss. "If Porterfield doesn't like it, we'll just build a moat to keep 'em out.

"You're my husband, and my lover," Ed added softly, stroking Rick's face. "And this is our home now. Nobody's gonna mess that up if I have anything to say about it."

# Chapter Eight

Life in the carriage house slowly began to evolve into a new routine with the usual amount of trial and error. Rick, who had bragged that he could now walk to the post office every morning, dutifully set his alarm clock back ten minutes to do just that. It lasted all of two days. On the third day, when Rick slept to his usual time and drove his car to work, Ed politely inquired whether Rick still planned to walk to work on a regular basis.

"I do enough walking on my route," Rick grumbled. "And besides, it's more convenient to have the car in case I need to run errands or stop by Claire's after work."

Ed solemnly agreed with Rick, and then proceeded to tease him for the rest of the week about the abandonment of his noble intentions.

Ed was making his own usual slow adjustment to new surroundings. He spent several restless nights on the new bed, occasionally waking up only to be startled by the alien room. He stubbed his toe on the dresser one dark night, stumbled down the stairs the next morning when he miscalculated the steps, and on more than one occasion absentmindedly drove to his house on Coleman Street after completing a job.

*Only twenty-eight years old, and already I'm set in my ways*, he thought.

He reminded himself, though, that he had gone through the same thing when he had moved into the Coleman Street house. It would all settle into his brain with time.

Although the new home was taking a good deal of getting used to, Ed had to admit he genuinely loved the apartment and life on the Penfield grounds in general. He seemed to take a great deal of comfort from the old buildings, which had stood for eighty-three years and would probably stand for another eighty-three. He had always loved older homes, and so far, living in one was as satisfying as he had hoped.

One Monday afternoon in mid-June, Ed was on the lower floor of the carriage house, hands on hips, surveying the space he hoped to use for his workshop. It seemed to be filled with eighty-three years worth of clutter, and after all the packing, throwing out, and hauling he had just completed, he was facing the project of clearing the space with little enthusiasm.

Ed had bought a portable radio cassette player so he could listen to the tapes Rick had made from Ed's old 45s. He had carefully set the stereo on a shelf attached to the stairway wall and ruefully reflected that it could be the only improvement he completed for the time being.

Cannibal and the Headhunters were chugging through "Land of 1000 Dances," and Ed was doing a very bad watusi to the beat, frowning at the wall space, trying to imagine the best locations for his father's tools. Bored with the watusi, he switched to the jerk. When he swung his left arm upward, he caught a glance of his watch and groaned. It was almost time for him to drive over to Coleman Street and show the house again.

Ed was having second thoughts about being a landlord. He had already shown the house three times and had been slightly horror stricken by his potential renters.

The first to answer his newspaper ad was a young couple with an infant. They seemed nice enough but cheerfully admitted that their sole source of income was the husband's unemployment check.

After that, another young couple appeared. They argued heatedly during Ed's house tour, and their six-year-old, who made Dennis the Menace appear positively saintly, pulled a curtain rod down, left the shower running, and slammed the front door so hard, Ed was afraid the glass would shatter.

The third applicant was a heavyset woman a few years younger than Ed. She wolfed down two Snickers bars, giggled repeatedly, and made it clear she had an interest in Ed other than as a landlord. He waved his left hand in her face several times, hoping she'd get the hint.

Ed regretfully shut off the portable stereo and pulled his keys out of his pocket. He jumped in the truck and backed out into the parking area. He paused for a moment, watching Rick, who had the day off, busily trimming the shrubbery next to the main house. He had wondered, despite Rick's assurances, whether he really knew what he was doing, but he seemed to be doing a good job. Ed tooted his horn and waved. Rick, smiling, waved his hedge clippers with one hand, showing Ed crossed fingers with the other.

Ed headed for Coleman Street, turning the radio to WFWQ. Musically he made the leap from 1965 to 1981, singing along with "Bette Davis Eyes."

"It's the new sound of the eighties," the disc jockey proclaimed, referring to the synthesizers and drum machines on the song. Ed, who had grown up with rock and roll, found it hard to believe guitars would actually go out of style.

He pulled into his driveway, looking nostalgically at his house. As happy as he was with the new place, he still missed this one. Mortgage payments or not, he couldn't help thinking he'd rather let it sit empty than rent it to someone who wouldn't appreciate it.

It looked as though his next potential renter was on time for the appointment. He noticed a rather haggard-looking middle-aged woman alighting from a bicycle in front of the house. Ed, sighing, walked through the side yard to meet her. His first impression of Dolores Herendeen wasn't too inspiring.

Ed introduced himself and quickly took a step back. Ms. Herendeen had obviously drunk her lunch, and the eighty-proof odor was quite strong. "It looks just wonderful," she slurred, pushing back her ill-kept hair. "And a garage! That will be great for my bike. So many thieves around these days," she grumbled, shaking her head at Ed.

"I take it you don't drive," Ed said tentatively.

"Not any more," she said tersely. "Can I see inside?"

Ed flipped through his keys with another sigh. He had a pretty good idea why Dolores didn't drive anymore. "This is lovely, just lovely," she muttered as he led her through the house. "I really need to move, you know. My landlord is so picky about things. It don't cost that much to clean carpets," she told Ed, looking most put upon.

Ed tried to keep his face as neutral as possible. "Would you like to see the upstairs?" he asked, hoping she'd decline.

"Oh, yes!" Dolores hauled herself up the stairs, clutching the banister tightly. "Lovely, lovely," she trilled at the top. "This'll be perfect for when my children come to visit. I don't have custody, you know."

"Really?"

"Oh, yes. My ex-husband bribed the judge, you know. Thinks he's such hot stuff. Oh, they were all in it together. Don't think I don't know it. Children," she said righteously, "belong with their mother. Go tell *that* to that judge."

Ed couldn't think of anything to say, but Dolores didn't wait for an answer.

"Are you going to mow the yard? I really don't have the time for that, you know. My landlord keeps complainin' about the weeds, but shouldn't that be his problem? I think my ex-husband pays him to pester me about all sorts of things. I pay my rent," she snorted. "What's wrong with a few weeds in the yard? I keep the house clean. Enough anyway."

She fished a cigarette pack out of her purse. "You don't live nearby, do you?" she asked suspiciously.

"Uh, no," Ed replied nervously. "I live north and west of here a few blocks."

"Well, then, I'm sure you're too busy to get involved with your tenant's business," she said, lighting up.

"I guess it depends," Ed said doubtfully, still very new at this.

"You certainly don't have to be over all the time telling me how to run my life," she said, head in the air. "I'm just fine! I don't care what my ex-husband tells you!" She took a deep drag from her cigarette.

"Why don't we go back downstairs?" Ed asked, nervously watching her cigarette. There wasn't an ashtray to be found in the house, and he was having nervous thoughts about his own carpeting.

Once downstairs, Dolores took another look around, tapping her cigarette over the kitchen sink, much to Ed's relief. "Well, it's just lovely." She peered into the refrigerator. "I don't know, though. I s'pose I should look at the other places on my list. They weren't as close as this one, though."

"Close to what?"

"Close to the liq—oh, never mind," she finished hastily.

"Why don't you check out those other places," Ed said smiling nervously. "I'd hate for you to make a rash decision."

"I'll be in touch," she said, moving toward the door. She turned around, frowning at Ed. "Are you married?" she asked abruptly.

"Yes, I am," Ed said hurriedly.

She nodded. "That figures. Well, you're too young for me anyway. Thanks for the tour, Mr. Stephens!"

Dolores Herendeen returned to her bicycle, mounting it unsteadily. Ed shook his head. He wanted nothing more than to go home and forget the whole thing, but another prospective tenant was due to arrive shortly.

Ed was running water in the kitchen sink, waving his arms to try to eliminate the smell of smoke, when he saw a respectable-looking sedan pull into the driveway next to his truck. A young man in a dark suit stepped out of the car, adjusting his tie. Ed's eyes grew larger. The man, who appeared to be in his early twenties, was quite attractive.

"I wonder what's wrong with him," Ed muttered, going to the door.

After a few minutes of pleasant conversation, Ed couldn't find anything the matter with Doug Morgan. He was as good-looking close up. He was a few inches shorter than Ed, slim and well built. His wavy blond hair and blue eyes were set off by a glowing tan. Ed had to remind himself he was a married man.

"This is great," Doug commented, checking out the rooms on the first floor. "Not too big; not too small. Close to work, too."

"What do you do?"

Doug grinned mischievously. "I'm an undertaker," he said, waiting for

Ed's reaction.

Ed was properly surprised. "Uh, then you must work for Reimer and Bayless," he said, referring to the funeral home four blocks down Coleman Street at its intersection with Main. It was located in an old Victorian home, not unlike Mrs. Penfield's.

"That's right." Doug smiled. "I did a couple years in the army after high school, then went to mortuary school. I know it grosses a lot of people out, but it's not a bad way to make a living. I've been living at the funeral home in the upstairs quarters, but my girlfriend hates it, so it's time to find a new place."

"Are you from Porterfield originally?" Ed asked curiously.

"No. I grew up near Chicago, in one of the western suburbs, actually. My girlfriend lives in Fort Wayne. She works there as a travel agent. She refuses to drive to Porterfield until I move out of the funeral home." He rolled his eyes. "Why people get so worked up about stuff like this is beyond me."

"Doesn't sound like you have much of a future with her," Ed said tentatively, thinking he was very glad Rick was a mailman.

Doug shrugged. "Maybe, maybe not. I'm not worried about it. What about the lawn chores around here?" he asked, changing the subject. "I'd be more than happy to take care of that for you. I was hoping to work on the landscaping at the funeral home, but they have that contracted out."

"That'd be great," Ed said in relief. "I'll even knock some money off the rent if I don't have to worry about it."

"Not a problem," Doug assured him. "If I wasn't an undertaker, I'd probably be a landscaper. This just pays better."

Ed continued his tour through the first floor, then upstairs. He showed Doug the gas furnace in the basement and took him outside to check out the garage and the yard. Doug nodded in satisfaction. "Yeah, this is just what I'm looking for."

He pulled a business card out of his suit pocket. "If you want, you can call the funeral home to see that I am who I say I am. Otherwise, I'd really like to talk about moving in, sir."

"Please, call me Ed," Ed said in embarrassment. He still wasn't old enough to appreciate the idea of being called "sir."

Doug chuckled. "Old army habit," he said. "Not to mention, that kind of respect comes in handy at work. You'd be surprised what great training the army is for funeral work."

"I can imagine," Ed said doubtfully. Actually, he had no desire to imagine it at all.

Doug looked at his watch. "I've got a funeral soon, so I should get going. Did you know a Mrs. Ruby Meggs?"

Ed shook his head.

"Oh. Seems like everyone in this town knows everyone else. Anyway, she's dead, and I have to make sure we get her safely to the cemetery today. Can I call you tonight?"

"Sure," Ed replied, trying to reconcile this cheerful, attractive young man with his somber profession.

Doug firmly shook Ed's hand. "Good to meet you, Ed. I look forward to talking to you again."

Ed watched in wonder as Doug strode to his car. He pulled out of the driveway, heading in the direction of the funeral home. Ed shook his head. "Geez, wait till I tell Rick about this one."

⋘•⋙

Ed hung up the phone. He and Rick had just finished supper that evening, and the phone had interrupted his dishwashing. "That was Doug Morgan," he told Rick. "He's coming over to talk about the lease. I think he really wants to take the place. What do you think?"

Rick looked up from the book he had been reading. " It's up to you. I certainly trust your judgment, and if you think he'll be good tenant, I'm sure he will be. It's your house, after all."

"Well, at least you'll get a chance to meet him before he signs. If you pick up on anything weird, stop me, okay?" Ed went back to the supper dishes.

Rick snickered. "Yeah, I'm kind of looking forward to meeting this cute mortician. I know that's not quite what you had in mind for the house, but he sounds responsible enough."

"We'll see. I have one little test for Mr. Undertaker," Ed said, scrubbing a pan.

"Oh?"

"Yeah. You'll see."

Doug Morgan arrived a half hour later. He admired the carriage house and the apartment. "I wish we had something like this at the funeral home," he said enviously. "What a great place to park the hearse."

He noticed Jett resting in one of the living room windows. "A black cat," he exclaimed. "Now, that would be great, too. It'd really freak out the mourners."

Ed laughed. Doug seemed to have a healthy attitude about his work, all right.

Rick came down the hall, and Ed grinned, thinking of his test. Doug had enjoyed telling Ed about his job; now it was Ed's turn to surprise him. "Doug, this is my husband, Rick Benton," he said, stressing the word husband. "Rick, this is Doug Morgan, who might take the house."

Doug, a startled look on his face, blinked a few times. He glanced from

Rick to Ed and back again. Ed enjoyed watching Doug struggle to maintain his composure. He was a bit disappointed when Doug's army training and mortician's professionalism quickly snapped into place. He gave Rick's hand a good shake, saying, "Nice to meet you. So how long have you two been together? Have you talked about prearrangements yet?"

Rick laughed. "Not too long, and no, we haven't. When the subject comes up, though, I promise we'll give you a call."

"Let's sit down and look over the lease," Ed said, pleased with Doug's reaction. He had wanted to know he wasn't renting his house to someone who might, at least outwardly, disapprove of his marriage. "Would you like something to drink? We've got some Pepsi and the usual stuff."

"I'd love a Pepsi." Doug grinned. "It was warm at the cemetery today, and as you can see, I haven't even bothered to change my clothes yet."

Rick grabbed a can of pop from the refrigerator, while Ed and Doug studied the lease on the coffee table. Mrs. Penfield's lawyer, Robert Mason, had given it to Ed, and now Ed tried to remember everything Mr. Mason had said.

Doug nodded complacently. "Yeah, this is all pretty standard. No problems. What time of the month do you want to get paid?"

The doorbell rang. Rick looked out the window and hollered, "Come in!"

He turned to the men on the sofa. "It's Gordy."

Gordy tromped up the stairs, yelling, "Hey guys!" through the open door. He walked in. "I was drivin' by, so I thought I'd stop in and see how it's goin'."

Gordy noticed the well-dressed young man on the sofa and glanced at both Ed and Rick, obviously surprised. "Hell, I'm sorry. I didn't know you had company."

Ed grinned at Gordy's reaction to the very handsome Doug Morgan. "Gord, this is Doug Morgan. He's going to rent our house. Doug, this is our good friend Gordy Smith."

Gordy walked closer to shake hands. "Good to meet you," he said in a more subdued tone than usual.

"Likewise," Doug grinned at him.

"Doug's a mortician," Rick said mischievously.

Gordy's face registered even greater surprise, and Ed resisted the impulse to giggle.

"Well," Gordy said, recovering. "If all the obits in the newspaper are any indication, you must be doing good business these days."

Doug nodded. "Oh, yes. They're croaking faster than we can plant 'em."

Gordy roared with laughter. "Now, that's my kind of undertaker."

"Have *you* thought about prearrangements, Mr. Smith?" Doug asked wickedly.

"Oh, hell, I just always thought they'd throw me in the back of a garbage truck and be done with it," Gordy said cheerfully, accepting the beer Rick handed him.

"I'm sure we could work something like that into the plans," Doug said, chuckling.

"C'mon, Gord," Rick said, shaking his head at him. "Let's go outside and let these guys finish their business."

Ed and Doug continued their discussion, which ended, happily, with a signed lease. Doug carefully wrote a check for the security deposit and first month's rent.

"Great," Ed said, smiling. He handed Doug Rick's old set of keys. "I guess that's it. Welcome to the house! I hope it's as good to you as it was to me."

"I'm sure it will be. You know, I looked at several places, but your house just had that feeling, you know? I think it'll work out fine."

He attached the keys to a ring he pulled out of his pocket. "I probably won't move in until the July Fourth weekend, if that's okay. Hopefully folks will stop dying for the holiday, and I can get it all done over a few days."

"That's cool. If you have any questions, or need any help, just call. I'm a handyman, and I pretty much make my own schedule. Keep that in mind if anything goes wrong, too. Don't hesitate to call."

Ed walked Doug back to his car, parked on Race Street. "Nice meeting you guys," Doug called to Rick and Gordy, who were sitting in the garden. "Come by the funeral home someday. I'll show you where we embalm the bodies."

Rick groaned, but Gordy roared his usual laugh. "You're on, man! I've always wondered how they did that."

Doug chuckled, shaking Ed's hand. "It's been a pleasure, Ed. I look forward to seeing you again."

"Same here," Ed said, watching him climb into his car. "Keep in touch, and I'll look forward to those rent checks."

Doug drove off, and Ed joined Rick and Gordy. "Shit," Gordy exclaimed. "Now, there's a man to get weak in the knees over. How the hell did you find him, Ed?"

"Calm down, cowboy," Ed told him, sitting down. "He's got a girlfriend."

"So what? A man can dream, can't he? Wow," Gordy said in appreciation.

"You were right, baby; he's one hunky undertaker," Rick said, laughing.

"Can't you just see the women in the funeral home trying to look all sad and mournful, secretly undressing him with their eyes?"

"I'd do a lot more than undress him," Gordy stated, raising his beer can. "Damn!"

"Well, I'll see if I can come up with an excuse for you to go over to the house," Ed said, smiling at his friend.

"Hell, I'll help him move in. I can think of lots of ways he can pay me."

"Gordy," Rick said, rolling his eyes. "You need to get laid. Bad!"

Gordy nodded in agreement. "Ya got that right. I'd better start looking around, or that undertaker's gonna find out how stiff I can be."

⋘•⋙

Ed adjusted the temperature on the bedroom air conditioner and flopped on the bed next to Rick with a sigh.

"I almost wish we had held out for central air-conditioning for this place, but it didn't seem right to have Mrs. Penfield pay for it. I tell you, our electric bill is gonna be gross this summer." As Ed had predicted, the heat of the warm June days rose into their second-story quarters every evening and, like an unwelcome houseguest, refused to leave until the wee hours of the morning.

"Well, look at the flipside," Rick said, looking up from his book. "We'll probably be warm and toasty next winter while everyone else is shivering."

"I hope so," Ed muttered.

Rick put his book aside. "Something bugging you?"

Ed shrugged. "Oh, I know it's dumb, but it seems really weird to have someone moving into the house."

Rick reached over and stroked Ed's hair. "It's natural, baby. Hell, I miss the house, too, but Doug seems like a good guy, and I don't think you have anything to worry about with him. He passed your little test, and if he has any problem with our relationship, I think he's too much of a gentleman to let it influence anything he might do at the house. I think he's too excited about finding a nice place to live to worry about what's going on here."

"Yeah, you're right." Ed allowed the soothing hand on his head to relax him. "It's just all been so much so fast. I'm still getting used to it."

"Life is change," Rick said as he massaged Ed's temples. "And I think all of our changes have been for the better. In fact . . ."

"What?"

"Oh, I was just thinking. When do you think you'll have your workshop set up downstairs?"

Ed groaned. "At the rate I'm going, probably not 'til the end of summer at the earliest. I'm burnt out on hauling junk around, but I'm gonna try to get that place cleaned out before we go to Cedar Point." During their moving process Ed and Rick had made plans for an early July overnight stay at the Ohio amusement park as a treat for all of their hard work.

"Hmmm." With a final pat on Ed's head, Rick rolled over and set his alarm clock. "Yuck; back to work tomorrow. Do you think you can handle all the work downstairs yourself?"

"I think so. Why? You already have projects lined up for me?" Ed teased with a tickle to Rick's side.

Rick giggled and pushed his hand away. "No. I was just wondering if you'd need my help with stuff."

"Don't worry about it. I know you have your hands full with work, checking up on the kids, and getting used to the yard and garden chores around here. Besides, Gordy said he'd help me haul Dad's tools over here on one of his days off."

"Good old Gordy," Rick murmured with a smile. "Did you see the way he was looking at Doug? He really does need to get laid. Better yet, he needs a boyfriend."

"Yeah. I'm guessing it's kind of hard for him to hang around us all the time and feel like a third wheel. Still, Mrs. Penfield said you were my reward for all the good things I had done, so maybe Gordy will get his reward, too."

"That reminds me. Mrs. P. came out for a chat while I was trimming the bushes. She asked if we would stop in and see her after dinner tomorrow night."

"What for? Anything wrong?"

"Nah, I think she just wants to see for herself that we're okay and that we're happy here." Rick moved closer to Ed and put an arm around him. "And I am happy here. Are you?"

Ed kissed him. "Yeah, I'm happy. Despite the heat, I'm happy 'cause we're together in our new home. And Mrs. Penfield's been great about letting us have our space. Mom had me worried that we'd be spending all of our time at the main house keeping her company, but she seems to respect our privacy as much as we respect hers.""

"Yeah," Rick said with a yawn. "She's been terrific. I don't think we need to worry about that. Baby, I know the changes have come fast and furious, but you're really okay, aren't you? I can't read that mind of yours, but sometimes I see a bewildered look on your face, you know, kind of like 'Where am I?' and 'Who is this guy in my bed?'"

Ed snickered. "I know where I am, and I sure know who the guy in my bed is. I'm just trying to get caught up, that's all. I'm getting there. I haven't stubbed my toe on this new bed or the dresser in three whole days."

Rick laughed as well. "Now, *that's* progress. I have to admit, it's all been pretty surprising for me, too. Remember our weekend at Spruce Lake and how we really talked about everything we wanted to do with our lives, and how to be more self-sufficient so we wouldn't have to worry so much about people disapproving of us?"

"Of course I remember."

"I'm still amazed at how this deal with Mrs. P. has kind of . . . I don't know . . . catapulted us farther ahead on those plans than I ever imagined. Like I said before, it's like it's all meant to be."

"Yeah. We've been really lucky," Ed said sleepily, letting his eyes close.

"Luck may be a lady instead of a gay man, but she's smiled on us for a long time now. Hopefully she'll keep smiling."

Ed opened his eyes and looked at Rick, who was sitting up in bed, staring into space above the dresser. "Are you worried about that? Luck, I mean?"

"No." Rick gave his head a shake. "Just thinking." His warm and tender special in place, he leaned over and kissed Ed. "I love you, baby. Good night."

"I love you, darlin'." Ed returned the kiss. "Good night. Don't stay up too late reading. Or thinking. Okay?"

"Okay."

⊰❋⊱

The next day was even warmer and more humid. Ed, hauling groceries into Mrs. Heston's house, thought sympathetically of Rick delivering mail in the summer heat.

Ed stowed Mrs. Heston's perishables in the refrigerator, then grabbed his toolbox from his truck. He wanted to check on the metal strip dividing her dining room carpet from the kitchen linoleum. It looked a bit loose to him, and he didn't want her snagging it with her walker.

Mrs. Heston, leaning on her walker, watched him with a pleased look. "Don't know what I'd do without you, Ed."

"Oh, it's no big deal," Ed muttered, embarrassed, as he usually was when someone praised him.

"There's something I've been meaning to ask you. If it's none of my business, you can tell me to shut my old trap. Won't hurt my feelings."

"What's on your mind?" he asked, looking up at her.

"That young man you're with, the one you moved in with over to Hilda Penfield's place. Does he have anything to do with that ring you've been wearing lately?"

Ed looked at his left hand, spread out on the floor. It was true; the general visual power of his clients wasn't the best, but he knew someone would notice it eventually. He was just amazed it had taken this long.

"Well, yes, Mrs. Heston," he said guardedly. "Rick gave me this ring."

Mrs. Heston slapped her walker. "I thought so. Now, don't you go bein' ashamed about it around me. Oh, I know most people don't cotton to such things, and I understand about that little story you told me a couple of months back, but I couldn't hold a bad thought in my head about you if I tried. You've done more for me than my own children have."

"Thanks, Mrs. Heston," he said in relief.

She shook her head in disgust. "None of my business, or anybody else's. You be as proud of that ring and that man as you want. He must care about you a lot."

Ed nodded, smiling. "Yes, he does."

"Good for you. I always thought it was a shame you were alone. I'm glad you've got someone."

She paused, thinking. "It tells me a lot, that you'd wear it to work. I s'pose there are some old buzzards in this town who might look down on you, tell you you're sinnin' or such, but don't worry about it. There's just as many like me, who thank the good Lord for Ed Stephens and what you do for us. I s'pect you'll always have more work than you need."

"I hope so," Ed said tentatively. "Yes, it does worry me sometimes, living with Rick in this town."

Mrs. Heston snorted. "Well! Anyone gives you any grief, you send 'em my way. I'll put 'em to rights."

Ed, chore completed, got to his feet. "Thanks again, Mrs. Heston. You're the best!"

"No, you're the best," she said, reaching out to give his arm a squeeze. "Don't let anyone else tell you otherwise, you hear?"

⋘•⋙

Ed was still feeling good about his talk with Mrs. Heston when he and Rick met with Mrs. Penfield that evening. The twilight air was quite muggy, so they settled in the back parlor instead of the usual garden meeting place. The house wasn't air-conditioned, but the first floor remained relatively cool with the help of a series of fans. Ed, his mind still on central air-conditioning, couldn't help but think it wouldn't be a bad idea for the main house, considering Mrs. Penfield's age and health. He feared it might be quite expensive, though, and decided to do a little private research on the subject.

"I'm not at all surprised at Aggie Heston's opinion of you, Ed," Mrs. Penfield was saying. "I believe a great many of your clients would feel the same way, and for those who don't, it's their loss. Please remember that."

Rick looked at him, warm and tender special in place. "His clients love him almost as much as I do," he commented. "I've never thought it would be a problem."

"Still," Ed said, "I don't want to push it."

"Yes, I can understand that, and I think it's wise. It does, however, raise a question.

"Rick," Mrs. Penfield said thoughtfully. "If Ed were to give you a ring such as the one he wears, would you feel comfortable wearing it to work?"

"Probably not," Rick said with a sigh.

Mrs. Penfield nodded. "As I thought." She looked at him seriously. "I recall you mentioning a potential career in real estate. Is this something you are still considering?"

Rick nodded. "Sure. Although," he said with a grin, "you've kept us pretty busy the past couple of months. I haven't given it much thought until the past few days."

Ed, eyebrows raised, turned to look at him. He didn't know Rick had been thinking about it at all.

"That's understandable," Mrs. Penfield said to Rick. "I myself had not given it much thought of late either. Yesterday, though, I was downtown, and I ran into yet another former student of mine, Vince Cummings. Ed"—she turned to him—"I'm sure that name is familiar to you."

Ed nodded. "Sure. Cummings Realty. Vince was, oh, about five or six years ahead of me in school, I think. I didn't know him, but I think his mom is in the garden club with mine."

Rick rolled his eyes. "This town. Everybody's connected to someone, one way or another."

"City slicker," Ed jeered.

Mrs. Penfield mock-frowned at them. "Our small-town ways may still come as a shock to you, Rick, but they do have their advantages. I had a very pleasant talk with Vince and mentioned your interest in pursing a career in real estate. He was quite frank with me regarding the current real estate market and the potential for a newcomer. I must admit, the prospects were not as optimistic as I had hoped."

Ed thought back to the articles he had read in *Time* magazine and the sluggish economy in general. "I guess with interest rates the way they are, no one's gonna buy a new home unless they have to do," he commented.

Mrs. Penfield nodded. "Vince told me he's actually let his part-time agents go for the time being. However, he feels that the housing market will turn around at some point, perhaps not soon or even within the year, but certainly within the next five years."

Rick drummed his fingers on the arm of his chair, looking very thoughtful. "Just out of curiosity, did you tell Mr. Cummings about Ed and me?"

"Yes, I did, as tactfully as possible. I do hope you don't feel as though I've betrayed a confidence, but I wanted a frank opinion on your prospects as a real estate agent in Porterfield."

"And?"

"And Vince seemed more concerned with a poor housing market than your sexual preference. He seemed to feel that if you continue to live in your current discreet fashion, it shouldn't be an overwhelming issue. Again, though, he stressed the fact that real estate isn't the best proposition for a steady income at this time."

"In other words," Rick sighed, "I shouldn't quit my day job."

"Exactly."

Rick looked so discouraged that Ed reached for his hand. He gave it a good squeeze. "Don't sweat it, darlin'. We've got plenty of time to get moving on your new career. Heck, I just rented the house yesterday. I'd like to collect a few rent checks before we try to sell it."

Mrs. Penfield, too, noted Rick's discouragement. "Ed's right, Rick. I made these inquiries merely to see what Vince would have to say. I certainly wasn't thinking of you rashly ending your postal career. I know you must worry about possible discrimination within the post office, and I share your desire for you to be self-employed as Ed is. However, as Aggie Heston has proven today, I firmly believe the majority of Porterfield will judge you both on your obvious merits and tactfully look the other way regarding your living arrangements."

"Mrs. Penfield's stamp of approval doesn't hurt either," Ed added, realizing it was true and wondering why he hadn't thought of it before.

Rick sighed. "I know. I was just hoping . . ." He suddenly sat up and smiled. "Do you think Mr. Cummings would mind if I stopped by his office for a talk?"

"Not at all. In fact, he told me to tell you to feel free to do just that. He is, he told me, not as busy as he would like to be these days and, being the good sort that he is, would be more than willing to share his thoughts and experience with you."

"Maybe I can least find out what all I'd need to do regarding real estate classes and obtaining a license," Rick said, his optimism returning.

Ed was glad to see it but wondered why Rick seemed so determined to move forward on a career with such currently murky prospects. He said as much to Rick when they were once again alone in the carriage-house apartment.

"Well, baby, I look at this way," Rick said, pulling Ed next to him on the living room sofa. "It's true that the economy stinks, and as far as I'm concerned, the Reagan administration isn't doing a damned thing to help or change it.

"But," he continued, "I've learned enough about economics from my dad the history teacher to know this stuff runs in cycles. Vince Cummings thinks the housing market will eventually improve, and your brother-in-law, Todd, down at the bank, said pretty much the same thing when he encouraged us through Laurie to accept Mrs. P.'s offer. Why not be ready for when things get better?"

Ed thought about that. "Yeah, you've got a point. I guess I was just surprised that you were thinking about it at all."

Rick frowned tenderly at him. "I wasn't holding anything back from you, baby. I wouldn't do that. I had every intention of talking to you about the whole real estate thing this week, but Mrs. P. beat me to the punch. I was thinking about it last night but decided we were both too tired to get into it. I wouldn't make any big decisions without consulting you. You know that, don't you?"

"Yeah, I know that," Ed said, settling himself in the usual comfort of Rick's arms. "It's just that we're barely settled here, and we've been living together for less than three months. I'd like to get used to all of this before we go charging off on something else."

Rick sighed and hugged Ed. "I know. I also know that because of all of the things I've done and been through, change probably comes a lot easier to me than it does to you. Your life was on a pretty even keel until I showed up. And this whole thing with moving here, well, it would be a lot for anyone to handle so soon after getting married. You've been great so far, and I'd like to think knowing I'm always here for you has made it easier as well."

"It has," Ed said, burying his face in Rick's chest.

"Well then. Mrs. P.'s generosity has, like I said last night, pushed us farther along on the road to our goals than we could have ever imagined that weekend at the lake. I know I get carried away with stuff sometimes, but since we're already this far, why not investigate where we can go next?"

"Huh?"

"You're going to spend your free time this summer making a workshop downstairs, right? That's your next step forward toward the goals we have for you. Is there anything wrong with me talking to Vince Cummings about what the next steps should be for me?"

"No," Ed muttered against Rick's T-shirt-covered chest.

Rick sighed. "Okay. I can see you still need time to adjust to all that's happened. How 'bout this? I promise I won't talk to Vince until after our Cedar Point trip. How's that?"

Ed pulled his head up and kissed Rick. "Yeah. Actually that does make me feel better. Is it okay with you, though? I don't want you to feel crappy just to make me more comfortable."

Rick laughed softly. "It's okay. Even though I'm excited about getting a real estate license, I'm not all that eager to start right this minute. Maybe I still need time to adjust to this place, too. The stubbed-toe curse passed on to me this morning. I banged my right foot against the foot of the bed pretty hard. It took all I could do not to holler and wake you up."

Ed giggled. "So what did you do instead?"

"Went into the bathroom, closed the door, and cussed a blue streak."

Ed pulled Rick's foot to where he could see it. "Well, it looks okay. Does it still hurt?"

Rick wiggled his toes. "It still hurts if a potential foot rub is involved."

Ed took the hint and began to massage Rick's wounded foot. Jett, annoyed that someone other than him was getting so much attention, jumped into Rick's lap. Rick petted the cat with one hand while he rubbed the back of Ed's neck with the other.

"This is nice," Rick murmured.

"Yeah, it is," Ed said, enjoying the scene: the two of them and their cat having an intimate, domestic moment in their own cozy and quiet home on a Tuesday night. This was the sort of thing he had dreamed about when he was alone: being close to the man he loved, sharing the ordinary events of everyday living.

"You know, my feet still kind of hurt, too," Ed said, swinging around on the sofa and putting his feet on either side of the purring cat. "You s'pose I could get the same service?"

"Absolutely," Rick said as he rearranged himself and Jett for a mutual foot massage.

"Yeah, this is nice," Rick repeated with a deep sigh of contentment. "Maybe you're right, baby. Maybe we need to sit still and count our blessings a few times before we go looking for more."

# Chapter Nine

Ed was busy unpacking his father's tools in the space for the proposed workshop. Gordy was supposedly helping, but he was actually leaning against Ed's truck and watching. He slurped away at a can of Pepsi and occasionally sang along with Steve Winwood as the Spencer Davis Group's "Gimme Some Lovin'," poured out of the portable stereo.

"Man, you've got the best tunes," he was saying. "I should make some tapes, too."

"Anytime," Ed said, setting up his father's old table saw. Gordy had helped him haul it from his mother's basement to the carriage house but refused to touch it after that. "I'd just break it or cut myself," he had grumbled.

A brief spell of cooler weather had invigorated Ed. He had spent several days going through the jumble of odds and ends in the lower floor of the carriage house and, after setting aside things worth saving, had made several trips to the Stratton County landfill with the rest of the junk. Once there had been room for his father's things, he had called Gordy to take him up on his offer to help move stuff one more time.

Gordy finished the last of his Pepsi and used the can to make a free throw at the garbage barrel in the corner. "Two points," he crowed. "I still got it. So when do you guys go to Cedar Point?"

"Thursday," Ed replied. "Rick finally has some vacation days. We're leaving Thursday morning. We'll spend the day in the park, and when we're all wiped out, we just have to walk over to the Hotel Breakers for the night. We'll drive home on Friday morning. Rick doesn't have to go back to work until Monday, so we're leaving the rest of the weekend clear, just in case something else comes up."

Ed stopped to wipe away some sweat. "I'm really looking forward to it. It seems like we've been working nonstop since Easter, and with Rick still thinking about those real estate classes, it's hard tellin' when we'll get another break."

"Shit, Benton selling real estate," Gordy snorted. "Now, that's something I didn't see comin'."

Ed shrugged. "Well, it hasn't come yet. We started talking about it as a new career for him several months ago, but I figured it wouldn't happen for a long time, especially with this move and all. But Mrs. Penfield talked to Vince Cummings about it, and now Rick's all hot to find out what he has to do to get a license."

"Damn," Gordy mumbled, bopping his head to the Buckinghams, which had come on after the Spencer Davis Group. "Like the song says, man, that's kind of a drag. I mean, carrying mail all day, then going to school at night."

"Yeah," Ed sighed. "Everyone's told him the housing market is in the toilet right now, but he's determined to have a license by the time it turns around. He's going to see Vince after we get back from our trip, and knowing Rick he'll probably sign up for classes as soon as he can."

"You don't sound too excited about it."

"I'm not," Ed said frankly. "I think he has enough to do already. And I'm afraid he'll get that license and start thinking about quitting his job, and we sure as hell can't afford that."

"Rick's not stupid. He wouldn't do anything that would mess up you guys' money, so I wouldn't worry about that. Hell, I just wouldn't want to be sitting in a classroom this time of year."

"Me either. But you know Rick; once he's got an idea in his head, he won't let it go."

Gordy left his perch by the truck to slip an arm around Ed's shoulders. "Hey, bud, don't let it bug ya, okay? Knowing you two, it'll all work out better than you thought. Rick's not a dumb ass, and neither are you. If nothing else, be proud of him. Most guys, namely me, don't have the balls to find a way out of that post office, so be glad you have one who's willing to work to make a better life for you guys."

"I know. I am proud of him. I just wish he'd wait awhile."

Ed reached for his own Pepsi, which had gotten warm. "Ugh," he grimaced, taking a sip. "I need a refill. What do you say we go upstairs? There's not much more I can get done here today, and I have to go over to Ruth Dorsey's and look at her damned kitchen sink."

"So," Ed said as they ascended the stairs, "you have any time off for the holiday weekend?"

"I sure do, and I'm gettin' the hell out of Dodge."

"Yeah? You got a road trip planned, too?"

"Yep! I'm going to Saugatuck and show off my new bod on Douglas Dunes. Hopefully I can take my pick of all the horny guys runnin' around.

Since your mouthy husband keeps saying I need to get laid, I'm gonna do just that."

Ed laughed. "That's great. Geez, we'll be on Lake Erie, riding roller coasters, and you'll be on Lake Michigan guy shopping."

"Whew," Gordy said once they were inside the apartment. He glanced with appreciation at the air conditioner. "I'm glad it's supposed to rain and cool off again tomorrow. I want the guys to be really hot, not the weather."

"Yeah, although seeing all those guys with their shirts off at Cedar Point is part of the fun."

"Listen to him, the happily married man! You should be gettin' it all the time."

"I do," Ed said smugly as he reached for two cold cans of Pepsi in the fridge. "But there's nothing wrong with enjoying the scenery, and Rick would tell you the same thing."

"Yeah? Well, okay, now I know why you rented your house to that hot undertaker. Now, that's what *I* call some scenery. For his sake, it's a good thing I'm going away this weekend, or I'd probably be over there with my binoculars. That guy needs to ditch the bitch and make the switch."

"Gord," Ed said, shaking his head, "you better get laid this weekend, 'cause if you scare that guy away before I get any more rent checks, I'm gonna be really pissed."

⋖⋗●⋖⋗

Ed reluctantly walked into Ruth Dorsey's kitchen an hour later. She was not, he had to admit, one of his favorite people. Her husband was an executive at Marsden Electric, where Ed had worked after high school. Since Marsden was the major employer in town, Ruth seemed to think her husband's position gave her a certain amount of status in Porterfield. Neither Ruth nor her husband had ever particularly impressed Ed.

The last time Ed had done any work for Ruth was the previous December. She had called in a panic begging him to paint her kitchen and dining room before her planned Christmas parties. Ed had not wanted to add a big painting job to his already hectic preholiday schedule, but she had managed to cajole him with the promise of full payment before Christmas and a substantial bonus. Ruth not only blew off payment before December 25, but when her check finally did arrive a month later, she had conveniently forgotten the promised bonus.

"Money doesn't automatically equal class," Rick had said at the time, and watching Ruth swoop down on him now, Ed had to agree.

"Oh, Eddie! I'm so glad you're here. That drippy faucet has been driving me crazy," Ruth exclaimed as her espadrilles clomped across the kitchen floor.

Ed gritted his teeth. He had always detested being called "Eddie" by anyone other than his late father.

Ruth's seriously middle-aged body was clad in shorts and a halter top. Ed, watching the aggressively tanned skin jiggle, could imagine what Gordy would have to say about it.

"You see what I mean?" She pushed the faucet handle back and forth. "I don't know what's the matter with it, but with the pool open this time of year, I certainly can't afford a leaky faucet."

Ed rolled his eyes. He mentally compared the volume of water in her tacky above-ground pool to the minor drip she indicated at the kitchen sink. *Just had to remind me she has a pool,* he thought, opening his toolbox.

He approached the sink, wrench in hand, Ruth hovering close to him in her usual overly intimate way. "Why, Eddie," she gushed. "What's that on your left hand? Did you sneak off and get married without telling me? Who's the lucky girl?"

Ed's grip on the wrench tightened. He thought back to his experience the week before with Mrs. Heston and debated what to say.

"Well, the lucky boy's name is Rick," he said calmly, going to work on the faucet.

Ruth giggled. "Oh, Eddie! Seriously. I suppose you mean Rita, as in Rita Waters, over at the factory. Lord knows, the woman isn't the most attractive thing in the world, but you shouldn't say that about her."

Ed turned to look at her in disbelief. "Rita Waters? No, I meant Rick. I'm married to another man" he said, at that moment not really caring what this pretentious, silly woman thought of him.

Ruth's eyes widened. "You're serious," she whispered. "But you're not . . ." She blinked at the outwardly masculine man standing in front of her, clad in T-shirt, jeans, and work boots, clutching a wrench.

Ed almost grinned. He could tell he'd blown away her stereotypical notions of a gay man. "We don't all dress in drag," he said, turning back to the sink.

"You're really serious," she said, shaking her head. Her face hardened. "I just don't believe it! You're really doing . . . *things* with another man, and you're not hiding it?"

Ed shrugged.

"Does your mother know about this? Goodness, does Hilda *Penfield* know about this? She must! I suppose this man is *living* with you at her place!"

"Yeah, she knows," Ed said, putting the wrench on the counter. He had a feeling he wouldn't be doing any work on Ruth Dorsey's kitchen faucet.

"Thank heaven that woman isn't teaching anymore. I'd see to it she was fired. Encouraging such a thing! Ed Stephens, you should be ashamed of yourself." She stared him, hands on hips, a look of disgust on her face.

Ed could feel the anger percolating in his stomach, along with a touch of nervousness. "No, I am not ashamed," he said with a calm he didn't feel.

"No, I suppose you're not," she sneered, backing away from him. "You're probably like those perverts flitting around on TV, proud of it."

Ed shrugged again. "I don't know about proud, but I won't apologize, if that's what you want."

"I don't want anything from you! You can just pack up that toolbox and get out of my house!" She pointed a gaudily jeweled finger at the back door.

Ed picked up his wrench and slowly returned it to his toolbox. "My pleasure," he mumbled.

"I just can't believe it. You've been working for me all this time, and I had no idea! A pervert here in my own home. Well, don't expect me to pay you for your time today."

Ed snickered. "Why should I expect that? You've never once paid me on time anyway."

Her mean, heavily made-up eyes narrowed at him. "I don't have to take that from you, you . . . fairy!"

"I may be a fairy, but at least I pay my bills on time," Ed snorted, slamming his toolbox shut.

"Well! Don't you leave here thinking you'll ever work for any decent people in this town ever again."

Ed's anger won out over his nervousness. "Decent?" His voice rose. "You call yourself decent? Hell, everyone in this town knows your husband is having an affair with his secretary and has been for years! And the way you spend every minute I'm in this house right next to me? All these years you've probably been hoping I'd make a move on you."

Ed could tell by the look on her face that what he had long suspected was the truth. Having it verified only increased his anger.

"Geez, even a straight man would have a hard time getting excited for a mess like you," he sneered.

He looked around the ostensibly modern kitchen. "You have this fancy house, and that ugly pool, and I'll bet not one bit of it is paid for. And yet you think you have the right to look down your nose at other people. If *decent* means I won't be working for phonies like you, then I'm all for it!"

Even with the tan, Ed could see her face was deadly pale. "How dare you," she snarled. "How dare you, a pervert, judge me!"

"I'm not judging; I'm just telling the truth. And the truth hurts, doesn't it?" he yelled.

"Well, you just take your truth and your perverted thoughts and get out of my house," she shouted.

"Gladly." Ed picked up his toolbox, purposely swinging it around to crash into the wall he had painted for her before Christmas.

Ruth jumped at the sound, but something about the look in his eyes told her not to comment.

"There's one more thing," Ed said, hand on the doorknob. "There's something I've been meaning to tell you for a long, long time, Ruth." He looked her right in the eye and smiled. "You're a bitch."

⋄⋅•⋅⋄

"Baby, we just crossed the Ohio state line," Rick said in the car two days later. He took Ed's hand. "We are officially out of Porterfield, out of Indiana, and we are going to have a good time. We are going to ride rides, eat too much, and probably get half sick, but we are going to have a good time, and Ruth Dorsey can go fuck herself. Okay?"

Ed sighed, squeezing Rick's hand. The past two days had been tense ones for him.

After he had calmed down that afternoon, he had called both Laurie and Norma, deciding it would be better for them to hear the story from him as opposed to someone else.

"Oh, Ed," Laurie groaned. "Don't worry about it. It's about time someone told that creep off. Besides, the way you called her on her shit? There's no way she's going to make trouble for you, 'cause she knows everything you said is true. So does everyone else in this town."

Norma, needless to say, had quite a few comments to make.

"Why that bleached-blond floozy," Norma gasped. "How dare she call my son a pervert? Why, I could tell you stories about that tramp that would make your hair stand on end. Just who does she think she is?"

Norma, as usual, barreled ahead without waiting for an answer. "She has no business sitting in judgment of anyone, let alone my son. Why, I have half a mind to march over there and pull that blond mess out by its gray roots. Talk about cheap! And horrible. Why, I remember the last Marsden Christmas party I went to with your father. That woman was drunk and making indecent proposals to half the men in the room. Not only that"—Norma paused before delivering her most damning indictment—"she's a Republican! A big, classless phony just like the rest of them."

Ed, smiling for the first time since the incident, said, "Thanks, Mom."

"Edward, don't you worry about this. If that woman says one thing about you to anyone, I'll deal with her. I always knew the day would come when I'd have to defend you, but to think I might have to do it with that tramp. Honestly!"

Ed, almost fearing for Ruth's safety, found himself laughing. "Mom, I can take care of myself. Don't go making a bad situation worse."

"Humph! I'm just telling you this isn't going to affect your business. Why, I could use this phone and get you four, five new clients by the end of the day."

"I may have just crossed Ruth Dorsey off my client list, but I still have more than enough work. But thanks, Mom. I really appreciate it."

"I know you do, Edward. That's why I'm here for you. I may not approve of what you're doing with your life one hundred percent, but no one—and I mean no one—can question your integrity or the hard work you do. That's my job," she finished primly.

Ed laughed again. "And if you ever stop criticizing what I do, then I'll know the world has finally come to an end."

Mrs. Penfield's reaction, while a good deal quieter than Norma's, had been much the same, and when Gordy was told of the incident he roared with laughter, saying, "Hell, Ed, you shoulda decked her with your toolbox!"

Even with the support and comfort of those close to him, he had jumped every time the phone rang, convinced it was a call from a client canceling his services. He had driven around town, sure everyone was staring at him. He had entered the homes of his regular clients hesitantly, braced for another confrontation.

It had been business as usual, though. No one had said a word. There had been no hurled insults from the streets. Either Ruth had kept his shocking revelation to herself, or the news had not spread beyond her own choosy inner circle.

Ed remembered a similar incident that past winter with one of Rick's coworkers, Jim Murkland, better known as Murk the Jerk. Once again, an individual who apparently wasn't well liked within the community had chosen to point a self-righteous finger. Ed knew, though, that in the minds of many, Ed's homosexuality trumped Ruth's cheap behavior on the sinning scale. Despite the great joy he had taken in telling her off, the experience had been unpleasant and unsettling. Worst of all, he suspected it would happen again, and again.

"Remember that night last winter at the cemetery, and all the stuff we talked about?" Rick frowned at the slow-moving semi truck in front of them. "We knew there would be tough times for us in that town, and we agreed to stick together and fight. You know I'll stand behind you no matter what happens, and there are plenty of other people who feel the same way. We'll go back to work on Monday, and the whole thing will have blown over."

Rick began to laugh. "I'm sorry," he said when he noticed Ed's glare. "I just wish I'd been there when you called her a bitch. I would have called her something much worse."

Ed found himself chuckling as well. Yes, that had been a triumphant moment. He, too, wished he'd thought of a few other things to call Ruth Dorsey.

Rick sighed impatiently at the truck traffic as they crawled along U.S. 224 in western Ohio. "Maybe we should have taken the toll road," he murmured. He reached for his car's tape player, turning up the volume. "Remember this one? We listened to it the first time I took you to Indy to meet my parents."

Argent's "Hold Your Head Up" began to play. Ed did remember. They had blasted the song, shouting the lyrics. Rick had claimed it had exorcised the leftover demons from his childhood once and for all.

Rick began to sing with the tape, and Ed joined in. As they had that December day, they shouted the chorus at the top of their lungs, heads held high.

Rick's grip on Ed's hand tightened. "We're gonna be just fine, baby. We have a home no one can take away from us, and we're smart enough to take care of ourselves, no matter what anyone says or does. Just keep holding that beautiful head of yours up, okay?"

"But what if—"

"No buts," Rick said firmly. "We are on vacation. If there are any buts to worry about, we will worry about them later."

Rick grinned, tapping the beat of the song on the steering wheel. "I wish I had 'Come Saturday Morning' on this tape. It may be Thursday, but it feels like Saturday morning. I'm going away with my husband, who happens to be my best friend as well, and we're gonna have a blast, just like the song says. Okay, Saturday friend?"

Ed reached across the car and kissed his cheek. "Okay. We're traveling for miles in our Thursday instead of Saturday smiles, and we'll always remember it, right?"

"I wish we were traveling a little faster," Rick grumbled, looking for an opportunity to pass the convoy of trucks ahead of them. "I'm ready to ride some roller coasters."

⸻ ● ⸻

Ed hadn't been to Cedar Point Amusement Park in Sandusky, Ohio, for many years, and when they approached the park from the causeway across Lake Erie, he felt his disturbing thoughts disappear. He had nothing but wonderful memories of the place from his visits with both family and high school friends.

The weather couldn't have been better. A cold front had moved across Indiana and Ohio the day before, ushering in cooler air. It was a sunny day, with a light breeze blowing across Lake Erie and the tiny peninsula.

After they checked into their hotel, Ed and Rick paid their park admissions and joined the crowds strolling the midways. Ed dragged Rick directly to the Blue Streak, the first roller coaster he had ever ridden. They endured an impatient wait in the long line but were finally on a train, ascending the first hill.

"You know," Ed said to Rick. "I once made Laurie cry on this thing. I had her convinced the support beams were broken, and the whole thing was gonna fall over with us on it."

Rick smirked at him. "I suppose you think you can pull that shit with me, too, huh?"

"No," Ed smirked back. "But I'm wondering if you're brave enough to go no-handed over the first hill."

"Is that a dare?"

"You bet."

"You're on, baby."

The train slowly rolled over the top of the summit, then hurtled downward. Ed, bracing himself with his feet, threw his hands in the air, letting go with a whoop of joy. The train hit the bottom of the hill, and then roared up the next.

"Jesus Christ," Rick hollered, bouncing around in the seat.

Ed glanced at him, laughing. He realized he was going to have to teach him how to ride with no hands. "Your feet," he shouted over the clattering of the roller coaster and the screams from the other riders. "You gotta brace yourself with your feet!"

They swooped through the rest of the coaster's course, laughing and hollering. "Oh, man, that was great," Rick said, still laughing when the train slammed into the station. "I wanna go on this again."

"We will," Ed promised. "I want to check out the other ones first." He sighed, throwing his head back. "I think I just blew a ton of carbon out of my engine."

"Good," Rick said, grinning at him. "Let's go ride another one of these monsters and blow out another ton, okay?"

It was a great day for both Ed and Rick. Aside from the boring waits they endured in the endless lines, they rode one ride after another, only stopping to eat something junky and nonnutritious. Ed was pleased to find Rick as enthusiastic about the rides as he was. He had never outgrown his excitement with carnival rides in general and was thrilled that Rick was enjoying them as much as he did.

They rode the big Gemini roller coaster at the back of the park, and Ed had to admit it was more exciting than the Blue Streak, although he suspected the smaller one would always be his favorite. After that, they climbed aboard the Witch's Wheel, exiting the ride a little dizzy from the experience.

"Damn," Rick said, holding on to the fence that surrounded the ride. "That was wild. I think I need something a little calmer."

He looked through the trees. "Can we ride that big Ferris wheel now? It doesn't look like it moves too fast. I need a break."

"Sure," Ed said, amazed at how the park's layout was returning to him. "I know the best way to get there."

He led Rick to the Frontier Town train station. They relaxed as the train took them back to the Midway station, depositing them directly in front of the Giant Wheel.

"I'm sure glad I'm here with someone who knows his way around," Rick commented, looking up at the top of the wheel.

Once they were seated in one of the wheel's gondolas, Ed sighed with contentment, enjoying the Lake Erie breeze as the ride slowly revolved. The Giant Wheel came to a stop, leaving them at the very top.

"Isn't it beautiful?" Ed murmured. The amusement park was spread out below them, with the city of Sandusky in the distance. To the north, the blue-green waters of Lake Erie stretched to the horizon.

Rick reached across the car and took Ed's hand. "You know, baby, if I wasn't strapped in with this safety belt, I'd come over there and give you a big kiss, right in front of God and everybody."

Ed squeezed his hand, feeling better than he had in days. "I love you, darlin'."

"I love you, too, baby," Rick said softly. "Just remember this: Nothing anyone says or does can really mess us up too much when we can have times like this."

He looked across the lake. "There's plenty of room for us, too, in this world."

"And Ruth Dorsey can go fuck herself," Ed said, giggling.

"Damn right!"

As dusk began to descend on the park, Ed and Rick sat tiredly on a bench, sharing a hot, doughy pretzel. Eating quietly, they watched the bright colored lights in motion on the Trabant and the Scrambler.

"It's been a wonderful day," Rick said. "I have to admit, though, my mailman legs are tired, and you picked up a little bit of sunburn. You wanna call it a day, or what? I really want to check out that boardwalk by the hotel before we go to bed."

Ed silently debated while they watched two cute college boys in T-shirts and brief shorts walk by. "You can't beat the guy watching here," he commented, remembering what he had said to Gordy earlier in the week.

Rick snickered. "Yeah, especially when they come off those water rides, shirts off and soaking wet."

Rick gazed around at the crowds, the lights, and the sky ride carrying passengers from one side of the park to other. "I know now why you like this place so much. It . . . it just has a feeling about it."

"I know. I've been to other amusement parks, but nothing beats Cedar Point. There's just something magical here. Maybe it's the lake, maybe it's something the Indians left behind years ago, but whatever it is, I love it."

"We'll come back next summer," Rick said positively. "By then maybe I'll be a big, successful real estate agent, and you'll be an even bigger, more successful handyman, doing woodworking on the side. We'll come back and do this again, okay?"

"Deal."

"You never answered my question, though. Are we done, or do you want to ride some more?"

Ed finished off the pretzel. "Just one more. I want to go on the Blue Streak one last time before we cash in."

Rick groaned. "Oh, all right."

"C'mon, old man," Ed jeered as he pulled Rick to his feet. "And don't forget to hang on the way I taught you."

⋘•⋙

Ed and Rick stood on the promenade in front of the Hotel Breakers. The breeze had died away, and the lake waves lapped gently against the shore. Since they had the place to themselves in the summer darkness, Ed slipped his arm around Rick, laying his head against his shoulder.

The clatter of the roller coasters and the screams of their riders drifted over the lake. Ed looked across the water, moonlight shimmering on its surface, with a feeling of peace growing inside him. "Remember our weekend at Spruce Lake?"

Rick chuckled. "Of course. This lake is just a *little* bigger, though."

Ed poked him. "Like that matters. But do you remember how we talked about having a cabin on a lake someday?"

Rick nodded. "Yep. It'll happen. Whether it's a swampy pond in Indiana or one of the Great Lakes, it'll happen."

"I hope so."

"It will. Why, just look at everything that's happened in the last three months. When we were at Spruce Lake, we had no way of knowing about all the changes coming. Now, thanks to Mrs. Penfield, our future is secure. I might be on the verge of a whole new career. You're building your workshop, and maybe someday you'll be able to knock way back on the handyman stuff and build your own things. Ruth Dorsey, or any of those hags she runs with, can't stop that."

"I know. I wasn't thinking so much about that. I was just thinking how happy I am when I'm away from home with you. I love our home, but there's something about being here that makes me love you, and our life together, even more."

Rick leaned over for a quick kiss. "That's what vacations are all about. If I didn't think they might kick us out of the hotel for the night, I'd shout across Lake Erie the way I shouted across Spruce Lake, letting the world know how much I love you."

Rick sighed. "Someday, maybe. Maybe someday I can shout those words across this lake and no one will care. For now, though, I'm just damned grateful for what we have."

Ed smiled into the darkness. "We're still pretty lucky guys, aren't we?"

"Yep. Oh, I suppose there will be more Ruth Dorseys, and times when we get mad as hell at each other. I know there will be. But no matter what happens, if I still have you, I'm still the luckiest guy in the world. Don't ever forget that."

Rick turned to Ed. "Now, I am exhausted, and I'm guessing that sunburn is starting to bother you, but what do you say we go into that grand hotel behind us, get naked, and make love?"

Ed pulled his arm tighter around Rick. "If you rub some lotion on my sunburn, you can do anything you want."

Ed glanced over his shoulder for one last look at Lake Erie. Thinking about what happened earlier in the week, he made a silent wish and threw it across the waters. *Please let it all work out for us, and let us be as much in love for the rest of our lives as we are tonight.*

It was, he thought, a lot to ask of any lake, no matter how great, and a pretty big demand for the universe in general. He still couldn't help but hope with all of his heart that it would come true.

# Chapter Ten

Ed and Rick arose late the next morning. They had a leisurely breakfast at the hotel, and then hit the road, Ed in the driver's seat of Rick's beat-up but dependable Monte Carlo.

Once Sandusky was behind them, Rick sighed and slumped in the passenger seat. "Thanks for sharing Cedar Point with me, baby. I had a wonderful time."

"You're welcome. I had a blast, too, darlin'."

Ed piloted the car westward on U.S. 6 toward Indiana. It had been a fun and relaxing break in their routines, but the closer they got to home, the more Ed's thoughts returned to the messy business with Ruth Dorsey. He couldn't help but wonder what, if anything, the woman had been up to during their absence from Porterfield.

"You know, we'll still have the whole Fourth of July weekend left when we get home," Rick said, interrupting his thoughts. "Is there anything else you want to do?"

Ed shifted in his seat, his sunburn bothering him. It didn't seem fair that Rick tanned so easily and all he seemed to do was burn.

"Nope," Ed replied. "How could we top yesterday? I'm okay with just hanging around the house, doing nothing."

"Well, we'll probably end up going to the fireworks tomorrow night with Claire and the kids, but if you think of something, speak up."

Ed found himself returning to his gloomy thoughts. It stuck in his head that U.S. 6 stretched from one end of the country to another. He had a sudden desire to keep driving west, all the way to the Pacific Ocean.

"Maybe we could just keep going," he said, giving voice to his thoughts. "You know, just see where this road takes us."

Rick sat up in his seat, reaching for Ed's hand. "Are you worrying again? I promise you, nothing Ruth Dorsey says or does is going to hurt us. Shit, if

I need to, I'll go over to her house and slay her, for the medieval dragon she is."

Ed smiled, picturing Rick galloping up to Ruth Dorsey's door on a white charger. "You mean you're my knight in shining armor?"

"Yes," Rick said adamantly. "Even if I have to go rent some chain mail to prove it."

Imagining that made Ed feel better, and he was able to redirect his thoughts to more pleasant things for the rest of the drive. It wasn't until they were heading into Porterfield on Highway 210 that those thoughts returned. He glanced at the WELCOME TO PORTERFIELD sign, half expecting it to say, FAGS NOT WELCOME.

He drove south on Race Street and pulled into their driveway. Everything looked the same. Jett was sunning himself in the garden; Effie Maude, who'd been in charge of feeding him, must have let him out.

They hauled their overnight bags out of the car and up the stairs, Jett on their heels. Once inside, they begin to settle in for the holiday weekend.

Ed looked over the mail Effie Maude had left for them with an impatient sigh. "I think I'll go see Mrs. Penfield."

Rick looked up at him with a sigh of his own. "Okay. I'll go over with you."

Mrs. Penfield was glad to see them and eager for details of their trip. "I'm pleased you had such a good time," she said when they finished the tale of their adventure.

"I rather hate to bring it up," she said reluctantly, "but I had a telephone call from that Dorsey woman." She snorted in disgust. "She attempted to give me a piece of her very tiny brain, while I managed to give her a very large piece of my much more agile brain. She obviously decided she was dealing with a woman deranged and hung up on me."

Rick chuckled. "See? We have the smart soldiers on our side."

"There were no other phone calls," Mrs. Penfield continued, "and no mention of it whatsoever at the Hospital Ladies Auxiliary luncheon I attended yesterday. The closest anyone came to the subject was when Annabelle Buxton remarked on how clever I was for talking two young, strong men into moving onto my property."

Rick looked smugly at Ed.

"Okay, okay, I'll calm down."

"I wish you would, Ed," Mrs. Penfield said. "I'm sure nothing will come of this. Oh, Ruth Dorsey might fancy herself Porterfield's answer to Anita Bryant, but I doubt she'll have much luck with any crusade she might begin. As you pointed out to her the other day, she has her own skeletons to keep well closeted."

She smiled fondly at Ed. "Now, go enjoy the rest of your long weekend. I'm sure when Monday comes, you'll have more work than you need."

So Ed decided to do just that. They went back to the carriage house, and Ed proceeded to hog the sofa, sprawling full-length with a library book. Rick settled in one of the easy chairs as he glanced through the newspaper, muttering in disgust over the latest news of the Reagan administration in Washington.

"Hey, look at this," Rick suddenly exclaimed, pointing to the television page. "One of your favorite movies is on the late show tonight."

Ed sat up. "Which one?"

"*The Sterile Cuckoo.* Isn't it great? We can watch it together, since I don't have to work tomorrow."

Ed laughed. "'Come Saturday Morning.' Isn't that something, after we were just talking about that song yesterday? Talk about timing."

They were both parked in front of the television set that night at eleven thirty, popcorn and Pepsi by their side. Ed sighed happily as "Come Saturday Morning" played over the opening credits. "I have to warn you, though. Old Crybaby Ed always falls apart over the ending of this one."

Rick looked at him, warm and tender special in place. "I honestly don't remember how it ends, so maybe I'll shed a few tears with you."

They contentedly watched the story unfold. Ed felt a few early tears come to his eyes when his favorite scenes came along—Pookie and Jerry running and frolicking across the rural autumn New York hillsides while "Come Saturday Morning" played again.

"I can't help it," he mumbled. "It reminds me of you and me at Spruce Lake, and again at Cedar Point. Every time I watched this movie, I wondered if I'd ever get to play like that with somebody special someday."

Rick put his arm around him. "I think I know how you feel, baby. I waited a long time to find you, too, so don't worry. I'll always be your Saturday friend."

The movie continued. Ed braced himself during the last commercial break. He swore to himself that he wouldn't cry over the movie's ending as he had in the past, but the tears began to fall during the last few minutes and were still falling when the Paramount logo flashed on the screen.

"I don't know why I love this movie so much," he sniffled. "The ending just breaks my heart."

Rick was doing a little sniffling of his own. He walked across the room and turned the television off. "Hmmm. I know I saw this movie when I was in college, but I sure don't remember being as moved by it as I was tonight. I think it's your fault. Somehow I feel safe enough with you to let all those emotions out, all the ones I kept to myself for so many years."

"Me, too. I don't remember crying all that much when I was younger, but since I met you..." Ed chuckled as he wiped his face.

"Well, as boys we were taught not to cry, you know. I guess we should just be grateful we're comfortable enough with each other to really let our true emotions show. I always seem to feel better after I do some weeping with you, baby."

Ed agreed. Somehow, the tears he wasn't afraid to shed in Rick's presence had managed to wash away his other concerns. He found himself truly relaxing for the first time since they had come home, confident not just in Rick's love and companionship but in the knowledge that Rick was firmly by his side, no matter what.

Claire and the kids came over the next day, and they had an impromptu weenie roast in the backyard. Then all of them, Mrs. Penfield included, piled into Claire's station wagon for the drive to the Stratton County 4-H Park to see to the annual fireworks display.

Ed found himself glancing around the crowd, wondering whether there were any odd looks or negative comments directed toward their party. No one seemed to be paying any attention, so he sat back and relaxed once again, enjoying the brilliant colors exploding in the sky over Porterfield.

They spent a quiet Sunday at home, and when Monday morning and Ed's first appointment of the day came upon him, he felt ready to face the world once again.

Mrs. West's house was his first stop. She was his most elderly client, and her usual fussing seemed reassuringly normal. She complained about the firecrackers keeping her up past her bedtime Saturday night and about the return of the heat and humidity. Ed confidently put together a wooden knickknack shelf for her—a gift from her daughter—wondering whether he could make something better himself.

Early that afternoon he drove downtown, parking his truck a block away from Wexler's Jewelers on West Commerce Street. He didn't want anyone to see him on his secret mission.

Ed had decided over the weekend to buy the gift Rick hoped he would buy for him someday, a gold neck chain. He wasn't really sure what had prompted his decision, whether it had something to do with his wish on Lake Erie or the image of Rick as his personal knight in shining armor. He just remembered Rick's demand that Ed not even think about purchasing the chain for him unless he was absolutely sure it was something he wanted to do, and for whatever reason, the desire to buy it had completely taken hold of him. The time had to be right, and Ed simply knew the time had come.

He wasn't giving it to Rick anytime soon, though. As he had waited until both his brain and his heart had told him he needed to purchase the gold chain, he would wait until the proper moment arrived to give the gift to Rick.

He examined the men's jewelry, smiling, quickly seeing what had caught Rick's eye earlier that year. It was a beautiful gold neck chain, and Ed knew it would look great on Rick. He was almost tempted to give it to him that night.

While old Mr. Wexler was wrapping his purchase, the door opened and a middle-aged, well-padded dowager walked in. Ed groaned silently. It was Eunice Ames.

Eunice Ames, of course, was his brother-in-law, Todd's, mother. She was an imposing woman, secure in her position within the town. Eunice had been a Hobson before she married, and the Hobsons had been among the first founders of Porterfield First National Bank. The Ameses had always been financially comfortable as well. Eunice was a strong and enthusiastic pillar of the community and prided herself on managing the social concerns of the Porterfield elite.

Ed wasn't overly fond of her. Oh, she had never been anything but pleasant to him and, as Laurie had told him, had certainly never said anything unkind behind his back, but Eunice's long-running feud with Norma usually left him siding with his mother out of reluctant family loyalty.

He also knew Eunice was well acquainted with Ruth Dorsey.

He turned toward the display counter, hunching his shoulders, wondering whether poor old Mr. Wexler was in any way prepared for the bomb that would surely shatter the hushed stillness of his little store.

"Edward?" Eunice called. "Is that you?"

Ed turned around, surprised to see her smiling at him.

"Hello, Eunice," he said tentatively. "What brings you to Wexler's today?"

She nodded toward the proprietor. "Mr. Wexler has been resetting the stones in my diamond earrings. They belonged to my great-grandmother, and I've been absolutely terrified to wear them, afraid I might lose one of the settings."

Mr. Wexler nodded in return. "I'll be right with you, Mrs. Ames."

"Take your time, take your time," Eunice replied with a languid wave of her hand. "It will give me a chance to catch up with Ed."

She walked closer to him. "I've been wanting to tell you how pleased I was to hear about your plans with the Penfield estate. You know, I survived several battles with Hilda Penfield during my years on the school board, but I must admit her common sense is improving with age. I think it's wonderful, her decision to leave her house to you and your friend. It's a great relief to the community, knowing one of our fine old houses will be well taken care of for years to come."

Ed blinked at her. "You know about that?"

"Oh, yes. Todd told me all about it and about how you're living there now. I'm sure with your talent you'll be able to do wonders with the place. Would you like to consider adding it to our annual Porterfield Historical Home Tour?"

"Uh," Ed said, trying not to stammer. "Well, it will be a long time before it actually belongs to us."

"Oh, I'm aware of that, but with you actually living there, on the grounds, I'm sure you'll be able to accomplish marvelous things with it."

She put a hand on his arm. "I also want you to know," she said in a much lower voice, "that I've spoken recently with Ruth Dorsey." Eunice shuddered. "Such a common, vulgar woman! She's always thought, because of her equally common husband's position, that she has somehow earned some sort of social privilege in Porterfield. The idea," Eunice huffed. "She and her husband weren't even raised in Porterfield, much less Stratton County. They come from the East *somewhere*. God only knows, and cares less.

"Imagine, the *things* she said about you. As if your choice of a companion was any of her business, or anyone else's for that matter. Todd told me your friend is a highly respectable, nice young man, and I for one have no reason to think otherwise."

Ed stared at her in shock. "I'm glad you feel that way," he managed to say.

She looked at him sternly. "Your family has lived in this town for decades, and Stephens is a name this town can look to with pride. Ed, your good works within the senior community have not gone unnoticed either. You're a valuable asset to Porterfield, and anyone who thinks otherwise has me to deal with."

Ed's mouth opened, but it took awhile before he was capable of speech. "Thanks, Eunice," he managed to whisper.

She smiled wickedly. "Oh, I probably shouldn't, but I'll thank you as well. I've detested that Dorsey woman for years, and you've finally given me the ammunition I needed to tell her exactly what I think of her to her face. I can only hope the next step is to drum her right off the board of the League of Women Voters.

"And Ed," she continued, "I've never called you for work at my home because I felt it might be taking advantage of our family connection, but if that woman's silly slander causes you any problems with your job, you give me a call. I'll make sure that between the Ameses and other *respectable* families in this town, you'll have more than enough money coming your way to make the Penfield house a showplace we all can be proud of."

"I . . . I really appreciate that," Ed stammered, still not believing his own ears.

"Don't give it another thought," she said with a gracious nod.

"Oh, speaking of the Historical Home Tour," she suddenly added, "I understand from Todd that your friend—Richard or Rick, is that right? He's interested in real estate and historical architecture, correct? What an asset a man with those interests would be on our committee! Do you think he'd be interested in volunteering?"

Ed finally gave up any pretense of cool and openly gaped at Eunice.

"I . . . well . . . I don't really know, but I could sure ask him."

"Do that, please, Ed. If he's willing to help us out with this year's tour, have him call me. There's no big rush; we've moved the tour to December this year so participants can decorate their homes for the holidays, and we're planning on a gift bazaar to help boost proceeds for the Historical Society. With the extra work involved this year, we could certainly use some new, young blood."

"I . . . I . . . I'll tell him when I see him at home." Ed clutched his bag a little tighter and managed a smile.

"Wonderful. I'll look forward to his call," she said as she turned to Mr. Wexler, who had returned to the counter, jewelry box in hand.

"Well, Howard," she said haughtily. "What have you managed to accomplish with Great-Grandmother's earrings?"

Ed remained near the counter for a moment, almost frozen, noting how his sweaty hands had left a wet spot on the traditional gray and purple Wexler's bag. He finally managed to unlock his legs and slowly moved toward the door, feeling a strong desire to return to his truck so he could sit down.

He paused at the door. "Good afternoon, Eunice," he called to her. "It was certainly nice talking with you."

She turned to him with a smile. "Oh, you, too, Edward. Do please greet Hilda for me, won't you?"

"I'll do that," he promised, pushing the door open.

Once inside his truck, he collapsed against the seat, rolling down the window to let out the hot, stale air. "I just can't believe it," he muttered. "Wait until I tell Rick. Wait until I tell Mrs. Penfield." He laughed. "Hell, wait until I tell *Mom*!"

⋘•⋙

"When I think of the trials I endured with that woman during her years on the school board," Mrs. Penfield said that evening, laughing. "And now I find I must change my opinion of her! I am indeed surprised but very pleased, Ed."

"Oh, you can still hate her in secret," Ed said with a grin. "I won't tell anyone."

"You see, baby?" Rick said smugly. "I knew this would all turn out all right."

Ed shrugged. Oh, Eunice Ames's support was undoubtedly a good thing, but he wondered how much weight she really carried within Porterfield. Still, Ed had managed to dump his least favorite client and somehow come out ahead in the long run. For that reason alone, he felt the weight he had been carrying since his encounter with Ruth Dorsey finally sliding off his shoulders.

"Okay," Ed said, smiling at them both. "I'll admit you were right. Now, how about some lemonade? I feel like celebrating."

"Yeah? We're celebrating? Well, the hell with the lemonade, then. I say this calls for something stronger. What do you think, Mrs. P.?"

Mrs. Penfield's laughter rang out across the yard. "By all means, Rick. Fix us all a properly celebratory drink."

They were sitting in the garden, sipping the sparkling wine Rick had brought forth from the carriage-house refrigerator and discussing the possibility of Rick joining the Porterfield Historical Home Tour committee, when Gordy's car pulled into the driveway. He approached them hesitantly, still not sure of his welcome with Mrs. Penfield. She happily greeted him, however, and soon he found himself sitting next to her, a glass of wine in his hand.

"It's good to see you, Gordon," she said, smiling at him. "What brings you our way this evening?"

"Oh," he said shifting uncomfortably. "There was just something I wanted to talk to the guys here about."

Ed grinned at him. He was sure Gordy was eager to share his ribald adventures at Saugatuck with them and couldn't find it within himself to provide even a G-rated version in front of Mrs. Penfield.

"Well, then," Mrs. Penfield said, slowly getting to her feet. "I'll leave you to your men talk. No, no." She waved off their protests. "It's time I went inside anyway.

"It's always a pleasure to see you, Gordon," she added with her mischievous grin. "What a relief it is to learn your grammar hasn't improved in all these years! Please feel free to visit here anytime. A friend of Ed and Rick's is definitely a friend of mine."

Ed and Rick giggled.

"You see?" Gordy muttered as she moved toward the house. "She still hates me."

Rick groaned. "Oh, Gord, she was *teasing*. Get over it, okay?"

Ed looked to make sure Mrs. Penfield was safely out of earshot. "Okay, now spill your guts. How many guys? How many times?"

Gordy shrugged. "Oh, I got my share."

Ed nudged Rick. "Listen to him, all modest all of a sudden."

"Yeah," Rick said. "What's the deal? C'mon, Gord. Give us the dirty details. We married folks have to live vicariously through our single friends, you know."

"Look, I was having a great time, getting laid left and right. I didn't meet anybody I'd want to take home to Mother, or even you dorks for that matter, but yeah, I got my rocks off. At least until Sunday afternoon."

Rick rolled his eyes. "Okay, so what happened Sunday afternoon? Did the great Gordy Smith actually get shot down?"

"No, but I heard something that made me slow down."

Gordy paused to light a cigarette. "Listen, you guys, this is serious. There's something I have to ask you about. Have you heard about any kind of 'gay flu'?"

"Huh?" Ed gave him a blank look.

"Gay flu," Rick repeated with a frown. "You mean they've come up with a strain that only we can get?"

"Yeah. I overheard these guys talking about it at Saugatuck. Seems like there are these gay guys who are getting this kind of flu. It turns into pneumonia or something, and they die."

Ed and Rick looked at each other, then at Gordy. "Aw, c'mon, Gordy," Rick said. "I think those guys were just kidding. I've never heard about anything like that."

Gordy shook his head, taking a long drag on his cigarette. "They weren't kiddin', believe me."

"How can there be some kind of pneumonia that only affects gay guys?" Ed asked, bewildered.

"I don't know. I was having a hell of a good time, getting laid left and right like I said, and then I heard about this. All I know is, guys are dying in New York City. Or maybe it was San Francisco."

"Are you sure you heard this right, Gord? How much did you have to drink that day?" Rick crossed his arms, looking quite skeptical.

"Fuck you, Benton. No, I wasn't drinking. I was having a quiet lunch by myself, recovering from the night before, when I heard these guys talking in the next booth. One of the guys was talking about a friend of his who had called him from New York. This friend had read some article in the *New York Times* about gay guys dying of some weird disease. Then the other guy in the booth said he had heard about some guys getting sick—I think it was in San Francisco or LA or some damned place—and he called it the 'gay flu.'"

Gordy looked at them, blowing smoke across the rose arbor. "So have you guys heard anything like that?"

"That's it? That's all you heard?" Ed wanted to know.

"Well, some asshole put some quarters in the jukebox and I couldn't hear the rest of the conversation."

"Then, no, I don't know anything about it," Ed said with a shudder. "I don't think I want to either."

"There's got to be a reasonable explanation for this," Rick said. "It's probably like that Legionnaires' disease thing from a few years ago. Remember? All these guys were probably hanging out at the same bathhouse, or something, like those guys at that hotel in Philly."

"There's another explanation," Gordy said, leaning toward them, his cigarette falling from his fingers to the ground. "It could be a government conspiracy, a way to kill off all the fags."

Rick snorted. "Did you overhear that, too? Hell, even as much as I hate the Reagan administration, I can't believe that."

"You got a better idea? All of a sudden gay guys are dropping dead, and no one else gets it! And how are they getting it, anyway?"

"Yeah," Ed said. "How could there be an illness that only gay guys get? That doesn't make any sense."

"Well, there's one possibility," Gordy said slowly, staring at them. "It could be sexual."

"You mean like gonorrhea or syphilis?" Ed shook his head. "Those don't kill you, at least not if you get to the doctor and get some medicine."

"Whatever this is, it kills you," Gordy said somberly.

"A new sex disease that only gay men get?" Ed put his wineglass down so he could stamp out Gordy's cigarette. "And it's like some kind of pneumonia? That's just . . . far out. I'm sorry, but it is."

"Well, if there's anything to it, I'm sure we'll read about it in one of our newspapers, or see it on the TV news," Rick said uncertainly.

Gordy snorted. "Yeah, right. If this is such big news, how come we haven't heard about it before? Besides, like anyone outside of New York City cares about a bunch of fags biting the dust."

"Maybe it's just some kind of coincidence," Rick said, reaching for Ed's hand.

"Gay guys are dying of some disease we've never heard of. You can call it a coincidence if you want, but I think there's more to it. You guys weren't there, listening to those men. Something's goin' on."

"Yeah, but it's got to be something the medical people can fix. Look at how far modern medicine's come. Besides, it's going on in New York or California," Ed said with a confidence he wasn't feeling. "It doesn't have anything to do with us, does it?" He looked to Rick for support.

"I sure hope not," Rick said quietly.

Gordy lit another cigarette. Rick sipped his wine, a pensive look on his face. Ed reached for his own wineglass but found he'd lost his taste for it.

*There's got to be a reasonable explanation for this.* Rick's words echoed in Ed's mind. Rick had to be right. Surely Gordy had been eavesdropping on the conversation of a couple of overwrought (and probably drunk) drama queens. They were most likely hypochondriacs to boot, Ed thought.

He did his best to reassure himself, but as dusk descended on them in the garden of the old house and the lightning bugs began to flash among the impatiens he had carefully watered only an hour before, something changed. Ed had the uncomfortable feeling that a shadow, which had nothing to do with the deepening twilight, had come over them, all three of them. And somehow that shadow seemed more sinister than anything they had yet to face.

# Chapter Eleven

Heat and humidity settled over Porterfield with no apparent intention of releasing their hot, sticky grasp on northern Indiana anytime soon.

*It's a bad case of the July mugs,* Tim Stephens would say. *Don't fight it; just give in to it, 'cause there's nothing you can do about it but sweat.*

So Ed did his best to accept it as he found himself sleepwalking through his usual Tuesday morning with Mrs. Heston, followed by a miserable afternoon replacing the spouting on the Rhodes house. He had not seen young Becky Rhodes since March and was surprised to find her noticeably pregnant and as unhappy about the weather as he. Bless her heart, though; she made frequent trips from the air-conditioned comfort of her home with cold beverages for Ed. Her optometrist husband came home early, heartily praised Ed's work, and proceeded to overpay him in gratitude. Ed drove home in a slightly better mood, looking forward to an evening in his own air-conditioned home.

Rick was home ahead of him, halfheartedly putting together a meal of Effie Maude's leftover meatloaf and some store-bought potato salad. After a day of delivering mail in the uncomfortable weather, he was as listless as Ed.

"I thought about making corn on the cob," he said apathetically, "but I couldn't even stand the thought of boiling water in this place. Too bad we don't have that microwave yet."

Ed was on his way to the bathroom and a cool shower when Rick stopped him. "By the way, I went in to talk to Vince Cummings after work. I'll tell you about it over dinner. Since his office is just down the street from the library, I stopped in there, too. After all that stuff Gordy was carrying on about last night, I decided to do a little research of my own."

Rick gestured toward the coffee table. Ed glanced over and saw a Xerox copy lying atop Rick's usual stack of magazines and books.

Rick said, "I wasn't convinced there had even been an article in the *New*

*York Times*, but sure enough, there was."

Ed picked up the Xerox and read the headline: "'Rare Cancer in Homosexuals.' What does cancer have to do with pneumonia?" he mumbled.

"Just read it."

Ed did. "Kaposi's sarcoma," he murmured. "I sure never heard of that." He scanned the rest of the article. "I don't get it. Gordy was talking about flu and pneumonia. This is a cancer."

Rick threw his hands in the air. "I don't understand it either. Only thing I can figure is maybe the guys Gordy was talking about had this cancer, and somehow their immune systems were so weak they caught pneumonia and died. I'm no doctor, so that's the only explanation I can think of. The spooky part is they don't know the cause or how to treat it."

"All of these guys had multiple sex partners, and some of them used drugs." Ed scratched his sweaty head. "And they all were connected to New York. Hmmm."

"Well, I guess that lets us out," Rick said. "We don't do drugs, and we don't sleep around, and we're a good five or six hundred miles from New York City." He put two plates on the table. "I don't think we should worry about it."

It occurred to Ed to say that neither one of them had been exactly celibate before they had met the previous fall but decided against it. He was not in the mood for a discussion of former sex partners or strange cancers.

"I gotta hit the shower." He looked down at his sweat-soaked T-shirt and cutoffs. "Do I have time?"

"Sure. We'll eat when you're ready."

Over their cold supper, Rick talked about his meeting with Vince Cummings.

"He's a nice guy, not really what I expected; just kind of laid back and friendly. I guess I was expecting some hard-sell guy; you know, like a car salesman with a big fake laugh and a handshake that about rips your arm off."

"I've heard that about him. Maybe that's why he's done so well." Ed took a big swig of his Pepsi and went to the refrigerator for more. "So what did he say about you getting a license?"

"Well, he told me what he told Mrs. P.: The market's soft and it's a bad time for a newcomer, but he also said that a lot of people are looking at real estate as a second career these days. Most of them are doing it part-time or on the side. He said a lot of women who are entering the workforce for the first time are looking at real estate."

Rick laughed. "He said since so many women are choosing real estate as a way to get liberated from housework, it's about time a liberated gay man went into the field."

"He really *said* that?"

"Yeah. Pretty cool, huh? Sure took me by surprise. Anyway, the next round of real estate classes start a week from tonight. I'm sure glad I went to see him when I did."

Ed almost choked on his meatloaf. "Next week? Already? Are you going to go?"

"Why not? It's either start now or wait 'til September. Or later. Why not get it over with?"

Ed pushed potato salad around on his plate. "I guess you're right," he said slowly. "But now, when it's so hot? When the kids are out of school? Are you really sure you want to add this to everything that's going on?"

"Baby, if I'm gonna get a license I'll have to go through these classes, pass 'em, *and* go through the state licensing exam. It's actually better that I do it now as far the kids are concerned. Mrs. Busby will be watching them every day until their school starts, so I don't need to be over there every day. As for the weather and everything else, so what? It'll always be something. At some point I just have to dig in and do it."

Rick showed Ed the material Vince had given him that afternoon. "See? The classes are two nights a week at IU-Purdue in Fort Wayne in Kettler Hall. Three hours every Tuesday and Thursday for nine weeks."

Rick sighed. "It's going to be tough. Vince warned me that a lot of people don't make it 'cause it's too hard for them. He said my lack of background in sales or real estate is against me, but that two years of college with good grades is a leg up. Thanks to my parents, teachers that they are, I know how to study when I need to, but it's going to be intense."

To Ed it sounded like a great deal of hard work with no real promise of a payoff in the end. He said as much.

"I know, but do you know how many people sweat through four or more years of college and never end up with a job that matches their degrees? Everything's a gamble, baby. When you started your own business, did you know for sure it would be successful enough to support you?"

"No," Ed admitted.

"Well then. Anyway, I'll have to pay for the class and the books, so money might be a little tight for the rest of the summer, and I'm not really sure how to get to the campus, but I'm excited about it. I've already planned to ask for as many Wednesdays and Fridays off as I can get so I won't be too wiped out from the late nights."

Rick looked at Ed soberly. "Here's the thing, baby. This *is* going to be hard. I can't do it unless I have your complete support. In addition to the classes, I'll have to do a lot of studying. I may need your help with my chores around here, and I probably won't be much fun for the next two months either. What do you think?"

Ed looked into Rick's eyes and saw his excitement at the prospect of a new career, but he also saw the uncertainty. Rick needed Ed's help if he was going to succeed with both the grueling classes and his gamble on a better life for them.

He thought about Rick's support the past week and everything Rick had done to ease his mind after the incident with Ruth Dorsey. He thought about the nagging concern in the back of his mind that a similar incident might occur again. Or worse, what if it happened at the post office? What if Rick lost his job? Wouldn't the possibility of a new career be good insurance if the worst happened?

Ed flashed back to their weekend at Spruce Lake and the plans they had made for their future. He had agreed wholeheartedly with Rick's idea to combine Ed's handyman skills and Rick's desire to go into real estate as a way of buying run-down houses, fixing them up, and selling them at a profit. He had been as enthusiastic as Rick at the thought of being less financially dependent on people who might not approve of them. So why was he hesitating now?

The past three months had been hectic. A lot had happened; there had been a good many changes. Ed just wanted to relax and enjoy the fact that he and Rick were together without pushing so hard to make it even better. However, Ed knew as long as the Ruth Dorseys of the world were determined to keep them down, they really couldn't relax. They had to be prepared for the worst, and unless they were willing to give up the life they loved in Porterfield, they would need to keep working toward a better future. Rick was right: Financial independence equaled freedom from Ruth Dorsey, Jim Murkland, and every other bigoted individual in Porterfield or anywhere else.

More important, Rick was Ed's husband. He looked at the ring on his hand and thought about the gold chain well hidden beneath a pile of sweaters in the bedroom. He had made a commitment to Rick, and part of that commitment was total support of Rick's dreams and goals, unless they were truly foolish. Rick's ideas for the future were practical, and he was willing to work hard to achieve them, not just for himself but for Ed as well.

Ed reached across the table and took Rick's hand. "Darlin', if you want to dive into this now, and you're willing to work your ass off when it's so damned hot, then I'm behind you a hundred percent. I'll take over your yard chores. I won't play the stereo while you're studying; hell, I'll even draw you a map to Kettler Hall at the university. I know how to get there. I once dated a guy who was going to school at IU-Purdue."

Ed pulled Rick's hand to his mouth for a kiss. "We're in this together," he said softly. "I'll do whatever I have to do for the next nine weeks to help you get that license."

The uncertainty faded from Rick's eyes. His warm and tender special glowing, he pulled Ed up from his chair and gathered him in his arms for a hug.

"Oh, baby," he whispered. "Thanks. It'll be hard, but we'll get through it. I'm doing this for us, you know."

"I know."

"I love you."

"I love you too, darlin'."

Rick kissed him, and then pushed him back with a mock frown on his face. "Now, about this guy you dated . . ."

Ed kissed him back. "Just a guy. Nobody important. He wasn't the cutest future real estate agent in Porterfield, Indiana."

Ed kissed him again. "He wasn't you, darlin'."

◈

Ed's noble thoughts of love, commitment, and support deserted him the next morning when the shrill buzz of Rick's alarm clock awoke him. It had been a restless night, thanks to the heat, and he was half tempted to roll over and almost accidentally slap Rick but thought better of it. He feigned sleep, thinking that if a new career for Rick meant the end of the five o'clock wake-up call, he'd endure whatever was necessary to make it happen.

He fell back into a deep sleep and groaned when his radio woke him up at seven thirty to the sound of "Bette Davis Eyes."

"Aw, crud, enough of Bette already," he mumbled, slamming his hand on the OFF button. "Isn't it time for a new number one song?"

He stumbled out of bed with a sigh that was almost a snarl. "Another good song they've run into the ground."

In retaliation he went into the living room and put a stack of old 45s on the stereo, sticking his copy of "Bette Davis Eyes" at the back of the record cabinet.

Although they had no windows facing east, the morning sun had heated the kitchen and living room to the point where anything other than cold cereal seemed unthinkable for breakfast. He poured a bowl of Frosted Flakes, serenaded by The Lovin' Spoonful's "Summer in the City." John Sebastian sang of people looking half dead and sidewalks hotter than a match from the heat.

"Include me in the half dead," Ed muttered, grateful he had a fairly easy day ahead of him.

He dawdled over breakfast and the morning newspaper. When his glance took in the Xeroxed article lying on the coffee table, he found himself walking into the living room to read it again. He was still vaguely troubled by the story, even though he couldn't really think of a connection between the rare cancer and himself, other than the fact that he was a gay man. The thought of a disease specifically targeting homosexuals bothered him, and he remembered Gordy's comments about a possible government conspiracy. It was improbable, he knew, but he couldn't help thinking the Ruth Dorseys of the world would approve.

The phone rang. He rose to answer it, the article still in his hand. He dropped it on the telephone table as he picked up the receiver. "Hello?"

"Ed? Is that you? This is Mary Tucker. I've got a problem."

Mary Tucker was the latest addition to what Gordy called "Ed's old-lady brigade." Her husband had died several months earlier and had left Mrs. Tucker confused and helpless when it came to maintaining her home. Her calls to Ed were becoming more frequent as time went by and more things required maintenance.

"What's going on?"

"I only have electricity in one-half of my house," she said anxiously. "I don't understand it. Shouldn't it all go out at once?"

"Have you checked the fuse box, or do you have circuit breakers?"

"The what?" she asked.

Ed sighed. Obviously Mr. Tucker had taken even the most basic household knowledge with him to his grave. "I'll be over as soon as I finish my breakfast."

He hung up, knowing her anxiety would only mount if he took his time getting there. He blew off his morning shave, deciding the world could just deal with a stubble-faced Ed Stephens for the day.

He clicked the stereo off midway through Barry Maguire's "Eve of Destruction." He looked at the record on the turntable, and then at the Xerox he had left on the telephone table.

"Oh, get a grip," he muttered, heading to the bedroom to dress.

Ed quickly found the problem at the Tucker house. A fuse had blown, probably overloaded from the ancient air conditioner he noted in the dining room window. He drove to the hardware store, wishing he had some air-conditioning of his own in his truck. Even at nine in the morning the heat and humidity were intense and promised only to get worse as the day went on.

He replaced the fuse, accepted Mary Tucker's profuse thanks, and headed to Mrs. West's house to look at a malfunctioning fan. The heat seemed to be causing problems for everyone.

Mrs. West's fan was as old, if not older, than Mrs. Tucker's air conditioner.

It was covered with dust, and Ed suspected the fan's motor was clogged with years' worth of crud.

"Mrs. West," he said patiently, "you have to clean these things every once in awhile."

She looked at him, horrified. "Put water on that motor? I'd never do such a thing!"

Ed acknowledged her phobia for all things electrical with a subtle eye roll. He happened to glance at a crumb-caked toaster next to her kitchen sink and sighed sharply. No amount of reassurance would change her opinion that her electrocution was imminent if she so much as pulled a plug. He added cleaning the toaster to his list of chores for her.

As he headed home for lunch, he went out of his way, curious to see how Doug Morgan was settling into Ed's former home. He pulled into the driveway behind the house on Coleman Street and noted, to his amusement, Doug mowing the front yard, clad in nothing but gym shorts. "Wouldn't Gordy have a fit," he said to himself, glad his friend was hard at work at the post office.

Doug saw Ed and waved, pushing the mower toward the driveway. He shut it off and it died with a noisy groan. "Hey, landlord," he said, grinning. "What's goin' on?"

"Nothing," Ed responded. "I just wanted to make sure you got moved in okay."

Doug nodded. "Yeah, everything's fine. No problems. I'm sure glad you left your air conditioner behind, though."

Ed smiled a little wistfully. He thought of how much cooler his little tree-shaded house was compared to the second-floor carriage-house apartment. For the first time since he and Rick had moved, he almost regretted it.

"Is it running okay? I've spent the morning dealing with shit like that."

Doug laughed. "It's fine. The heat's getting to everyone, though. Had a lady pass out at a funeral yesterday, and it wasn't from grief."

Ed chuckled and glanced at the yard, remembering the sight of it frozen under a blanket of snow. "Why is it," he said, thinking aloud, "that July only looks good in January, and January only looks good in July?"

Doug wiped some sweat from his dark blond hair. "I don't know, but I wouldn't mind throwing myself in a snowdrift about now."

"Me, too." Ed suddenly saw himself under a pile of heavy blankets, his arms around Rick. He sighed. "Well, shit. It can't stay hot forever. I'd kill for a Popsicle about now, though."

"I hear that. Where's that stupid ice cream truck when you need it? I hear that thing rolling up and the down the streets, playing 'Pop Goes the Weasel' until I'm ready to shoot out the speakers. But when you really want it, where is it?" Doug snickered.

"Oh, hell, it's probably broken down, too. Hey, I'll let you get back to the mowing. I just wanted to make sure everything's okay."

"It's great," Doug assured him. "My girlfriend's actually coming down for the weekend, now that I have a death-free home. So believe me, you'll get no complaints from me."

Ed climbed back into his truck with a smile, wishing for Gordy's sake the handsome mortician was more interested in men than women, but still glad he'd found such a nice guy as a tenant. With one last look at his house, he drove home for lunch.

Ed's afternoon was finished after a few quick maintenance jobs. Once home for the day, he flopped on the couch with one of the Popsicles he had stopped to buy at the IGA, idly watching TV, puzzling over the plotlines on *All My Children*. He thought Erica's new boyfriend bore a striking resemblance to the guy from *Petticoat Junction* Rick had lusted for as a teenager. It just had to be the same guy, he decided, watching Erica argue with Brandon. He considered teasing Rick about it but knew Rick would just bitch about him wasting time watching soap operas. Laurie had watched *All My Children* for years, and in her enthusiasm for the show had encouraged Ed to watch it as well during his idle afternoons.

The soaps ended and he remained in front of the TV, the oppressive heat keeping him from thoughts of more strenuous activity. He wanted to get more work done establishing his workshop but couldn't bear the stuffy first floor of the carriage house. Any yard work that needed doing, he thought, could damn well wait until the next cloudy day.

Rick appeared after five o'clock. He had taken Judy to Fort Wayne for an orthodontist's appointment after work, and he had the look of a man who had spent most of his day delivering mail in the heat and then enduring a sixty-mile round-trip in the company of a twelve-year-old with aching teeth.

Rick opened the freezer and quickly glommed onto one of Ed's Popsicles. He sneered at the refrigerator's contents in disgust. "There isn't anything in here I feel like making for supper," he grumbled.

He looked at Ed sprawled on the sofa. "What are you up to?"

Ed rolled his eyes. "What does it look like? I'm watching TV."

"What are you watching?"

"*The Brady Bunch*."

Rick snorted. "Is that the best you can do? What are those six monsters up to now?"

"They're fighting over trading stamps."

"Oh, brother!" Rick slammed the refrigerator door. "What a great way to spend a Wednesday afternoon."

Ed looked at him. "It's hot, and I'm tired. What's wrong with watching TV? I don't feel like doing anything else."

Rick licked his Popsicle. "I get enough of that sappy-shit TV over at Claire's. I don't expect to put up with it at home."

"I suppose I could turn it over to PBS," Ed snapped. "Maybe *Sesame Street* is on. That's educational."

"Still don't know how to count to twenty, huh?" Rick snickered.

"Piss off," Ed retorted, now thoroughly annoyed. "You make fun of almost everything I watch on TV. I can't watch game shows anymore 'cause you bitch about how stupid they are. You make fun of my mom behind her back because she likes *Dallas*. I'm sorry, Mr. Two Years of College, but you married into a family of *stupids*, okay?"

He glared at Rick. "For your information, I was watching *All My Children* today, too. I can hardly wait to hear what you have to say about that!"

Rick glared right back at him over his Popsicle. "The least you could do is read a book instead of wasting your time on that junk. And you're not stupid!"

"You make me feel stupid sometimes, just because I don't like a lot of the stuff you read. I didn't want to read those John Jakes books, and you wouldn't let me hear the end of it. Then you made fun of me for reading *A Tree Grows in Brooklyn*, telling me *you* had read it in junior high. Big fuckin' deal! It's a good story!"

"I did not make fun of you," Rick replied, his voice raised. "Reading that is a lot better than the shit on the boob tube."

He gestured at the TV. "I mean, look at that. Building a house of cards to see who gets custody of some stupid trading stamps? Shit!"

"Aha," Ed crowed. "How did you know that's what they're doing unless you've seen it before?"

Rick smiled an extremely smug smile. "Jack used to watch it. Every day."

Ed's eyes grew big. "Oh, so that's it. I'm as stupid as your ex-lover, right?"

Rick shrugged, still smiling. "You said it; I didn't."

Ed stared at him, wishing he had something to throw. "Fuck. You," he said very slowly and very distinctly.

Rick's smile disappeared. He threw what was left of his Popsicle in the sink. "You can just get your own damn supper," he hissed. He stormed down the hall, and Ed heard the bathroom door slam.

Ed was trying to think of an answer to that when he heard the door open. "And don't be calling Gino's for a pizza either. We can't afford it," Rick hollered.

"Oh, yeah?" Ed hollered back. "I'll eat whatever I damn well want to!"

The bathroom door slammed again, followed by the sound of the shower. Ed sat up on the sofa, seething. He couldn't believe Rick would in any way compare him to Jack. "How dare he?" he mumbled, kicking at the coffee table. "And since when can't we afford a pizza? Just because he has to pay for those stupid classes, he's acting like we're down to our last dime."

Ed stood up and began pacing. "Who put him in charge of our money anyway?" he grumbled. He glanced at the TV, where the Brady girls were on the verge of redeeming the trading stamps they had won from the boys. He was about to turn the TV off but instead turned up the volume, hoping it would bug the shit out of Rick when he left the bathroom.

He stomped down the hall to the bedroom and grabbed his keys and wallet. He paused at the bathroom door. "I'm leaving!"

"Good!" Rick shouted from the shower.

Ed stormed down the stairs, thinking he'd go to the P & J Root Beer Stand and eat in the truck. Air-conditioning or no air-conditioning, he didn't feel like dealing with anyone other than a carhop right now.

He pulled open the carriage-house door and almost collided with Josh, who was standing by the door, holding on to his bike.

"Josh," Ed exclaimed. "What are you doing way over here?"

Josh, who resembled Rick more than his father, looked up at Ed. "I'm running away!"

*Aw, crud*, Ed moaned to himself. "What for?"

"I'm tired of living in a house full of girls," he said, kicking his bicycle tire.

Ed sighed, feeling he had just fallen into a *Brady Bunch* episode of his own. "I can understand that, Josh," he said, trying to sound like a TV father. "Being the only boy can be tough, but I'm sure your mom's worried about you. Does she know you're here?"

"No," Josh muttered, stubbing his sneaker against the driveway.

Ed, sweaty and disgusted, looked at Josh, wondering what to do. His anger with Rick left him feeling incapable of dealing with an angry nine-year-old. His first impulse was to throw both the kid and his bike in the back of the truck and head over to Claire's, but he knew that wouldn't solve anything. However, he wasn't in any mood to go back upstairs either.

"Can't I stay with you and Uncle Rick?" Josh looked at Ed with the eyes of a misunderstood boy. "I'm sick of girls."

Ed's anger melted. *What a pushover I am*, he thought. "Well," he said gently, "maybe for tonight anyway, and only if we call your mom and let her know where you are, okay?"

Josh thought that over. "Okay," he reluctantly agreed.

Ed helped Josh put his bike in the carriage house and led him upstairs. He handed him a Popsicle, waiting uneasily for Rick to emerge from the bathroom.

Josh plopped himself happily on the sofa, watching the closing credits of *The Brady Bunch*. A voiceover announcer invited viewers to stay tuned for *Leave It to Beaver*. Ed groaned to himself, wondering what Rick would have to say about that.

He heard the bathroom door open, and Rick came down the hall wearing a pair of gym shorts not unlike Doug Morgan's. Any other time Ed would have enjoyed the sight, but he was still mad at him. Rick raised his eyebrows at Ed, who pointed into the living room. Rick looked around the corner at Josh, who was humming along with the *Leave It to Beaver* theme.

"What's going on?" Rick sighed, still visibly perturbed with Ed.

"He ran away from home," Ed whispered.

Rick's eyes closed. "Oh, shit! That's just what I need today."

Rick shook his head, sighed once more, and sat on the sofa next to Josh. "Hey, kid," he said cheerfully. "What seems to be the trouble?"

Josh tore himself away from Beaver and Wally. "Mom and Judy and Jane think they can boss me all the time. I don't wanna live there anymore!"

*So you wanna live here with your bossy uncle?* Ed thought.

"That's just the way girls are," Rick said to Josh. "You have to ignore them, that's all. Yes, you have to do what your mother tells you, but don't let the girls bother you."

"Uncle Ed said I could stay here," Josh said, slurping his Popsicle.

"He did, did he?" Rick asked, turning to Ed.

"I told him he could stay here tonight," Ed said quickly.

Ed noticed Rick fighting to keep a smile off his face. "Well, I suppose that's okay, as long as your mother knows about it," he said, reaching for the phone.

"I'm not going back there," Josh said definitely.

"We'll talk about it," Rick said soothingly, punching in Claire's number.

Ed, getting hungry, went to the refrigerator for another Popsicle. He eavesdropped on Rick's conversation with Claire, hearing him tell her not to worry, that Josh was fine, and either he or Ed would bring him home the next day. Josh looked at his uncle with suspicion at that but said nothing.

Rick hung up the phone. "Have you had anything to eat yet?"

"No."

Rick sighed. "That figures. Oh, well, we'll come up with something for you."

"Look," Ed said, feeling terribly embarrassed for some reason. "I was just on my way to the P & J for Spanish dogs. How 'bout I bring home enough for everyone, with some fries, too?"

"Yeah!" Josh shouted, eyes shining.

Rick lost the battle with his smile. "That would be great," he said softly.

Ed wasn't quite ready to smile back at him but nodded pleasantly. "Be back in a flash," he said, rattling his keys.

Later, after Josh had made his way through a sizable share of the P & J's version of chili dogs and cheese fries, he returned to the TV, engrossed in a rerun of *Little House on the Prairie*. Ed and Rick were still at the table, Ed picking at the sticky cheese on the French fry container, trying to avoid Rick's eyes.

Rick looked thoughtfully at Josh. "Maybe I should get him started on the *Little House* books. I think he's old enough to appreciate them."

"Aren't those for girls?" Ed was still put out with Rick's enrichment reading programs.

Rick frowned at him. "There's nothing wrong with boys reading those books. I did. I fail to see how a series of books about a pioneer family, told through the eyes of one of the daughters, will in any way damage the kid, or bring his sexuality into question. It's that kind of thinking that makes life hard for people like you and me."

"Excuse *me*," Ed replied. "I was reading Henry Huggins books at his age, but I guess that's not historical enough."

Rick reached across the table for Ed's hand. "Baby, can we call a cease-fire while Josh is here?" He grinned. "I read those Henry Huggins stories, too. And loved them."

Ed found a grin sneaking onto his own face. "Deal." He squeezed Rick's hand.

When the Ingalls family disappeared from the television screen, Rick sat down with Josh. "Okay. What brought this on today, anyway?"

Josh shrugged. "Nothing."

Rick crossed his arms. "Come on, Josh. Tell me why you're more upset with the girls than usual."

Josh swung his legs in embarrassment. "Oh, I'm just tired of Judy having Angie over. They always act so snotty. The only friend I have to come over is Eric, and he's at his grandma's for the whole summer. And Jane's just a big baby. She gets whatever she wants! Mom can do girl stuff with them, but she doesn't know how to do stuff I want to do."

Ed braced himself for one of Rick's guilt attacks. "Well, that's not a problem, Josh," he said, trying to prevent it. "When you need to do guy stuff, just call us. That's what we're here for."

Rick looked at Ed in gratitude. "He's right. You don't have to be shy about that, just 'cause I'm not living in your house anymore."

Josh's eyes brightened. "Can you teach me how to bowl?"

"Bowl?" Rick asked, puzzled.

"Yeah. There's a bowling league for kids at the Porterfield Bowl-O-Rama. It starts when school does. Eric wants to go, but I don't know how to bowl."

"I can take care of that," Ed said confidently. Rick looked at him, surprised. "Sure. I bowled in a league when I worked at Marsden. I'm not the greatest at it, but I can teach you how to roll a strike."

"Neat! Can we go tomorrow?"

"Well, I don't know about tomorrow, but we'll do it soon. I promise."

"When?" Josh persisted.

Ed laughed. "Okay, how 'bout next Tuesday night? Uncle Rick has his first real estate class, so we'll have a boy's night out without him. We can go every Tuesday night until school starts. Heck, you'll be a better bowler than Eric by then." Ed happened to know the Porterfield Bowl-O-Rama had a summer family bowling special every Tuesday night, and as far as he was concerned, Josh was family.

"Wow. Can I get my own ball and everything?"

"I don't know about that," Rick said. "Let's make sure you like it first, okay? They'll have plenty of balls at the Bowl-O-Rama for you to use. I think." He looked at Ed. "I have to admit, I've never done much bowling."

"Sure they do. I'll even teach you how to keep score. That's the hard part."

Rick grinned at Ed, relieved and obviously very grateful. "Can you wait until Tuesday night?" he asked Josh.

Josh nodded. "We can go in Ed's truck, too, right?"

"Absolutely."

"And the girls can't go, right?"

"No girls allowed," Ed said firmly. "We'll drink pop, smoke cigars, and tell mean stories about them."

Josh laughed happily. "Neat!"

Rick rolled his eyes at Ed. "Don't forget, Josh, Mrs. Penfield invited you over sometime to play in her attic. When the weather cools off, you can do that, too."

Josh smiled, pleased. "Can I stay over here sometimes? I'll bet it'll make Judy mad."

"I don't see why not," Rick said. "Just ask your mom first in the future, okay?"

Josh shrugged. "Okay. If I have to."

"You have to," Rick said, giving him a playful poke on the arm. "How 'bout this? When I get off work Saturday, let's you and I go to Fort Wayne and see that *Raiders of the Lost Ark* movie you've been wanting to see. No girls. We guys have to stick together."

"Thanks," Josh said, giving his uncle a hug.

Ed smiled at them both, thinking that for someone who hated *The Brady Bunch,* Rick was pretty good at creating Brady moments.

They made a bed on the sofa for Josh. He was as tired from the heat as anyone else, and that, along with the high emotion of the day, made him ready to crash at Rick's bedtime.

Ed gingerly approached their bedroom, slightly annoyed with Josh for ruining his own plans to sleep on the couch. He settled on his side of the bed, as close to the edge as possible.

Rick, glancing at him, put his book on the nightstand. He reached once again for Ed's hand. "Baby, I'm sorry," he said softly. "I had no right to say the things I said earlier. Will you forgive me?"

Ed let out a very long sigh, slumping down on the bed. "Yeah, I forgive you. I'm sorry, too, for being such a jerk. I'm just tired of the heat, that's all."

"I know," Rick said with a sigh of his own. "I don't think I would have snapped at you so badly if it wasn't so hot. You were right about one thing, that's for sure. It gets a little hot up here in the summer."

Ed chuckled ruefully. "In more ways than one. Oh, darlin', don't worry about it. I think we were past due for that. No hard feelings, okay?"

"None at all," Rick said, tentatively kissing him. "Oh, baby, I really am sorry," he whispered. "Please don't ever think I think you're stupid. It's because you're so smart, I guess, that I get it into my head to push you a little bit. I know I shouldn't, but I just want you to be everything you can be."

"So it's okay for smart people to watch dumb television when they're tired?" Ed tentatively put an arm around him.

Rick put both arms around him for a hug. "Yes. The only reason I get so crazy with the TV is because Jack had it going all the time when we lived together. The difference is, he *was* stupid." Rick snorted. "I think that's why I get irritated with the game shows. He couldn't even come up with the joke answers on *Match Game*. He'd just sit there and howl about what a queen Charles Nelson Reilly was. I couldn't ever have an intelligent conversation with him, the way I do with you."

Rick kissed him again. "I'm sorry, and I promise to remember who I'm with now. You're nothing like Jack, and don't ever think you are."

"Okay," said Ed, wanting to drop the subject of Jack. "Maybe we're still getting used to each other."

Rick nodded. "Yeah, I think we are. So much has happened in the past few months. Oh, I wouldn't change any of it, but I guess it's taking more getting used to than I thought, and I'm nervous about those classes. A lot of people bomb out on their first try at a license, and I don't want to go through it more than once."

"You're worried about the money, too, aren't you?"

"Yes. I know the money for these classes is an investment in our future, but it bugs me to think we won't really be saving anything this month. I don't want us to fight over money. I can handle arguing over *The Brady Bunch*, but not money. That tears too many couples apart."

Rick shrugged. "That's why I haven't bothered to look at microwave ovens, and that's why I don't even want to call Gino's for pizza. I want us to have as much money as possible tucked away for when we really need it."

Ed gave him a squeeze. "Yeah, I know. But you're doing this for both of us, not just you. It scares me, too, but we agreed this was a good thing for you to do."

Rick stretched out on the bed and groaned. "I know, I know. I think I'll feel better once I start the class and see how hard it really is. I hope to hell it cools off before then.

"And thanks for agreeing to take Josh bowling. I can't tell you how much that means to me."

"No problem. I'm looking forward to it. I might even ask Gordy if he wants to go, too. You know, the more guys, the merrier. I'm sorry it's on your school night, but it's the cheap night at the Bowl-O-Rama, so we won't spend as much money."

Despite the heat, Rick pulled Ed very close to him. "It's okay. I know I'm uptight about the money, but if it'll make Josh happy, I don't care."

He looked at Ed, warm and tender special glowing. "I love you so much, baby. Even when I yell at you, I still love you more than I can say."

"I love you, too, darlin'. Sometimes I wanna push you down the stairs, but I still love you." Ed kissed him. "My mom warned me there'd be days like this."

Rick laughed. "She did, huh? Well, I guess she should know. We may still be new at it, but we're not doing too badly. Didn't someone once sing something about the best part of breaking up was making up?"

Ed smirked at him. "What did you have in mind?"

Rick nodded toward the living room. "Well, considering our little houseguest, I guess lovemaking is out of the question, but can you stand the heat enough to hold me close for awhile?"

Ed looked at Rick, the man he loved, the man who shared his life, the man who was helping him to learn what marriage was all about. Oh, sometimes Rick frustrated the hell out of him, but at that moment he wouldn't have traded him for anyone or anything.

Ed smiled at him. "I can take the heat for that, darlin'. I promise."

# Chapter Twelve

Ed had almost fallen back to sleep after Rick's alarm the next morning when he felt a hand on his arm.

"Baby, I hate to wake you up, but I need to know your plans for Josh today. I need to call Mrs. Busby."

Ed opened his eyes to see Rick standing next to the bed, dressed for work. "Did anyone ever tell you how sexy you look in those mailman shorts?"

Rick grinned. "Thanks, but I need to know about Josh."

Ed yawned. "I don't have any appointments this morning, so I thought I'd take him home after lunch. I figured if he stayed here long enough, he might actually wanna go home."

Rick bent over and kissed him. "You're something else, you know that? I really appreciate this."

"Yeah, yeah," Ed mumbled, turning over. "Go to work. Maybe I can actually sleep for another ten minutes before he wakes me up."

"I'll see you this afternoon. I love you, baby, and I'm sorry for—"

"If you start to apologize again, I'm gonna get out of this bed and kick your ass. I love you, too. Now, go to work!"

With one more kiss, but no more words, Rick slipped out the door.

It was another hot, humid day. Ed was relieved that Josh was content to sprawl on the sofa with Jett watching TV while he used the morning to catch up on his client records for his usual end-of-the-month billing.

Ed suggested a picnic lunch, hoping Josh would decline, but his eyes lit up at the idea. Resigned to a sweaty meal, Ed packed a grocery bag with some bologna sandwiches, bananas, potato chips, and Oreos.

"Can't we take some of the Popsicles, too?" Josh asked.

"Bud, they'd be nothing but a puddle of orange water by the time we get to where we're going."

"Where are we going?"

"You'll see."

Ed took the road out of town that followed Stratton Creek. About a mile out was a small county roadside rest area. It was located on a shady bend in the creek, and there were a few picnic tables scattered under the trees. Ed led Josh to one, handing him a lukewarm Pepsi. They sat down to their lunch, looking at the water, which wasn't more than a few feet deep.

Ed had not been looking forward to eating a bologna sandwich in the extreme heat and humidity, but he had to admit it wasn't so bad. There was a nice breeze blowing, and he noticed some clouds scudding across the sky. He suspected there would be thunderstorms by the end of the day.

"Ed, are there any fish in this creek?"

"Oh, maybe some tiny ones. It's not very deep, you know."

"Do you know how to fish?"

"No. My dad didn't like to fish."

"Did you like your dad?"

"Yes."

"Was he a good dad?"

"The best."

"You're lucky."

"I s'pose so."

"Do you think my dad will come back?"

Ed looked at Josh. He was tall for his age and skinny. He looked the way Rick described himself at that age. Ed sighed, thinking of Rick's lonely childhood and his own childhood struggles. "I don't know, Josh. I really don't."

"Can I tell you a secret?"

"Okay."

"I don't think I want him to come back."

"That's okay. I mean, it's okay to think that way, and I promise I won't tell anyone."

"Dad never wanted to do anything with me. He just wanted to drink beer and watch TV. I like TV, but I like other things, too."

"What other things?"

"The things I can do with you and Uncle Rick. Dad never took me to the movies, or to the library. I really like the books Uncle Rick picks out. And you're gonna teach me to bowl. I bet Dad wouldn't do that."

Ed felt badly for his nasty thoughts on Rick's reading suggestions. "Do you like other sports, Josh?"

"Oh, they're okay. I'm not very good at them, though. I like games better."

Ed sighed again, thinking of the hell he went through as a nonathletic kid. "Well, bowling is cool. I think you'll have a lot of fun with that."

"I'm glad Uncle Rick moved here, and that he's with you. It's like having two dads. Is it okay if I pretend you guys are my dads?"

Ed almost snickered, thinking of what some people would say about that, a nine-year-old boy pretending two gay men were his fathers. "Sure, I don't see why not. I wouldn't tell anyone, though. A lot of people get weird about that stuff. Tell you what. You can think of us as your dads in private."

"That's cool."

"Josh, does it bother you that Uncle Rick moved out?"

"A little bit."

"Well, you know you can call or come over anytime you want, right?"

"Yeah. I do now."

"Good."

"I'm just afraid Dad will come back, and I won't get to see you guys anymore."

Ed looked at Josh, who was carefully peeling a banana. He often wondered how much Josh understood about his relationship with Rick.

"Why wouldn't you be able to see us anymore? I mean, if your dad came back?"

Josh shrugged. "'Cause he was mean. 'Cause he didn't like Uncle Rick."

"Do you know why he didn't like Uncle Rick?"

"Yeah, 'cause he's a fag. That's what Dad always called him."

"Do you know what that is?"

"I think so."

Ed wasn't sure he wanted to get into a discussion of homosexuality with a nine-year-old but decided for his own sake he'd better learn what was going on in the kid's mind. "Can you tell me what it means, Josh?"

Josh reached for some Oreos. "It means a guy who likes other guys, instead of girls."

"Yeah, that's right."

"Are you a fag, too, Uncle Ed?"

"Yeah."

"I thought so."

"Does that bother you?"

"No. I guess it bothers a lot of people, though."

"What makes you say that?"

"Judy told me not to tell anyone, 'cause lots of people hate fags. So I don't tell anyone. I don't want anyone to take Uncle Rick away from me. Or you."

"Well, it stinks, but Judy's right. It's better if you keep it to yourself, okay?"

"Sure."

"I wouldn't worry too much about your dad. I know your mom is doing some legal stuff with Mr. Mason. He's a lawyer, and he's going to fix it so you don't have to worry about it anymore."

"Yeah, she's gonna get a divorce from Dad, right?"

"Yeah, and some other stuff. When it's all over with, your dad won't be able to bother you anymore. Maybe I shouldn't tell you that, but I didn't want you to worry about it."

"Okay.."

Ed looked at Josh, amazed at how their lives had become entangled. He knew Rick sometimes thought he put up with his nephew and nieces out of obligation to Rick, but he genuinely liked all three of them, and his own secret, shared with no one, was that he liked Josh the best. Being a nine-year-old boy's pretend Dad was pretty damned cool, and certainly nothing he had ever pictured happening to him.

He worried, though. He saw a lot of Rick and himself in Josh and only hoped the kid would turn out to be straight. "Josh?"

"Yeah?"

"Do you like girls? I don't mean your sisters, but, like, the girls at school?"

"Yeah. I don't think I'm a fag."

Ed breathed a guarded sigh of relief, knowing Josh still had the terror of puberty ahead of him. "Well, if you ever want to talk about girls, or any of that stuff, you can talk to Uncle Rick and me. Some of that crud gets confusing."

"Okay."

"And Josh? *Fag* isn't a very nice word. Uncle Rick and I are homosexuals, or what a lot of people call gay men. *Fag* is what someone calls us when they're being mean."

Josh thought about that. "Okay, then what should I call you?"

Ed smiled at him. "How 'bout just 'Uncle Ed'? I think that takes care of things, without a lot of details nobody else needs to worry about."

"Neat."

Ed looked at the sky, which had gotten steadily darker during their picnic. "Well, bud, I think I better take you home. Looks like it's going to rain."

"Can we do this again sometime?"

"Sure." Ed began stuffing the garbage in the grocery bag. "We're going bowling Tuesday night, don't forget. I'll see you then. Can I ask my friend Gordy to come with us?"

"Is he a good bowler?"

"I think so."

"Okay, he can come."

Ed dropped Josh off at his house just as a thunderstorm rolled into Porterfield. He drove home slowly, the windshield wipers unable to keep up with the deluge. He pulled into the garage but instead of going upstairs he stood by the open garage doors, watching the storm. He would be late getting to his first appointment, but considering he was to restring the Hausers' outdoor clothesline, he thought they wouldn't be too upset. He watched the rain falling across the garden in sheets, blown by gusts of wind, hoping Rick was somewhere under cover.

His thoughts turned to his conversation with Josh. As much as he enjoyed the boy's company, he worried what other people might think. It angered him to think of people who would discourage Josh, the son of a deadbeat dad, from having a close relationship with his gay uncle and his gay uncle's lover. It didn't seem fair to anyone in the situation, but as Rick had once said, life wasn't fair, even, or equal.

He thought of his own nephew, Bobby, who idolized his father. Todd was a father worth idolizing—a good man and a good husband who was crazy about his kids. Ed thought of Hank Romanowski, Josh's father—a drunk, a cheat, and possibly a drug dealer. He wondered whether the millions of people in the world who automatically condemned Rick and himself would rather Josh grow up with no male role models at all, as opposed to spending time with two grown men who genuinely loved and cared for him. He suspected they probably would.

He thought of how pleased Josh was to spend the night with his two pretend dads, and how much it meant to Josh that Ed would take him for a bologna-sandwich picnic on a hot day and promise to teach him how to bowl. Hell, he even got a kick out of riding in Ed's truck. He shook his head in disgust at those people whose self-righteousness couldn't or wouldn't allow them to look deep into the heart of a little boy who didn't care if his uncle was a fag. He was just glad to have a man around who cared what happened to him.

The rain was slowing down, and Ed could see patches of sunlight in the west. He looked down at his work boots, anticipating the grass stains they'd have after he fixed the Hausers' clothesline in their wet yard.

"Well, life just stinks sometimes, doesn't it?" he muttered as he walked to his truck.

⋆•⋆

Rick was home when Ed, grubby and grass-stained, walked in at the end of the day. Rick, looking fresh from the shower, was relaxing on the sofa in last night's gym shorts, reading the paper. He looked up at Ed's entrance, smiling. "Hey, baby."

"Hey yourself," Ed responded, staring thoughtfully at him. He shook his head. "What is it with you and shorts anyway? Damn, you've got great legs."

"You're looking pretty studly yourself, sport, standing there in those cutoffs and dirty work boots."

Ed grinned at him. "Okay. Are we gonna do it now, after I take a shower, or after supper?"

Rick gave that some serious thought. "I think I can wait until after supper, which is cold fried chicken and cucumber salad, thanks to my new favorite woman in the world, Effie Maude."

"Beats the bologna sandwich I had for lunch," Ed said, walking down the hall.

"Huh?"

"I'll tell you over supper."

As they sat down to enjoy Effie Maude's chicken, rain began to drum on the roof. Thunder rumbled hard enough to make the plates on the table tremble.

"Well, if the weather guessers are right, this should be the end of the heat for awhile," Rick said.

"I hope so," Ed said fervently, helping himself to salad.

"What was that about a bologna sandwich?"

"Oh." Ed chuckled. He told Rick about his picnic with Josh and the conversation they'd had.

Rick shook his head, sighing. "How do you do it? I've been trying to think of a tactful way to find out what Josh thought about us for the longest time, and you get him to talk without even trying."

"I think he wanted to talk," Ed said. "I also think he felt more comfortable talking to me about it. That's cool, though. He's a good kid, and I don't think you have anything to worry about."

Rick poked at a chicken thigh with his fork. "Ed," he said, looking at his plate, "about last night—"

"No more apologies!"

Rick looked at him. "This isn't an apology. It's just something I want to say, okay?"

Ed rolled his eyes. "Okay."

Rick's eyes returned to his plate. "Well. I was so mad at you when you stormed out of here last night. I planned on staying mad all night, too, even it meant I had to sleep on the couch. Then you show up with Josh, and he tells me you'd told him he could spend the night, even though you were as mad at me as I was at you."

Rick looked up at Ed, his warm and tender special beginning to show. "It just reminded me how much I love you. Most people wouldn't have bothered. They just woulda taken the kid home and not even bothered to tell me he was here. You didn't do that, and I don't think you could do that."

"Don't go pinning a medal on me," Ed protested. "I thought about it."

"Yeah, you thought about it, but you didn't do it. You did what you did 'cause you really care about Josh, and that means a lot to me. Here's the other thing, though. I wanted you to know I realized something else later. Even if Josh hadn't've shown up, I wouldn't have stayed mad at you." The warm and tender special was glowing strong now. "Baby, I don't think I *can* stay mad at you."

Ed reached across the table for Rick's hand. "I'll remember that the next time you get really pissed at me, okay?" He squeezed Rick's hand. "I don't know how mad I still was after Josh showed up. I was mad at you, but mad at myself, too, for hurting you. Remember that Carpenters' song 'Hurting Each Other'? Why do people in love hurt each other?"

Rick sighed. "I don't know, but they do. We'll probably do it again someday, so I just want you to know if I hurt you when I'm mad about something, it's . . . I don't know . . . temporary, I guess."

"That goes for me, too," Ed said, still pondering why people in love do the things they do. He shook his head. He'd had enough deep thoughts for one day. "Oh, well. Enough of this. As soon as I finish off this fried chicken, since we have no nine-year-old houseguests, I'm gonna show you how much I love you, and I promise it won't hurt a bit."

"Oh, I don't know about that. Some hurtin' feels kinda good."

"Whatever you want, darlin'. I aim to please."

Rick gripped his hand. "You always do, baby. You always do."

⋘•⋙

The following Tuesday evening, a nervous Rick prepared for his first real estate class. Ed gave him an extra kiss for good luck, told him he'd be fine, and sent him on his way.

Ed left shortly after, driving north to pick up Gordy before heading west to collect Josh for the promised evening of bowling.

"How crappy do I have bowl to keep the kid happy?" Gordy wanted to know.

"Oh, a few gutter balls oughta do it," Ed responded, grinning at him. "I'm just glad you wanted to come along. I figure two teachers are better than one."

"Gets me out of the house," Gordy said, blowing smoke out the window. "Besides, that kid needs all the help he can get, having Hank Romanowski for a dad."

"You got that right." Ed sighed.

He pulled into the driveway of Claire's house in the Westside Hills subdivision. Josh, clearly excited, was waiting on the front steps, Claire by his side. Gordy earned Josh's immediate friendship and hero worship by picking him up, throwing him over his shoulder, and depositing him in the back of the truck.

"Any other garbage we gotta pick up here, lady?" he hollered at Claire, who was laughing on the front steps.

"I've got two more bags, if you want them," she called.

Gordy peered into the truck bed. "Considering how this one smells, one's bad enough. Keep 'em!"

Josh banged on the window. "Can I ride back here, Uncle Ed?"

"No," Ed shouted, pretending to look angry. "Your mom would kill me. Gordy, put him in the cab. Geez!"

Gordy heaved a sigh. "Yes, boss." He hauled Josh out of the truck bed and shoved him on the truck seat next to Ed.

"We'll be back by nine," Ed called to Claire.

"Okay. Thanks," she said, waving.

Josh was still giggling as Ed slammed his foot on the accelerator. The truck roared backward out of the driveway. He shifted gears, slammed his foot on the accelerator again, and burned some rubber on Willow Lane. "Boy's night out has officially begun," he announced, turning up the volume on the radio. AC/DC's "Back in Black" blared out of the speakers.

"Hell, yes," Gordy hollered, slapping the truck door to the beat. "We are gonna get loose from the noose. Did you remember the beer?" he asked Josh, who giggled some more.

Gordy lit another cigarette.

"Uncle Ed, I thought we were gonna smoke cigars tonight. Gordy has a cigarette," Josh yelled over AC/DC.

"Aw, let him have his stinky cigarettes," Ed yelled back.

He pulled down his sun visor. "I got the good stuff for us," he said, handing Josh two bubble gum cigars.

"Hell, yes," Josh hollered.

Gordy roared with laughter as Ed reached across the truck to slap him upside the head. "You get me in trouble with his mom, your ass is mine, bud!"

"Promises, promises," Gordy retorted.

"What?" Josh asked, unwrapping his cigar.

"It just means I'm gonna beat him up," Ed said hurriedly, with a glare at Gordy, who smiled in stunned innocence.

"Don't worry about it," Gordy said to Josh. "We can both take him, easy."

"Geez, I'm beginning to wish I'd left you at home where you belong," Ed said, slowing for a stop sign.

"We'll whip his butt on the lanes, too," Gordy said to Josh, who almost choked on his bubble gum.

"Gordy's fun." Josh coughed, looking at Ed.

"Is that what he is?" Ed grumbled. "I'd been wondering about that."

AC/DC was followed by Hot Chocolate and "You Sexy Thing." Ed, stunned to hear a mid-seventies dance tune on the radio, cranked it up even louder. Ed and Gordy sang along, much to Josh's delight. Ed bopped back and forth behind the steering wheel, Josh banged on the dashboard, and Gordy snapped his fingers out the window.

A carload of teenage girls pulled up next to them at a traffic light, giggling. "We're booked for the night, ladies. Some other time, huh?" Gordy hollered as the light turned green.

"Aw, crud, they'll probably follow us now," Ed said, hitting the gas. He roared down Main Street, ten miles over the speed limit, Gordy and Josh laughing hysterically. He debated whether to make the turn into the Bowl-O-Rama's parking lot, but the girls, realizing they were dealing with lunatics, drove on to the P & J for what Ed knew would be a slow circuit to see who was hanging out.

"Okay, calm down," Ed said, parking the truck. "You two think you can behave yourselves?"

"This is supposed to be a respectable place," Gordy said confidentially to Josh. "We better do what he says."

"It isn't gonna be respectable once I walk in with you two clowns." Ed slammed his door.

He caught a glimpse of Josh's face and felt great. Josh had probably had more fun in the last ten minutes than he'd had in the last ten months, and they hadn't even rented bowling shoes yet. *Gordy, I love you,* he thought, knowing he couldn't have pulled off such rowdy behavior without him.

Once they were established on lane 17, Ed began to instruct Josh on the finer points of bowling. Gordy, bored with that, picked up a ball and promptly rolled it into the gutter.

"Don't do that," he said. "That's all you need to know. Hell, let's start a game."

Josh was a little shaky and uncertain at first but by the tenth frame of the first game was getting the knack of basic bowling.

"You're doing fine," Ed encouraged him as they started a second game. "It's when you try to get fancy with it, like this big dork, that you get in trouble."

"I'll show you who's a dork," Gordy grumbled. He went to the line, took an exaggerated stance, and simply to piss Ed off, somehow managed to roll a strike.

"Beat that," he crowed, rubbing his fingers on his T-shirt and blowing on them.

"Yeah, Uncle Ed. Beat that," said Josh, who'd clearly adopted yet another dad sometime during the evening.

"One gutter ball, coming up," Ed said, stepping up for his turn.

"Ed Stephens," yelled a male voice.

Ed turned around and almost dropped his ball. It was Ted Gillis, an old friend from high school. Ed hadn't seen him in years.

"Ted?" Ed's face registered both delight and hesitation. He was sure it was Ted, but he'd always been overweight, and this new version of Ted was looking trim indeed in khaki shorts and a sports shirt.

Ted laughed. "Yeah, it's me. Not as much me as there used to be. The wife put me on a diet."

Ed walked to him for a good handshake. "Well, it sure worked. You look great! What are you doing in Porterfield? I thought you were living in Wisconsin."

Ted nodded, grinning. "Oh, we still do. We're here visiting my folks, letting them have a good look at their grandkids." He gestured toward his family, several lanes away.

He looked past Ed to Josh, who was trying to figure out the scorekeeping. "Don't tell me this is yours?"

Ed blushed. "Oh, no! No! This is . . . uh—"

Josh looked up. "He's my uncle Ed," he said, smiling happily.

"Oh," Ted said. "One of Laurie's kids."

"Uh, no," Ed said, feeling the blush on his face. "He's the son of a friend. The *uncle* is just . . . uh . . . honorary."

"I get it," Ted said smiling slyly. "Divorcé. Say no more."

Ed was debating whether to correct him when he caught a glimpse of Gordy, who was watching with great interest. "Uh, you remember Gordy Smith, don't you, Ted?"

"Sure," Ted said, stepping down to the bowling lanes to shake Gordy's hand. "I didn't know you two were friends."

Gordy, with a veiled glance at Ed, nodded at Ted. "Ed and I have been hangin' out for awhile. Good to see you again, Ted. You still selling cars up there in Wisconsin?"

Ted began talking about his job, and the moment for Ed to explain his relationship to Josh passed. He noticed, with relief, Josh tuning out of the boring adult conversation. Ted wanted to know whether Ed was still doing the handyman thing and asked Gordy about the post office.

Ed felt extremely uncomfortable, and he wasn't exactly sure why. Was it because he had allowed Ted to believe Josh was the son of a girlfriend, or was it because he was afraid Ted would somehow figure out the truth? He was relieved when one of Ted's kids called for him.

"Time for Dad to add up the score again," Ted said with a shrug. "It's sure good to see you, Ed. If we weren't booked up for the week, I'd say let's get together, talk about old times."

"You mean, like, the time I puked all over your car?" Ed laughed.

"Yeah." Ted laughed with him. "The good stuff. Next time we're in town, I'll give you a call, okay?"

"Sure," Ed said, still uncomfortable but feeling strangely nostalgic.

Ted rejoined his family. Ed watched him go with a frown on his face.

"You okay?" Gordy whispered.

"Yeah, that was just . . . weird."

Gordy nodded. "Yeah, I've been there."

They looked at each other, two gay men in a small town, wondering who knew, who didn't, who deserved to know, and who would shit their pants if they knew.

Josh looked up from the score table, puzzled as to why his two playmates had become so serious. "It's still your turn, Uncle Ed," he said tentatively.

"Yeah," Ed said, giving his head a shake. "Gotta see if I can break a hundred!"

Gordy snorted. "Yeah, right. You'll be lucky if you hit seventy-five. C'mon, let's watch you screw it up!"

"Eat my dust, dork," Ed said. He rolled the ball down the center of the lane. It hit the pins dead on, leaving a seven/ten split. Ed groaned as Josh giggled in delight, and Gordy roared with mocking laughter.

"I take it back," Gordy said. "You'll be lucky if you hit fifty. The kid here's gonna do better than you!"

"Yeah, I'm gonna beat you, Uncle Ed," Josh smirked.

Ed laughed with them, but as he watched Ted Gillis with his family, he knew some of the fun had gone out of his evening.

⋘•⋙

Ed and Gordy were sitting in Ed's truck in the parking lot of Gordy's apartment building. Ed's still-current radio favorite, "Sweetheart" from Franke & The Knockouts, was playing softly on the radio. Ed absentmindedly tapped the beat on the steering wheel, singing "who treats you like a star" softly while Gordy blew smoke out the open window.

"Gord," Ed said quietly when the song ended. "I feel like such a jerk. Why is that?"

Gordy shrugged. "Hell, I don't know. Were you obligated to tell Ted the kid was the nephew of your male lover?"

"I don't know. Was I? How would I have handled it if Rick was there instead of you?"

"Don't let it bug you so much. You were just covering your ass."

Ed looked at his hand tapping the beat of the next song on the steering wheel. "Geez! What if he'd noticed my ring? Then what would I have said?"

Gordy took a deep drag and exhaled slowly. "Ed, he didn't notice it. Stop spazzin'. Look, you weren't just protecting yourself; you were protecting me, and I appreciate that. As much as I love hangin' out with you and Rick, I'm still not ready to be known as the town queer. Hell, I probably never will be. There's the kid to think about, too. You said yourself, when you invited me out tonight, that people would probably shit if they knew a couple of fags were teaching him how to bowl. That kid had a blast tonight. Getting into a big hassle with Ted woulda spoiled that for him."

Ed sighed. "I s'pose you're right. It's just every time I think I have a handle on all of this, something happens to make me doubt myself, and . . . well, everything."

"You mean bein' with Rick?"

"No. Being with Rick in Porterfield."

"You told me you guys were cool on that."

"I thought we were. No, I thought *I* was. Dammit." Ed slapped the steering wheel. "It never gets easy, does it?"

Gordy pitched his cigarette out the window. "Nope," he said, looking at his friend. "It never does."

# Chapter Thirteen

Rick, sighing with contentment, rolled closer to Ed on the bed. "Finally, a morning when neither of us has to get up and be somewhere."

Ed smiled drowsily. "I'm glad God and the postal service take Sunday off."

The window air conditioner hummed on low. It wasn't quite as warm as it had been earlier in July, and it was comfortable in the bedroom, comfortable enough for Ed to enjoy being under the covers, arms around his husband.

He thought back to those Sundays spent with Rick while they had been dating—magical, golden days when the only things that had mattered were each other and what fun they could have together. These days, Ed felt so caught up in their day-to-day routine he had a hard time finding the magic. He wouldn't trade being married to Rick for anything, but he had to admit, he missed the excitement of their dating days.

He remembered moving from Monday to Friday, counting the days until the weekend and his time with Rick. He remembered the feeling when Rick would walk through his door on Saturday afternoon, ready to begin their private time together. He wondered, a little sadly, if he'd ever be that happy again. Oh, he was happy now, but it was a different kind of happiness. There was a great deal of security and contentment, which he thought was wonderful; it simply lacked the thrill of those earlier months with Rick. He suddenly understood why couples talked about needing to spice up their marriages.

"More than three months, baby," Rick murmured in his ear. "Do you still love me?"

Ed was pleased to see their romantic ESP still seemed to be working. "Boy, do I ever. It's different, though, isn't it?"

"Yeah, it is. We're too damn busy these days. I looked forward to actually living with you so much, I never stopped to think about the boring parts. I hate to admit it, but sometimes I wish we were still on Coleman Street, still just seeing each other on the weekends and occasionally during the week. Do you hate me for that?"

Ed chuckled, shaking his head. "No. I was thinking the exact same thing. I think I know now why they keep breaking up couples on soap operas. The dating part is just more interesting than the married part."

Rick laughed out loud. "How 'bout that. I guess *All My Children* does come in handy sometimes. Serves me right for being such an asshole about it."

"You're not an asshole. You just get carried away, that's all."

"You're right. I do get carried away with things. Do you regret us moving over here so soon and me taking the plunge with these classes? Maybe we should have waited awhile, even a year, to really settle into marriage and really get used to each other."

Ed, who had thought just that when Rick was determined to enroll in his real estate courses, closed his eyes and stifled a groan. However, he was in no mood to spoil their relaxed Sunday morning with further discussion on the subject.

"Oh, I don't regret it," he said lightly. "Maybe we should have waited, but everything's working out okay. I think I'm about as used to you as I'm gonna get. Much as I miss my house, I really do love living here. It's like Mrs. Penfield and Effie Maude are those two women in *The Enchanted Cottage*. Did you ever see that movie?"

"I don't think so."

"Well, it's an old one, from the forties, I think. Anyway, it's very sad and very happy, but there's this cottage where lovers go to start their marriages. I used to watch it, thinking how fun it would be to start a marriage there, safe in this cozy place, with people to look after me and my lover. This whole thing, us being here, is kind of enchanted."

"That it is, baby. I've felt enchanted since the day I met you." Rick kissed Ed slowly and tenderly. "You definitely turned this frog into a prince, even if I don't act very princely sometimes."

"Even princes have their bad days," Ed said returning the kiss. "How 'bout, for old times' sake, you get up and make a big ole handyman's Sunday breakfast? It will be your Get out of Jail Free card for the next time you start telling me what to do."

Rick heaved an exaggerated sigh. "I should have known I'd have to pay someday for my sins. What does the handyman want to eat, anyway?"

"He wants pancakes."

"You got it," Rick said, pushing away the covers. "I'll even throw in a piece of bacon or two, how's that?"

"I knew there was a reason I loved you!"

While he was wolfing down Rick's pancakes, Ed flipped through the Sunday paper. "How 'bout we spend the afternoon in an air-conditioned movie theater? I'd love to see that new John Carpenter movie."

"John Carpenter?" Rick asked warily.

"Oh, darlin'. It's not a slasher movie. It's a sci-fi flick with Kurt Russell. It's called *Escape from New York*. All of New York City has been turned into a prison, and he has to, well, escape from it."

Rick sighed. "As much as I want to spend the whole day with you, I really should study for my class this week. This buying and selling stuff is new to me. It's a lot more complicated than I thought. I'm going to pass that licensing exam on the first try, no matter what."

"Is it that hard?" Ed carefully poured more syrup on his pancakes, hoping Rick wouldn't see his disappointment.

"Oh, I don't know if *hard* is the word; it's just a hell of a lot different from sorting and delivering mail. It's been a long time since I've sat in a classroom. I had a hard time concentrating these past couple of weeks, although I guess the weather doesn't help either."

Rick reached for the bacon. "Why don't you call Gordy and see if he wants to go? That'll give me the afternoon to study, and then maybe the three of us can splurge and go out for supper. Besides, I'm already driving to Fort Wayne twice a week. I'm not really in the mood for it."

"Geez, you're doing all the work, and I have all the fun," Ed said, thinking of his standing Tuesday bowling date with Josh.

Rick shook his head. "That's not true. You're doing all the work for Mrs. Penfield and helping Effie Maude when she needs it. You deserve some fun. I just wish it could be with me."

Ed resigned himself to a Rick-free afternoon. "Okay. I'll call Gordy. I have an idea, though, for this week." He giggled. "I don't know how much fun it would be, but it'd be an excuse to spend some time with the kids."

Rick smirked at him. "What are you thinking?"

"The Stratton County 4-H Fair is this week. I thought maybe we could go one night and take the kids. You know, eat some supper at the 4-H Junior Leaders booth and go on some rides. The kids would love it."

Rick's warm and tender special was going strong. "I think that's a great idea. Don's giving me Wednesday off, so we can go that night. I won't be too tired. Josh'll be in heaven, getting to spend two nights in a row with his new favorite uncle."

"Gordy is his new favorite uncle. That poor guy made such a hit, he'll probably have to go bowling with us every week. I think I've slipped to second place. Anyway, it gives me a good excuse to go on the rides without feeling like an old fool."

Rick snickered. "Ah, I should have known you had an ulterior motive." He shook his head. "Sure you're not afraid you'll run into another high school buddy?" he teased.

Ed rolled his eyes. "Well, if we do, I'll just tell him we're a couple of divorced dads, spending time with our kids. How's that?"

"Whatever works," Rick said, giving him a kiss with syrup-sticky lips. "As long as everything's okay with us, as far as I'm concerned you can tell them anything."

⋘•⋙

It was still warm, but the air was blissfully less humid Wednesday night. As Rick pulled his car into the fairgrounds, Ed took in the scene, feeling a comforting sense of tradition as his eyes scanned the small carnival, the livestock arena, and the crowds moving through the exhibit areas.

Judy had her friend Angie with her, and being typical twelve-year-olds, they would have rather died than be seen in the company of grown-ups or younger kids. After promising Rick to eat a halfway nutritious supper, and swearing to be back at the car in exactly two hours, they took off toward the carnival, heads together, giggling.

"Well, let's go see what kind of grub they got this year," Ed said to Josh and Jane, who were excited enough about the change in their usual routine to be on their best behavior.

The 4-H Junior Leaders menu of hot dogs and fries was quickly voted down in favor of the Stratton County Homemakers, who were featuring pork barbecue sandwiches and homemade cake. Ed and Rick had just settled the children at a table under the cookhouse pavilion when Ed heard a familiar voice behind him.

"Hey, look who's here!"

Ed turned around and saw his brother-in-law, Todd. He was out of his usual banker's clothes, and his short frame was informally clad in shorts, T-shirt, and sandals. A big smile stretched across his deeply tanned face as he gestured to Laurie, Bobby, and Lesley, who were trailing him.

"Can we join you guys?"

The children, who were acquainted from school, huddled at one end of the table, slurping milk and red Jell-O, trying to gross each other out as they described the smells wafting from the livestock area. Todd and Rick went into an immediate discussion about the current real estate market, which left Laurie for Ed, although she wasn't the best of company. She picked at her food and gave short, absentminded answers to Ed's questions.

"Geez, what's your problem?" Ed teased. "Time of the month?"

Laurie scowled. "That, too."

"Huh?"

She jerked her head toward her husband, who was busy explaining Porterfield First National's mortgage applications to Rick. "Mommy and Daddy had a little disagreement tonight. The reason he latched on to you guys so fast was so he wouldn't have to deal with me."

Ed lowered his voice. "What's the fight about?"

Laurie glanced again at Todd, and then at the children. "Let's go for a walk," she whispered.

Ed stood up. "Hey, there's Joel and Becky Rhodes over by the Catholic Church fish sandwich stand," he said in a loud voice. "C'mon, Laurie; I want you to meet them."

The others at the table ignored Ed and Laurie as they left the covered dining area and wandered toward the shady stand of oak trees where local nonprofit agencies were peddling sandwiches and snacks.

"So what's up?" Ed asked as he grinned and waved at the Rhodeses.

Laurie sighed and kicked at an acorn. "Oh, he still doesn't want me to go back to work full-time this fall."

Laurie had completed secretarial school shortly after her marriage to Todd. She had immediately gone to work at Robert Mason's law firm in downtown Porterfield and had returned on a part-time basis after the birth of Lesley, her youngest.

"Why doesn't he want you to work full-time?"

"Oh, he says we don't need the money, which I think is his subtle way of saying his parents would help us out if we got in a jam. Plus, I'm hearing some male chauvinist pig sneak in, too. He seems to think his children will turn into delinquents if their mother isn't at home all the time."

"Lots of mothers are working these days," Ed remarked. Rick had told him there were more women than men in his real estate class.

"Of course they are. I don't care what any of those jerks in the Moral Majority say. It takes two incomes to keep a family going these days. It's not about being liberated anymore; it's about dollars and cents."

Ed laughed. "Rick calls Jerry Falwell Jerry *Foul*well."

"Yeah. Suckering people out of money to kill ERA and bashing decent men like you and Rick. He's pretty foul, all right."

Laurie shook her head in frustration. "As for me, sure, most families don't have Earl and Eunice Ames to fall back on, but what difference should that make? You know Mom and Dad taught us to be independent and take care of ourselves. I don't want to spend the rest of my life taking handouts from my in-laws. And what am I supposed to do all day while the kids are in school? Housework? Volunteer? I suppose that's what Todd wants, me joining his mother's committees and being the perfect Porterfield society matron. Well, my last name may be Ames, but I'm still Norma Stephens's daughter, and I'm a little too outspoken to put up with all the crap that goes on in those groups."

She suddenly laughed. "I'm glad Eunice is after Rick to volunteer for the home tour. At least I'm off the hook with that one!"

"Yeah, and the main reason he's going to do it is to get acquainted with those people in case the day comes he needs to sell one of them a house," Ed said with a chuckle. "He sure isn't doing it to kill time. He doesn't have enough of that as it is."

"See? Rick's doing it to help provide for your future. What's wrong with me earning enough money so we have a stash put back in case Bobby and Lesley want to go to college someday?"

"I don't know." Ed leaned against a tree and shuffled his feet through a pile of acorn caps. "You'd think Todd had been around you and Mom long enough to know how headstrong you both are. Do you think he'll give in, or is it going to be a big deal? And speaking of Mom, what does she say?"

Laurie laughed again. "Believe it or not, she's on my side. You know she quit her job at Patterson's when she got pregnant with you because that's what women were expected to do back then. She told me she's always regretted it and that I'm a fool if I let Todd get his way on this one."

Ed laughed with her. "So what's going to happen?"

"Oh, we'll work it out, one way or another. If he absolutely refuses to give in, I'll stay on part-time. You know: compromise."

She gave Ed a level look. "That's what we married folks have to do: compromise. A lot. You figured that one out yet?"

Ed thought about agreeing with Rick to move into the carriage house and supporting Rick's decision to go ahead with his real estate classes. He had secretly felt he'd been giving in, but perhaps it actually had been compromising. "Yeah, I think compromise has become an important word in my vocabulary."

"That's good to know. I'm not about to give up on my marriage because of something like this, and I know you wouldn't either. Too many people do that—bail at the first argument. Fortunately Mom and Dad set a good example for us. Dad always said something worth having was worth fighting for, and even though I wouldn't mind shoving Todd into one of those smelly pigpens right now, I'm not about to give up on him."

Ed noticed Rick and Todd looking their way. He gestured for Laurie to head back.

"Well, keep me posted, okay?"

"I will. Shoot, if I lose my temper and bash Todd with the iron, I'll call you to post bail for me."

Ed laughed and changed the subject to *Escape from New York*. "It's a little too intense for the kids, but Gordy and I sure enjoyed it."

"The only movie my men have allowed me to see all summer is *Raiders*. I didn't know anything else was playing. Besides," she said, giving him a poke as they approached the table, "after all those dumb horror movies you've made me sit through over the years, I'm not too sure I'd go see any movie you recommend."

Rick looked up from his conversation with Todd. "I heard that," he said empathetically. "Thank God he's got Gordy for those now. I had been dreading Halloween all year, thinking I would have to spend it watching Jamie Lee Curtis get terrorized again by a guy with a big knife."

"Humph." Ed sulked as he sat down to finish his cake. "You guys just don't know how to have fun."

*Compromise,* he thought, smiling to himself. He knew Rick hated the slasher movies he enjoyed, but he also knew Rick would sit through them if Gordy wasn't around to share the movies with Ed. There were, he thought, all kinds of compromise in a marriage.

Once everyone had devoured their cake, they split up, the Ameses on their way to the arena to cheer on one of Todd's cousins in the Miss Stratton County contest, and Jane clamoring for a ride on the merry-go-round.

"Rick, why don't you take her over to the kiddie rides," Ed said, looking thoughtfully at Josh. "I want to show Josh something. We'll meet you there in a little bit."

Ed led Josh through the 4-H exhibit buildings. "You can join 4-H when you're ten," he told him. "Do you think you'd like to do stuff like this?"

"I thought you had to live on a farm to be in 4-H," Josh said, admiring the electrical projects that had fascinated Ed as a boy.

"Nope," Ed said. "Lots of this stuff is stuff town kids can do. If you think you want to join next year, I'll stop by the extension office and find out about town clubs, okay?"

Josh nodded. "Okay. I'll think about it." Ed was relieved, thinking a 4-H club would be a great way for Josh to make some additional friends.

They rejoined Rick and Jane, and after Ed and Josh had spun themselves dizzy on the Tilt-A-Whirl, the Scrambler, and the Octopus, they were ready to call it a night.

Ed told Rick his idea about Josh and 4-H once they were alone in the car. Rick smiled at Ed, shaking his head. "Baby, I think you're about the best thing to happen to that kid, after me. Growing up in the city, I would have never thought of that."

Ed was pleased. "Well, when he told me he didn't care much about sports, I kept thinking he needed something else to do when the other boys get caught up in basketball and stuff. He doesn't seem to be very musical, so I thought 4-H might be a great way for him to explore different things."

Rick sighed, taking his hand. "Baby, you're about the best pretend dad any kid ever had. I hope Laurie's kids know how lucky they are to have you for an uncle."

Ed shrugged. "Well, considering how miserable you and I were when we were kids, the least I can do is try to help them enjoy being kids more than we did."

"Yeah, I know what you mean. I think that's one of the reasons I agreed to move here in the first place. I wanted the kids to have a good life even if their dad was gone."

"Still," Rick said as he pulled into their driveway, "I'd much rather spend time with Claire's kids, or Laurie's, than have any of our own. I know I thought about that when we were dating, but now that we're actually living together, building a life and all that, I can't imagine having to raise a kid as well."

Ed agreed. As always, when he thought of his life before Rick, he realized he had taken on a lot of responsibility along with Rick's love. He had promised to love Rick for better or worse, but the idea of adding a kid to that equation almost made him dizzy again.

He enjoyed the nieces and nephews, but he was always relieved when it was time to deposit them where they belonged once the fun was done. Pretend dad or not, he wasn't at all sure he was cut out for fatherhood.

Loving another man may have given him a pass on the responsibility of parenting, but he felt he more than made up for it with the worry he had about people's opinions of his marriage.

"I guess everything in life is a trade-off," he mused aloud as Rick pulled into the garage.

"Hmmm?"

"Oh, you know. The straights have to worry about raising kids, but we have to worry about what people think of us."

"And," Rick said with a leer, reaching across the car to provocatively rub Ed's crotch, "they have to worry about birth control, and we don't."

"Sounds like you've got plans for the rest of the evening," Ed said as he slipped his own hand into Rick's private zone.

"Baby, I have every intention of taking you for a ride, and I promise it'll be a hell of a lot better than the Octopus!"

Ed thought back to his discussion with Rick that past Sunday morning as they climbed the stairs to their home. Oh, maybe the romance between them had cooled a little bit, but the passion hadn't completely died. Ed could only imagine what would happen to that passion if they were taking turns dealing with a screaming baby.

*Even with the compromises and the trade-offs, we have an okay life,* he thought, remembering that wish he'd made on Lake Erie. It wasn't perfect, but it wasn't rotten either.

*And maybe that's the lesson,* he continued to think. *Maybe a lot of folks aren't willing to settle for that big, boring place between perfect and rotten.*

*I'm sure glad I did,* he told himself as Rick took his hand and led him to the bedroom.

❖

Ed went about his handyman appointments in a peaceful mood the next day. He spent the morning at Mary Tucker's house doing as much preventative maintenance as possible, hoping it might slow the stream of emergency calls he was receiving from her. She followed him around the house, wringing her hands, repeatedly telling him how Harold had taken care of all this stuff and she really should learn how to do it herself. Ed nodded complacently and agreed over and over, fully realizing she was too busy talking to pay the slightest bit of attention to anything he was doing.

After lunch he walked over to Oak Street to take care of some chores for the Rinkenbergers. He planted a tulip tree sapling in the front yard while Chauncey Rinkenberger leaned on his cane and told Ed repeatedly that he just didn't have the strength to handle a shovel these days. Mr. Rinkenberger stood to one side of the hole Ed had dug and instructed Ed as to exactly how the tree should be settled into the ground. Ed, who'd planted a few trees in his day, nodded agreeably and followed directions while old Chauncey told him several times how the tulip was the Indiana state tree, and what a pitiful shame it was that there were so few of them in Porterfield.

Ed managed to escape indoors to haul bags of water-softener salt to the basement before Mr. Rinkenberger thought of any other lawn and garden chores for him to do. He happily cleared away snow in the winter for his older clients but had long ago learned to say no to any regular landscaping work. He had mowed lawns every summer as an adolescent and had no desire to do so now.

He was about to slip out the back door when Bernita Rinkenberger caught him and insisted he stay long enough for a piece of her rhubarb pie. For an elderly lady, she had an amazing amount of determination when it came to sharing her usually lackluster baking, and she managed to shove him into a kitchen chair before he could beg off. Ed was no big fan of rhubarb, but he managed to get a piece of it down with a glass of milk while Bernita told him there simply wasn't any decent rhubarb to be found anywhere in Porterfield, and how she had to have her sister-in-law bring it to her from her home in central Indiana.

He finished his day farther down Oak Street at Mrs. Ilinski's house. His tranquil mood still not shattered by client demands and nattering, he didn't even bother to argue when she begged him to mow her yard.

"The boy that's been doing it all summer is away at church camp," she fretted, staring at her yard, which was covered in buckhorn. "The grass isn't growing so much, but those weeds are awful."

Ed agreed. He thought the yard needed an herbicide more than a cutting, but in his calm state of mind, he merely went to the garage to haul out her old Toro without bothering to go into the usual speech about his no-lawn-chores policy.

So Ed walked back to his house late that afternoon a bit grass stained but feeling as though he had indeed spent the day as the caring, helpful, respected Porterfield citizen both Mrs. Penfield and Eunice Ames claimed he was.

As he ambled into the driveway, pausing to see whether the impatiens needing watering again, he saw Effie Maude come out of the main house, heading his way. He met her halfway on the garden walk.

"Ed, can you keep an eye on Mrs. P. tonight?" she asked anxiously. "Her 'ritis is givin' her fits today. I called Doc Weisberg, and he came over and gave her a shot, but her knees are plaguing her something awful."

"Well, sure. I can check on her. Is there anything special I should do for her?"

"No. I've got her all set up downstairs, like always when it gets bad. I've got supper goin', and there's enough for you boys if you want to eat in the house. I just want to make sure she's not alone if she needs anything. She says she's just fine, but I know better."

Ed noted the worried look on Effie Maude's face and at last his peaceful mood fell apart. "Why is she feeling so crummy all of a sudden?"

Effie Maude sighed, a concerned frown cutting deeper into her already wrinkled face. "Oh, it just happens from time to time. The 'ritis flares up for some reason. Always seems to catch her by surprise, even though she should be used to it by now. It makes her blue and tired, ya know, dealin' with the pain and all. Older she gets, the less strength she seems to have to fight it."

She laid a gentle hand on Ed's arm. "She manages to hide it from most folks, 'cept me, but since you're livin' here now, you're gonna see it more."

*It's all part of the bargain Rick and I made*, Ed thought, taking a deep breath and letting it out.

"Okay. Don't worry about it," he said, slipping an arm around Effie Maude's sizable shoulders and guiding her toward the back door. "Rick's got his class tonight, so I'll spend the evening over here, and I'll even crash in the parlor if I have to."

Effie Maude was shaking her head. "I'm so glad she talked you boys into movin' in here. Takes such a load offa my mind. I'm wonderin', though, if I should still go to my niece's weddin' in Ohio this weekend."

"Yes," Ed said sternly. "You've been looking forward to seeing your family. Mrs. Penfield would have a fit if she knew you canceled the trip. Rick and I can keep an eye on her for the next few days."

Effie Maude looked a little dubious. "Well, if you say so. I know she's a-hurtin' bad with this, but she just won't admit it. Sometimes the pain medicine just don't cut it when she gets this way. If it gets worse, you can call Doc Weisberg, and he'll send a nurse over to watch her. I don't know. Maybe I shouldn't go."

"Effie, you can't do everything. We don't know how long Mrs. Penfield is going to be dealing with this. That's one of the reasons Rick and I are here. You have to keep up with your life, too, you know." He sighed. "There may come a day when we really do need you here, no matter what. For now, I think you should go ahead with your plans."

Effie Maude managed a grim smile. "You're a good man, Ed, both you and Rick. I'll probably worry the whole blame time, but I guess I'll go. I'll leave ya a phone number, just in case."

Ed hurried off to the carriage house to change his clothes and leave a note for Rick. He went back to the main house to get any other necessary instructions before Effie Maude left for the day. She showed him the meal she had prepared, finger to her lips. "She finally dropped off to sleep, so I don't wanna wake her. Just make sure she eats something when she wakes up, you hear?"

Ed promised. Effie Maude reluctantly left the house, driving away slowly in her ancient pickup truck. Ed looked in on Mrs. Penfield, who was asleep in the study. She always stayed in that room when the arthritis was too bad for her to climb the stairs to her room.

Rick appeared shortly thereafter. They had a quiet supper in the kitchen, talking in low voices about Mrs. Penfield and making a schedule to make sure one or the other would be on the property throughout the next few days.

"I'll come home right after work tomorrow, so you can get in a few hours on that paint job for the Rhodeses," Rick said, frowning. "They won't mind if you split it up over a couple of days, will they?"

"I don't think so. It's not much, and I can probably finish it on Saturday afternoon, after you get off work. They're pretty easygoing."

"I knew this would happen sooner or later," Rick said with a sigh. "I was just hoping for later. Do you think—"

"No," Ed said firmly. "She probably was overdoing it, is my guess. Don't start thinking the worst. I'm sure she'll be better in a few days."

Rick still looked pensive, but Ed, more worried than he would let on, didn't bother to further reassure him. When it was time for Rick to drive to Fort Wayne, Ed all but pushed him out the door, telling him over and over again that he would be fine alone with Mrs. Penfield.

"Can you imagine what she'd say if you skipped one of those classes?" Ed asked him. "Why, despite the pain, she'd get out of bed and deck you."

Rick finally left, driving down Spruce Street almost as slowly as Effie Maude had. Once Ed was sure he was out of sight, he returned to the house. He walked the first-floor rooms, avoiding the study. He still wasn't used to the idea of the house belonging to them someday, and he wasn't about to believe it would be anytime soon, but he found himself studying the faded wallpaper, the cracks in the walls, and the worn carpet on the stairs, unable to stop himself from planning long-term renovation.

He had always loved the old house, and his feelings for it were growing stronger over time, but the price to pay for owning it—Mrs. Penfield's death—seemed too high to pay. He almost wished she had changed her will but not bothered to tell them about it. They'd still be in his little house on Coleman Street, planning for a future still unknown and exciting. On nights such as this, he felt like a vulture, waiting for the inevitable.

Mrs. Penfield awoke not long after Rick had left. Ed brought her some food, and much to his relief she ate some of it. The pain medication had taken hold, she said, but she looked pale and uncomfortable to him.

"I think I'll go raid the linen closet for some sheets," Ed told her. "I'm going to make up that big sofa in the front parlor and stay there tonight."

"Oh, Ed, that isn't necessary," Mrs. Penfield scolded. "Many is the night I've managed on my own here, and the carriage house is just a phone call away," she said, indicating the phone on her bedside table. "I'd feel foolish and overprotected, and you'd certainly get a better night's sleep in your own bed."

Ed argued a bit longer, but she convinced him to return to the carriage house at bedtime. "It's comfort enough to know how close the two of you are."

"Okay," Ed sighed. "If you're sure."

"I'm very sure. Ed, I'm extremely relieved you and Rick accepted my offer of the carriage-house apartment. It has taken a great burden from my mind in many ways. However, there simply is no reason for you to alter your lives any more than you already have."

"Well," Ed said, trying to be cheerful, "it's not like you're going anywhere anytime soon."

Mrs. Penfield's usual spry countenance crumbled. "No, I don't suppose

I'll be leaving this earth anytime soon," she said quietly. "I will be honest with you, though, Ed. Sometimes the constant battle against my foe makes me very weak. There are times when the thought of everlasting peace, and an everlasting break from the pain, sounds very blessed indeed."

Despite the warm July night, Ed felt a chill. It was the first time Mrs. Penfield had ever said such a thing to him. He simply couldn't imagine a pain so intense and constant that death would seem a blessing.

Ed also couldn't help but wonder, with him and Rick living on the property, whether Mrs. Penfield was now willing to let her foe win the battle once and for all.

# Chapter Fourteen

Mrs. Penfield continued to languish. Ed and Rick took turns staying with her through Friday. On Saturday morning, well after Rick had left for work, Ed checked on her and found her a bit stronger but unwilling to eat much of the breakfast he had prepared. With his limited cooking skills, he wasn't at all sure what to prepare for an ailing old woman, so he bit the bullet and decided to call in the reserves. He telephoned his mother and asked for help.

Norma, of course, was glad of an excuse to cook for someone, but she wasn't about to let Ed know that. She appeared midafternoon with a bag of groceries, grumbling as usual.

"I knew I'd get roped into helping with that old woman eventually."

Ed refused to rise to the bait. "Thanks, Mom. You're the best. If anyone can get her to eat a good meal, it's you."

Norma acknowledged that with a matter-of-fact nod. She waved away the money Ed offered. "It wasn't that much. Don't worry about it. I'll think of something you can do for me in return."

Ed had no doubt of that. He left Norma banging pots and pans in the big kitchen to check once again on Mrs. Penfield. He was pleased to find her awake and behaving more like her usual self than she had in days.

"I should be angry with you, Ed, for calling your mother to cook for me," Mrs. Penfield said with a bright smile. "I must admit, however, I'm looking forward to whatever she prepares. You've told me enough about her kitchen talents over the years to know it should be wonderful."

"You seem to be feeling better."

Her smiled broadened. "Yes, I am. I do believe the worst is past. My goal now is to join you all for that meal in the dining room."

Ed, relieved, returned to the kitchen. He had heard Rick come through the back door. "Your turn to go to work," Rick greeted him.

Ed grinned at Rick, who was chugging his way through a glass of water.

"She's feeling a lot better. I think we can actually relax for awhile."

"That figures," Norma snorted, pulling a chicken apart. "I come to the rescue, and now she's better. If I didn't already have this started, I'd just go home."

Ed and Rick smirked at each other behind her back. "Oh, Mom, I think the reason she feels better is 'cause she's looking forward to your cooking. You're not going anywhere."

"Humph!"

"Look at it this way, Norma," Rick teased. "You're saving your son from a takeout meal from the P & J. I've been too busy to buy groceries or cook anything, so that's probably what he would have gotten tonight."

"So what else is new?" said Norma, hands on hips. "Ed's practically lived at that place every summer since he's had his driver's license. Honestly, you can smell the grease at my house. I'd hate to know your cholesterol count, Ed Stephens. Yours, too, Rick. He's probably got you addicted to that trash, too."

"It does come in handy sometimes," Rick admitted, scratching a mosquito bite on his leg. "Still, I try to keep him away from it as much as possible. I promise."

"Geez," Ed mumbled. "If you two are finished discussing my diet, I have some painting to do."

"Oh, get out of here," Norma said, hacking away at the chicken. "Just make sure you're home by six. If you're not, we're eating without you."

"Need any help, Norma?" Rick asked, peering into her grocery bag.

"No. You get out of here, too. I don't want you underfoot. Go put some lotion on those mosquito bites. I don't want you scratching at the dinner table."

With a grin, Rick followed Ed to the back door. "In that case, I'll go medicate my bites and change my clothes. Give me a holler across the backyard if you need me."

"You can count on that," Norma muttered, throwing chicken parts into a stew pot.

Ed finished his painting job at the Rhodes house and was home by six. He was pleased to see Rick helping Mrs. Penfield to the dining room table, determinedly sending his dark thoughts of Thursday night to the back of his mind.

They all sat down and began to eat Norma's excellent chicken stew, showering her with compliments. She responded graciously, and Ed could see, despite her thoughts on their living arrangements, that she had enjoyed cooking in the main house's kitchen, and how secretly impressed she was with the house in general. Ed was sure the farm girl who had grown up poor during the Depression had often imagined herself in such a grand place. Perhaps he came by his own dreams of such a home honestly.

"I am feeling so much better," Mrs. Penfield said, "I believe I shall attempt to attend church in the morning. Could I talk one of you gentlemen into acting as my chauffeur?"

"I'll do it," Ed offered. "Rick probably wants to study all day."

"How are the classes going, Rick?"

"Not bad," Rick said, helping himself to more stew. "Oh, it was a little confusing at first, but I'm getting the hang of it." He shook his head. "I wonder if every state has the same regulations as Indiana. You wouldn't think buying and selling property would be such a big deal."

"You just make sure you learn how to do it properly," Norma said sharply. "The last thing you need is to get carted off to jail for real estate fraud."

Ed snickered. "That's my mom, always looking on the bright side."

"You have my word of honor, Norma," Rick teased. "I promise to bring no additional scandal to the Stephens family. I've done enough damage already."

"Oh, we've survived it," she mumbled. "I had the pleasure of cutting that Dorsey woman dead on Commerce Street the other day. How dare a cheap woman like that criticize a hardworking member of my family."

"I believe, Norma, despite their concerns, our boys here will find Ruth Dorsey to be the minority in Porterfield," Mrs. Penfield said gently. "There has always been a practical live-and-let-live attitude in this town. Although I've never been fond of her, I'm inclined to agree with Eunice Ames. I believe Ed and Rick's contributions to the community far outweigh any apprehension over their personal relationship."

"Eunice Ames," Norma snorted. "I never thought I'd live to see the day she would defend a Stephens."

"Oh, Mom, isn't it about time you buried the hatchet with her?" Ed asked wearily.

"She started it," Norma sniffed. "From the day she implied your father and I could have provided a nicer wedding for your sister and Todd, I've been dodging her catty remarks. Her nerve is as big as her bank account."

"Well, she's done all right by me," Ed stated flatly. "I'm officially retiring from the feud. The next time you two get into a hair-pulling fight, you can find another referee."

"You'd think your first loyalty would be to your mother," Norma said, offended.

"You see what I've put up with for almost twenty-nine years?" Ed asked Mrs. Penfield. "I can't win!"

Mrs. Penfield chuckled. "Norma, I honestly believe the last thing you need question is Ed's loyalty to you. There were many times over the years I called him for help, and he told me he would see to my problem *after* he had completed his work for you."

"I'd like to think he knows what side his bread is buttered on," Norma said, looking suspiciously at her son.

"I certainly do," Rick jumped in. "And as long as it's your bread, Norma, you have my loyalty, my heart, and my taste buds. If Mrs. Ames makes even the slightest remark about you while I'm working on her home tour committee, I'll happily tell her to go to hell for you."

"Traitor," Ed fired at him.

"I'm no traitor, and I'm no fool," Rick said to the table at large. "I'm not about to stop the flow of chocolate chip cookies from Norma's house to ours."

"My son-in-law, the charmer," Norma sneered, although everyone could see she was pleased. "Think you can pull an Eddie Haskell on me? Just for that, you can do the dishes, Rick Benton!"

"My pleasure," Rick said, laughing.

"Mom likes you best," Ed said to Rick, invoking an old Smothers Brothers routine.

"You're both full of prunes," Norma grumbled, passing her biscuits again. "Eat up, eat up! There's plenty, and I'm not taking it home."

❧•❧

The next morning, Ed drove Mrs. Penfield to the Presbyterian Church she had attended for years. He helped her out of Rick's car and saw her safely up a short flight of steps, knowing someone else would come to her aid inside.

"Would you care to stay for the service, Ed?" she teased.

Ed looked at his old T-shirt and shorts. "Well, I'm certainly not dressed for it."

"Perhaps not, but I've had the feeling you might be in need of some prayer and meditation yourself these days."

Ed shrugged. "I'll go home and sit in the garden until it's time to pick you up. I can't think of a better place for prayer and meditation."

"You do that," she said gently. "Please don't worry. I know you have a tendency to do so, and I want to assure you, it's not necessary. I know things have moved quickly for you these past months, and I know I gave you a bit of a scare these past few days, but I'm feeling much better. These spells occasionally get the best of me. I do my best to retain a brave face for the world, but since you're now living on the property, I simply am unable to hide it from you and Rick. However, as you have seen for yourself, I manage to rally after a day or so. I'm afraid you'll have to contend with this old woman for quite some time yet."

Ed grinned at her. "Believe me, that's no problem."

He drove home slowly, enjoying the warm sunshine and the sleepy, quiet feeling of Porterfield on a Sunday morning. After another hearty Sunday breakfast prepared by Rick, he settled in the rose arbor, library book in hand. It lay closed in his lap, however, as he repeated Mrs. Penfield's words to himself.

"She's right," he whispered. "I just need to let my brain catch up to everything that's happened this summer."

He was slumped on the bench, eyes closed, content to enjoy the Sunday quiet, when Rick hollered at him out the living room window.

"Phone call! Don't panic; it's not work. It's Laurie."

Ed hurried into the carriage house, hoping for good news regarding her ongoing battle with Todd. "I thought you'd want to know," Laurie said in a low voice, "that a détente has been reached in the Full-Time Work War."

"Well, I'm relieved to here that. What happened?"

"God works in mysterious ways." She giggled softly. "The transmission completely crapped out in my Oldsmobile. Todd decided it would be cheaper in the long run to get another car instead of repairing this one. With as much tact as possible, I let him know the only way we could afford it was if I worked full-time this fall. He grumbled for a while but he finally agreed that it might be a good idea. 'We'll try it for six months and see how it goes,' he told me, like a king granting a favor. Oh, well. I got my way and he still thinks he's the head of the house, so it worked out. It does, however, bring up another issue."

"What's that?"

"Well, now that I finally made it to the Promised Land, you know, both kids out of diapers and in school full-time, I've decided my next project is to talk Todd into getting himself snipped."

"Huh?"

"A vasectomy, brother dear, something you don't need to worry about."

"Geez," Ed muttered, feeling a sympathy pain in his groin. "That might take some doing."

"Yeah, I'm sure it will, but we agreed on just two kids, and accidents happen, usually when you really think you're done and you're ready to put the baby clothes in a garage sale. I'll just have to work my womanly wiles on him. I've still got 'em, somewhere."

Ed groaned. "Good luck, Shortshit. You're gonna need it!"

She giggled again. "Oh, well, for the time being, at least, I can go to my class reunion next month, look at all my pregnant classmates, and know I have something to look forward to other than toilet training."

"Class reunion? Yuck," said Ed, who'd found his ten-year reunion the summer before to be an uncomfortable bore. "Have fun."

"I will. The class of seventy-one *was* more fun than yours," Laurie teased. "I'd better get off the phone, though, before Todd gets suspicious. Thanks for listening the other day, and I'll talk to you later, okay?"

"Sure thing," Ed promised, hanging up. He shook his head with a smile, happy for Laurie and pleased to think all the latest crises were solved for the moment.

"What was that all about?" Rick asked from the kitchen table.

"Oh, just a brother-sister discussion," Ed told him. "Nothing you need to worry about."

He glanced at Jett, who was performing his usual morning wash in his favorite chair. "I just remembered, though, that we haven't done anything about the c-a-t," he spelled, not wanting to attract Jett's attention.

"*That's* what you were talking about with Laurie?" Rick looked confused.

Ed laughed, feeling the weight of the past few days slide off his shoulders. "Kinda. Just be glad we can't reproduce, darlin'."

Rick gave him a puzzled look, then shrugged. "Whatever. Anyway, I'm glad you had an excuse to come inside. I see in the paper that the original 1939 *Goodbye, Mr. Chips* is on television this afternoon. I think I'm going to shove these books aside and watch it. Want to join me?"

"Sure," Ed replied, happy at the thought of sharing an afternoon and a movie with Rick.

"It's my turn to warn you," Rick said that afternoon, turning on the television. "I may cry over the end of this one." He laughed. "You bring it out in me. Not that I'm complaining."

"We're just a couple of sappy queers," Ed said, pulling Rick onto the sofa. "I don't know if I've seen this all the way through or not, so get the Kleenex handy."

Sure enough, they were both misty-eyed at the film's conclusion. "What a wonderful movie," Ed sighed. "Boy, they don't make 'em like that anymore, do they?"

"Nope. It's a shame, too. Oh, I love the movies nowadays, but nothing beats those old MGM and Warner Brothers classics. The book is great, too."

Ed smirked at him. "Okay. Get it for me the next time you're at the library."

"You sure?" Rick teased. "I don't want to be accused of controlling your reading again."

"No, I'd like to read it. If it's half as good as the movie, I'm sure I'll like it."

"I think you will," Rick said with a kiss. "Isn't this nice? Almost like our old Sundays together."

"Yeah. The weekend turned out pretty good after all, didn't it?"

Ed stretched and yawned. "This summer's been like those roller coasters we rode at Cedar Point. Up and down, up and down. . . . Geez." He shook his head.

"Yeah, things have kind of been at sixes and sevens."

"Huh?"

"Oh, it's something my grandmother used to say. I'm not sure exactly what she meant, but I always thought it meant being caught off guard by good and bad stuff happening together, or one right after the other."

"Well, that's been this summer all right. Some good, some bad . . ."

"In other words," Rick said with his warm and tender special in place, "it's real life. That's what this summer has been, which reminds of me of my grandfather, who used to say you have to roll with the punches."

Ed sighed contentedly and pulled Jett into his lap. "Yep, we've been doing that, haven't we? Rolling with the punches. Except for you," he told the cat, who purred and kneaded Ed's belly. "You've had it pretty easy with both of us, *and* Effie Maude, to spoil you rotten. Speaking of Effie Maude, since she'll be back tomorrow to keep an eye on Mrs. Penfield, I can go paint those ugly shutters the Hausers bought with a clear conscience."

"Still," Rick said with a frown, "I think something is missing from this weekend."

Ed looked around the room. "Huh?"

Rick slid his hand under Ed's T-shirt. "How quickly they forget! Before I'm even tempted to look at that textbook again, I'd like to go lie down with my husband."

"Oh. That! Well," Ed considered, "I guess I could be talked into that."

"I can assure you," Rick said, nuzzling Ed's neck, "I can be very persuasive."

"Oh, I know, darlin', I know. You've persuaded me into all kinds of stuff."

"Any regrets, baby?"

Ed looked at Rick, noticing his warm and tender special had changed into a smile of pure lust and seduction. *I don't think this marriage needs any extra spice yet*, he thought, sliding a hand under the waistband of Rick's shorts, and also thinking that compromise and occasionally giving in wasn't so bad if afternoons like this one were part of the bargain.

"No, darlin'. No regrets. None at all."

⋘•⋙

Ed drove to the Hauser house the next day in a better-than-average

Monday mood. He was a bit dubious over their decision to add shutters to the front of their house, and more than a little skeptical about the color of paint they had chosen, but he cheerfully painted away, glad to have the first coat done by day's end.

Tuesday morning he headed to Mrs. Heston's house as he always did. As he drove to East Clark Street, he went over his jobs for the week, hoping to have the shutters finished soon enough to have a day to himself. He was anxious to get more work done on his workshop, which had been neglected during the hot, busy July days.

He stuck his nose in Mrs. Heston's kitchen door, expecting her to be waiting for him, grocery list in hand. The kitchen was empty. Frowning, Ed pulled the door open. "Mrs. Heston?"

There was no answer. Ed uneasily entered the house. Never, in the six years he'd been helping her, had she failed to be ready for their weekly trip to the store. He called again from the kitchen, and again there was no answer. He walked through the dining room to the living room. There was nothing unusual to be seen, except for the absence of Mrs. Heston.

A terrible thought grew in his mind. He slowly walked to her bedroom, cautiously peering around the half-open door. He gasped, grabbing the door for support.

"Aw, crud." His head went down, eyes closed, as he tried desperately to convince himself that what he saw simply couldn't be.

"Oh, Mrs. Heston," he sighed, sadly shaking his head.

⁂

After both a Porterfield police officer and County Coroner Stuart Reimer had questioned Ed, he was allowed to leave Mrs. Heston's house. He went immediately home, unable to think of painting for the rest of the day. He collapsed on the sofa, dry-eyed but shaken. Jett, sensing something, jumped into his lap. Ed petted the cat, grateful for his company.

Ed was no stranger to death. As a boy, he'd learned his way around the Reimer and Bayless Funeral Home during the four funerals for his grandparents. He vividly remembered the June morning, three years earlier, when his mother's telephone call had awakened him with the news of his father's sudden passing.

Mrs. Heston, of course, was not a family member, but she might as well have been. Ed thought of how she had become his first regular client when he had decided against returning to his factory job. Her enthusiasm and help in obtaining other clients for him had enabled him to ditch any regrets about his decision to become a handyman, and he had thanked her repeatedly over the past six years.

Ed sighed, stroking the cat. Oh, he had always been grateful for that, but only this summer she had given him another reason to be grateful, when she had immediately accepted his marriage to Rick, no questions asked.

Ed reviewed the past six years and the clients who had preceded Mrs. Heston in death. Ed dealt almost exclusively with the elderly, and he was used to the idea of losing a customer in this way, but somehow he'd never pictured Mrs. Heston as one of them. True, she had a multitude of health problems, and her walker had been all but permanently attached to her, but her feisty, salty personality seemed somehow able to outwit death.

"What in the hell am I going to do on Tuesday mornings?" he asked Jett. Jett purred in response, and Ed hugged him, wishing Rick was home.

The grapevine of Ed's old-lady brigade was active. As he spent the afternoon on the sofa, both Mrs. West and Mrs. Tucker called, offering condolences and canceling appointments for the week. Ed spoke to both of them quietly, assuring them he'd see to their chores after funeral arrangements had been made. He couldn't help but wonder whether the death of someone their age brought on thoughts of their own.

Rick walked in the door shortly after three, obviously surprised to see Ed at home. He looked from the stereo, softly playing the Youngbloods' "Get Together," to Ed, sprawled on the sofa.

"What's wrong?" he asked, concern showing on his face.

"Mrs. Heston died. I found her this morning when I went over to her house."

"Oh, baby!" Rick sat on the sofa, taking Ed in his arms. "Oh, baby, I'm so sorry," he said, holding him close. "What happened?"

"She just died in her sleep. Her heart gave out."

Ed snuggled deeper into Rick's arms, grateful for his presence. "Why wasn't I expecting it? With everything she had wrong with her, why didn't I think it might happen at any time?"

"She was a lively old broad, that's why," Rick murmured, stroking his hair. "You had no reason to think about it. I'm just so sorry you had to be the one to, you know . . ."

"Yeah. I've never had to go through that before. I'll tell you, I can go the rest of my life without being questioned by a coroner again."

Ed buried his head in Rick's neck. "I'm so glad you're here."

"Me too, baby," Rick said softly.

The phone rang. With a sigh, Rick let go of Ed to answer it. "Hello? Oh, hi. Yeah, he's here. Just a minute."

Rick handed the receiver to Ed. "It's Doug Morgan," he whispered.

"Hi, Doug," Ed said, as Rick put his arm around again him.

"Hi, Ed. There's nothing wrong at the house. I'm calling in a professional capacity. I'm with the family of Agnes Heston, and they've requested your services as a pallbearer. Would you be willing?"

"Oh." Ed was surprised. "Well, sure. I can do that."

"I know it would mean a lot to them," Doug said respectfully. "Apparently she was very fond of you. I'm sure they'll be honored that you've accepted."

Ed almost cracked his first smile of the day, amused at the difference between the Doug he knew informally and the professional funeral director.

"Calling will be Thursday afternoon and evening, and the service will be here at the funeral home, Friday morning at ten thirty," Doug continued. "If you have any questions, you give me a call."

"I'll do that, and unfortunately, I'll see you later in the week." Ed handed the receiver to Rick, who replaced it on the phone. "They want me to be a pallbearer," Ed told him.

"I think that's nice," Rick said, hugging him. "It shows how much her family thought of you. Do you want me to take off work and go to the funeral with you? When is it?"

"Friday morning, and no, you don't have to do that. You didn't really know her." Ed sighed. "I think I'd just as soon go by myself."

"Well, you let me know if you change your mind, okay?" Rick kissed him gently.

"Okay. Thanks, darlin'."

"Don't you get any ideas about dying on me anytime soon, you hear? I couldn't live without you."

"I won't if you won't." Ed returned Rick's kiss, so grateful for this living, breathing man who loved him.

⊰·●·⊱

Norma showed up the next morning, bearing a freshly baked, foil-wrapped meatloaf. "I thought this might come in handy, considering," she said, shoving it in the refrigerator.

Ed, dressed in his painting clothes, found himself smiling. "Mom, you take food to the family of the deceased, not the handyman."

"As far as I'm concerned, that woman was your family. Why, if wasn't for her, you'd still be at that factory, probably hating it even more than you did back then."

Norma slammed the refrigerator door. "She was a nice lady, and I'm just as sad as anyone to see her go."

"Thanks, Mom. As always, I appreciate it. Do you want to go to the calling with me Thursday night? Rick will be in Fort Wayne for his class."

Norma nodded. "Yes, I'll go with you." She narrowed her eyes at him. "Is

Rick standing by you these days?"

"Oh, Mom," Ed groaned. "Of course he is. He even offered to take off work and go to the funeral with me. I just don't see any reason for him to miss work, or his class, for this. He didn't even know her. And yes, he's been great since he found out what happened. I'm almost mad at you, thinking he would be any other way."

"I'm just checking," Norma said, head in the air. "What about that funeral? You want me to go to that, too?"

"No. They've asked me to be a pallbearer, so I'll probably have to sit up front with the family. Besides, I'd rather go alone," Ed added, hoping she wouldn't ask why.

Norma nodded, sighing. "This time of year and all, I can't help thinking of that awful day three years ago. Let me tell you something, Edward. It doesn't matter how old you are; it never gets easier."

Ed looked at her, knowing how much she still missed his father. "I'm beginning to see that, Mom. I'm also beginning to wonder if anything gets easier."

"I wonder that myself," she grumbled. She looked at him critically. "Where on earth are you going dressed like that?"

"The Hausers. I'm hoping to get their painting finished before the funeral."

"I see. Well, I'll let you go, then. You give me a call Thursday night when you want to go to the funeral home."

"I will. Thanks again, Mom."

Ed followed her down the stairs and out into the bright, late July sunshine. "I'm really beginning to hate summer," he muttered to himself.

⋘•⋙

"Oh, Ed, I'm so glad you've come," Geraldine, Mrs. Heston's eldest daughter, said Thursday evening. "Mother just thought the world of you!"

She gave Ed a warm hug. "I can't tell you how indebted the whole family feels to you, keeping an eye on her all these years."

"I was happy to do it. I liked her a lot." Ed smiled.

"Now, I don't want you to be offended," Geraldine said seriously, "but I insist on paying you for whatever Mother owed you for this month."

Ed help up a hand to protest, but she gently pushed it away. "No, Ed. That's how Mother would want it. When you have her bill ready, you just send it on to me, you hear?"

Ed nodded. "Okay. I guess she'd probably come back and haunt us both, otherwise."

Geraldine managed a chuckle. "Yes. She probably would."

Another family member was signaling for Geraldine's attention, so she left him with one more hug. Ed looked around, unable to avoid the memories of his father's wake right in this very room. He looked for Norma. She was on the other side of the room, busily talking with acquaintances.

He saw Doug enter the room, ushering in newcomers. Doug caught Ed's eye and gave him a secret wink. Ed smiled, relieved to know Doug's sense of humor allowed him to laugh at his own professional demeanor.

Ed gingerly approached the casket, thinking he'd seen quite enough Tuesday morning but feeling that custom demanded it. He was relieved to note that Doug, or someone else at Reimer and Bayless, had done a nice job, and he was comforted to see her looking much more at peace than she had the other day.

The next day, dressed in his one dark suit, Ed did his duty with the other pallbearers. Once the casket was at rest above the freshly dug grave, Ed stepped back behind the family for the minister's final prayer.

This last day of July was warm and breezy, and Ed felt the wind whipping his suit coat. His attention wandered from the minister's remarks as his glance roamed the sprawling Porterfield town cemetery. There was something he had to do before he left, and he hoped he could sneak away without attracting notice.

After the service's conclusion, Ed assured the family he would join them shortly for the funeral dinner at Mrs. Heston's home. As mourners returned to their cars, Ed walked off in the other direction. He'd purposely parked his truck away from Mrs. Heston's grave.

He walked over a hill, past old monuments, around century-old trees, and with a sigh, halted at the site of a graveside service he'd attended three years earlier.

Careful of his good clothes, Ed squatted on his heels, reading the words engraved on the simple granite marker: TIMOTHY J. STEPHENS JANUARY 17, 1928–JUNE 2, 1978.

"Hi, Dad," he said quietly. "It didn't seem right to come out here and not stop by."

The wind ruffled his hair. Two blue jays quarreled in the trees behind him. Ed looked around, but aside from the birds, he was alone.

"I'm sorry I didn't come out last month," he said, rubbing his hand over the grass. "Rick and I were so busy moving, I forgot. I know you don't mind, though. I think you'd be happy about us living at the carriage house. I know that, 'cause Mom thinks it's a bad idea, so naturally you'd be on my side."

Ed grinned, thinking of that. "I never understood how two different people could have such a good marriage, but you and Mom sure did. I hope mine with Rick is just as good. I think we're off to a good start, although it's been a little crazy so far. There's been a lot going on, but I guess you know that.

"I sure wish you could have met Rick. It's funny, how sometimes he reminds me of Mom, but most of the time he reminds me of you. I know you'd like him. It helps a lot, too, knowing you would have understood. Mom told me the two of you had talked about it. I know you'd be glad I found someone as special as him. He loves me so much, Dad. I didn't know anyone could love me as much as he does. I honestly believe he'll be with me until, well, until I end up here.

"I love him, too, Dad. He's a good man, and exactly the guy I hoped I'd meet someday. The way he just showed up, delivering my mail last fall, I've sometimes wondered if you didn't send him to me. That's the kind of thing you would have done. If you did, I want to say thanks. I promise to be as good to him as he is to me."

Ed closed his eyes. "I still really miss you, Dad. There are times I wish I could talk to you. Mom does her best, but you know how she is. There are times I just need to know you're still behind me, like when I decided not to go back to the factory. You knew I wasn't happy with that job, so you told me I could stay with you and Mom until I had my handyman business going well."

Ed, his eyes still closed, laughed. "I still haven't told Mom you gave me the money for the down payment on my truck. I thought sure she'd figure it out after you died, but if she did, she never let on. It's still running, still going strong. It's getting old, and sometimes I worry about it, but maybe you're keeping an eye on it, too.

"Say hi to Mrs. Heston for me, okay? I never felt like I really thanked her enough for all she did for me, especially where Rick is concerned. She never batted an eye when I told her who gave me the ring I'm wearing. Make sure she knows how much that meant to me."

Ed's eyes opened. He stared at the tombstone for a while and sighed. "I guess I should get going. They're expecting me for the funeral dinner. I'll bet they have deviled eggs. Remember how much you loved deviled eggs? I'll have one for you, okay?"

He stood up, brushing the grass from his hands. "Bye, Dad. Thanks for listening. I promise not to wait so long to come again."

Ed walked slowly back to his truck. The mourners were gone, and he could see workers removing the tent over the grave. He turned his head, concentrating on getting his key into the ignition.

The radio came on when he started the engine. "Time," the Alan Parsons Project's hit from that summer, was playing. Ed sat quietly, listening to the words.

*Goodbye my friends, Maybe for forever*
*Goodbye my friends, The stars wait for me*
*Who knows where we shall meet again*
*If ever*
*But time*
*Keeps flowing like a river (on and on)*
*To the sea, to the sea*

Ed gripped the steering wheel, his head down. The tears he'd held in since Tuesday morning were finally able to fall as he mourned both the recent loss of his friend and the still-painful loss of his father.

When the tears ceased, he wiped his face and put the truck in gear. He drove out of the cemetery, toward the people who continued to bless his life today, quietly missing those who'd gone before him.

# Chapter Fifteen

Ed remained understandably subdued over the weekend. Rick watched him closely but said nothing. Ed was glad Rick had the sense to let him be sad without making a big deal about it.

August began that weekend, and Ed was relieved to see July end. Although August was usually as hot as July, Ed enjoyed the high-summer feeling of August, with the myriad insects chirping in the bushes, the gardens in full bloom, and the dusty, hazy air that seemed so much a part of the month.

His mood brightened somewhat by the end of the weekend but came crashing down again come Tuesday morning, the first since Mrs. Heston's funeral. He wandered aimlessly around the carriage-house apartment, feeling lost. He had spent so many Tuesday mornings cruising the aisles of the IGA, he felt out of place anywhere else. Somehow, scheduling other work didn't feel right. At last an idea came to him. He walked downstairs and returned to the project of re-creating his father's workshop. It seemed appropriate, considering his visit with his father the week before.

Rick came home from work that afternoon to find Ed happily hanging tools on the pegboard he'd attached to the back wall of the carriage house.

"Lookin' good," he said, hugging Ed from behind. "How soon do you think you'll be done in here?"

"I'm not sure." Ed thoughtfully surveyed the space. "I'm thinking of putting up a partition between this area and the parking area," he said, pointing. "That would give me another wall and make it feel less like a garage."

"Sounds good," Rick said with a nod.

"You know what else I wish I had, though? I really wish I had a desk down here. It's funny, now that I think about it. I used my kitchen table in the other house for all my handyman business for years, but suddenly I wish I had a desk of my own. It would be a great place to keep all that work stuff, and I'd love to have a place in here where I could sit and draw sketches and plans of the things I want to make."

"Didn't your dad have one?"

"No. Oh, you've seen that little desk in Mom's living room, but that was mostly hers. Dad had an old kitchen table he used in the basement. I could ask Mom for it, but I'd really like to have something of my own."

Rick smiled at him. "One of those old rolltop desks, I'll bet."

Ed grinned back at him. "Yeah. I've always liked them. Wouldn't that look great in here? Well," he conceded, "not great, but it would make it into an office, as well as a workshop. Best of all, if it was a rolltop desk, I could close it to keep the sawdust out."

Rick laughed. "That's my man, always thinking practically. Well, I suppose we could look around for one somewhere."

"Mrs. Heston had a beautiful rolltop desk," Ed said wistfully.

"Hmmm. I wonder—" Rick began.

"No!" Ed was adamant. "I wouldn't think of asking her family about something like that. Besides, I'm sure someone in the family wants it."

Rick shrugged. "Okay, okay. Don't get upset. Listen, we'll just start watching the auction notices, and maybe stop by some of those secondhand furniture stores in Fort Wayne sometime. There's bound to be a nice one out there somewhere."

"Maybe," Ed said doubtfully. "Oh, well. It's not that important. I can certainly get to work in here without it, now that I've got all of Dad's tools and stuff over here. It's really just a matter of finding the time and getting up the nerve to mess up with some wood. I'm really out of practice."

"It'll come back to you," Rick said confidently. "I have a feeling, once you get started on something, your dad will help guide you through it."

"Wouldn't that be nice." Ed sighed. "Still, I'd like to find someone else, someone still with us I could watch for a while, and pick up a few more skills."

"The perfect person will turn up, same as that desk. I predict it," Rick said, grabbing Ed for a kiss. "Oh, you've had some bumpy moments this summer, but I think our luck will hold out. Why, right about the time I'm sitting for that license exam, you'll probably stumble over some . . . some carpenter-type genius who'd love to have you learn from him."

"Geez, that'd be right around my birthday next month," Ed mused. "Wouldn't that be something?"

"Your birthday," Rick said, smiling. "Yeah, that'd be a nice birthday present. Speaking of which, be thinking of what you'd like to have, present-wise, okay?"

"Oh, it's still more than a month and a half away, and I don't want you spending a lot of money on me," Ed scolded, grabbing him around the waist. "It's not that important. As long as I've got you, that's all I really need."

"Yeah, you were definitely my favorite birthday present this year," Rick agreed, warm and tender special in place. "I'd really like to get you something special, though. I can, can't I, if I don't spend a lot of money?"

"Considering all you got from me was a gift certificate to the bookstore, I hope you find something cheap," Ed said with a chuckle.

"Baby, I don't do anything cheap. Inexpensive, maybe, but never cheap." Rick kissed him again. "There is nothing cheap about you, and I promise to make it a nice birthday and stay within our budget."

"You'd better! Now, why don't you let me get back to work? Go change out of that sexy postal uniform before I do something right here, in broad daylight, that we'll both regret."

Ed was still thinking of the workshop at the dinner table that evening. He responded to Rick's comments and questions absentmindedly until he noticed Rick giving him the look he'd been giving him that past weekend. He pulled his mind to the present, not wanting Rick to think he was brooding over Mrs. Heston's death.

"By the way," Rick said, once he knew he had Ed's full attention, "what do you have on your schedule for Friday?"

"Hmm? Well, nothing at the moment. This whole week is actually pretty quiet."

"Good. Why don't you keep it that way?"

"What for?"

Rick grinned mysteriously. "Oh, just a little idea I got from someone at work today. I have the day off, and I think it's time we got away from everything for a day. How do you feel about that?"

"Sure. I'm always up to a day away with you. What did you have in mind?"

"I'm not telling," Rick said, obviously enjoying Ed's puzzlement. "Just think of it as a 'Come Saturday Morning' kind of day on a Friday. And," he added cryptically, "a Magical Mystery Tour as well."

"Oh, c'mon. What are you cookin' up, here?"

"You'll see. Actually, I'm not a hundred percent sure. I have to check on a few things, but for right now just plan on leaving the whole day free for us, okay?"

"Something to look forward to, just like the old days. Okay, darlin', you're on."

Rick left for his Tuesday night class, and Ed washed the dishes, wondering what Rick was planning. He didn't have the slightest idea what someone at the post office could have said to give Rick an idea for a special day for them.

He was so lost in thought, he almost dropped a plate when he glanced at the clock. He was going to be late picking up Josh for their standing Tuesday night bowling date. He dried his hands, leaving a sink full of pots and pans. He was so intent on getting to Claire's house before Josh began to worry, he forgot all about Rick's secret plans.

Rick said no more the next two days, but when he appeared Thursday afternoon with Claire's big thermal cooler, Ed's curiosity was once again aroused.

"What's going on?" he needled Rick. "Where are you taking me tomorrow?"

"No hints, no clues, no nothing," Rick said flatly. "The only thing you have to do is put your portable tape player in my car and wear comfortable clothes. That's all I'm saying."

"Hmm, something outdoors, I'll bet," Ed teased. "I could tickle you, or something worse."

"Do your worst," Rick dared. "You're not getting any information out of me. Just be ready to have a good time."

Ed, knowing Rick was going to a certain amount of trouble to get him excited, was now eagerly anticipating the Magical Mystery Tour. He knew Rick was doing whatever it was he was doing to lift Ed out of the depression that had settled over him since Mrs. Heston's death, and he loved him even more for it.

"I am one lucky guy," he told himself that evening, working on his overdue end-of-the-month billing.

When Ed awoke the next morning, Rick was long gone. Rick had managed to slip out of bed, and out of the house, without waking Ed. He wandered into the kitchen, now thoroughly confused. He saw the thermal picnic cooler on one of the kitchen chairs and was going to open it, but a big sign, in Rick's handwriting said, NO PEEKING!

"All right," Ed said to Jett. "You saw him messing around in here. What's he up to?"

Jett gave Ed a look that said he should know better than to ask. "I should have known," Ed mockingly sneered at him. "You're in on this, too."

He heard Rick's car pull into the driveway as he was finishing breakfast. Rick came bounding up the stairs, demanding that Ed wait in one of the other rooms while he finished filling the cooler. Ed did as he was told, enjoying the mystery more than he was willing to admit.

"What is this anyway, *Mission: Impossible*?" he grumbled, slamming the bathroom door behind him.

"Yeah, and if you don't get a move on in there, you're gonna self-destruct in five seconds," Rick hollered through the closed door. "As soon as I get this in the car, we'll be ready to go."

Ed hurriedly brushed his teeth and shaved. He pulled on a T-shirt, shorts, and his sneakers. He ran downstairs, leaving behind an annoyed Jett, who was regally disturbed by all of Ed's noise.

Ed grabbed his stereo from the almost-finished workshop, along with a few mix tapes. He jumped in the car, where Rick was impatiently tapping his fingers on the steering wheel. "Okay, I am now ready to go. So where are we going?"

Rick gave him a very smug smile. "You'll see. Just sit back and enjoy the ride."

Ed heaved a very put-upon sigh. "I feel like I'm being kidnapped."

"You are. Deal with it, okay?"

"Alllll right," Ed groaned as Rick pulled out of the driveway, heading north.

It was a perfect summer day, warm and sunny, but not humid. Ed felt lighter the moment they left the Porterfield city limits. He turned on the radio, happily singing along to Blondie's "Rapture." Rick joined him, and their awful singing voices soared over Debbie Harry's vocal.

"Man, she wouldn't have to dye her hair blond if she could hear us butchering her song, huh?" Rick laughed.

"Yeah, we'd turn it completely white," Ed shouted, feeling, for some reason, happy enough to fly. It was great to be away from home and work, wonderful to be with the man he loved, and although he hated to admit it, genuinely exciting to *not* know where they were going.

Rick drove steadily north, bypassing Fort Wayne. For a moment Ed wondered if he was going to Spruce Lake in Michigan, where they had proposed to each other the previous spring, but certainly Rick would have taken the interstate highway if that were the case. Ed hummed happily with the music on the radio, from Blondie, to Journey's new one, to an old Fleetwood Mac tune. By this time he was enjoying himself so much he didn't really care about the destination.

Once they were well north and west of Porterfield, Rick slowed the car, looking for a turnoff.

"Aha," Ed said in delight as they entered an Indiana state park. "We're going for a hike and a picnic, right?"

"Wrong," Rick gloated. "Oh, you got the picnic part right, but that's it."

Ed watched with interest as Rick carefully drove through the park. He seemed to be on the lookout for a specific signpost. Ed read the signs as they passed them but still couldn't figure out exactly where Rick was heading.

He was therefore surprised when a lake suddenly appeared, and Rick pulled into a parking lot nearby.

"The Magical Mystery Tour has reached it destination," Rick said grandly, indicating the lake.

Ed looked over the shimmering blue-green water of the lake, confused. "You mean we're going on a boat trip?"

Rick grinned. "You're warm. Look at that dock over there."

Ed looked. A young woman dressed in park-employee clothes seemed to be renting canoes.

"You mean we're going out in a canoe?" Ed asked, his eyes growing large.

"Yep," Rick said, pleased. "Do you know how to paddle a canoe?"

"I think so," Ed said doubtfully. "I mean, my friend Steve had one when we kids. We used to mess around in Stratton Creek with it. Do *you* know how to paddle a canoe?"

"Believe it or not, yes, I do." Rick said smugly. "My dad had a canoe for years, and we used to paddle it down the White River in Indy. It's like riding a bike, baby. You don't forget. This lake is just part of a chain. There's all sorts of other, smaller lakes and connecting channels. We can spend the whole day exploring them. C'mon!"

Ed, a little dubious about his canoe-paddling abilities, helped Rick unload the car. Soon they were both in a rented canoe, along with the cooler, Ed's stereo, and a blanket Rick had hidden in the trunk.

"Have fun," the young woman called, shoving them away from the dock.

"If my tape player falls in this lake, I'm gonna kill you." Ed gingerly stuck his paddle in the water.

"Oh, don't worry," said Rick, steering in the front. "Just watch what I do, and we'll be fine."

Ed found, to his surprise, that Rick was right. It was like riding a bike. The necessary motions came back to him, and within a few minutes they were slowly gliding through the center of the lake.

"I hope they don't allow speedboats," Ed said, noticing no other watercraft on the lake.

"This is a state park, so I kinda doubt it." Rick turned around with a grin. "You okay, baby?"

"Yeah, I am now." Ed relaxed enough to enjoy the sensation of being on the water as he watched the passing scenery. He saw two men fishing from the lake's edge and smiled at the sight of a crane flapping its wings and flying away from a patch of water lilies.

"Darlin', this was a wonderful surprise. Thanks!"

"You like your Magical Mystery Tour?"

"Yes. How did you get this idea, anyway?"

"Well," Rick said, gently guiding the canoe away from the lakeshore, "I overheard a couple of the guys talking about it at work the other day. Seems one of them has a camper, and he and his family come up here a lot throughout the summer. He was telling Don about the canoes, and it hit me I hadn't been on a canoe trip in, oh, I don't know how many years. Not since my dad sold his canoe, anyway. I'd also been thinking that we needed a day off, away from home, so I thought it would be fun, especially since I'd never been here. I hoped you hadn't either, so it would be like we talked about last winter. You know, when we said we'd have Saturdays when we'd go places we'd never been and have fun."

"'Come Saturday Morning.'" Ed sighed with contentment. "Brilliant. I don't care if it's Friday. It feels like Saturday, just like when we were at Cedar Point. I just wish we had the song with us."

Rick turned around again, his warm and tender special glowing. "That has already been taken care of. You'll find out when we stop to eat."

They drifted across the lake, bothering to paddle hard only when the canoe moved too close to the lakeshore or they encountered another canoe. Rick spied a narrow channel ahead, almost hidden by the water lilies.

"Look up there. Wanna paddle that way and see where it takes us?"

"Sure," Ed said, feeling very Lewis and Clark. Oh, they weren't charting the Louisiana Purchase, but he was feeling a good deal more adventurous than usual.

They entered the channel, having a brief moment of panic when Ed's paddle got entangled in some underwater vines. He managed to free it, and they slowly floated through the narrow passage, the thick woods closing in on both sides.

"I almost feel like I'm in a bayou," Ed murmured, Louisiana still on his mind.

"Yeah, aside from the same old maple and oak trees, it's hard to believe we're still in northern Indiana."

They rounded a curve, and Rick spotted a barren patch of ground at the water's edge.

"How 'bout that?" he said, steering the canoe that way. "It's a perfect place to ground the canoe. We can pull it ashore, then look for a place to eat our lunch, okay?"

Ed agreed. Once they had reached the shore, he jumped out, steadying the canoe. Rick climbed out, and together they pulled it onto dry land.

"Geez," Ed whispered. "Do you think we can find a space big enough for the blanket? I can't believe how thick these trees are."

The woods were especially dense, and between the trees and the thick undergrowth, they lost sight of the water and the canoe only a few steps away. They walked slowly and carefully, mindful of getting lost. The foliage was a deep shade of summer green, and the air pungent and cool with the odor of earth and vegetation. The air itself almost looked green, Ed thought, trailing Rick. He stepped over a thorny bush, wishing he'd worn jeans.

A few feet farther, Rick came across a small clearing inside a ring of maple trees. He asked Ed to spread the blanket, while he commenced unpacking the cooler.

"Okay, Mr. No Peeking," Ed teased. "What all have you got in there?"

"Let's see. Insect repellant, in case the mosquitoes start bothering us." Rick removed a spray can of Off from the cooler. "Some cream for the sunburn you're probably gonna get; a very special tape for the stereo—"

"You got any food in there?" Ed interrupted, suddenly feeling starved.

Rick smirked at him. "Yeah, more bologna sandwiches! The food is part of the surprise, smart-ass. I placed a very special to-go order from the Cozy Hearth Café. I was getting it when you woke up this morning. I just happen to have your favorite roast beef on rye with horseradish sauce, some pickles, potato salad, cold Pepsi-Cola, and, thanks to a secret deal with your mother, some chocolate chip cookies for dessert."

"Umm," Ed moaned hungrily. "Not only are you brilliant; you're one hell of a picnic planner. Hand it over!"

As Ed attacked his sandwich, Rick put the tape he had hidden away into the stereo. Ed smiled, shaking his head, as "Come Saturday Morning" began to play.

"Darlin'," he said with his mouth full, "you always say I'm something else. You know what? You're something else, too. When did you make this tape?"

Rick, bashfully pleased at his success in surprising Ed, grinned at the ground. "Saturday before last, when your mom threw me out of the kitchen. Remember? You were away painting, and I thought it would be a good time to make this tape. I'd been planning it as something I was going to give you for your birthday, but I decided today would be just as good. I couldn't wait."

"I suppose the rest of the songs on it are a surprise, too." Ed happily leaned back against a tree.

"Yep. They're all songs that make me think of you." Rick leaned against another tree. "Enough talking. Let's enjoy our food and the music."

They did just that. They ate until they were full, Ed smiling as one favorite song after another played softly. He looked at Rick resting against his tree, wondering whether anyone else in the world had a man as wonderful as he did. This whole day, one surprise after another, was the finest he'd had since their vacation at Cedar Point. No, he amended; it was even better than Cedar

Point, because Rick had worked so hard to make it a day to treasure for both of them.

Ed put his empty Pepsi can in the cooler and settled himself between Rick's legs. Rick's arms went around him, and Ed sighed, his eyes closed.

"This is incredible. I haven't felt this relaxed in ages."

"Me, too." Rick said quietly, giving him a squeeze.

The last song on side one of the tape faded out. Rick reached over and reversed the tape for side two. Ed drowsily wondered what song would come on next and was pleasantly surprised when he recognized the beginning of Exile's "Kiss You All Over."

"I forgot I even had that record," he said, turning around to smile at Rick.

"I didn't." Rick's arms tightened around Ed. "The minute I thought of this tape, I knew it had to be on it. I remember hearing this song on the radio, back when it was popular, wishing I had someone to play this song for."

"Hmmm. You mean you wanna kiss me all over?"

"Yeah. Baby, you think you can slide out of those clothes?"

"I will if you will."

*Gonna wrap my arms around you*
*Hold you next to me*
*Oh, babe, I wanna taste your lips*
*I wanna fill your fantasy, yeah*

"You ever done it in the woods before?"
"Nope."
"Me either."

*I don't know what I'd do without you, babe*
*Don't know where I'd be*
*You're not just another lover*
*No, you're everything to me*

Ed stretched out on the blanket, and Rick fell on top of him. "I'm glad this is another first time we can share together," he whispered before their lips came together.

"You said we'd go places and do things we hadn't done before."

"Yeah, baby. I'm not exactly sure where we're going right this minute, but I have a feeling it's gonna be one hell of a journey."

*I wanna kiss you all over*

*And over again*
*I wanna kiss you all over*
*Till the night closes in*
*Till the night closes in*

◆

The tape player clicked. Ed lay in Rick's arms, staring at the leaf canopy above them.

"Tape's finished, darlin'."

"I know. I don't care either. I don't want to move."

"Me either."

"I love you, baby."

"I love you, too. Is it just me, just this place, or was that, like, the best ever?"

"I think it was."

"I can't believe no canoes came by."

"It's fate. We were meant to be here like this today. I wouldn't have stopped, even if I'd heard someone."

"I couldn't have stopped."

"You think we can ever top this 'Come Saturday Morning'?"

"I don't know, but I sure intend to try."

"The day's not over yet. We still have more lakes to explore."

"Do we have to? Can we just stay here for awhile, then go back?"

"Sure, baby. Whatever you want. Still glad you married me?"

"Yes."

Ed's eyes closed. He was tempted to fall asleep. He felt Rick move, and he opened his eyes. Rick was looking at his watch.

"I can't believe you're doing that," Ed teased softly.

"Well, we have to have that canoe back before our time runs out on it."

"How much time do we have?"

Rick kissed him again. "Time for lots more kisses, and maybe another Pepsi. I'm kinda thirsty after all that."

"Aw, crud. If you're gonna get up, you might as well get me one, too."

They quietly sipped their pop. Ed looked at their clothes, lying in a tangled heap at the edge of the blanket. *I can't believe it,* he thought. *We just made love under the trees; two guys showing how much they love each other like it was the most natural thing in the world, and I feel like I could do it again.* He shook his head in amazement.

Rick grinned at him. "Whatcha thinking?"

Ed looked at him for a moment. "Oh, just thinking I'll probably remember this afternoon for the rest of my life."

"Me, too. I hope I'm thinking about this the moment I die. I sure would die happy."

"You are not dying for a very long time," Ed said sternly. "Remember? We decided that last week."

"Yes, sir. I have no intentions of dying. I don't want to miss a single moment with you, especially if we have more like this one."

The sun slowly made its way to the west. Reluctantly they pulled their clothes back on and collected their things.

"I hope the canoe's still there," Rick said with a chuckle.

It was. They climbed aboard and slowly paddled their way back to the dock.

"Do I look sunburned?" Ed asked, in the front of the canoe this time.

"No. I think we spent so much time in the woods, you probably don't have to worry about it."

They surrendered the canoe at the dock and languidly packed the car. Ed slammed his door shut, feeling a little wistful. "Is the Magical Mystery Tour over?"

Rick shrugged. "Well, that's all I had planned. Any ideas?"

Ed thought, staring across the lake. "No," he said finally. "I guess we should just go home. You have to go to work tomorrow."

Checking first for an audience, Rick leaned across the car and kissed him. "Okay. Be thinking about what you want to do for supper. Anything you want."

"Okay."

They were quiet on the long drive home. Ed watched the farm fields fly by, barely noticing the ripening corn and soybeans. He could think only of their time in the woods and how Rick had been right about one thing: If for some reason he were to die at this moment, he would die a very happy man.

The Carpenters came on the radio with a new song, "Touch Me When We're Dancing."

"It's good to have the Carpenters back on the radio, isn't it?" Ed asked. "I think of us when I hear this song."

Rick nodded, slowing down for the late afternoon traffic. "Me, too. I don't think there's a romantic song ever made that doesn't make me think of us. I mean, here we are, just two average guys in Bum Fuck Egypt, Indiana, and yet sometimes I feel we're the two greatest lovers the world has ever known."

"If only the rest of the world knew," Ed chuckled. "Oh, I guess most couples feel that way."

"Do they?" Rick asked thoughtfully. "I wonder about that. I mean, I don't want to brag or anything, but I wonder how many guys go to the trouble I went to, planning this day for us. The only reason I did it was 'cause I knew it would make you happy. I'd do anything to see the look on your face when you're really happy."

"Really? It's that special?"

"Yes. The way your eyes shine when you're happy just blows me away. I never get tired of seeing it."

"You know what I see when you're happy?"

"What?"

"I see how much I love you. It's like your face is a mirror, and I see how much I love you, how much I care about you. I never get tired of seeing that either."

"You make me very, very happy, baby."

"All the time?"

Rick snickered. "Don't push it, okay? We may be the greatest lovers the world has ever known, but we ain't perfect. Remember that argument we had last month? Something tells me it isn't the last one we'll ever have."

Ed laughed. "Oh, you had to spoil it with some reality. Okay. I'm glad I make you happy *almost* all the time. How's that?"

"It'll do just fine."

When Porterfield was before them, Rick asked Ed again for his thoughts on an evening meal. "Oh, darlin', I don't want to go to some restaurant or have to share you with anyone. Can we just order a pizza? We can grab it from the guy, then pretend it just magically appeared or something."

"Okay. That sounds really good, and no, I'm not gonna bitch about the cost. Not today, anyway."

"Actually," Ed said, once they were upstairs, behind their two doors, "I could really use a shower. Care to join me?"

Rick's eyebrows rose. "Get naked with you under a warm shower?" He nodded thoughtfully. "Yeah, I think I can do that."

Ed stood under the spray of water, eyes closed, feeling Rick massage his back with a bar of soap. "Oh, that's so wonderful."

"I can't wait until you soap me up."

"I want to do a lot more than rub soap on you."

"You do? Again?"

"Absolutely. Is there a rule that says we're restricted to once a day?"

"Hmmm. Not on a day like this." Rick carefully placed the soap in its dish and turned Ed around for a kiss. "What do you want to do?"

"Everything we did earlier, and more. I want you just as bad as I did then."

"Go for it, baby. I'm all yours."

Ed kissed him, feeling their passion reignite. "I think you're right," he whispered. "I think we are the greatest lovers in the world."

Later that evening, pizza eaten, they sat together on the sofa in the soft summer darkness while Rick's special tape played on the stereo.

"I'll always remember this day, darlin'."

"I'm glad, baby."

Rick stroked Ed's hand, rubbing his fingers over the ring he had given Ed. Ed thought of the gold chain he had purchased for Rick, still well hidden in a dresser drawer under some seldom-worn sweaters. He thought about digging it out and giving it to him right now but decided against it. This day had been a special gift from Rick to him. He knew the gold chain was just as special but thought maybe it should wait for a day he created for Rick.

"I shouldn't say it," Rick interrupted his thoughts, "but do you feel better than you did a week ago?"

"Yes. I can't help but think Mrs. Heston is in a better place now, free of that damned walker. I also think she's happy for us, the same way I think Dad is happy for us."

"I know they are."

Ed smiled as another old favorite song began on the stereo.

"This song is so sappy, but I love it, and it's perfect for us," he said as "Betcha by Golly Wow" by the Stylistics flowed smoothly from the speakers.

"Like I said. Every love song applies."

"Especially this one. You're the one that I've been waiting for. And my love for you will keep growin' strong. Forever."

# Chapter Sixteen

August was a pleasant change from the hectic months of June and July. Ed found the quiet chain of warm, hazy days a relief after the drama of early summer. His job slowed down to routine activities, and he found the time to finish his carriage-house workshop.

He spent several days drawing plans for the partition wall between the workshop and the parking area. When he was sure he knew what he was doing, he bought the supplies and, with a little help from Rick, finished the construction during an especially warm and humid weekend.

The heat abated at the beginning of the next week, and a refreshing, cool breeze began to blow through Porterfield. Ed spent Monday afternoon happily slapping paint on the partition as his radio played a wonderful mix of old and new songs. He had recently discovered a radio station that played, it seemed, one old song for every new one. The AM signal was a little weak, but Ed loved hearing his old favorites and the current hits as well.

Mrs. Penfield, cane in hand, came out to the carriage house to admire his work. "You've done a beautiful job, Ed," she said approvingly. "I've no doubt you'll be able to create some attractive pieces here."

"Thanks," Ed said, with his usual blush.

Mrs. Penfield's gaze roamed the first floor of her carriage house, and garden, and came to a rest on Ed. "I know you believe you and Rick have the better part of the bargain in our arrangement, but I quite feel it's the other way around. It gives me great pleasure to see the carriage house being put to such good use these days. The gardens and the grounds look better than they have in years, and I suspect your cheerful presence has added a few years to my life as well."

"Aw . . ." Ed blushed harder. "I'm just glad it's all working out. Rick and I are happy here, and this workshop and Rick's decision to begin real estate classes wouldn't have happened without your help. I guess it's what they call a mutually advantageous arrangement."

Mrs. Penfield laughed. "That it is, Ed. Oh, I know there were doubts on both sides, but it is working out beautifully.

"By the way," she said, changing the subject, "any word from Rick's parents? I recall you mentioning I may finally have the opportunity of meeting them soon."

"Yeah." Ed dipped his brush in the paint can. "They're coming up Labor Day weekend. They've been as busy as we have this summer, what with teaching summer school and that trip they took across Canada. Rick talked to them the other night, and they said they really want to see the place before the new school term starts. Rick was thinking, if it's not too hot, maybe we'd have an old-fashioned Labor Day barbecue in the backyard."

"Wonderful." Mrs. Penfield nodded. "Let me know what I can do to help. I can only hope having three teachers in attendance will not turn your barbecue into a dull affair, the conversation centered on educational methods and such."

"Oh, I'm not worried about it," Ed said with a grin. "Rick's used to it after all these years, and I don't care as long as everyone gets along."

"I'm sure we will all behave," Mrs. Penfield chuckled. "Although you might be surprised at some of the rowdy teacher gatherings I have attended over the years."

"Yeah, I always heard the teacher's lounge was a den of sin."

"I wouldn't go that far. Still, there are a few of us who know how to enjoy ourselves. It should be a good time, and I'm looking forward to it."

Mrs. Penfield watched Ed move his ladder. "Well, I don't want to interrupt your painting any longer. Good luck with your workshop, Ed, although I have a feeling you won't need it."

When Rick came home from work that day, he found Ed standing outside the carriage-house door, a pair of scissors in hand.

"What's up?" Rick said, grinning in puzzlement.

Ed handed Rick the scissors. "This is the ribbon-cutting ceremony."

He indicated a red Christmas ribbon he'd attached to one side of the partition, stretching across the workshop space to the stairway wall. "After you do the honors, Ed's workshop will be officially open for business."

Rick shook his head, handing the scissors back to Ed. "No. You should cut it. It's your workshop."

"It may be *my* workshop, but it was your idea."

Ed gently shoved the scissors into Rick's hand. "Darlin', if you hadn't've come into my life, I'd be doing exactly what I was doing a year ago, wondering if things were ever going to change. Well, they have. A lot! None of it would have happened without you, so I want you to cut the ribbon, for good luck."

Rick's warm and tender special was at full mast. "Okay, if you insist."

He stood, scissors poised over the ribbon. "Hmmm. What should I say?" He thought for a moment. "I hereby declare the Ed Stephens Workshop officially completed and open for business. May he create woodworks of dazzling beauty and greatness within its walls."

Rick cut the ribbon, and as it slumped to the floor, he walked into the room, beckoning Ed to follow him. He put the scissors on the workbench and opened his arms. Ed stepped in them for a hug.

"That was great, darlin'. I only hope you're right."

"I am," Rick said positively. "I know once you get started you're going to have a lot of fun here, and maybe even make some money."

He cocked his head toward the radio. The Supremes' "I Hear a Symphony" was playing. "From one Supremes fan to another, may I have this dance? We haven't danced together in ages, and it seems appropriate today."

They held each other close, swaying slowly together near the workbench. "I don't know if this one-man band is up to a symphony," Ed murmured, "but I sure love the music you have me making these days."

"Bach and Beethoven are rolling in their graves in envy," Rick said softly. "Even Motown can't make sweeter music than you do. This may have been my idea, but you did the work, and I think you're going to be surprised at what you can do."

"It's like you say about me," Ed whispered. "As long as you're behind me, I think I can do anything. The first project is for you, you know. I'm going to build that bookcase I've talked about for so long. I see it at the end of the hall upstairs, under the window. You can keep your favorite books there, and on top will be a picture frame, with the enlargement of a picture Claire took of us in front of the carriage house the day after we moved in."

"I can't wait to see it," Rick said with a kiss. "It will be something I treasure forever."

"I just hope it doesn't come out looking like an eighth-grade shop project," Ed snickered.

"It will be as beautiful as the man who makes it," Rick insisted. "It will symbolize another part of our dreams. We're going to be strong, self-sufficient, and the envy of Porterfield."

"We'll be so successful Ruth Dorsey will move out of town in disgust, right?"

"Absolutely. Keep dreamin' big, baby. Keep dreamin' big."

⋘•⋙

That night as Ed washed their dinner dishes, Rick dumped his real estate class work on the table with a sigh.

"One exam down, two to go," he groaned, pulling out a chair.

"You worried about the next test? You did okay on the first one."

"Oh, I'm not worried, just a little anxious. You know, three people have dropped out of that class 'cause they were so disappointed by their grades on the first exam. That seemed kind of dumb to me, as they average the three test scores together, but I guess they decided they just couldn't cut it."

"Wow." Ed attacked the frying pan with an SOS pad. "I'm glad I've got such a smart husband, then."

"I don't know about me being smart, but I sure as hell am determined. I swear this investment in time, money, concentration, *and* gas to Fort Wayne and back twice a week is going to pay off."

"Oh, that reminds me," Ed said a bit reluctantly. "I didn't want to mention it earlier in case I'd spoil your appetite, but we've been invited to Fort Wayne Saturday night."

"What for? And by who?"

"My friend Glen," Ed explained. "You know, the one we had dinner with last fall at the fish restaurant? His birthday is this week, and he's having a party at Carlton's Saturday night."

Rick rolled his eyes. "A birthday party at a gay bar. What fun!"

"Well, he finally broke up with Michael, so I think he arranged this party to cheer himself up and start the hunt for a new man."

"That Michael." Rick snickered and shook his head. "What a snotty little queen he was. I can't help but think Glen's better off without him."

"Yeah, I didn't like him either, but knowing Glen he'll find another Michael to replace him. He likes 'em young."

"Shit, when I think of all the Michaels I knew when I was going to the bars in Indy," Rick said in disgust. "Snotty, arrogant little twerps who didn't have a goddamned clue. As for gay bars in general, now that I have you I don't care if I ever set foot in one again. The only reason I ever went in the first place was to find a decent guy, and usually all I ever met were a bunch of drunken cockhounds. Baby, do we really have to go to this party?"

Ed wasn't all that thrilled with the idea either but felt a certain obligation to an old friend.

"We just need to put in an appearance. The party doesn't start until ten. We can run up there, wish Glen a happy birthday, and pull the country-bumpkin thing and tell him we always go to bed early. He'll make fun of us for that, and then we can go home.

"Besides," Ed continued, playfully putting his wet hands on Rick's neck, "if he hadn't've agreed to send that special-delivery letter I dreamed up as a way of talking to you, we might not be having this discussion right now. And are you forgetting? You met me in a gay bar; Carlton's, to be exact."

Rick pushed Ed's hands away with a big grin on his face. "Get my notes wet and you are in serious trouble, baby. Yeah, but only after you cooked up that scheme with the special-delivery letter. I was mooning over you so much after I delivered that letter that I wouldn't have gone if Claire hadn't've pushed me out of the house, determined to see me make some friends."

"And *I* wouldn't have gone if Glen hadn't've invited me to join him and Michael that night, 'cause I was so depressed wondering if the sexy new mailman was really gay or not. So you see, we do kinda owe him. Just for a little while. I promise."

"Oh, all right," Rick moaned. "Now, get your wet paws off my neck and back in the dishwater, okay? I've got to study."

"Yes, dear." Ed flicked one last drop of water on Rick as he turned back to the sink.

"Maybe I'll ask Gordy to go with us. That would certainly liven up the evening."

"Okay," Rick mumbled, intently reading.

Ed took the hint and quietly finished the dishes.

The next night he told Gordy about the party. Gordy was joining Ed and Josh once again for their Tuesday night bowling date. Ed expected Gordy to cheerfully agree to accompany them to Carlton's that weekend, as he usually did when any kind of fun was proposed, and was surprised when Gordy seemed uninterested in the invitation.

"Not to sound bitchy or anything," Ed said as they drove across town to pick up Josh, "but do you have anything better to do on a Saturday night?"

Instead of the smart-ass retort Ed was expecting, Gordy shifted in his seat, looking embarrassed. "I don't want you to go makin' a big deal out of this, but I met this guy."

Ed took his eyes off the road to look at Gordy. "Really? That's great!"

"I don't know how great it is yet," Gordy said, lighting a cigarette. "He's a couple of years older than me. He's been married, and he has a couple of kids. That kinda freaked me out when he told me. Anyway, I met him at Carlton's a couple of weekends ago. He's been down here twice since. He says he likes getting out of Fort Wayne, but I'm guessing it's so no one he knows will see us together."

"Yeah, well, you're not the most out-and-proud guy around either, ya know."

"Yeah," Gordy grumbled. "I know. But kids! Man, can you see me as a stepfather?"

"Yes," Ed said firmly. "The way you are with Josh? You'd be great. We're kinda jumping the gun, though, aren't we?"

"I know, I know. I'm just looking ahead. It's weird. This is the first guy

I've, like, dated, in years. Mostly it's just sex and good times, but when I'm with this guy, it's like a real date. We go to dinner; we watch TV. He spends the night. Shit, I don't know how to act."

Ed pulled into Claire's driveway. "Do you like him? I mean, really like him?"

Gordy squirmed a bit, puffing away on his cigarette. Ed knew it wasn't very nice of him, but he enjoyed seeing Gordy look uncomfortable. It was a big change from his usual roaring, cocky self.

"I don't know how much I like him," Gordy said, grinding the cigarette out in the truck's ashtray. "I mean, I do, but I think he likes me a lot more than I like him. I'm not sure yet. It's all too new for me."

"Yeah, I was pretty freaked out when Rick and I got together," Ed said. "But I knew I liked him. Hell, I knew I liked him a lot."

"That's the difference," Gordy said, his voice back to normal. "You two getting together was like something out of a movie. You were ready for it, too. I don't know if I am. I say I am, but I'll tell you, it's a big change, waking up to a good-looking guy in the morning."

"Tell me about it." Ed laughed.

Josh came out the front door, waving at them. "Look, no talk about this in front of the kid," Gordy said in a low voice. "Do you think, though, I might be able to bring this guy over to your place sometime? I wanna see what you think."

"Sure. I wanna meet him. Hey, I've got an idea," Ed said in a low voice as Josh ran toward the truck. "Why don't you bring him over for dinner Saturday evening? Then if you want to go to the party with us, we can make it like a double date. That would make it a lot more fun for Rick and me."

Gordy nodded, looking thoughtful. "Okay. I'll let you know," he said quickly as he opened his door for Josh.

Ed watched Gordy and Josh engaging in their usual horseplay, thinking any kid would be lucky to have Gordy for a stepdad.

He couldn't help but wonder, though, if this guy was Gordy's prince or one of those damned frogs that needed to be kissed before the prince came along.

◆

The next day Ed needed to make a hardware run for a job he was doing for Mrs. Tucker, but instead of going to the hardware store downtown, he headed to the west side for a stop at Rankin's lumberyard. He had the plans he'd drawn for the bookcase in his pocket, and he decided he was ready to purchase the wood.

He walked into the lumber-supply building, deeply inhaling the scent of fresh-cut wood and sawdust. It had always been a wonderful smell to him, and it brought back memories of working on projects with his father.

"Well," he said to himself, "if I flop as a woodworker, maybe I can get a job selling lumber."

He investigated various types of wood. He wanted only the best but was afraid of spending too much money. *It'd be just my luck to screw it up and have to start over,* he thought. After a long discussion with Bill, one of the lumberyard guys, he finally settled on white pine. He was pretty sure, with the right stain or paint, it could be made to look as rich as a more expensive type of wood.

He approved the boards Bill selected and eagerly stowed them in his truck bed. After he finished his job for Mrs. Tucker, he carried the wood into the workshop. He stared at the boards scattered across his workbench.

"Well," he said, taking a deep breath, "here goes nothing."

With a pencil and a yardstick, he began measuring the boards for cuts. Soon he was engrossed in his work, even ignoring the radio, as he found his father's woodworking tips coming back to him.

Rick found him there, still hard at it, at the end of the day. "You see?" Rick crowed. "I knew it'd all come back to you, just like paddling a canoe."

Ed grinned. "So far, so good, anyway. I haven't gotten to the hard parts yet."

"The hard part," Rick said, brushing sawdust off Ed's shirt, "will be tearing you away from this place to go to your paying jobs."

"Oh, don't worry about that. I have to get the work done around here and keep the money coming in while my man gets his license to sell real estate someday."

"You're something else, baby; you really are. I don't think I'd be surviving these classes without your support and hard work around here."

"I hope Gordy is as lucky as I am," Rick said, kissing him. "He told me this morning that he and his new guy would be happy to come over for dinner Saturday night. I can't wait to see what he's dug up."

"Oh, good. Do you s'pose we should splurge and buy something expensive for dinner?"

Rick frowned. "I don't know. I wanna meet this guy before I decide he's worth an expensive cut of meat. How 'bout we do spaghetti with your mom's sauce recipe?"

"Yeah, Gordy's new cut of meat may turn out to be less than grade A." Ed laughed. "Okay, let's do that. I'll tell Gordy to stop by the liquor store and pick up a nice bottle of wine. That'll confuse him. I'm sure he only knows his way to the beer cooler. He'll be so busy worrying about that, he won't have time to be nervous about us meeting this guy."

Gordy arrived promptly at six o'clock that Saturday evening, leading his date a bit sheepishly into the carriage-house apartment. "Guys, this is Ken. Ken, this is Ed," he said, nodding to Ed at the door, "and that's Rick, messin' around at the stove."

"It's good to meet you both," said Ken, shaking Ed's hand with a bright smile.

Rick put down his spaghetti sauce spoon and went to door for a handshake as well. He looked at Ed out of the corner of his eye, and Ed knew Rick was thinking the same thing he was. This Ken was definitely grade A in the looks department.

He appeared to be in his mid-thirties, a little older than Gordy, as he had told Ed earlier that week, but Gordy had not mentioned that Ken was tall, deeply tanned, well built, and ruggedly handsome, possessing a mouthful of perfect teeth, which shone brilliantly when he smiled. Ed felt quite plain and pale next to him, and he could see that Rick, despite his summer tan, felt the same way.

"Would you like something to drink before dinner?" Ed asked him, hoping their guests had not picked up on the glance he had shared with Rick.

"That would be great," Ken said, still smiling, "but I'd love a tour of the rest of this place. When Gordy told me you lived in a carriage house, I wasn't sure what to expect, but I really like it."

"Ed, why don't you show him around while I stir this glop," Rick said, going back to the stove. "If your mom finds out I've screwed up her sauce, I'll never hear the end of it."

Ed turned to Ken, who was nodding at the stereo. "I see you like the Stones as much as Gordy does."

"Oh, I always stack those albums on when Gordy comes over." Ed grinned.

"They're okay," Ken said. "I'm more into country music myself."

Ed gave Gordy a stricken look. Aside from the occasional crossover hit, he was not a big fan of country music and couldn't imagine dating a man who was.

Gordy shrugged, rolling his eyes. "It's not so bad," was all he said.

Ed, pushing aside his misgivings about Ken's taste in music, gave him the official carriage-house tour, first floor and second. Ken was quietly impressed.

"You two have a really good setup here," he said, looking out a bedroom window.

"We like it."

Ken turned from the window. His eyes went to the pictures of both Rick's and Ed's nieces and nephews on the dresser.

"Oh, you've both got kids, too," he said with that toothpaste-ad smile.

"Uh, no." Ed shook his head. "Those are nieces and nephews, our sisters' kids. We spend a lot of time with Rick's. Their—" He was about to say their father had abandoned them but decided against it. "They're really great kids. I've been teaching Josh, there, the boy in that picture, how to bowl."

"Oh!" Ken's smile faded. "That's great. Your sisters are okay with that?"

"Sure. Why wouldn't they be?"

Ken shrugged uncomfortably. "I just wondered. You know how families can be."

Ed assumed Ken was referring to his ex-wife, but he wasn't about to get into that subject with someone he'd just met.

"Rick and I have been lucky with our families," he said, walking to the bedroom door. "How 'bout something to drink now?"

Over dinner, Ed and Rick learned that Ken sold commercial airtime for a radio station. Ed immediately pelted him with questions about the music programming, and Ken, who'd obviously been asked those questions many times, answered with easy grace and his big smile. Rick had questions about the psychology of selling, and Ken was happy to share his own ideas with him.

Gordy, who was good deal more subdued than usual, watched the other three with a grin when he wasn't slurping up spaghetti. Ed was pleased to notice the situation hadn't affected Gordy's appetite. The evening was going well, and Ed was happy Gordy seemed to have found such a handsome, personable boyfriend.

When Ken reached for the wine bottle, Ed's attention was drawn to his left hand. He frowned, noticing a distinct tan line on the man's ring finger. He puzzled over that, wondering just how long Ken had been divorced. Ed couldn't help but think Ken's finger looked much like his own when he slipped his ring off to paint.

He glanced at Gordy, who had jumped into the conversation with a crack about the psychology of selling postage stamps. Surely, he thought, Gordy's noticed that tan line and asked about it.

*Damn, it's like something out of a soap opera*, Ed thought, *a married guy pretending to be single and cheating on his wife.*

"Of course, the big difference between selling radio airtime and houses," Ken was saying, "is that I usually have to convince a client that radio spots are something he needs, where your potential customers are generally already in the market for a new home. That should give you a big leg up on me."

"That's true," Rick said thoughtfully. "Still, I'm sure I'm going to have to spend some time convincing people who think they don't need a new home that they do."

"I'm sure you'll do fine," Ken said with a chuckle. "Anyone who can turn an old carriage house into a home as nice as this should be able to charm the stubborn ones into seeing the advantages."

"When the day comes that I'm actually selling real estate, maybe I should take Ed with me on my house tours," Rick said with a fond glance at him. "Almost everything we did up here was his idea."

Ken looked rather stunned at that notion, and Ed once again looked at his left hand. He didn't expect a recently divorced man with children to be waving a gay-pride flag, but if he had come out enough to date other men, you'd think he would know Rick was teasing.

"I got it," Gordy roared. "Instead of taking Ed with you, just tell 'em if they buy the house they get his handyman services free for six months."

"*What?*" Ed squawked, and they all laughed.

The conversation moved on. Ed hated himself for it, but that tan line genuinely bothered him. He'd had a few experiences—none of them pleasant—with married men, and he found himself wondering whether there wasn't more to Ken's story than Gordy knew. He debated whether to say anything to Gordy, wishing he could get Rick aside and ask his advice.

Ed looked at Rick. If he had noticed anything unusual, his face didn't betray it. He seemed to have fallen under the spell of Ken's good looks and charming personality, Ed thought sourly, the same way he had until suspicion had crept into his mind. Ed wanted only the best for Gordy, and he had a sudden sneaky feeling Ken wasn't it.

*Don't make a scene*, he scolded himself. *If you gotta stick your nose in it, at least wait until tomorrow, when this guy's back in Fort Wayne where he belongs.*

Ed had decided to keep his mouth firmly shut when Ken's next comment drew his attention.

"I have to admit, I really admire your courage, Rick," he said, looking at the table. "It takes guts to think about a new career, selling, as an out gay man. I don't know if I could do it."

"Well, I don't plan on wearing a pink triangle on my suit jacket," Rick said uneasily. "Still, I won't lie about it either, if someone asks. That's just the chance I'll have to take."

"Some of the people I see on a regular basis," Ken said, shaking his head, "always seem to have a new joke for me. If it's not a Polish joke, it's one about fags. I'd probably lose half my client list if they knew."

"Sometimes people surprise you," Ed said, thinking of Mrs. Heston.

"Not very often," Ken said flatly.

"I don't blame Ken a bit," Gordy stated. "He's right about one thing, though. Benton's got balls for what he's doing."

Rick shrugged. "Yeah, well, I may end up losing my balls over all of this someday, but I'm not gonna deny my marriage to Ed to anyone. If some of them want to make it an issue, I'll just wait for the ones who won't."

"*Marriage?*" Ken asked in surprise. "You call it a marriage?"

"Yes," Rick said defensively. "As far as we're concerned, we're married. It may not be legal, but who gives a shit?"

He reached for Ed's hand. "It's the commitment that counts, not the marriage license."

Ken's eyes were drawn to the clasped hands on the table. Ed saw him look from Ed's ring to his own hand. The vague suspicion in Ed's mind became stronger. At that moment, he was positive Ken was not divorced; he was sure Ken had lied to Gordy.

Ed looked at Gordy, who was watching Ken with a thoughtful expression.

"I've always said these two are an inspiration," Gordy said slowly. "If they can pull it off, there's hope for the rest of us."

"Well," Ken laughed nervously, putting his hands in his lap. "Best of luck to you both."

"Thanks," Ed said, staring at Ken.

"Anybody want some more wine?" Rick tried to defuse the tense moment. "There's plenty more spaghetti and sauce, too."

"Oh, the hell with that wine already," Gordy said in his usual tone of voice. "How 'bout a beer, huh?"

"I have to admit, that sounds good," Ken said, smiling at Gordy.

"Comin' right up." Rick headed for the refrigerator.

Rick, Gordy, and Ken settled in the living room with beers, while Ed busied himself with cleanup duty, his back to the other three. He wasn't sure how to approach the topic with Gordy, especially with Ken in the room, but he wanted to know how much Gordy knew. He no longer cared if he made a scene. If this guy was lying, he wanted Gordy to know before things went any farther.

Ken excused himself and headed for the bathroom. Ed, seeing his chance, beckoned Gordy into the kitchen. "Gord," he said quietly, "have you noticed that tan line on Ken's ring finger?"

Gordy's eyes darkened. "What about it?"

"Well, just how long has he been divorced? Or, how long has he *told* you he's been divorced?"

"What are you sayin', Ed?" Gordy asked defensively. "Just come right out and say it."

"I think he's still married. That tan line looks awfully fresh to me, and he got nervous when he saw me staring at it."

Gordy looked stunned. "Why the hell would he lie about it?"

"Do you want to date a man married to a woman, Gord?"

"No!"

"Well, there's your answer. This guy wants his cake and wants to eat it, too. He doesn't want to make the hard choices we made."

Gordy's face hardened. "I'm such a fuckin' dope," he muttered, walking back into the living room.

"Gordy," Ed hissed, not wanting Ken to hear. "I'm sorry, but I had to say something."

"What's going on?" Rick asked, confused.

"Your husband just taught me a lesson," Gordy said, picking up his beer bottle. "One I thought I had already learned."

He drained the bottle's contents. "Thanks, Ed," he said gently. "I knew there was a reason I wanted you both to meet this guy."

Rick looked from Ed to Gordy. "I repeat: What's going on?"

Ken walked into the room. "I'll tell you later," Gordy said grimly, looking at his handsome, would-be boyfriend.

"Private joke?" Ken asked, his oh-so-successful smile flashing.

"Yeah," Gordy snorted. "As usual, I'm the punch line."

He stood up. "It's about time we left these guys alone for awhile. How 'bout we go back to my place?"

Ken looked taken aback. "Okay. I thought we were going to a party at Carlton's."

Gordy had a dazzling smile of his own when he wanted to use it. He did now.

"We can't really do all the things I've got in mind at a party. Why don't we go back to my place and maybe get down to doing them?"

Gordy turned to Rick, who had stood up, still looking perplexed by the sudden turn of events. Gordy hugged him. "Thanks! I'll call ya tomorrow, okay?"

"Okay," Rick answered, returning the hug.

Gordy walked to the kitchen. He gave Ed an even bigger hug. "Thanks, buddy," he whispered. "This guy's in for one hell of a night."

"What are you going to do?" Ed worriedly whispered back.

Gordy grinned. "You'll see. Don't sweat it. I'm okay. I'll call you tomorrow."

There were handshakes with Ken, and within a few minutes they departed, Rick watching them descend the stairs, shaking his head. "I don't get it," he said to Ed, his expression changing from confused to annoyed. "What in the hell did you say to him?"

Ed threw his dishtowel on the counter, and then rubbed his eyes. "Darlin', didn't you see the tan line that guy had on his ring finger?"

Rick frowned. "No," he said doubtfully. "We knew he was divorced, though."

Ed snorted. "Yeah, right. Divorced. I don't think so. Geez, after the shit I went through with married men, I know one when I see one. He was lying to Gordy about being divorced. I think Gordy wanted to get him alone so he could ask him for himself."

Rick sighed. "Oh, poor Gordy. He was probably as taken in by that smile as I was. You gotta admit, he's one hot guy."

"Yeah, a hot liar," Ed said angrily. "If he wants to cheat on his wife with guys, that's his business, but he's not gonna do it with one of my best friends! Crud, you'd think he'd at least rub some QT on his finger to cover his tracks."

"And Gordy never noticed it? The tan line, I mean?"

Ed went to the refrigerator. He was suddenly in need of a beer himself.

"He wanted to believe what Ken told him. Do you blame him? Yeah, the guy's hot, charming, and God knows what else. Gordy's tired of being alone, so he saw what he wanted to see."

"Yeah," Rick said slowly. "I guess I've done that, too. I sure did it with Jack."

Ed reached for the bottle opener. "Oh, well. Gordy wasn't in love with him, not even close. I think, somewhere in that big heart of his, he knew something wasn't right. I think that's why he brought him over here."

Ed chugged his beer. "I just hate being the whistle-blower."

"You did the right thing, baby," Rick said, putting an arm around him. "Better he should know now than later. Still," Rick snickered. "I would love to be a fly on the wall of Gordy's place right now."

"Yeah," Ed said, surprised at his own snickering. "But we have a birthday party to go to, remember?"

"Oh. Yeah." Rick knocked back the rest of his beer and sighed. "Gordy met Ken at Carlton's, didn't he?"

"Yep."

"Humph," Rick snorted, hands on hips, looking and sounding very much like Norma. "And *that's* what I hate about gay bars!"

⋲⋗•⋖⋘

Gordy didn't call the next day. He came over.

"Beautiful morning, isn't it?" Gordy strolled into the apartment and parked himself in the middle of the sofa next to Jett.

"I don't know. Is it?" Rick asked tentatively.

Gordy smiled at his friends. "Well, it is for me. So how'd the party go last night?"

"It was okay," Ed said impatiently, eager for details about Gordy's evening. "Everyone was pretty well lit by the time we got there, but the music was good. So was the cake. And I think Glen's found himself a new boyfriend already. Rick even liked this one."

"Oh?" Gordy glanced from Rick to Ed. "Did you check his marital status?" he asked with a wicked grin.

"Yeah, yeah, he's single; a bit on the goofy side, but a nice guy."

"His dad's a Realtor," Rick put in. "We actually had a good discussion about the business. I think Glen got lucky this time."

"Well, good for him," Gordy muttered as he concentrated on petting the cat.

"So what happened?" Rick wanted to know.

"Yeah, Gord, c'mon. Spill!"

Gordy looked up and his face broke into his usual big smile.

"I had some of the hottest sex of my life last night, then had the pleasure of throwing the guy out of my apartment." He laughed. "Shit! He didn't see that comin'!"

"All right, Smith, what did you do?" Rick asked with a grin.

"Yeah." Ed swatted him with the Sunday paper. "I knew you were up to something when you left here last night."

Gordy went to the counter and helped himself to a cup of coffee.

"Well, I don't have to tell you guys what I saw in him," he said, sitting at the table. "Damn! He's a good salesman, too. I bought that divorce story because he made it sound so good."

Gordy shrugged. "He was crazy about me, so I took a chance. Why should he lie about being married, right? It would have come out eventually, so I believed him.

"Anyway, thanks to Ed here, I put the pieces together. I wasn't so much mad as I was just disgusted. With myself, I mean. Hell, I knew better, should have paid more attention, but I just didn't want to see it. I mean, if it was just sex, maybe I coulda justified it, but it wasn't. This guy told me he wanted to start a relationship. Now, how in the hell was he going to do that?"

Ed and Rick looked at each other.

"Beats me," Ed said.

"Yeah! What fantasy world was he living in? What was he gonna do, tell me he loved me, then tell me about the little woman?

"That poor broad," Gordy said, shaking his head. "I'll bet you anything

I'm not the first. Guy as good-looking as that can have any guy he wants. Shit, he doesn't have to get divorced. I'm sure there's some sap out there who'll put up with being the other woman. Well, not Gordy Smith.

"So we get back to my place last night," Gordy continued. "I decided to send him off with a little present to remember me by." He roared his usual laugh. "Oh, he'll remember all right! He'll remember every time he goes to sit down today. I'll be he's never had it that good. That bastard will be walking funny for a week. I'll bet the wife'll think he's got hemorrhoids!"

"Gordy," Ed exclaimed, laughing.

"Oh, man." Rick was laughing too.

"Ah, don't worry. The dumb shit loved every minute of it. I've never been into getting rough, but that's what he wanted, so he got it. I was happy to oblige."

Gordy shook his head, remembering. "Afterward he went to take a shower. I went through his pants pockets, and sure enough, there was his wedding ring. I was so mad at that point I was ready to drag him out of my shower, naked, and throw him out in the street. But I waited 'til he came back to bed. He curled up next to me, all ready to spend the night. I can't even imagine what he tells his wife on nights like that.

"When he was good and comfortable, I asked him right out: Are you divorced, or what? He hemmed and hawed around but finally admitted the truth. Then he started all this blah-blah bullshit about how he couldn't afford to leave his wife; that she knew about it, etcetera. Yeah, I'll just bet she does! Anyway, I told him to take his sexy ass and get the hell out, and find some other guy with a moth-eaten letter jacket to bang him."

"Wow," Ed said, imagining the scene. "That's so cool, Gord. I mean, to hit him with it when he least expected it."

"It was kinda mean, but I don't blame you a bit." Rick chuckled.

"He deserved it," Gordy said flatly. "I s'pose I deserve worse for falling for his bullshit, but at least it's over with."

Ed put an arm around him. "You deserve only the best, bud, and you'll find it someday.

"I can tell you," he continued, looking at Rick, "there's a prince at the end of that line of frogs."

"Maybe," Gordy sighed. "I just hope mine doesn't come complete with a princess."

## Chapter Seventeen

Ed hoped to have Rick's bookcase done by the time his parents came to visit, but a sudden rush of handyman emergencies kept him from it.

"Don't sweat it," Rick told him. "Between touring the house and hearing all of our good news from this summer, they'll be too busy being impressed with everything else."

John and Vera, Rick's parents, were driving from Indianapolis to Porterfield the Saturday of Labor Day weekend. As they planned to spend the night with Claire and the kids, Rick invited them to the Penfield place for Saturday evening dinner. Mrs. Penfield urged him to include Claire and the children as well. Ed, when he went to pick up Josh for their last Tuesday night bowling session of the summer, passed this news on to Claire.

"Rick wants to play backyard chef again," he told her. "Mrs. Penfield, though, insists we all eat in her dining room, since there will be so many of us. Still, don't worry about the kids breaking anything. Rick told her, dining room or not, we're gonna use paper plates."

Claire laughed. "Good thinking on his part. You can tell he put in some serious time around here. Can I bring anything?"

"Rick told me to tell you you're in charge of dessert."

She nodded. "I can handle that."

Josh came out of his room with his friend Eric with him. "Can Eric go with us tonight, Uncle Ed?"

"Sure! You can show him how much you've learned this summer."

"Thanks, Ed, for teaching Josh to bowl this summer," Claire said. "Although I may change my mind in the next few weeks. I have to have them out at the Bowl-O-Rama at eight every Saturday morning."

"Uncles do the fun part," Ed said, laughing, "and Moms do the hard part."

"Tell me about it," Claire said wryly. "Oh, well. At least they're back in school now. Hard to believe the summer's almost over, isn't it?"

"Yeah," Ed agreed. "I can't believe today is September first. Well, guys, you ready to go?"

Ed had not spent any time with Eric and was happy to find him much like Josh—quiet and respectful. He was also comforted to see that Josh had a friend who seemed to share a lot of his interests.

Josh's hard work on the lanes paid off that night. He solidly beat Eric in the first two games.

"Gee, I wish I hadn't've been gone all summer," Eric said wistfully. "Maybe if I could have bowled with you guys, I'd be better at it."

"Here," Ed said, picking up a ball. "Let me show you a few things."

Eric's score improved in the third game. Ed nodded in satisfaction.

"You are gonna be the two best guys in the league. Don't worry about it. You'll wipe up the lanes with those other fourth graders. Heck, you'll probably even beat the fifth graders!"

The boys were bashfully pleased at Ed's praise. He dropped them off at Josh's house and drove across town feeling pleased with himself as well. He hadn't done a bad job with this pretend dad stuff at all.

Thinking of his success with Josh over the summer, he no longer cared about finishing the bookcase before the Bentons' visit. There was certainly enough evidence to prove Ed and Rick were doing fine together in Porterfield, despite John and Vera's concerns over a gay couple living in a small town. Ed remembered the heated discussion on that particular topic during their visit for Rick's birthday in March—and Rick's anger—and hoped to make it through the holiday weekend without a repeat of it.

Ed was busy tidying up the backyard and garden the next day when Doug Morgan stopped by with the month's rent check. "Big plans for the weekend?" Doug asked, watching Ed washing the lawn chairs.

"Yeah. Rick's family, including his parents, is coming over for a barbecue. His parents have never seen this place before, so I want it looking good."

Doug glanced around the garden. "Looks good to me."

Ed paused in his work to study Doug. He didn't seem to be his usual cheerful self. "You have plans for the weekend?" he asked tentatively.

Doug shrugged. "No. Just work. Nothing better to do."

He looked away. "I guess you might as well know, my girlfriend dumped me. Just couldn't handle the mortician thing."

"Aw, Doug, I'm sorry," Ed said sympathetically.

"I'll live," Doug said, attempting, and failing, to smile.

"You know, you're more than welcome to join us here Saturday night," Ed offered. "I know family stuff isn't that exciting, but the more the merrier." Ed couldn't help wishing Doug was either older, or Claire younger. If it wasn't for the age difference, he thought they might enjoy each other's company.

Doug shook his head. "No, but thanks. I'm on call at the funeral home. Someone always kicks the bucket over a holiday weekend, so I'm sure I'll end up spending most of my time there."

"Well, if you change your mind, just come over. I'm sure there will be plenty to eat. Rick and I don't have any plans for the rest of the weekend, so if you just wanna hang out, you're welcome for that, too."

Doug's handsome face cracked a smile for real. "Thanks. I think that's above and beyond the call of landlord duty—entertaining your tenant—but I might take you up on that. It's kind of hard making friends in a town like this."

"I know," Ed said, nodding. "Rick went through the same thing when he moved here. Anyway, if you don't mind hangin' out with a couple of fags, you're always welcome."

"Thanks." Doug shook his head again. "I'm sure you've figured out that doesn't matter to me. You're the nicest people I've met yet in Porterfield. But then again," he said, sounding more like the Doug Ed was used to, "most of the people I meet are either dead or in mourning."

Ed chuckled. "It's not a nonstop party over here, but we're still breathing. Come over some night when Rick doesn't have class, and we'll play some cards or something."

"It's a deal." Doug looked at his watch. "Well, time to get back to the dead zone. I'll give you a call sometime, okay?"

"Great." Ed watched Doug take off down Race Street in his sober, inconspicuous mortician's sedan, thinking that the friendship and support both he and Rick had acquired over the summer from various Porterfield citizens would give John and Vera even less to worry about.

Gordy was invited to the barbecue as well but declined the invitation.

"I'm going up to my dad's cabin, maybe do some fishin'," he told Ed over the phone.

"Alone?"

Gordy snorted. "Yeah! What'd ya think? I was gonna call Ken? He's probably already busy linin' up his next sucker. Hell, after that scene I'm happy being alone for a few days. I think it'll do me some good."

"Well, if you say so," Ed said doubtfully. "Still, if you change your mind, or come home early, you come see us, okay?"

"Sure. Maybe I'll stop by on Labor Day. Beats watchin' that damn telethon."

"Geez, I'm glad to know we're more fun than Jerry Lewis," Ed grumbled.

"Hell, yes! Tell ya what, if I catch anything, I'll bring you a fish, too,"

Gordy said wickedly, knowing Ed's distaste for fish.

"I knew you'd find a way to get even with me," Ed groaned. "Do me a favor. Instead of giving it to us, just go stick it in Ruth Dorsey's mailbox."

⋘•⋙

Saturday arrived sunny, warm, and humid with the possibility of a thunderstorm hanging in the heavy air. Weather-wise, it seemed to be like almost every other Labor Day weekend Ed could remember. Rick went ahead with his barbecue plans, and while he was busy setting up the charcoal grill, Ed messed around in the kitchen, throwing together a baked bean casserole. He had the stereo radio going full blast for his new favorite radio song, Robbie Patton's "Don't Give It Up." He sang along with Robbie about keeping the fire hot as he fried some bacon for the casserole.

"I don't think our fire needs to get any hotter," Rick said, grabbing him from behind.

Ed, startled, stumbled and fell backward against Rick.

"Are you talking about the fire on the grill or the fire between us?"

Rick's arms tightened around Ed. "Well, both, actually. I was mainly referring to us, though."

"So your parents have nothing to worry about, right?"

Rick heaved a sigh. "You'd think. We're doing great here with Mrs. P., my classes are going well, you're too busy working for people who don't judge you to spend any time in your workshop, Claire's divorce is going through, the kids are just fine, and those baked beans look delicious. So what's to bitch about? I'm sure they'll think of something. They'll probably get back on the 'bigoted and prejudiced small town' routine. For bleeding-heart liberals, they can be awfully damned conservative. You'd think we were taking out ads in the paper and flying a gay-pride flag out our bedroom window."

"Don't start," Ed commanded. "We are going to have a nice evening. If your parents start that shit again, you are going to ignore it."

"Okay," Rick reluctantly agreed. "If only for the sake of everyone's digestion, I promise to keep my mouth shut."

Mrs. Penfield, in her usual rose arbor seat, was anxiously scanning the sky when the Bentons and the Romanowskis arrived.

"Perhaps we should eat earlier than we had planned, Rick," she suggested. "My arthritis tells me we'll see a storm before the night is out."

The guests swarmed into the garden, and greetings and introductions filled the air.

"I'm so happy to finally meet you," Vera Benton exclaimed to Mrs. Penfield. Vera bent over to take Mrs. Penfield's hand. "I think it's wonderful what you're doing for the boys."

"The boys are quite wonderful as well," Mrs. Penfield assured her.

John Benton beamed at Mrs. Penfield. "Allow me to thank you for taking such good care of my family. You've made a big hit not just with Rick but with the grandchildren as well. Joshua spent a good part of the afternoon showing me the treasures he unearthed from your attic."

"He was certainly welcome to them," Mrs. Penfield said with a chuckle. "As Ed and Rick can tell you, we have more Penfield artifacts scattered about the property than we can possibly put to any practical use."

"Ed," Rick called from the grill, "Mrs. P. thinks we should eat early in case it rains. Will you show Mom and Dad around while I get things going?"

Judy butted in. "Uncle Ed, I want to show Grandma and Grandpa the house, okay?"

Ed, his hands full with the chocolate cake Claire had baked, grinned at her. "Go ahead, kid. I need to deposit this and check on my baked beans."

Judy, anxious to prove she knew her way around the main house, ushered her grandparents through the back door, while Josh and Jane settled near Mrs. Penfield in the rose arbor, eagerly telling her about their first week back at school.

Ed headed to the carriage house with Claire on his heels. Once they were upstairs, Ed carefully placed the rich-smelling cake on the table.

"Umm, chocolate sheet cake." He took a deep sniff. "You must put in a dash of cinnamon like Mom does."

Claire nodded. "Actually it's her recipe. Rick got it from your mom and gave it to me when he was watching the kids after school this week. I was hoping it would satisfy Mom's sweet tooth and give her less to bitch about, but just in case I brought this along." She opened a grocery bag and pulled out two bottles of wine.

"You're gonna get her drunk?"

Claire opened the refrigerator and shoved the bottles behind the milk carton. "No, the wine is for us—you, Rick, and me—if they start in again. We drink enough of this, we won't care what they say anymore, but if it doesn't work we can always smash the empty bottles over Mom and Dad's heads."

Claire slammed the refrigerator door so hard the bottles rattled inside. "They've already tag-teamed me this afternoon, so I can only assume you and Rick are next on their hit list."

Ed groaned. "Aw, crud. They were so nice when we drove down in April to get Rick's stuff, I was hoping they were done worrying about us."

"Well, you know, that's what Mom does best. Worry. They both got me alone this afternoon to ask about the divorce proceedings. After I assured them Bob Mason knew what he was doing, Mom started in on all the children of divorce in her classroom and how worried she was about Judy, Josh, and

Jane. Then Dad, who has never passed up an opportunity to bad-mouth Hank in the last thirteen years, told me it was about time I officially got rid of him, but was I really prepared to be a single mom?"

Claire shook her head in annoyance. "Can you believe that? He's wanted me to ditch Hank since the day I met him, and now he throws *that* at me? I told them how much the kids' grades had improved this past year with Rick helping them with their homework and encouraging them all to read more, and how they've all got nice friends, and how generally comfortable and less worried they are since Hank's been gone. I mentioned how much Josh had enjoyed bowling with you and Gordy this summer, and how much it means to him to have adult men to hang out with. Then I saw the look on Dad's face, and I could just tell what he was thinking."

"What?"

"Oh, you know, did I really know what I was doing, letting Josh spend so much time with a bunch of gay men? To prove it, he asked me if I had met any decent stepfather material here in Porterfield."

"Well, that's a legitimate question," Ed said uncertainly, preferring to think Claire was wrong about John's intentions.

"Maybe it is," Claire allowed, "but it all comes down to the same old thing: Dad thinking I don't know what the hell I'm doing, and how can a woman alone raise three kids, and how much better it would all be if I had a man. I told him I had been propositioned by plenty of guys while I was cleaning their teeth, but all of them wanted to meet me out of town so their wives wouldn't find out, and the only decent men I was currently acquainted with in Porterfield were you, Rick, and Gordy."

Ed sighed, tempted to reach for a knife and start in on the cake. "I don't get it. They don't really have a problem with Rick being gay, or with him being with me, and it's obvious we're all doing just fine, so why do they get so worked up about stuff? Geez, my mom may be opinionated and mouthy, but after she says what she thinks, she always ends up supporting me and Laurie."

Claire shrugged. "That's just their way. It's always been like that. Oh, they love us to death and would do anything for us, but since neither Rick nor I have ever done exactly what they thought we should do, they worry that we've made bad decisions and are going to ruin our lives. For some reason they have a hard time letting go. I guess it's a family thing. I remember our grandparents being like that, too.

"Take Mom," Claire continued, leaning against the kitchen sink while Ed pulled his casserole out of the oven. "Since I had shut Dad down with my crack about married guys hitting on me, she suggested, as she always does, that perhaps I start thinking about moving back to Indianapolis, how there were more eligible men there, and how the name Romanowski wouldn't mean anything, but just in case, had I asked Bob Mason about changing my name back to Benton? Maybe I should change the children's names, too? Her implication, of course, was that I probably never would find a man in Porterfield with Hank or his last name on my track record, and of course if I moved back to Indy she could keep an eye on me and make sure I was doing what she wanted me to do. Aarghh!"

The last of Ed's earlier optimism faded away. He glanced out the living room window and saw Judy finishing her house and grounds tour in the garden. John and Vera were taking seats in the rose arbor while Mrs. Penfield poured lemonade for everyone. Rick was cheerfully flipping burgers on the grill with Josh's help. Ed thought he heard thunder in the distance. It seemed appropriate. The scene in the yard appeared peaceful enough, but if Claire was right, emotional storm clouds were building.

He went to the fridge to uncork one of Claire's wine bottles, hesitated, and reached instead for the cabinet above the refrigerator. He pulled out a bottle of vodka.

"The hell with the wine," he said, unscrewing the bottle cap. "I think we may need something stronger."

Claire sighed. "Make mine a double."

◆

Despite Ed's concerns, the evening proceeded pleasantly enough. Ed and Claire, calmer and a bit giggly from their private cocktail session, returned to the party in time for dinner, which everyone enjoyed in the big dining room of the main house. The occasional rumble of thunder remained well to the south of Porterfield, and any threat of storms within the family seemed to abate as well.

After everyone had eaten their fill of hamburgers, beans, and salad, Ed rose from the table to retrieve the chocolate cake he had left in the carriage house. John and Vera tagged along, eager to see the apartment.

"Between this building and the main house, I understand why Rick became so interested in Victorian architecture," John murmured, admiring the stained-glass windows. "This place is amazing."

"Well, we'll have a lot of work to do on it someday," Ed told him. "For right now, we're content with what we have here in our apartment."

"How are things going with Mrs. Penfield and your arrangement?" Vera asked.

"Just great," Ed assured her. "Oh, I had some doubts when we first decided to move, but we haven't had any problems at all. We both love living here, and Mrs. Penfield's happier than she's been in years."

"I'm glad to hear that," Vera said with a sigh. "I had my concerns as well. It's such a marvelous opportunity, though, I can see why you didn't want to pass on it."

"Has Mrs. Penfield changed her will, as Rick told us?" John wanted to know. "Will all of this *really* belong to the two of you someday?"

"Well, yes," Ed said uncomfortably.

"Incredible," John mumbled. "A woman our son barely knows wills him her house. Life is certainly full of surprises."

"Well," Ed said. "Her son, George Junior, died in the Korean War. She's kind of adopted Rick and me in his place, I guess." He shrugged. "She doesn't have any family at all."

"Obviously," John snorted. "She wouldn't be doing this for you otherwise."

Ed was glad Rick was out of earshot for that comment and decided the subject needed to be changed. "Would you like to see what I'm doing downstairs with my workshop?"

Ed was pointing out his progress on his bookcase for Rick when Vera's glance fell on his left hand.

"That's a very attractive ring you're wearing, Ed. Did Rick give that to you?"

"Yes," he mumbled, wishing he'd taken it off before they arrived.

"Do you intend to give one to him as well?"

"No," Ed said quietly. "He doesn't want one."

Vera sighed. "I suppose that's for the best, considering his job. I'd hate to think what people would say."

"That's not the reason," Ed said in a firm but polite tone of voice. He didn't want to start an argument, but he felt both Vera and John needed to know workplace prejudice wasn't the real issue.

"Rick doesn't like rings. He gave this to me as a sign of his commitment to me, and I'm very honored to wear it. When the time comes, I'll give Rick something just as meaningful."

Vera laid a hand on his arm. "I wasn't questioning your devotion to our son, Ed," she gently said. "I just worry about—"

"I know," Ed interrupted. "But we're doing just fine, really. There's nothing for you to worry about. With Mrs. Penfield's help we're moving ahead on our goals, and no one seems to have a problem with what we're doing."

He thought of Ruth Dorsey but figured what they didn't know wouldn't worry them. "Rick told you about the volunteer work he's going to be doing for the Porterfield Historical Home Tour," he continued. "Eunice Ames is one of the big movers and shakers in town, and with her support I'm sure Rick will have a great head start when he gets his real estate license."

"We'll see," John commented. "Still, I hope you boys are being careful, as you promised to be."

"We are."

Ed was pleased when John and Vera dropped the subject and began to praise the partially completed bookcase, but he wondered whether the Bentons planned to return to the matter before the evening was over.

Over dessert Rick told his parents about his classes in Fort Wayne, and how he had to pass only one more test to finish successfully.

"Then I'll be able to go to Indy the first Saturday in October and take the licensing exam," he said confidently. "If I pass, and I certainly plan to, I'll be a genuine, licensed real estate agent in the state of Indiana."

Vera looked at her son in concern. "Don't you think, though, you'll be overworked, delivering mail, keeping an eye on the children for your sister, and attempting to sell property on the side?"

"Oh, Mom," Claire groaned.

"It's my belief, Mrs. Benton," Mrs. Penfield put in smoothly, "that Rick intends to refrain from actually entering the real estate field until the current market improves and an appropriate opportunity arises."

Rick shot grateful looks at both his sister and Mrs. Penfield but obviously intended to answer his mother's question himself.

"Mrs. P.'s right, Mom," he said, reaching for his lemonade glass. Ed almost wished he had included Rick in the vodka he and Claire had shared earlier.

"I'm not about to jeopardize my income or my sanity by trying to take the Porterfield real estate market by storm. I just wanted to get the licensing process out of the way so I'd be ready. For now I'm happy to continue building what I hope is a future working relationship with Vince Cummings, and make some connections working with Eunice Ames on her home tour committee."

Rick glanced at Ed. "We're both excited about our plans to buy fixer-uppers and resell them, but we're still aware of my possible handicap. I know Porterfield isn't going to love me overnight, so I'm taking my time, making sure I move carefully."

Vera looked at the children, who were following the discussion with interest. "If that's the case, then everything should be fine," she said, obviously not eager to talk about Rick's "handicap" in front of Judy, Josh, and Jane. "Mrs. Penfield, I couldn't help but notice the beautiful china in your breakfront. Is it Havilland, by any chance?"

Mrs. Penfield told her it was and began to go into its history. Judy rolled her eyes at Ed, who grinned and kicked her good-naturedly under the table, relieved once again to have the conversation move away from a topic of which he was thoroughly tired.

After dessert, Vera and Claire insisted on taking charge of the cleanup, drafting Judy and Jane to help. Mrs. Penfield accompanied them to the kitchen for more conversation, while Josh, flashlight in hand, headed to the attic in hopes of finding more of the old toys he had discovered on an earlier visit.

John pulled out his pipe and headed for the front parlor, motioning Ed and Rick to join him. Ed followed Rick and John out of the dining room, hoping for more inane party chatter, as opposed to another rehash of their living arrangements or future in Porterfield.

"Son," John said once they had taken seats, "are you sure you want to go through with this? Real estate is a notoriously chancy business. I hate to think of you throwing away your benefits from the government on such a risky enterprise."

"Dad," Rick said patiently, "my goal is to become self-employed someday. That isn't going to happen if I stay with the postal service the rest of my life. Yes, I know this is a risk, but it's one I'm willing to take."

John turned to Ed. "How do you feel about this?"

"He's my husband, and I support him," Ed said firmly.

"Even though you may end up supporting him financially?"

Rick looked stunned. "Shit, Dad, are you that convinced I'm gonna be a flop at this?"

"I didn't say that," John said impatiently. "I'm making sure Ed understands the possibilities here. I can't help but think the provisions of Mrs. Penfield's will, and her rent-free accommodations here, have gone to your heads."

"For your information," Rick said in a low voice, "we do not live here rent free. We do a lot of work around this place. Or rather, I should say *Ed* has been doing a lot of work around here while I've been going to classes and studying. He's been great about it, but then again, he knows it will pay off for us both someday."

John snorted. "You mean when that old woman dies?"

"Dad," Rick shouted. "I can't believe you said that! Is that what you think? I'm just playing around, waiting to own this house?"

"I don't know. *Is* that what you're doing?"

Ed looked at John in horror. He couldn't believe what he was hearing. Any thoughts of refereeing this skirmish were abandoned as he aligned himself solidly with Rick.

"Rick isn't playing," Ed said quietly, trying to mask his anger. "He's been working his butt off with this all summer. Mrs. Penfield, me, and even Vince Cummings, are proud of what he's accomplished. Those classes are hard, and Rick's managed to get good grades and hasn't missed a day of work."

He paused for a moment, looking John in the eye. "We are not broke. We are not living on charity. Yes, Mrs. Penfield has been good to us, but we are supporting ourselves. Rick wants to be self-employed so his sexual orientation won't be as much of an issue as it could be now. It's made a big difference for me, and I know it will for him, too."

John shook his head in disgust. "Postal service or real estate? What's the difference? With everyone in this town eventually knowing the truth about you two, do you honestly think anyone will use your services as a real estate agent, or continue to take advantage of Ed's handyman service?"

"There it is again," Rick said in disgust. "A fag can't survive in Porterfield. Dad, it wouldn't be any different in Indianapolis. Why don't you just come right out and say it: You don't think a fag can be successful at anything unless he stays in the closet."

"Don't put words in my mouth, Richard," John said calmly. "I just feel you haven't given this enough time or thought. Go ahead and take your licensing exam. Then, in a year or so, if the economy improves, perhaps you can dabble in it as a second income. Wait until you know for sure this is a viable possibility."

"Wait?" Rick shouted. "What the hell for? You mean wait like you did? You waited to go for your PhD, and you waited so long you decided against it. You put off writing that book you always wanted to write about Indiana's role in the Civil War, and you still haven't written page one. What am I supposed to do, wait until I'm your age and I don't care anymore?"

"We're not discussing me; we are discussing you."

"I think maybe we are discussing you. Just because you were too cautious and put off everything you wanted to do, you think I should, too."

"I do not think that at all," John said defensively, but Ed was sure Rick had hit a nerve. "I *do* think you shouldn't throw away an honest career because you had one lucky break, thanks to the generosity of a lonely old woman."

"Mrs. Penfield and her generosity have nothing to do with this," Rick informed him. "I had decided to pursue this career long before we knew anything about that will. Jesus! This is just like the time I told you I wasn't going to finish college but was going to work for the post office full-time. You were convinced I was ruining my life then, and now you think I'm so goddamned dumb the post office is the best I can do."

"I think real estate is a poor choice. Surely there is some other, safer, line of work you could investigate."

"Maybe I should become a hairdresser," Rick said sarcastically. "Isn't that what fags are supposed to do? Gee, maybe I could own my own shop someday."

"If you choose to live your life as an outspoken gay man," John said quietly, "you will have to live with the consequences as well. In the meantime, are you willing to live on Ed's modest handyman income?"

"Don't drag Ed into this," Rick yelled.

"He's already in it," John yelled in return. "I was hoping he had more sense than you did!"

Rick's anger suddenly diminished. He slumped in his chair, a defeated look on his face. "I've never been the son you wanted," he said bitterly. "No wonder you always think I'm going to fail at whatever I do."

John looked stunned. "Rick," he whispered. "That's just not so! I'm merely concerned for your welfare."

"Yeah. Just like Mom always is, convinced I'm gonna get queer-bashed and sent home to her in shame and bandages."

Ed, seething from that "modest income" comment, looked at Rick, angered further by the expression on his face. He was about to ask John just what *his* salary was as an Indianapolis public school teacher when Rick abruptly got up and walked out of the room. He disappeared into the front hall, and Ed could hear the front screen door slam as lightning suddenly illuminated the house. An ominous rumble of thunder followed moments later, overriding the droning of the cicadas from the oak trees in the front yard.

Ed looked at John in disgust. "Nice goin', John."

John sighed. "Ed, I'm sure you want to go after him, but please wait a moment. You must know by now how pleased Vera and I are to have you in our family. We think the world of you, and frankly, we've also hoped your good sense would be a positive influence on Richard. Are you as confident about this real estate scheme as he is?"

Ed's first impulse was to defend Rick at any cost, but he suddenly decided honesty might be a better way of diffusing the situation.

"I've had my doubts," he said slowly. "I don't think Rick should do anything now, and he agrees with me. But as for the future, who knows? I think if we keep moving forward, working toward our goals, it'll work out eventually."

"It's just such a gamble—" John began, but Ed held up a hand to cut him off.

"I know that. I also know that no one wins in Vegas if they don't put some money on the table. Life is the same way sometimes. *My* dad told me that when I decided to start my handyman business. He knew I could fall on my face, but he told me to go ahead and try it."

"I don't know if the situations are comparable."

Ed shrugged. "Maybe not, but one thing sure is. Dad supported me and told me he had my back. Why can't you do that with Rick instead of always belittling his ideas?"

John, who had finally gotten around to lighting his pipe, almost dropped his matches. "Is that what you think I'm doing?"

"Doesn't matter what I think. It's what Rick thinks that counts."

And with that, Ed stood up and walked into the front hall, following Rick's path out of the house.

He hurried down the front steps and anxiously scanned the western sky. Heavy, dark clouds were racing to the east as a steadily stronger wind rattled the oak leaves and sighed through the pines.

Ed, hoping to avoid notice from anyone in the kitchen, crept along the west side of the house. He ducked behind the tossing pines and made his way to the carriage house. He sighed in relief when he saw that Rick's car was still in the garage. He was about to head upstairs when he heard the radio in his workshop. An old Guess Who song was fighting its way through the storm-related static on the AM signal. Ed paused and peered into the gloom and saw Rick in the back, idly fingering the tools hanging from the pegboard.

Another lightning flash, this one much closer, lit the workshop. The radio squawked in response. Rick looked up and saw Ed at the open door. They both winced as booming thunder immediately followed.

"Looks like we're really in for it," Ed said.

"Yeah. The radio says there's a severe thunderstorm warning for Stratton County."

Ed looked back at the main house and saw, by the light of the kitchen, the children running through the house to close windows before the rain began.

"I should probably get our windows shut upstairs," Ed said over the noise of the wind and the radio. "Will you come upstairs with me, darlin'?"

Rick shrugged. He paused for a moment, and then followed Ed up the stairs.

Ed slowly ascended the stairs. He really did want to close the living room windows, but he was also thinking about the gold neck chain that had remained hidden for two months now. He had wanted to give it to Rick on some sort of special occasion but thought that giving it to him now might show Rick just how much he supported him and his plans, private doubts or not.

But as he was walking into their home, he suddenly changed his mind. He knew Rick wasn't at all concerned about Ed's support, but rather the lack of support from his father. Giving Rick the chain at this time wouldn't solve that, and would, perhaps, even make the situation worse. Ed didn't want Rick to think he would give him such an important gift as a way of making him forget what his father had said, and the hurt Rick obviously felt.

Ed went to close the windows, looking around the room for Jett. He was nowhere to be seen. Ed figured the cat had already retreated to his usual hiding place during thunderstorms—under the bed. Rick stood by the record cabinet Ed's father had made, stroking it much the way he had been touching the tools downstairs.

"Your dad must have been one hell of a guy," he said as Ed closed the second window and turned to him.

"He was."

"Why can't all dads be like that?" Rick asked bitterly.

"Your dad is a great guy, too. He's just concerned about your future. Any dad would be."

"Sure has a funny way of showing it."

Ed, again distracted by the lightning now flashing repeatedly in the sky over Porterfield, took Rick by the hand and led him away from the windows.

"Well, our dads must not have gone to the same dad school," Ed said, putting his arm around Rick's shoulders, "but he loves you and cares about you. He could have completely rejected you when you told him you were gay, but he didn't. Gordy's dad? Gordy's told me more than once that he never plans to tell him he's gay 'cause he knows he'll be disowned, kicked out of the family. What if you had to deal with that?"

"Yeah, I know," Rick sighed. "This is just his way of showing his love for me, telling me what an idiot I'm being for thinking I can be successful at something other than delivering mail."

"He doesn't think you're an idiot."

"Maybe, maybe not. I sure do sometimes."

Ed looked at him in complete surprise. Rick actually grinned.

"Yeah, sometimes I think I'm an idiot, baby. Sometimes I think Dad's absolutely right about all of this. The stuff he was saying earlier isn't anything I haven't thought about over the past few months, and I've wondered if I wasn't just wasting my time, and yours."

A gust of wind, accompanied by a loud cracking sound and a thump, sent them both to the windows. A large limb from an old maple tree in the neighbor's yard had fallen through a gap in the pines and was now resting on the rose arbor.

"Aw, crud," Ed muttered as rain suddenly began to fall across the yard in sheets. "I knew I should have bought a chainsaw when I had the chance. Now we're gonna have to hire someone to clean that up before it crushes the latticework on the arbor."

"It's always something, isn't it, baby?"

"Yeah, but we always get through it," Ed said tentatively. "Don't we? What you said about being an idiot, you're not thinking something stupid like dropping out of that class now that you're so close to finishing, are you?"

Rick sighed. "No, I was just admitting that this whole plan we've made for our future scares me sometimes. Having Dad say what he said just made it worse."

"Well, it's okay to be scared as long as you admit it to me, but don't go thinking you're an idiot. I wouldn't have married an idiot, and I sure as hell wouldn't have agreed to someday fix up run-down houses for an idiot to sell either."

"You still have your doubts, too, though, don't you?"

"Sure. I had a lot of doubts when I started my handyman business, but it worked out. I think this will, too, eventually. The future's always scary. You know, a part of me wishes we could just stay where we are and live happily ever after, but it doesn't work that way. I hate to admit it, but you don't change anything if you don't take a chance once in a while. Taking chances got me out of a factory job I hated, and taking a chance got me you, too."

"I hope you kept your receipt," Rick teased, pulling Ed to him for a hug. "If you decide you don't want me anymore, you can take me back to the store. Maybe they'll even give you a cash refund."

Ed laughed. "I'm not too worried about that. As long as we're really here for each other, I think we'll be fine. You know what I think, though? I think you've been working so damned hard on that class through this hot weather, and going back to the routine of having to go to Claire's after work every day to watch the kids after school, that you're getting a lot more tired than you're willing to admit."

"Maybe you're right," Rick said ruefully. "Maybe what Dad said wouldn't have gotten to me so much if I wasn't."

While the storm raged outside, Ed enjoyed the protection of the carriage house and Rick's arms. Maybe, he thought, it was time for him to provide a break in the action for Rick, as Rick had done for him after Mrs. Heston's death.

"I've got an idea," Ed said slowly as he watched the rain pelt the garden. "When you pass that state exam in October, why don't we go away together? October is the anniversary of when we first met, you know. We could celebrate you getting your license and the fact that we're together and married." And, he thought, it would be a perfect opportunity at last to give Rick the gold chain.

"Hmmm." Rick's face looked a good deal brighter than it had when he had walked out of the main house. "That sounds like fun. What do you have in mind for a destination?"

"Well, we could go back to Spruce Lake, if Gordy can get us permission to use the cabin again. Or maybe we could go even farther north, maybe all the way to Mackinac Island. Have you ever been there? Mom and Dad took Laurie and me there once when we were kids, and I loved it. And just think how pretty it'd be in October with the leaves changing."

Rick smiled nostalgically. "Yeah, our family went there once when Claire and I were little, too, but it would be fun to go back, spend some time on the island, and drive over that big bridge. I'd love to share all of that with you, baby. Sign me up."

Ed, pleased at Rick's reaction, kissed him. "Okay. Don't worry about a thing except passing that last test and the state exam. I'll take care of everything, and we'll have something wonderful to look forward to in a month. Not something scary like the future, but just a getaway where we can relax and enjoy ourselves."

While they had been talking, the thunder and lightning had quickly moved off to the east, and now the volume of water falling from the sky began to diminish.

"Looks like the worst is over," Rick commented.

"This time," Ed snickered.

Rick laughed with him. "Yeah, this time. But you're right; somehow we always manage to get through it."

"Yeah, now we just have to go clean up the damage."

"Huh? I thought you said you'd have to hire someone to take care of that limb."

"I didn't mean the limb. I meant your dad."

"Oh." Rick's smile faded. "Yeah. I guess I'd better clear the air before they leave, huh?"

"Yes," Ed said firmly. "As you've said before, we just have to prove them wrong. We can't do it tonight, but we will when the time is right. For now just let them both know you appreciate their concern, and let it go, okay?"

"Okay."

Ed took Rick's hand and led him down the stairs and into the rain-cooled air outside. As they stopped to inspect the rose arbor, the back door opened and Vera appeared.

"Oh, thank heaven," she said, relieved to see them. "Were you in the carriage house all this time? I was afraid you were out in the storm."

"We're fine," Ed called across the yard. "Well, almost," he said gesturing to the rose arbor and then smirking at Rick.

"I know, I know," Rick said under his breath. "I'm going."

Rick started for the house but paused a few feet away, his warm and tender special glowing through the dusk at Ed.

"You're something else, you know that, baby?"

"Nah. I'm just trying to be a good husband."

# Chapter Eighteen

Ed was determined to continue being a good husband the rest of the weekend by finishing Rick's bookcase, but that tree limb leaning on the rose arbor bothered him. He feared its weight would crush the delicate woodwork of the arbor if it were left too long, so he spent the early part of Sunday afternoon calling the few people he knew who owned a chainsaw. It seemed most of Porterfield had left town for the weekend, as no one he called was home. In desperation he finally called Carl Botts, a former classmate who owned and operated a tree service.

"I'm sorry, Ed, but Carl went to Chicago with some of his buddies for a Cubs game," his wife, Jill (also a former classmate), told him on the phone. "Why don't you try Clyde Croasdale? He has a chainsaw, and he's probably home this weekend."

"Who?"

"Clyde Croasdale. He's Claudine Croasdale's brother. You know who she is, don't you?"

Ed thought for a moment, and then mumbled, "Yeah, I know who you're talking about."

Claudine Croasdale, an older maiden lady, had worked for the Penney's store in downtown Porterfield for as long as Ed could remember. As children, Ed and Laurie had been routinely dragged into the store every August by Norma for back-to-school shopping. Norma had always asked for Claudine's help. They had grown up on farms a mile or so apart in rural Stratton County, and in addition to finding the proper school clothing for Ed and Laurie, had spent a good deal of time exchanging both memories and current gossip while Ed and Laurie fidgeted and told each other how ugly they looked in their new clothes.

"Well," Jill was saying, "Clyde moved in with his sister a few months ago. He's a widower, retired, and happens to have a chainsaw. When Carl's short of help he calls Clyde, and Carl says he knows what he's doing. It couldn't hurt to call him."

"I guess I'll do that," Ed told her. "Do you happen to have his number?"

Jill gave it to him; Ed thanked her and hung up. He called the number with low expectations but figured he didn't have much to lose at this point.

"Why, sure, I'd be glad to help you," Clyde Croasdale said after Ed explained who he was and his situation with the maple limb. "It would give me something to do this afternoon. The old Penfield place? I know where that is. I can be over in a half hour or so if you're ready for me."

Ed assured him he was and happily hung up the phone once again.

"Looks like I'm gonna get rid of that tree limb today," he told Rick, who was at the table studying.

"That's nice," Rick mumbled. "Need any help?"

"Nope. Keep studying, real estate boy. After what we went through with your dad last night, I want you to ace that last test."

Ed went downstairs to take a closer look at the maple limb before Clyde arrived, thinking of the previous evening. Both John and Rick had apologized to each other, but the deeper communication Ed hoped would develop between them didn't occur. When John and Vera left, the air had been cleared, as Rick promised it would be, but Ed pessimistically braced himself for another confrontation the next time they were together. He wasn't at all happy about it but realized thirty years of father-son conflicts couldn't be resolved in one weekend.

He was pulling the ladder from the garage when a blue Chevy pickup truck, several model years older than Ed's, rolled to a stop at the Race Street curb. A middle-aged man got out, grabbed a chainsaw from the truck bed, and walked up the drive. He introduced himself to Ed as Clyde Croasdale with a hearty handshake. Clyde was of medium height with a stocky and powerful-looking build. His gray hair was thinning on top, and his face was rather careworn, but Ed guessed the man was probably in his mid-fifties, a little early, Ed thought, for retirement.

As the two of them looked over the fallen limb, Clyde explained how he happened to be living with his sister and at loose ends on a holiday weekend afternoon.

He was, he told Ed, a retired police officer. He'd worked on the Milwaukee, Wisconsin, police force since he had left the army after World War II. He had taken a bullet in his left knee during a shoot-out several years earlier, which had left him unable to continue his work on the street. He'd taken a desk job until his wife had passed away of cancer in late 1980. With his children grown and married and busy with lives of their own, he had decided to take an early retirement and return to Indiana.

"Claudine has some health problems of her own," he said, steadying the ladder, "and she's been alone all these years since our parents died. It seemed better for us to look out for each other than continue living alone, so far apart."

The family farm had been sold when their parents died, and Claudine had used her share of the proceeds to buy a home on North Michigan Street, near Laurie's house on Elm. There was ample room for both of them to go about their own business and for Clyde to indulge himself in his various hobbies.

"A lot of men don't do so well with retirement and time on their hands," he said to Ed, "but I enjoy it. I've always had a lot of outside interests. You about have to, with police work. It can really get you down, but thanks to gardening, woodworking, and boating I managed to keep my perspective. I sold my boat when I moved here, but I'm thinking about getting a new one next summer and taking it north of Fort Wayne to Lake Wawasee or Lake Webster."

"Woodworking?" Ed's ears pricked up at the word.

"Sure. My grandfather was a whittler, a real artist with a knife and a piece of wood. He taught me what he knew, and over the years I moved from a knife to power tools."

"Wow. My dad was the same way."

"I've had a little basement workshop for years," Clyde said as he studied the arbor latticework. "I see your concern here, Ed, but whoever built this arbor built it to last. Whoever did it knew their way around wood, too. Anyway, I brought all of my tools with me when I moved, and now Claudine's basement is where I work on that stuff."

Ed laughed. "I just re-created my dad's basement workshop over in the carriage house."

"Really?" Clyde asked with interest. "That's great. I'd like to see it when we're done here."

Clyde then went to work, and Ed quickly saw that he indeed knew what he was doing. Ed found himself reduced to the role of assistant, holding the ladder and collecting the debris that fell away as Clyde confidently cut the limb away from the arbor.

"This would make good firewood," Clyde remarked as he sawed through the main section of the limb. So Ed fetched his ax and chopped some logs for Mrs. Penfield's fireplace.

When they were finished with the chore, Ed wiped away some sweat and invited Clyde into the carriage house for a cold drink, an offer Clyde eagerly accepted. Ed ran upstairs to grab a beer for Clyde and a Pepsi for himself.

"This guy's really something," he told Rick as he rushed past the table.

"He's into wood, too, so I'm gonna show him what I'm doing with your bookcase."

"That's nice, baby," Rick murmured, not looking up from his books.

Drinks in hand, Ed gave Clyde the official workshop tour. Clyde admired the selection of tools and carefully inspected Ed's work in progress.

"You're doing a real good job here, Ed," Clyde told him, rubbing his hand overone of the shelves and nodding with satisfaction.

Ed picked up a piece of wood from the other side of the workbench. "I want to rout this piece out and attach it to the front, to give the whole thing a little more flair, but I keep putting off cutting in the design I have in mind. I guess I'm afraid I'll mess it up. It's been years since I even tried."

Clyde took the wood and studied Ed's pencil marks. "Well, as my son always says, that's no sweat."

To Ed's astonishment, Clyde slapped the wood on the table saw, flipped the power switch, and went to work, skillfully cutting along the lines Ed had drawn.

"Don't be afraid of making a mistake," Clyde shouted over the noise of the saw. "You can always sand it out, or just get another piece of wood."

"I'll be damned," Ed muttered to himself, remembering his father saying something similar years before.

Clyde finished the cut, shut the saw off, and showed Ed what he had done. When Ed murmured his thanks, Clyde grinned and handed the board to Ed. His feeling of déjà vu continued when Clyde said, "Now, why don't you rout out those grooves so we can see if it will fit properly."

Ed, feeling as though he'd stepped back fifteen years in time, did just that.

"Looks good," Clyde said after they had attached the decorative piece to the top of the bookcase. "Some sanding, staining, and a good varnish and you'll have a real nice piece here."

Ed thanked Clyde profusely for his help, but Clyde waved it off. "This is fun for me. I was glad to help out. You come over to the house sometime and I'll show you the cedar chest I'm working on for Claudine. I've never worked with cedar before, but I'm enjoying it."

"That's just the kind of stuff I've always wanted to do," Ed admitted. "I'd love to come over and see what you're doing if you're sure it's no trouble."

"No trouble at all. I'm glad to meet a young man who enjoys working with wood. My son never took to it, so I'd be more than happy to kick around the shop with you, show you a few things, maybe even collaborate on a project or two."

Clyde left shortly after, saying he had an early supper date with some friends he'd made from the Porterfield Police Department. He refused any payment for his work on the tree limb but did agree to call Ed if a handyman problem he couldn't handle came up at his sister's house.

"But don't wait 'til something breaks down to come over," Clyde urged as he went to his truck. "I want to show you that chest."

Ed waved as the truck rolled down Race and turned the corner onto Spruce. He felt a bit dazed by the unexpected events of the afternoon but was relieved to have the fallen limb taken care of and genuinely excited at the prospect of meeting someone who might be able to resurrect his dormant skills with wood, and perhaps even improve upon them.

He wandered into the workshop as he heard Rick clattering down the stairs. Rick burst into the workshop, jingling the car keys in his hand.

"It's time for a study break," he announced. "How about a quick spin out to the P & J for some Spanish dogs? Hey," he exclaimed, noticing the bookcase. "You got a lot done with that today. You showing off for the tree guy, baby?"

"Nope," Ed said, shaking his head with a smile. "I think he was showing off for me. Not only that; I think I may have found the guy who can help me get serious about this stuff."

Rick's warm and tender special spread across his face. "And just in time for your birthday, like I said. How 'bout that?"

Ed gave the bookcase a satisfied pat and went to give Rick a big hug. "Yeah, how 'bout that. Now, Jeane Dixon, how 'bout those Spanish dogs?"

❧•❦

Two days later Ed led Mrs. Penfield into the dim workshop. He snapped on the light and waved his arm toward the workbench. "There it is!" He indicated the finished bookcase. "What do you think?"

Mrs. Penfield, leaning on her cane, studied first the bookcase, then Ed, who anxiously awaited her opinion. She nodded in great satisfaction. "It's beautiful, Ed. If I didn't know better, I would think you had brought it home from the showroom of Fletcher Furniture."

"A labor of love," he said, pleased with Mrs. Penfield's response.

It was an attractive piece. Although not as big as Ed's original vision, it would fit perfectly under the hallway window upstairs. Ed's hard work was apparent in its obvious sturdiness, and his careful sanding and staining showed in the burnished glow of the wood.

Inspired by Clyde Croasdale's help, Ed had completed the project in a burst of energy on Labor Day. Now, the day after, he was eager to move it upstairs and surprise Rick when he returned from work.

Mrs. Penfield moved slowly forward. She reached out to rub the bookcase's finish, smiling. "A labor of love perhaps, but more important, did you enjoy it?"

"Yes, I did. More than I thought I would." Ed cocked his head, admiring his own work. "It's been years since I did anything like this, but I swear Dad was in here with me, telling me what to do until I met Clyde. Then he got me over the hard parts so all I had to do yesterday was the finish work."

He laughed. "Okay, you and Rick were right all along. Meeting Clyde the way I did proves this is meant to be."

Ed, noticing that Mrs. Penfield seemed a bit unsteady, led her out of the workshop to her favorite seat in the rose arbor.

"If I'm going to do more complicated projects, though, I'll definitely need some help," he told her once he'd sat next to her. "Bookcases are one thing, but I'm going to need someone with more experience to help me with the things I'm thinking about."

"And what might those things be?" Mrs. Penfield's faded blue eyes were twinkling behind her glasses.

"Oh, I'd really like to make cabinets, like Rick suggested. Chests, too. Thing is, the most complicated stuff I think my dad ever made was my record cabinet and a big dollhouse for Laurie. Clyde's working on a cedar chest for his sister, so I hope he can steer me in the right direction."

"Well, I'm delighted you seem to have found the proper instructor."

"Maybe," Ed said doubtfully. "I like Clyde, and I wouldn't have the bookcase finished now without his help, but I kind of hate to impose on him."

Mrs. Penfield laughed. "If Mr. Croasdale's retirement is anything like mine, I can assure you he would consider your eagerness to learn a pleasure as opposed to an imposition."

"We'll see." Ed shrugged. "Right now I'm more concerned with Rick getting through with that class."

"Don't put it off too long, Ed. I know your twenty-ninth birthday is a few weeks away, and you feel as though you have all the time in the world, but I can promise you that time somehow moves a lot faster after a certain age. You've proven to yourself that you have talent and skill with woodworking, so I do hope you'll continue to make the most of it."

"I will. I'm not about to neglect my handyman work, though. I can only imagine what Mom would say about me trying to make money from woodworking, and after what we went through with Rick's parents the other night, I don't want to make any more waves."

Much to Ed's surprise, he had learned from Rick late Saturday night that during the storm Mrs. Penfield had spoken to both John and Vera about their concern regarding Rick's possible career change. Neither Rick nor Ed knew exactly what was said, but apparently Mrs. Penfield's words had considerably eased their worries.

"I always said I wanted Mrs. P. to give them a good talking-to," Rick had told Ed Saturday night before they went to bed.

"Why is it," he said now to Mrs. Penfield, "that you seem to have more confidence in us than our parents do?"

She pondered Ed's question. "Perhaps it's my many years of teaching. My job has always been to instruct, educate, and encourage. I would never encourage a child beyond what I considered his abilities to be, and I'm certainly not doing that with Rick or yourself. Rick will be an excellent real estate agent someday because he has the interest and the ability. You will be a wonderful craftsman with wood as well. You've already proven that."

"But Rick's parents are teachers, too."

"Yes, they are, but they are parents first. A parent's job is to worry, Ed." Mrs. Penfield shrugged. "My perspective on this might be entirely different if George Junior had lived. I would like to think I would be encouraging and supportive of whatever he wanted to do, but who knows? Parents have a hard time being rational where their own offspring are concerned. I have a certain amount of distance with Rick and yourself. Haven't you noticed that distance yourself, dealing with your nieces and nephews?"

"I guess so."

Mrs. Penfield looked thoughtful. "I also suspect the Bentons have been disappointed with the choices both Rick and Claire have made over the years. It's unfortunate but common. Parents have a tendency to create high expectations for their children. Give them time, Ed. Claire's doing a wonderful job of rebuilding her life and raising her children, and we both know, despite the uncertainties of the real estate business, that Rick can make a success of it. It may be rough going at first, but I am sure my confidence in him is not misplaced. Don't worry about it, and see to it Rick isn't worrying over it as well."

"I will." He grinned at her. "Distraction number one will be ready and waiting in the upstairs hall when he comes home from work."

Ed managed to get the bookcase up the narrow stairs and in place by himself. He shook his head and smiled, more pleased than he could say to display the results of his own work. Oh, Ed derived a lot of satisfaction from completing the chores his handyman clients gave him, but to have actually created a piece of furniture—something practical yet attractive—was a feeling deeper and even more satisfying. He realized that a big part of him would be very happy to spend the rest of his workdays puttering in his workshop, handyman job forgotten.

He sighed, knowing that wouldn't happen for quite some time, but content nonetheless to have discovered a possible new career. And, he reminded himself, it would have never happened without Rick's encouragement and support.

Ed was ready and waiting when Rick returned that day. He made Rick cover his eyes as he led him down the hall to the bookcase.

"Okay," Ed said when he had Rick stationed in front of it. "You can open your eyes."

Rick eyes opened slowly, then widened in surprise and joy. "Oh, baby," he whispered. He abruptly turned his head toward the wall.

"What's wrong?" Ed asked in alarm, afraid Rick didn't like it.

Rick, his eyes still averted, sniffled. "I just don't want to cry again, that's all. We're . . . we're always blubbering over each other, and it gets embarrassing," he choked out.

Ed put his arms around him, and Rick lost the battle with his tears.

"It's beautiful," he sniffed. "I love it! I just can't believe someone would work so hard to do something like this for me."

"A labor of love," Ed said for the second time that day, stroking Rick's back. "I gotta admit, I was hoping you'd like it, but I wasn't expecting this."

It took awhile, but Rick got himself under control. He hesitantly reached out a hand to the bookcase, shaking his head.

"Don't you understand? You *made* this for me! With your own two hands." He shrugged, and smiled through his tears.

Ed was blushing as he usually did when praised. "Well, I had some help."

"Just a little. You started this whole thing thinking of me, and you made it happen."

Ed was very pleased with Rick's reaction and his words.

"I think I know what you mean, darlin'. I'm glad you love it. The reason I worked so hard on it was because it's for you. It wouldn't have happened without you. Remember that Saturday, way back in December, when you first asked me if I ever thought about doing this kind of work? Well, look. Another Saturday dream come true for us. On a Tuesday."

Ed snorted, an amused look on his face. "How come none of this shit ever happens on Saturday?"

Rick laughed, wiping his eyes. "Oh, I don't know, and I don't care, as long the dreams keep coming true."

He opened his arms wide and hugged the bookcase, then turned to hug Ed. "Thank you, Ed. Thank you for the bookcase, and for everything."

Ed hugged him back and added a kiss. "You're very welcome."

"I can't wait to stock this with books." Rick ran his hands along the shelves. "You know, there's a boxful in the closet I was saving just for this day. I wish I didn't have class tonight."

He looked at his watch. "Oh, maybe I've got some time to sit here and play if you don't mind takeout for supper tonight."

"Fine with me. Play all you want. I'll go get us something from the P & J again."

Rick went to the hall closet and hauled out a cardboard carton. "Well, it's a great day. We have the first completed project from the Ed Stephens Workshop. What's next?"

"Nothing."

"What?" Rick almost dropped the carton. "What do you mean, nothing?"

Ed laughed at the expression on Rick's face. "What I mean is I'll be too busy to do much of anything there for awhile. Fall's coming, and I have a lot of work to do. With you busy studying for that exam, I'm going to have to see to all the winterizing chores around here myself, not to mention all the stuff I'll have to do for the old-lady brigade and the house on Coleman Street."

Rick frowned. "You don't have to do all the work around here. I'll help you with it. Just because I'm working hard toward getting that license doesn't mean I can't do anything. I don't want you to give up the fun you have in your workshop."

Ed took the carton from Rick and placed it on the floor in front of the bookcase. He drew Rick toward him for another hug.

"Don't worry about it. Look, this whole real estate thing is important, and I want you to concentrate on it. We can't do everything at once, and when winter comes I'll have lots of time to mess around downstairs. Besides, I really *don't* know what I want to do next."

He shrugged. "Now I've got all fall to think about it, and I can spend some time visiting Clyde to see what he's doing. When the work slows down, the way it always does, I'll have some ideas."

Rick looked unconvinced. "It doesn't seem right, especially now that you have someone to work with. None of these opportunities would have come to me without you. I don't want you sacrificing anything for me."

"I'm not sacrificing. Just postponing. My turn will come."

Ed looked at the ring on his left hand. "Right now the good husband's job is to support his man until he's an official licensed real estate agent."

Rick hugged him hard. "Okay, if you say so. I'm going to make you very proud of me, though. I promise."

"Hey, I already am." Ed kissed him slowly and tenderly. "I know you're gonna make me even prouder, too."

❧●❦

After Rick left for his class, Ed went outside to water the gardens. He had noticed the impatiens were in need of a good soak.

"Drink up, you greedy bitches," he grumbled, aiming the hose's spray over their wilting heads. In his opinion impatiens were properly named. If you didn't give them all the water they wanted, they pouted.

The cicadas roared in the oak trees, and the crickets happily chirped away in the garden, now at its end-of-summer best despite the languishing impatiens. Ed couldn't help but think of the frosts and freezes to come, and the day when he'd pull up plants and prepare the flower beds for a long winter's nap. He then envisioned contented meetings with Mrs. Penfield as they planned for next summer's garden. Already he was plotting a replacement for the impatiens, which were beautiful but required more attention than Ed felt they deserved.

*Mrs. Penfield's right,* he thought as he surveyed the garden. *Time does start to move faster when you're older. I can't believe it's been almost a year since the day I first saw Rick delivering my mail.*

Although Ed had no control over the passage of time, he was comforted by nature's yearly cycle of birth, growth, death, and rebirth. As Rick had imagined shortly after they had moved into the carriage house, Ed could see them together conferring on spring plantings in this very garden for many years to come.

*I hope so, anyway,* he thought as he coiled up the hose, wondering what to do next. It seemed odd to be at loose ends on a Tuesday night after so many Tuesdays spent bowling with Josh. Thinking of the fun he'd had at the Bowl-O-Rama with Josh made him think of Gordy, so he decided to go upstairs and call his friend and invite him over for a drink and some conversation.

As he entered the apartment, it occurred to Ed that Gordy hadn't stopped by on Labor Day as he said he might. Ed shrugged, assuming the fish must have been really biting over the weekend.

He flipped on the radio as he reached for the phone. "Arthur's Theme" by Christopher Cross was playing, which reminded Ed that Rick had mentioned he wanted to see the Dudley Moore movie that weekend if he managed to get enough studying done. Ed decided he'd invite Gordy along for that as well.

"Hell-lo." Gordy answered the phone as he always did.

"Hey, Gord. It's Ed. If you're not doing anything, you wanna come over? It seems weird not having anything to do on a Tuesday night."

"Uh, thanks, Ed, but I'm kinda busy tonight."

Ed was surprised. "Oh, okay," he said slowly. "So how was Spruce Lake?"

Gordy, who was seldom, if ever, at a loss for words, was silent for several moments, surprising Ed even further.

"Actually," Gordy finally said, "I didn't go. Had a little change of plans."

"Is anything wrong?"

"No. Hell, no. Listen, Ed, I don't want you freakin' out on me here, but I met another guy. I wasn't lookin' for it, and I sure didn't expect it, but I met someone, and we spent most of the weekend together."

Ed grabbed the telephone table for support. "Really? Out of the blue? That's great! But if you weren't out looking, did you meet him here in *Porterfield*?"

"Maybe, maybe not. I'd rather not say."

"Well, why the hell not? I'm your best bud, aren't I? Don't I get any details?"

"Hey! I told you not to freak out. I'm freaked out enough as it is. Listen, I promise to tell you everything sometime, but just not now, okay? He's . . . well, he's careful about stuff the way I am. We're playing it close to the vest right now. I think we both want to see where this is going."

Ed blinked a few times, wondering what to say. He walked to the stereo and turned the volume down on a radio commercial, which made him think of Ken.

"He's not married, is he?" Ed asked suspiciously.

"Christ, no! Believe me, I checked that out first thing. No, he's just not ready to be all open about stuff. I can understand that, can't you?"

"Well, yeah, I guess so. After what happened last month I just want you to be happy, that's all."

"If happy is being weak in the knees and scared and turning up the radio for those stupid love songs you like so much and feeling like an asshole, then I'm happy all right," Gordy said, sounding closer to normal.

"So you're seeing him tonight?" Ed asked, thinking he had nothing better to do than sneak over to the Stratton Avenue Apartments and spy on Gordy's door to see who showed up.

"Yeah, I'm seeing him tonight, and don't you get any ideas," Gordy said, reading Ed's mind.

"I wouldn't do that," Ed said in a self-righteous huff. Actually, he really wouldn't. He wouldn't want anyone doing it to him, so he wouldn't do it either, but his curiosity had gotten the better of him for a moment.

"You damn well better not, bud." Gordy snickered. "You do anything to mess this up, and I'll have your ass."

"I won't. If this guy is something special I want it to work out as much as you do. Really, Gord, you know that."

"I know. That's why you *are* my best bud. Just wish me luck, okay?"

"I do. Good luck. Gordy," Ed said, and then paused. "Gord, you really like this guy, don't you?"

"Yeah," Gordy answered quietly. "I really do. I don't know if it's anything like the Ed and Rick Adventure, but there's something special goin' on, ya know?"

"Apparently," Ed said just as quietly. He didn't know what else to say, as he knew Gordy wouldn't answer any of the questions crowding his mind.

"Well," he finally said, "have fun tonight. And keep me posted when you're ready, okay?"

"I will, bud. I promise. And since I know you're gonna tell Rick about this, tell him to keep his big mouth shut at the post office tomorrow. I'll tell you both about this when I'm damn good and ready."

"Okay. I promise."

Ed and Gordy exchanged good-byes. Ed hung up the phone and reached once again for the radio volume. Another one of those stupid love songs that Ed enjoyed and Gordy was paying attention to these days was playing, "The Look of Love" by Sergio Mendes and Brazil '66. Ed wondered whether Gordy had found the look of love in this mystery man's eyes, the same way Ed had found it in Rick's.

He wandered over to the window thinking he had forgotten to ask Gordy to join them for the movies that weekend but realizing Gordy probably had other more interesting plans. He smiled, suddenly feeling wistful. Ed couldn't turn back the clock, and he didn't want to, but he couldn't help but envy the excitement Gordy was feeling. Those early days of his relationship with Rick were some of the most exciting ones he'd ever had.

He stared out into the late summer twilight, listening to the bugs and admiring the garden below him, observing nature's current moment on its yearly cycle, still feeling a little wistful but very content as well. The Ed and Rick Adventure, as Gordy called it, was nearly a year old and progressing forward nicely in its own cycle. Hopefully Gordy's new adventure would provide the same opportunities for Gordy as well.

# Chapter Nineteen

On a Thursday night in mid-September, Rick returned home tired but triumphant from his final real estate class. He had passed all three of the exams with better-than-average grades and was now eligible to move on to the state licensing exam in Indianapolis.

"Am I glad that's over," he sighed, throwing his books and notebook on the coffee table.

"Why don't we put those books in some dark corner of the closet?" Ed teased as he gave Rick a congratulatory hug. "I'm as tired of looking at them as you are."

"I know, but I'll need to skim through them again before that exam in Indy, so I'd better leave 'em in plain sight.

"But not tonight," Rick groaned as he slumped onto the sofa, dragging Ed with him. "Now that it's over with, all I want to do is collapse. I didn't realize how uptight I'd been until now. I just want to go to bed and sleep as late as possible tomorrow."

And he did. He was sound asleep and snoring within a half hour and was still at it when Ed ventured out of bed the next morning. Ed went about his morning routine attempting to be as thoughtful as Rick usually was. When he left the bathroom after his morning shower and shave he was surprised to hear the television in the living room. He was about to apologize for waking Rick up when he saw Rick, clad in his shabby bathrobe, sprawled on the sofa watching *That Girl*.

"Well, what's this?" Ed mock-barked, hands on his hips. "A smart person watching dumb TV?"

Rick made a poor attempt at looking abashed. "Well, *That Girl* doesn't count," he mumbled as a grin snuck onto his face. "We both like this show."

Ed watched Ann Marie try to explain to Donald Hollinger why she was in jail wearing a leopard-skin cavewoman's costume. It was true. *That Girl* was one of the few television shows they had in common. The reruns had recently begun airing every morning at eight thirty, and Ed had been watching them with a guilty relish while Rick was at work. He was relieved to find out Ann's single-girl-in-the-city exploits were to be considered acceptable viewing at the carriage house.

"Besides, after all the studying I've done, I think I deserve a little light entertainment."

Ed couldn't argue with that but couldn't resist a small tweak at Rick's nerves. "Well, *Family Affair* comes on next, and I know you wouldn't want to miss that."

Rick rolled his eyes. "I think the TV will be turned off at nine. That sad little girl who OD'd in real life, and that creepy old-lady doll she carried around? Yuck!"

"Anyway," Rick said as he stretched and reached for a cup of coffee, "I have better things to do today. Since you're going to be out of the house, I have some secret phone calls to make."

"Secret?"

"Yeah. It has to do with the fact that a certain someone is having a birthday next week, so grab your toolbox and get your sexy ass out of here, okay? I've got plans to make."

"Speaking of plans, did you remember to ask Don for a couple of vacation days next month for our trip?" Ed had been busy the past week gathering information from the Michigan Tourism Bureau and planning their getaway to Mackinac Island for the weekend after the state licensing exam.

Rick looked vague. "Oh, no. I forgot. Guess I was too worried about passing that last test."

"Well, if you see him tomorrow make sure you put in for those days. It's less than a month away now." Ed was a little perturbed that Rick didn't seem to be as excited about the trip as he was but figured he had nothing to bitch about if Rick was busy making secret plans for his birthday.

"Okay," Rick said, his eyes back on the television.

Ed was still hoping for a more enthusiastic response but decided it was too early in the day to nag. After a quick kiss on the top of Rick's head, he went downstairs, hopped into his truck, and drove the two blocks to his mother's house. Norma had asked him to stop by and pick up some stuff she wanted him to deliver to the Ladies Hospital Auxiliary discount store.

When he pulled into his mother's driveway, he saw several overflowing bags and boxes on the back steps. He was placing them in the truck bed when Norma appeared at the back door.

"Ed? That's not all of it. I want you to take that easy chair from your sister's old room, too."

"Mom," he said patiently as he put the last bag in the truck, "the ladies aid store doesn't sell furniture, just old clothes and knickknacks."

"Well, take it somewhere else, then. I've decided to set up my sewing machine in there for the winter because the light's better. I don't have room for it, and your sister doesn't want it."

Ed wasn't surprised to hear that. The chair in question, a decidedly uncomfortable easy chair in a loud paisley print, had been purchased by Norma for Laurie's bedroom in the late sixties. Norma, it turned out, was the only member of the family who liked it. Tim, Ed, and Laurie had privately agreed that it was ugly, and Laurie had been resisting Norma's attempts to move it to her house for years.

"I guess I'll just haul it to the dump, then," Ed sighed, walking toward the house.

"The dump! That perfectly good chair? Are you sure you don't want it for your place?"

Ed shuddered at the thought. "I'll make sure it finds a good home," he lied.

He hurried upstairs and, with Norma watching to make sure he didn't scratch the stairway wallpaper, managed to get it out of the house and into his truck.

"You need anything else today, Mom?" he asked as he sat down at the kitchen table to rest for a moment.

"No. I'll be calling you by the end of the month, though. I've decided to go through that basement again and get rid of more junk you and Laurie don't want and I'm tired of looking at."

Ed was grateful he had removed all of his father's tools earlier in the summer. He thought of Clyde Croasdale and looked up from the piece of homemade coffee cake Norma was placing in front of him.

"Hey, I met someone last week I think you know."

"Who's that?"

"You know old Claudine Croasdale at Penney's? Her brother Clyde is living with her now. He helped me take care of a limb that fell on the rose arbor."

Norma's mouth fell open. "Clyde *Croasdale*? What on earth is he doing in Porterfield?"

"He's retired and his wife died last year. He moved back home to keep an eye on his sister. Apparently she's not doing so well these days."

Norma was shaking her head. "Clyde Croasdale, after all these years. Humph." Her usually sharp-featured face softened into a silly grin, and a faraway look came into her eyes.

Ed, taken aback by this side of his mother he seldom saw, put two and two together and crowed, "Is he an old boyfriend, Mom?"

"Don't be ridiculous," she snapped, making a quick return to the present.

"Well, did you go out with him?" Ed needled, thoroughly enjoying the idea of making her uncomfortable instead of the other way around for a change.

"I was not sweet on him," she said indignantly. "As for going out, if you consider going in a group to town to see *Mrs. Miniver* when I was thirteen and he was seventeen, then I suppose we did. I always said that movie goosed him into enlisting after he turned eighteen instead of waiting to be drafted like other farm boys. Why, with his father so crippled up with gout, Clyde could have gotten a deferment to run the family farm, but he went anyway."

"So he went off to the war and ended up in Milwaukee as a policeman. Didn't he ever come back to the farm?"

Norma, still looking indignant, explained. "He took off the day after his eighteenth birthday, breaking his mother's heart. Then he met one of those women who hung around USO halls and collected men like charms for their bracelets. According to Claudine, he fell hard for her and the minute he was discharged came back to marry her. This woman didn't like or approve of farm life, so they settled in her hometown up in Wisconsin. He ended up with the police, and that's that."

Ed closely studied his mother's face and smiled. "I think you *were* sweet on him."

Norma crossed her arms over her chest and glared at him. "Whether I was or not, it's all water under the bridge. I moved to town after the war, married your father, and had a perfectly good life. That's the end of the story."

"Except you're a widow now, and he's a widower."

"Ed Stephens," she gasped. "How can you even think such a thing with your father gone just three years? Who do you think I am, Scarlett O'Hara?"

Ed laughed. "No, but you're still a reasonably young, good-looking woman. I miss Dad as much as you and Laurie do, but sometimes Laurie and I wonder if you'll ever get married again."

"Humph. Well, I haven't been wondering, so just put the thought out of your head, and I'll tell that sister of yours the same thing when I see her tonight when I go over there to babysit. You hear me?"

"Yes, Mom," Ed said, dropping the smile from his face in favor of a more solemn expression.

"Now, finish your coffee cake and get out of here. I've got things to do this morning."

Norma got up from the table and marched into the dining room, a can of Pledge and a dust rag in her hand. Ed savored the excellent pastry, spent a moment anticipating the chocolate birthday cake his mother would surely bake for him next week, and enjoyed the thought that he had finally, after years of trying, managed to make his mother squirm the way she often did him.

❦

Rick shook Ed awake on the morning of his twenty-ninth birthday.

"Wake up, baby. I know you don't have any appointments today, but I made one for you. Laurie's coming by in a while to take you out for brunch. I have stuff to do while you're gone." Rick had arranged to take the day off as well.

Ed yawned, squinting at the clock. "Aw, crud. Since it's my birthday I thought *you'd* be making breakfast for me today."

Rick, still bent over the bed, kissed his forehead. "Well, I was going to, but I needed to get you out of the house for a while, so Laurie stepped in to help. She's taking you to the Cozy Hearth at nine, so you'd better get dressed."

❦

Ed happily dug into a heaping plate of pancakes at the Cozy Hearth Café. He beamed at Laurie across the table. "Thanks for taking me out for breakfast this morning. I know it's something Rick asked you to do, so I really appreciate it."

Laurie smiled at him over her coffee cup. "My pleasure. My brother's birthday seemed like a great excuse to take part of the morning off from work. Besides, with me being busy getting the kids ready for a new school year, and working full-time now, we haven't had a chance to sit and talk for ages."

"That's true," Ed said, savoring pancakes almost as good as Rick's. "But I gotta ask you: I'm not going home to some surprise party, am I?"

Laurie laughed. "No. Oh, Rick has a surprise for you, but it's not a party. As far as I know, the only party planned is for this evening at Mrs. Penfield's, and you know about that. Relax and enjoy those pancakes." She rolled her eyes. "I wish I could eat like that. They'd go straight to my hips."

"You shouldn't count calories on your birthday." Ed poured more syrup. "At least I don't. So what else is going on with you these days?"

Laurie updated him on her family: Lesley's excitement about first grade, Bobby's exploits in the third, and her own satisfaction at working full-time again.

"It's been a bit of a shock, you know, having to schedule everything for the kids outside of work hours, and still having to get all the housework done, but Mom, despite her bitching, has been great, helping out when she can. But I've been meaning to ask you, what did you say to get her all worked up about the idea of getting married again?"

Ed laughed and told her about Clyde Croasdale.

"So Mom has a romantic past other than Dad," Laurie marveled. "When I used to ask her if there were any other men in her life, she made it sound like she lived in a nunnery, not on a farm."

"Well, I think she thought about Clyde a lot more than he thought about her. And he was older, too."

"Hmmm. I'll bet she had a real crush on him."

Laurie tapped her fingers against her coffee cup. "You know what? You should have Clyde come over to your workshop when you know Mom's coming over, to see what happens."

Ed almost choked on his pancakes. "Are you crazy? She'd never let me hear the end of it. I'd be paying for that for the rest of my life!"

Laurie giggled. "Probably. But it'd be worth it to see the look on her face."

Ed, imagining that scene, giggled as well.

"No, I'm staying out of it. The way Porterfield is, they'll run into each other sooner or later. For right now I think I'll visit Clyde at his house instead of the other way around."

"Yeah, birthday boy, you're probably right. You don't want to piss off Mom until after you've had the chocolate cake she makes for you every year."

Laurie, still shaking her head in amusement, glanced at Ed's plate.

"You about done with those things? I should get back to work, and I'm sure by now Rick's surprise is ready."

"You know what it is?"

"Yes, I do, but I'm not telling."

Ed gave her a suspicious look. "It doesn't have anything to do with that awful chair I hauled out of Mom's last week, does it?"

"No, but you're a little warm. Finish eating those things, and you'll find out soon enough."

❧•❧

When Laurie dropped Ed off in front of the carriage house, he was surprised to see his truck in the driveway, as it had been parked in the garage when he left. He was about to head upstairs when Rick appeared at the door.

"Don't move," he commanded.

"You mean I have to spend the rest of my birthday standing here in the driveway?"

"No, smart-ass." Rick walked over to him. He covered Ed's eyes with his hands and slowly led him to the door. "I've got a surprise for you in here. You'll see it the minute you walk in, and I'm not about to miss the look on your face."

Once inside, Rick positioned Ed just inside his workshop. "You ready?"

Ed laughed, enjoying the suspense. "Oh, I suppose we could stand here like this all day, but yeah, I think I'm ready."

"Okay. Happy birthday!"

Rick took his hands away, and Ed blinked to adjust his eyes. His mouth fell open in surprise. "Rick," he gasped. "I don't believe it!"

A rolltop desk had been placed next to the partition wall he had built the month before. It was a beautiful desk, made of oak, and obviously not new, as it had the warm, mellow glow of age. Ed hesitantly walked toward the desk, and then reached out to touch it, as if he didn't believe it was really there.

"Do you like it, baby?" Rick asked anxiously.

"Like it?" Ed turned his incredulous face to Rick. "I love it! I can't believe you did this."

He turned back to the desk and suddenly realized he had seen it before.

"This is Mrs. Heston's desk! What the hell?" He shook his head, wondering just what all Rick had been up to in the last month.

Rick laughed in relief. "Oh, it's a long story." He put his arms around him. "It's your desk now. It's from both Mrs. Heston and me. Happy birthday."

Ed buried his face in Rick's neck, thrilled at the gift but a little annoyed with him. "I told you not to bother her family about this! What did you do?"

Rick hugged him. "I promise I didn't bother them. Geraldine, Mrs. Heston's daughter, called here last month one afternoon while you were still at work. She wanted to make sure you were sending her mother's bill to her. Remember how late you were with your July billing? I told her it was on its way, and then *politely* inquired about the desk. When she realized I wanted it for you, she all but gave it to me. She said no one in the family wanted it, and she didn't know what to do with it. She said she thought her mother would be very happy to see it go to you. I didn't want to just take it, so I finally got her to agree to a token payment. So I didn't spend a lot of money, and I think it made Geraldine happy for you to have it."

Ed was quite moved, thinking of Mrs. Heston and her daughter's kindness.

"Oh, darlin', thank you. I don't know what to say."

Rick gently pushed Ed into the chair that accompanied the desk. "You don't have to say anything. Just enjoy it. What goes around comes around, you know. You've worked hard for your clients all these years. Sure, you get paid to do it, but they appreciate the things you do for them more than you know. I began to see that a long time ago, when I met some of them on my route. Geraldine said she knew her mother would want you to have this desk, and I'll bet the rest of the old-lady brigade would feel the same way."

Rick stooped down to hug him again. "You're a good man, Ed Stephens," he whispered. "You've given of yourself without hesitation all these years, so now the world's starting to give back. Think of this desk as a blessing from all of us who love you and are grateful for all you do. Whether you're a handyman all your life, or if you decide to give it up to build furniture, you'll have this to remember how much good you've done for the old folks in this town."

Ed wiped his eyes. "Thank you," he repeated. He knew if he tried to say anything else he'd start to bawl.

"You're welcome. However, I do want to apologize for borrowing your truck without asking. I had Laurie get you out of here so I could meet Geraldine's husband at Mrs. Heston's house. We loaded the desk in the truck and brought it back over here just before you came home."

Ed giggled, still wiping away tears. "That's okay."

"Since this desk is not just from me, I've got another present for you later on, and all *it* cost me was a postage stamp and a long-distance phone call." Rick gave him a kiss, obviously very pleased with himself and his surprises.

"What else are you up to?"

"You'll find out this evening." Rick carefully rolled the desk's lid up. "Man, it's a beauty, all right. I can see why you liked it so much."

"I love it." Ed returned Rick's kiss. "I just love it. I've always wanted a desk just like this, almost as much as I always wanted a man just like you. Already this is the best birthday I've ever had."

"I'm glad, baby. You know how much I love you, and how much I love making you happy. I hope I'm around to make you happy for lots more birthdays."

"Me, too." Ed hugged Rick hard. "I love you, darlin'. Thanks for making my life so wonderful." He sat back in his new chair with a sigh, admiring his new desk.

"You know, it's only eleven o'clock," Rick said. "My next surprise isn't 'til after six, right before that party Mrs. Penfield has planned. What do you want to do with the rest of the day? Anything you want. I didn't want to plan the whole day away, in case there was something special you wanted to do."

Ed's brow crinkled in thought. "Well, aside from stocking my new desk with all my business stuff, there is something I'd like to do."

"What's that?"

"Well, do you remember your birthday?"

"Of course."

"Do you remember what we did after I made you dinner and we danced in the living room?"

Rick's eyes widened. "I remember. Are you trying to tell me you'd like me to remove my clothes and meet you in the bedroom?"

"Yeah." Ed pulled Rick to him for another kiss. "I wanna do everything we did that night, 'cause you said we'd do it all again on my birthday. Oh, I know we've done that stuff since then, but you *did* promise it would happen again today."

Rick nodded solemnly. "I did promise."

"So meet me upstairs in about ten minutes?"

Rick grinned. "Hell, I'll be ready in five."

⋘•⋙

By early evening, Ed was feeling thoroughly spoiled. After a passionate and erotic lovemaking session with his husband, the mail had arrived with a flood of birthday cards. There were cards from his clients and Uncle Chester and Aunt Eleanor; he was especially pleased to receive one from Rick's parents, which included a very generous birthday check as well. He showed it to Rick, who looked as pleased as Ed felt.

Although he thought the day had been grand enough already, he couldn't help but look forward to dinner at Mrs. Penfield's. Effie Maude was making her specialty, fried chicken, and both Norma and Gordy had been invited. The other family members—Claire and her children and Laurie, Todd, and their kids—were invited for cake and ice cream.

Ed was dressed and ready to go to the big house for dinner by six o'clock and was surprised when Rick told him to sit on the sofa and wait awhile. "I've got your other present to give you first."

Rick turned the radio to WFWQ. A new program, *The '60's at 6*, came on. Mystified but enjoying the music, Ed sat patiently through golden oldies from Gary Puckett & the Union Gap and Lesley Gore.

"Darlin', you know how much I love these songs, but what are you up to?"

"You'll see," Rick said with a grin.

"And now on *The '60's at 6* we have a special birthday dedication," the disc jockey said. "This next song is going out to Ed in Porterfield. It's one of his favorite groups, and it's from his darlin' with love. Happy birthday, Ed! Here's the Mamas and the Papas for you."

Ed's mouth fell open in surprise for the second time that day as "Dedicated to the One I Love" began to play on the radio.

"Well, what do you know? No one ever dedicated a song to me on the radio before!"

"I thought so." Rick's grin grew bigger. "And it *is* dedicated to the one I love, baby."

Rick joined him on the sofa. He put his arm around Ed as they sat and listened to the song. Ed shook his head in amazement, feeling as though he was hearing it for the first time. When the song ended and the radio station jingle played, he pulled Rick to him for a kiss.

"That was so cool," he whispered. "That was just as great as the desk. Thank you."

Rick held him close. "It occurred to me that someone who listened to the radio as much as you have all these years should have a special song played for him."

"How'd you get that guy to do it? And why'd you pick that song? I love that song, but why'd you pick it?"

Rick laughed, again pleased with his success in surprising Ed.

"Well, remember this morning when I said it only cost me a stamp and a phone call? I wrote that disc jockey a letter last week, asking him to do this. Then last night, when you were over at the main house, I called him and confirmed it with him. He seems to be a pretty nice guy. He said he'd be happy to do it for me, and it would be the third song on the show, so we'd have time to get over to the house for dinner.

"As for the song, well, I remembered you telling me how your dad would sneak you extra money to buy records at Woolworth's, and how he liked the Mamas and the Papas almost as much as you did. It just seemed appropriate."

Ed smiled at him, sad and happy at the same time. "I wish you had known Dad. He would have thought this was cool, too. Thanks, darlin'. Hearing that . . . well, it was wonderful. It's almost like Dad was here for this birthday."

"I'm glad you liked your present," Rick said stroking his face.

"It was better than anything you could have bought me."

"Hey," Gordy shouted from the driveway. "You guys up there? Get your butts over here. We're all hungry!"

Rick laughed again. "I think our tender moment has come to an end."

Ed laughed, too. "That's okay." He gave Rick another kiss. "Trust me. It's one moment I'll never forget."

⋘•⋙

The rest of the evening was just as wonderful. Although everyone had been forbidden to bring presents, Norma gave him a new bathrobe.

"It's a mother's right," she said, handing him the box. "Now, when you go home, throw that old one away. I don't ever want to see it again."

Gordy was in an exceptionally good mood, and Ed caught him looking at his watch a few times.

"Okay, I might as well admit it. I have a date later this evening," he said when Ed called him on it.

"The mystery man?" Ed teased.

"Yeah, and don't bug me about it. Since things are goin' so good, you'll find out soon enough."

The whole group was clustered in the dining room when Effie Maude called Ed to the phone in the front hall.

"Ed?" It was Vera, Rick's mother. "We just wanted to call and wish you a happy birthday, since we couldn't come to the party."

"Yes, Ed, happy birthday," John added from their extension phone.

"Why, thanks for calling," Ed replied. He motioned for Rick to join him in the hall. "And thanks so much for the card and the check. You didn't have to do it, but I sure appreciate it."

"It was our pleasure," John said.

"Yes, it certainly was," Vera said. "You know, Ed, we're pleased you're with Rick and that things are going so well for the two of you. Rick's been very happy since you've been together, and that means a lot to us."

"Well, Rick makes me pretty happy, too," Ed said, looking at him. "You won't believe what all he did for my birthday." He told them about the desk and the song dedication.

"He's standing right here," he added, knowing he was putting Rick on the spot but feeling that Rick needed to talk with his parents. "Would you like to talk to him?"

He handed the phone to Rick, who frowned but accepted the receiver. "Hi, Mom; hi, Dad," he said. "Thanks for being so good to Ed for his birthday."

Rick listened for a while, and then smiled. "Well, it means a lot to me that you approve of our marriage."

Laurie stepped into the hall and grabbed Ed's arm.

"C'mon, you need to cut the cake. The kids are getting restless."

Ed left Rick at the phone and returned to the dining room, where Norma was removing the birthday candles he'd blown out earlier.

Everyone was enjoying Norma's always-delicious chocolate cake when Rick returned to the dining room. Ed looked up and almost dropped his fork at the expression on Rick's face. His eyes were dark with anger, something Ed rarely saw.

Ed set his fork down and hurried over to him before anyone else noticed.

"What's wrong?" he asked anxiously.

Rick took a deep breath and made an effort to smile. "Nothing. Just another disagreement with the folks."

"What about?"

Rick let out a long whooshing sigh and the anger seemed to dissolve with it. "It's your birthday, baby. I don't want to spoil it with more of my family bullshit."

"But—"

"But nothing. We'll talk about it later."

"Hey," Rick heartily called out to Josh and Bobby, who were sneaking second helpings of cake. "Save some of that for me, okay?"

Ed retrieved his own piece of cake from the dining room table as he watched Rick kidding with the boys. It appeared as though nothing at all was bothering him, but Ed knew his man well enough by now to know he had been, and still was, deeply troubled by his parents' phone call.

Ed silently finished his dessert, immune to the cheerful conversation around him. He suspected once his birthday was officially over, he'd be back on good-husband duty again.

# Chapter Twenty

Ed spent most of the next day worrying about Rick and the latest episode with his parents. However, when Rick came home in his usual jubilant Saturday end-of-the-workweek mood, Ed felt better. He thought perhaps Rick had worked out his negative emotions while walking his mail route, something he often did when he was bothered by something.

Still, Ed wondered whether anything John or Vera had said on the phone the night before continued to fester in Rick's mind. After Rick was happily settled on the sofa with a glass of cold Pepsi and Jett in his lap, Ed sat down across from him, determined to find out what had been said.

"Oh, baby, it was the same old shit," Rick muttered when Ed point-blank asked what had once again set him off against his parents.

"Despite anything you or I said, or Mrs. P. said, they still think I'm making the biggest mistake of my life with this real estate thing. That's bad enough, but I was really pissed that they chose your birthday as the time to go into it again. I should have hung up the damned phone after I thanked them for your birthday check."

"Why are they still going on about that?" Ed was mystified. He had thought the matter was as settled as it possibly could be.

"I don't know, and I don't intend to worry about it. I don't want you to worry about it either. A week from today I take that state exam, and I don't want any of their negativity to jinx that.

"So enough of them and their worrying, okay? How 'bout we keep celebrating your birthday? You wanna go to Fort Wayne for dinner and a movie? We still haven't seen *Arthur*, and I'd really like to see it before it leaves the theaters."

Ed narrowed his eyes at Rick. "Can we afford it?" He couldn't help but think Rick was offering Ed bait to change the subject.

Rick laughed and his warm and tender special spread across his face. "Oh, man, I should have never hollered at you that day about ordering a pizza. Yes, dear, we can afford it. I had planned to spend more money on your birthday than I did, so one night out isn't gonna break our bank."

"Shouldn't we be saving money for our Michigan trip?" Ed wasn't ready to give in yet.

"Use the check my worrywart parents sent," Rick answered with a smirk. "Unless you had something you really wanted to buy with it."

"No, I had planned to save that money for our trip," Ed said slowly.

"Well then. Let's go to that Redwood place and try those great sausage-roll things Gordy told us about. Then we'll go watch the movie everyone else says is so funny. I could use a few good laughs."

"Oh, okay." Ed, despite his suspicion that Rick was withholding information from him, was cheered by the idea of a Saturday night date with his husband. Aside from Glen's birthday party the month before, they hadn't really been out on a Saturday night since they had been married.

"It'll be like the old days," Ed said, moving from his chair to the sofa next to Rick.

Rick put his drink down and put an arm around Ed. "Yeah, just like the old days. You're still my favorite Saturday night date, you know."

"You're mine, too, darlin'." Ed kissed Rick and gave up his resolution to pry deeper into the Benton family drama since Rick was determined to let it go. If he ever really needed to know more, Ed thought, he'd find out someday. For now he was ready to leave it alone and enjoy himself.

◆

Ed awoke the next morning to the musty smell of a furnace running for the first time in months. He had felt a definite autumn chill in the air when they had returned home from their movie date but hadn't thought it was quite that cold.

The smell of bacon and eggs frying competed with the furnace odor. Rick was already up and obviously counting on the lure of breakfast to draw Ed out of bed. With a sigh Ed slipped on his new bathrobe and stumbled into the kitchen for his morning glass of orange juice. As was usually the case, he had been so busy doing winterizing chores for his clients, he had neglected to do the furnace checks and filter changes at home.

"I hope you didn't make plans for me today," he mumbled to Rick after a half-awake kiss.

"Nope," Rick replied as he flipped the sizzling bacon. "I was going to study for next weekend. Why? What's up?"

Ed chugged some of the juice Rick had set out for him. "Well, I really want to go over the furnace downstairs, and the one in the main house. I should probably check the one on Coleman Street, too. I remember showing Doug how it runs, but I didn't show him how to change filters. He can probably do it himself, but I'd feel better if I went over there."

Rick's warm and tender special lit up his face as he shook his head. "And you call me a responsibility freak. I can't help but think the furnaces won't blow up before tomorrow morning, but if you're determined to do all that on a Sunday, at least hang around long enough to make a dent in all this food I'm making."

"Oh, don't worry. I have no intention of letting it go to waste." To prove it, Ed snatched a piece of bacon draining on a paper towel and fled to the bathroom before Rick could swat him with his greasy spatula.

After they had both enjoyed Rick's Sunday breakfast, Ed got up to take over the cleanup chores, but Rick stopped him.

"Don't sweat it. Go ahead and do your furnace stuff. When I need a break from the books I'll take care of this. If we time it right, maybe we can do something later this afternoon."

"Now, there's a good idea," Ed said as he detoured from the kitchen sink to the telephone to call Doug.

There was no answer at Doug's. Ed shrugged as he hung up the phone. "He's probably at work. Oh, well. I'll take care of the furnaces here, then call again."

Doug still didn't answer the phone when Ed tried again around noontime. He considered calling the funeral home, but if Doug was busy embalming the recently deceased, Ed didn't really want to know about it. Impatient to get the chore behind him, Ed grabbed his keys for the house and drove over to Coleman Street, composing in his head the note he'd leave Doug to explain why he'd entered the house.

Doug's car was in the driveway. Ed, puzzled, parked his truck next to it and slowly approached the house. He found the back door unlocked and could hear music coming from the living room. Ed paused for a moment, feeling like a Peeping Tom as he identified the song playing, Donna Summer's "I Love You." He wouldn't have thought Doug was a fan of disco.

He was about to turn around and leave when he caught a glimpse of Doug walking through the living room to the kitchen. Ed opened the back door a little wider and called out.

"Doug? It's just me, Ed. I want to check on the furnace. You didn't answer the phone, so I thought you weren't home. If it's a bad time, I'll come back later."

Doug, his dark blond hair tousled, was clad in pajama bottoms and an old army T-shirt. He managed a sleepy grin at Ed as he beckoned him inside.

"Nah, it's okay. It's my day off, so I was ignoring the phone. Actually I was going to check on the furnace later today, so I'm glad you came over."

Ed hesitantly climbed the steps from the back door into the kitchen, feeling like an intruder in the house he'd called his own for so long. He heard footsteps coming from the bedroom and blushed.

"Aw, crud, you're not alone. I'm sorry, man, I'll come back later."

"You don't have to do that, bud," Gordy said as he rounded the corner into the kitchen.

Ed's mouth fell open. He blinked rapidly at the sight of Gordy Smith standing before him wearing nothing but a pair of boxer shorts and a huge, shit-eating grin.

"Guess it's about time you found out who the mystery guy is," Gordy said as he reached for Doug to give him a long, lingering kiss.

Ed watched this display of obvious mutual affection with his mouth still gaping and his brown eyes open wide. He reached out a hand to the nearest wall to steady himself as the kiss finally came to an end.

"Surprise," Gordy said with a smirk as he held Doug close to him.

"Yeah, surprise," Doug echoed sheepishly as he gazed up at Gordy, his eyes glowing.

"I gotta sit down." Ed pulled out one of Doug's kitchen chairs and did just that. He looked at the two of them, shaking his head.

"Gordon, you have some serious explaining to do. You, too, Mr. I've-Got-a-Girlfriend Mortician!"

⋘•⋙

"I'm really sorry, Ed. I should have been honest with you from the beginning," Doug said after they were all seated in the living room, Doug and Gordy with mugs of coffee and Ed with another glass of juice.

"Needless to say, I was deep in the closet while I was in the army," Doug continued. "I finally came out when I was doing mortician school in Chicago. When I got this job in Porterfield, I kind of went back into the closet. I just didn't know if I could be out in a small town. That night when you introduced Rick to me as your husband, I about fell over in shock. I was going to tell you the truth, but I was afraid. I didn't know you well enough to know whether you'd tell anyone or not. You and Rick seemed so comfortable together I was afraid everyone knew about you guys, and I hadn't been at the funeral home long enough to know if I could get away with being out or not. You know?"

Ed nodded. He did understand.

"Then this big lug walked in," Doug said with an affectionate grin at Gordy, who grinned back at him. "Wow! At first I figured he was gay because he was friends with you, but this being a small town, who could tell for sure? Lots of gay guys have straight friends. Boy, did I have some fun fantasies about him all summer."

"While I was doing the same thing," Gordy snickered.

Ed nodded again with a grin of his own. He was fully aware of Gordy's attraction to Doug.

Gordy took up the story. "After I dumped Ken I was ready to swear off guys for a while. That's why I was gonna go to Spruce Lake by myself, remember? Then one of my dad's fishing buddies died right before Labor Day. I decided to go to the calling Friday night and leave Saturday morning."

"So you guys met up at the funeral home."

"Yeah. After I'd paid my respects, I walked out back where they park the hearse to have a smoke. Doug followed me out there. We started talkin' and feelin' each other out. I finally got gutsy enough to say how cute he was, and the next thing I know we're back here really gettin' to know each other. I still figured I'd be goin' to the lake the next day, but after spending some time with this guy, there was no way in hell I was goin' up there by myself, and since he had to work all weekend, I just hung around so I could be with him when he was free."

"I'll be damned," Ed said, shaking his head.

"Yeah, I know. Pretty damned unexpected. If it had just been some wham-bam thing, it wouldn't have been a big deal, but this ain't no wham-bam."

"I sure hope not." Doug beamed at Gordy, who pulled Doug closer to him on the sofa.

"Wow," Ed murmured, and sipped his juice. He was having a hard time taking it in. His good friend Gordy and his tenant, the handsome mortician, had been carrying on a secret romance practically under his nose. He had never guessed, never even suspected.

"What is it about this house?" Ed gazed around the room where he had first met Rick face-to-face.

"I don't know, but I'm sure glad you left some of the luck behind. Just this morning," Doug said, tearing his eyes away from Gordy, "I was telling him we should come clean with you and Rick. So when I saw you coming up the back walk, we decided it was time you knew what was going on."

"And I couldn't resist the chance to freak you out a little bit." Gordy chuckled.

"Well, that you did. Freak me out, I mean. Rick's gonna pee his pants when I tell him!"

There was, however, still one part of the mystery Ed didn't understand. He mock-glared at Doug. "So what about the girlfriend you kept telling me about? Did you just make that up?"

Doug looked rather ashamed. "Well, yes and no. It was actually a guy, a college guy I met at Carlton's in Fort Wayne. I just switched the gender to cover my ass. The rest of it, though, his being creeped out by the funeral home thing and him dumping me last month a few weeks before Gordy and I got together, yeah, that was true."

"The guy was a dork," Gordy roared in his usual way. "He had no sense of humor and was stupid enough to let go of the best-lookin' guy in the world. Course I'm glad he did, though."

"Me, too." Doug turned his head for Gordy's kiss, another long and apparently very satisfying one.

Ed rolled his eyes. "Geez, look at 'em, making out again. You're just getting even for all the times Rick and I kissed in front of you, aren't you?"

"Nope," Gordy whispered, stroking Doug's face. "I'm just doin' what I like doin' best these days."

Ed smiled. The sight of his big cocky friend behaving tenderly, and so obviously in love, was a sight he'd occasionally imagined but somehow never thought he'd see. His shock at the situation was wearing off, replaced by a warm tide of good feelings for both of them. Gordy had apparently found the right guy Ed had told him he would find someday, and Ed couldn't have been more pleased about it.

Ed stood up. "Well, this is the best surprise I've had since my birthday presents from Rick, but I still need to change those furnace filters. Then I'm going home and tell Rick, because I can't wait to see *his* reaction."

"I think we should celebrate," Gordy said. "What are you guys doin' tonight?"

"Nothing special at the moment."

"Okay, then let's the four of us go out for dinner. In Fort Wayne. My treat. It's about time I had a guy with me when I hang out with you guys."

Doug shook his head. "No, it's my treat. It'll be my way of apologizing for not being honest from the beginning. Maybe if I had been, we'd have been together sooner."

Gordy gave Doug's arm an affectionate poke. "I don't care about that as long as I got you now. What do you say, Ed? You wanna go out and watch Doug and me make cow eyes at each other all night?"

Ed groaned. "I don't know how much food I'll be able to choke down watching that, but yeah, I'm up for it. Let me call home and see what Rick thinks about it."

He went to the phone and punched in his home number.

"Hello?"

"Hey, darlin'. How's the studying? Got those dishes done yet?"

"Not yet, but I'm working on it. Something wrong at Doug's?"

Ed grinned. "Oh, not at all, but we've been invited out for dinner tonight.

Doug's treat. I was just calling to see if you were interested."

"Well, sure. Sounds great. I'm just surprised Doug wants to take us out. What's the occasion?"

"No special occasion, but it'll be four of us, not just three."

"Huh? Who else is going?"

Ed laughed. "Are you sitting down? Have I got some news for you!"

⋘•⋙

"I still don't believe it," Rick said that night as they were getting ready for bed. "Gordy and Doug! I know we just spent the evening with them, but my mind is still blown. I never would have put those two together. Doug had me completely fooled."

"I know." Ed pulled the covers back on the bed and giggled. "They sure are cute together, though, aren't they?"

Rick snorted. "They're acting the way we did when we first got together, I guess. Do you suppose we were that sickening?"

"Yes," Ed said firmly. "We were."

Ed had enjoyed their double date at a popular Mexican restaurant. He had savored the chorizo burritos and fideo soup and had gotten a real kick out of watching Gordy and Doug caught up in the mushy, lovey-dovey behavior of a new and exciting romance. It had brought back some wonderful memories of his own early times with Rick.

"You know, I may be used to you now, darlin', but I still think you're the most handsome man in the whole world."

"Yeah?" Rick flopped on the bed and reached out to pull Ed next to him. "Well, I still think you're the cutest handyman in Porterfield, Indiana, *and* the whole world. I don't think that'll ever change."

"Even when I'm sixty-four?" Ed asked, thinking of an old Beatles tune.

"Oh, I think you'll still be as sexy as you are now, baby." Rick's warm and tender special backed up his statement, and as further evidence he gave Ed the kind of kiss Ed had seen Gordy and Doug sharing earlier in the day.

"Do you think they'll end up like us? Gordy's almost ten years older than Doug, you know."

Rick looked thoughtful. "Oh, that shouldn't make a difference if they really love each other and have a future together. Time will tell if it works out for them. I'm not gonna waste any time on predictions. I'm just glad they're together now."

Rick reluctantly let Ed go to turn around and set his alarm clock. "I just hope they can get over that whole gay-couple-in-a–small-town thing like we have."

"Have we gotten past it?"

Rick shrugged. "I'd like to think so. I'm working on that committee with Eunice Ames. She introduces me to everyone as Ed Stephens's companion, and no one seems to be overly bothered by it."

"I know. But people can take that a lot of different ways. Besides, those people are too busy being polite and social to stir up trouble. I guess it's the less-dignified people I worry about."

Rick sighed. "Hopefully I won't be selling houses to the less dignified someday. Still, working on that committee has proven to me that there are plenty of people, even in Porterfield, who are more concerned with who you are, as opposed to whom you sleep with."

"And if anyone tried to give Gordy any shit, he'd probably just threaten to pound 'em into the ground anyway."

Rick laughed. "Yeah, probably. But if they start getting scared the way I did last winter, we'll just bring them over here so Mrs. P. can give them her strength-through-adversity speech. Sure worked for us."

"Yeah, the stuff she's said has helped a lot, but I still worry sometimes. Don't you?"

Rick looked thoughtful. "Oh, sometimes. Not as much as I used to. That committee work and talking with Vince Cummings have been real eye-openers for me. I wish my parents could see some of it. There are a lot of people in this town who have accepted me, and you, at face value. I know everyone won't, but so what? That's the same for everybody. There's always going to be people who don't like you based on something stupid: money, religion, geography, or politics. Ours just happens to be sexual orientation. I keep thinking if we don't make a big deal of it—and we aren't—most people will just let it go. We're not necking on the courthouse square, and we weren't waving pride flags in the Stratton County 4-H parade last summer. Mrs. P.'s right. Live and let live seems to be theme around here."

"Most of the time," Ed said, thinking of Ruth Dorsey.

"Yeah, most of the time. If we keep working hard, someday all of the dreams we have together will become reality, and people will just respect us even more for accomplishing them."

"Yeah, I s'pose you're right." Ed dreamily slid under the covers thinking of a day in the future when he was busy making the things he hoped to make and sell in his workshop; Rick giving up his postal service job to sell houses full-time; and the two of them having enough money saved to buy a lake cottage . . . maybe even a boat to go with it.

Or, he thought, remembering the Magical Mystery Tour, a canoe.

Rick plumped his pillow and slid down next to Ed. "I've always said, sometimes you just get lucky. I've felt lucky ever since I met you, so who knows? Maybe another lucky break is coming up for us."

"Really? What makes you think so?"

"Well, this whole thing with us being here, and everything Mrs. P. has done for us. It gave us a head start on the future we didn't expect, so when we start building on it, things will come together just as well, I hope."

"Yeah." Ed thought back to the beginning of last autumn, when he first saw his Dream Man delivering the mail, and Mrs. Penfield was simply his former English teacher and one of his favorite handyman clients.

"Yeah, I sure didn't see any of this coming," Ed sighed as he snuggled close to Rick.

Rick snickered as he turned off the light. "Well, let's hope the next thing you don't see coming isn't a mack truck headin' for us dead-on."

"You know what, though?" Ed murmured as he stared into the sudden darkness. "Even if we don't get another lucky break, I'm happy. I may still worry about stuff, but I'm grateful for what we've got."

"Me, too, baby. But I'm not ready to give up. I hope you aren't either."

"Oh, no," Ed said quickly. "I just meant I can enjoy what I have without needing a whole lot more."

"Well then." Rick slid his arms around him. "I guess it's a good thing I came along to light a fire under you, Ed Stephens, so the rest of the world will find out what a talented man you are."

Ed settled into Rick's arms with a sigh. Yes, he supposed he was even grateful for that fire Rick kept stoking, but every now and again he still wished Rick could slow down and just enjoy as well.

# Chapter Twenty-one

Ed was up earlier than usual the next Saturday morning, but he didn't care. This was a big day, the day Rick had been looking forward to for months. Rick was going to Indianapolis for his real estate licensing exam.

Ed watched Rick put on his new suit. They had agreed that a future real estate agent needed to look the part, so they had made room in their budget for Rick to splurge on the proper attire from Gibson's Menswear in downtown Porterfield.

"You know, guys in business suits never impressed me until you got one. I can't believe how sexy you look."

Rick grinned in the mirror as he adjusted his tie. "Now, don't start that kind of talk, or I won't get out of here on time."

"You sure you don't want me to go with you?"

"No. I'll be fine." Rick smiled. "I know you'll be here at home sending me good-luck vibes, and besides, there really isn't anything for you to do except hang around while I'm taking the test."

"You could drop me off at your parents' house," Ed said tentatively. "I could visit with them until you're finished."

Rick scowled in the mirror, not bothering to respond.

"So you're not even going to stop and see them while you're in town?"

"Nope."

Ed sighed. "They'll want to know how the exam went."

"Let 'em call if they want to know."

"I thought you were over what happened Labor Day weekend and that phone call on my birthday. Why are you being such an asshole about this?"

Rick reached for his suit jacket. "Look. Maybe we kissed and made up before they left town, but that phone call proves they still think I'm making a mistake with this. I don't want to stop by there and watch them pretend to be happy for me, and I don't want you getting caught in the middle of it. They'll come around eventually. It really isn't any different than when I left school to become a mailman. They were cool with that after time, and this will be the same way. For right now I'd rather concentrate on you and the other people who are excited about this, okay?"

"Okay." Ed wasn't entirely okay with it but decided not to pursue the matter.

Ed crawled out of bed and gently hugged Rick, careful not to wrinkle his new suit. "I guess I should stay home anyway. I've got plenty of yard work to do, and I want to spend some time making myself look good, 'cause when you come home in victory, I'm gonna take my man out for another celebration dinner. Damn the cost, too."

Rick kissed him. "If you say so." He kissed him again, and then looked at his watch.

"Well, shit. I should probably hit the road. I want to be there in plenty of time. Baby, do you s'pose you can tell me you love me once, just for some more good luck?"

"I love you, darlin'." Ed gave him a very long, affectionate kiss. "If my love was all you needed to ace that test, you wouldn't even have to open the book."

"Oh, I love you, too." He hugged Ed tightly. "I'll come home as soon as I know I've passed."

"You will. Go knock 'em dead."

Ed walked him to the door. He then went back to the bedroom to watch Rick pull out of the garage. He waved as Rick pulled onto Race Street and heaved a big sigh once Rick was out of sight. He was sure Rick would pass the test but knew he wouldn't relax until Rick was home again, hopefully through once and for all with the whole real estate license process.

Jett walked into the bedroom. He gave a brief meow, his yellow-green eyes fixed on Ed. Ed patted the bed next him, and with one leap Jett was beside him. Ed pulled the cat into his lap and stroked his sleek, black fur. "How do you always seem to know when I need some attention?" he asked Jett, who purred in response.

He pondered where to take Rick for dinner that night. Ed wasn't a huge fan of fancy restaurants, and there wasn't much to choose from in Porterfield. Still, he wanted to show Rick how proud he was of his hard work, and he felt such a well-dressed member of the Porterfield Historical Home Tour Committee deserved to be seen somewhere nice.

He couldn't help but wonder, though, what would happen after Rick had his license. There had not been any real improvement in the housing market, and there was no immediate reason for Rick to even think of leaving the postal service. Ed also had no desire to sell his own home. Now that Doug and Gordy were a couple and perhaps even building a life together, he didn't want to sell the house out from under them unless it was to the two of them, and he knew any chance of that was a long way off.

*I hope this whole real estate license thing wasn't all for nothing,* he thought, tickling Jett's ears. *I hope Rick doesn't get discouraged when he has the license and no way to utilize it.*

"Well, then, I guess I'll just be back on good-husband duty, propping him up and telling him how wonderful he is," Ed said to Jett, who began to wash his whiskers.

Ed was glad to see the cat in a good mood, because what Jett didn't know and wouldn't know until it happened on Monday was that Ed had scheduled a little outpatient surgery at the vet's. Jett's increasingly heated arguments with the neighborhood tomcats over the female who lived on the next block had forced Ed and Rick to deal with a situation they had put off for too long.

"One cat is enough," Rick had said, shaking his head at Jett's wounds from the latest fight. "We don't need to get stuck raising his offspring."

Ed had agreed, but he was dreading the trip to the vet's.

He carefully settled Jett on the bed and got up to put on his yard-work clothes. *Enough with the thinking and worrying already; you've got a yard to mow, and if you're lucky it will be the last time this season.*

He whistled "One Man Band" to himself as he tied his grass-stained sneakers. *Keep this up, and the music you make for Rick will go out of tune.*

He went downstairs and pushed the lawnmower out of the carriage house, thinking of Rick on his way to Indianapolis. Ed hoped that he wasn't too nervous and that the test would go well. He knew Rick was doing this as much for Ed as for himself, and while he may have been dubious about the immediate value of the entire enterprise, Ed was genuinely grateful for Rick's hard work and couldn't wait to show him how just how grateful he really was.

⁂

Ed had his yard work finished by midafternoon. He spent the rest of the day pacing around the apartment, putting records on the stereo and taking them off again, and doing a half-assed job of dusting the furniture. He ran his dust rag over the record cabinet and on an impulse pulled out Kool & the Gang's "Celebration" to play when Rick burst through the door with the good news.

He was placing the record on the turntable when he saw Rick's car pull in the driveway. Rick didn't bother to pull into the garage. He jumped out of the car and, seeing Ed watching from the window, waved a piece of paper in the air. "I passed," he hollered in triumph. He ran for the door.

Ed met him halfway on the stairs with a big hug that almost knocked Rick over backward. "Whoa, baby," Rick shouted, grabbing for the railing.

"Way to go, darlin'." Ed gave him a kiss filled with pride at Rick's accomplishment. His dark thoughts from earlier in the day vanished in his joy over Rick's success. "Congratulations! I've got Indiana's newest and best real estate agent right here in my arms."

Rick returned the kiss, just as excited. "Well, thanks, but why don't we go upstairs before Indiana's newest real estate agent, or his handyman, falls down and breaks a leg."

Ed took Rick by the hand, leading him into the apartment, where he promptly kissed him again. He reluctantly let Rick go long enough to put "Celebration" on the turntable. "Tell me. Was the test hard? When do you get your license?"

Rick laughed as he threw his suit coat over a kitchen chair. "Let me sit down. I'm wiped out from that long drive."

He got himself a can of Pepsi from the refrigerator and plopped himself on the sofa. "No, the test wasn't too hard," he said after he'd had a sip of his pop. "All that studying really paid off. I know some of the people sitting for that exam were sweating it, but once I looked it over I knew I would do okay. They'll send me my license after it's been printed. That"—he indicated the paper he had waved earlier—"is my receipt and temporary license. So yeah, it's a done deal."

Ed sighed with relief. From the moment Rick had started his real estate classes, he had been waiting for this moment. Finally! No more classes, no more studying, and no more worrying about whether he'd pass or fail.

Ed jumped to his feet, too happy to have the three-month ordeal finished to sit still. "So where do you wanna go for dinner tonight? The sky's the limit."

Rick slumped against the sofa, a look of relief on his face as well. "You know what? I'd be really happy with just a Gino's special here at home. It's been a long day, and I'd love to get out of this suit and just relax. Besides, now that this is over with, I'm starting to look forward to our trip next weekend. We went out twice last weekend, so why don't we save the money and the big celebration until we're up north?"

Ed was pleased by Rick's response, glad to know he was finally looking forward to their Michigan excursion as much as Ed was. "Okay," he said with a mock frown. "If that's what you want, I'll call in an order after a while."

"That's all I want. Now that I have this little piece of paper, all I want for the moment is a pizza and my man to share it with me. Okay?"

"Deal."

Ed admired the temporary license and the man holding it. "You're something else, darlin'," he whispered.

"And hearing you say that," said Rick as he drew Ed into a hug, "makes this day complete."

⋘•⋙

Norma never needed an excuse to cook a big meal but, upon hearing the good news about Rick's licensing exam, insisted Ed and Rick come over the next day for an old-fashioned Sunday dinner.

"You may think I'm being Eddie Haskell again," Rick told her as he helped himself to more pot roast and mashed potatoes, "but I still say you're the best cook in Porterfield. Even better than Effie Maude, but if you repeat that last part I'll deny it."

Norma, obviously more pleased by the comment than she wanted to let on, muttered, "Well, it's good to be appreciated. So tell me, Rick. Now that you have this license, what are you going to do with it?"

Rick sighed. "I guess I'll frame it, hang it on the wall, and go back to the post office where I belong tomorrow."

Norma nodded. "That's sensible. I'm just as proud as Ed here that you passed that course and got your license, but there's no reason to quit a perfectly good job until you have something to move on to. That big-mouthed Don Hoffmeyer treating you okay at the post office?"

"Oh, sure. I don't have any complaints about my job; I'm just eager to start my new career."

He gave Norma a big smile. "How 'bout it, Norma? Wanna have me sell your house so I can get started?"

She snorted. "Honestly! I've never yet met a real estate agent who wasn't after everyone to sell their property. If you're already nagging your poor mother-in-law, then I s'pose you're off to a good start."

Later, after Rick had retired to the living room with the Sunday paper, Ed helped his mother clear the table.

"Ed," she said in a low voice, "you were awfully quiet when I was asking Rick about his future. How do you feel about this whole thing?"

Ed shrugged as he scraped leftover corn pudding into a plastic container, wishing Norma wouldn't put him on the spot when he was so contentedly full of good food.

"I don't know, Mom." He concentrated on carefully burping the Tupperware as Norma had taught him to do. "I guess," he blurted in a moment of rare honesty with her, "that a part of me hopes that now that he's got the license he'll go back to the post office tomorrow like he says and shut up about the whole thing."

Norma glanced at him as though she had a suspicion confirmed. "I thought so."

"Don't get me wrong," he said hastily. "I've been behind him a hundred percent on this whole thing. I've supported him and encouraged him all I could, but sometimes I wish we could just relax and enjoy what we've got without always pushing so hard toward the future."

"Humph." Norma shook her head as she stacked plates for Ed to wash. "A lot of men are like that, always pushing for more than they've got, acting like they have to prove something to the world. Sad thing is, a lot of women are acting like that too nowadays. That's just the way men are; always have been, always will be."

"Rick didn't use to be like that," Ed protested.

"Oh, for Pete's sake, he was, too. You just didn't see it. You were so busy making him out to be exactly what you wanted that you didn't notice the things that bothered you. Everybody does that. Why, I remember being absolutely shocked at some of the things I discovered about your father after we were married. Took me a while to get used to it, believe me. You will, too. It's all a part of being married."

"Yeah. I hate to admit it, Mom, but you were right. Some of it's harder than I thought it would be."

"Of course I was right," she said smugly. "Your mother is always right, and don't you forget it, young man. Still, I do understand. Now, you, Ed, you take after your father. I've always said he could have run that Marsden factory single-handed, but he settled for being a plant division manager. It wasn't that he wasn't ambitious like all men are, but he was content to have his family well taken care of, and he didn't want the added fuss and stress. You're like that. You've managed to make a good life for yourself, but you're not worried about being something you aren't. You won't go to your grave like a lot of men thinking you didn't accomplish enough."

"Rick says he has to light a fire under me to keep me going."

"Hmmm." Norma frowned. "Is that so? Well, Edward, you'd better find a good way to turn down the heat when that fire gets too hot."

Norma began to run water into the sink. She reached for the dishwashing liquid and turned to Ed. "Now, before you start on these dishes, you fetch me the cloth from the dining room table for the laundry," she commanded. "Don't think I didn't see that gravy stain you were trying to hide. Honestly, twenty-nine years old and you still can't put gravy on your potatoes without making a mess."

Ed, relieved that the mother-son talk seemed to be over, cheerfully headed to the dining room on his chore. "I guess I'm just like Dad about that," he called over his shoulder.

"You got that right! That man was a gravy spiller from the day I met him.

Must be a man thing. I sometimes wonder what the good Lord had in mind when he made men."

"You know what, Mom?" Ed handed her the tablecloth with a sigh. "I sometimes wonder that myself."

⋄•⋄

Monday morning Ed was standing in the living room, staring at Jett, who was engaged in his morning wash. Ed was trying to decide on the best way to transport Jett to the veterinarian's office. Jett didn't much care for traveling, and Ed, who was dreading the whole thing anyway, was wondering how to get him into the truck with as little fuss as possible. He was about to go downstairs and grab one of the cardboard boxes left over from their move when the phone rang.

"Ed?" It was Rick, calling from the post office. "I'm sure glad I caught you. Listen, can you do you me a big, big favor this afternoon?"

"I don't know. What is it?"

"Well, Vince Cummings just stopped by to see me. He managed to catch me right when I getting ready to start my route. Anyway, he wanted to congratulate me on passing the exam, and then said he has something he wants to talk to me about. He asked if I could come over after work, but I'm supposed to drive Judy to the orthodontist. I know your afternoon is clear, so could you please take her? The other kids are going to Mrs. Busby's after school, so you don't have to worry about that, and I'm really curious to know what Vince has to say."

Ed silently groaned. Yes, his afternoon was free, the first work-free afternoon he'd had in a while. He had happily made plans to spend most of it at Clyde's workshop, checking on the progress of the cedar chest and hopefully acquiring some hands-on experience with such a project.

"Well," Ed said slowly, "I guess I can take her. I was going to go to Clyde's, but—"

"I would really appreciate it, and I promise to make it up to you sometime. Vince seemed excited, so who knows? Maybe something has happened that would actually give me a chance to put that license to good use."

Ed couldn't imagine what could have happened to change the real estate market in Porterfield so suddenly and was privately perturbed at Vince for getting Rick stirred up again.

"Okay," he sighed. "I'll take Judy to Fort Wayne. What time do I have to pick her up?"

"Be at the junior high about three fifteen. She'll be waiting for you. The appointment's at four fifteen. Thank you, Ed." He lowered his voice and whispered into the phone, "Thank you, baby. You're the best, and hopefully

I'll have some good news for you this evening."

Ed hung up the phone feeling both annoyed and virtuous. He hated to give up his afternoon at Clyde's, but if it meant that much to Rick, he'd make the sacrifice. Plus, if he didn't have to be at the school until after three, he might have time for a brief visit with Clyde.

*That news had better be good,* he thought as he once again turned his attentions to Jett.

◆

By the time Ed brought his truck to a halt in front of the old Porterfield Junior High School building, he was in the crabbiest mood he'd experienced in quite some time. Getting Jett to the vet had been a worse ordeal than he'd anticipated, and the doctor had been running behind schedule as well. Once he finally had the cat safely home, Jett—groggy and grumpy—made it clear he had little intention of ever having anything to do with Ed ever again. Ed knew he'd get over it, but it was upsetting just the same.

Ed had eaten his lunch on the run and had rushed through an easy chore for Mrs. West, but he simply didn't have the time to stop by Clyde's for anything more than a quick look at the cedar chest, so he had called Clyde and told him he hoped to be able to stop by later in the week.

Judy was waiting for him on the front steps he had routinely climbed through the seventh, eighth, and ninth grades. Aside from her surprise that Ed and not Rick was taking her to Fort Wayne, she didn't have much to say, except to complain about her home ec teacher, "the lamest old bag ever." With their bad moods in sync, Ed and Judy made the trip to Fort Wayne with WFWQ turned up loud and a minimum of conversation.

While Judy was having her wires tightened, Ed decided to take Judy down the road to Ayr-Way and buy them both some records. Maybe wasting a few dollars would improve both of their dispositions. Judy was more than pleased at the suggested detour, and they both hopped back into the truck in a slightly better frame of mind.

"But just one apiece," Ed said, looking through his wallet. "I don't have as much money on me as I thought."

Ed grabbed the last copy of Robbie Patton's "Don't Give It Up," and Judy, without hesitating, picked up "Private Eyes" from Hall & Oates. "I love it. It reminds me of 'Bette Davis Eyes.'"

Ed snickered. "Hmmm. Bette Davis eyes. Private eyes. Same synthesizer sounds. I think it did for Daryl and John, too."

They were actually giggling together as they got ready for the trip home. Ed put the truck in reverse to back out of the parking space he'd found near the storefront, but the truck didn't move. Frowning, he tapped the gas again.

The truck whined and after some hesitation finally jerked backward.

"Aw, crud," he muttered.

"What's wrong?" Judy asked as she retrieved the bag with their records, which had fallen to the floor.

"Transmission," he said briefly, his short-lived good mood deflating.

He shifted through the gears and with some under-the-breath pleading finally maneuvered the truck out of the parking space and toward the highway.

"Shit," he exclaimed, breaking his vow never to use profanity around the children.

He glanced at Judy. "Sorry."

She rolled her eyes. "I know what it means, Uncle Ed. I've heard it before, believe me. Will we make it home?"

"Yeah, we'll make it home as long as I don't have to drive in reverse. The reverse gear on the transmission is giving out. My family must have a transmission curse. Laurie's died a few months ago, so now it's my turn." He shook his head. "This is not a cheap fix."

Judy was concerned enough to turn down the radio volume. "Can't you get a new truck?"

Ed let go with a rueful laugh. "Well, as much as I'd like that, it's not too practical. No, I'm afraid my poor old truck is starting to show its age, and I'm just gonna have to start paying for it. I'll have to park on the street tonight and take it out to Wagner's in the morning."

"Gee, I'm sorry," Judy said, shooting him a sympathetic look. "It's been a crummy day for you, hasn't it?"

"Yeah," Ed replied with a sigh. "I sure hope it doesn't get any worse."

⋘•⋙

After dropping Judy off in front of her house as opposed to pulling in the driveway, Ed drove home, turning on the headlights in the autumn dusk. The earlier darkness combined with the overcast skies seemed to be a perfect reflection of his gloomy state of mind. He parked the truck on Race Street and again tested the reverse gear. After several coaxing attempts, the truck moved backward a few feet. He realized it had been a bit balky the past few weeks, but he hadn't given it much thought. Now he was all too painfully aware of it as he mentally went over their budget and thought about the money he had planned to spend that weekend in Michigan.

As he trudged in disgust up the stairs, he noticed that Rick was home ahead of him. He was so lost in thought over the potential cost of the transmission repair, he had almost forgotten Rick's meeting with Vince and was surprised to see Rick waiting for him at the table, a bottle of sparkling wine and two glasses in front of him.

"Hey, baby!" Rick jumped up from the table to meet Ed at the door with a hug and a kiss.

"Hi." Ed halfheartedly returned the kiss and turned to hang his jean jacket on the clothes tree near the door. He tossed his new record on the table, narrowly missing the wine bottle.

"Something wrong?"

"Yeah. Truck transmission," Ed said, tiredly rubbing his face.

"Oh." Rick looked rather uncertain for a moment, but then smiled. "Well, that sucks, but maybe my news will make up for it."

Ed flopped in one of the easy chairs. Jett, in the other one, gave Ed a dirty look and turned his back to him. "Okay, so what's this big news?"

"Well," Rick said grandly, settling across from Ed on the sofa, "I have been offered a job!"

Ed gave him a puzzled look. "Huh? Vince offered you a job?"

"No, Vince did not offer me job; Walt Granger did."

"Who's that?" Ed asked impatiently, in no mood for guessing games.

"He's a real estate broker in Indianapolis, a gay real estate broker. Remember how I was surprised that Vince didn't seem fazed about me being gay? Well, he's known this guy for years. He just happened to be talking to him last week about a house in Indy and mentioned me. It seems Walt's business is doing great. He's built up a thriving gay clientele in Indy, guys like us—couples and singles—who buy mostly old houses and then gentrify them. He's been looking for an assistant to help him handle the business. So while I was at Vince's this afternoon we called him, and he all but gave me the job over the phone!"

Ed just stared, trying to comprehend what Rick was saying. "This guy who's never even laid eyes on you is offering you a job as his assistant selling houses in Indianapolis?"

"Yeah! Well, of course he wants to meet in person and make sure it would all work out. He wants me to come down this weekend so he can show me around and see if we'd be a good fit to work together."

"This weekend," Ed said flatly. "So I guess the Mackinac trip is shot." The thought of the trip he'd been planning and looking forward to for a month falling apart was the icing on the cake of an already miserable day for Ed. He got up from his chair and stomped to the window, his back to Rick.

"Oh, baby, we can take a trip anytime. This is a golden opportunity, and those don't come along every day."

"Neither do vacations," Ed muttered. "I've suspected all along you didn't really want to go. And after all the planning I did to see to it we'd have a good time. I even sent money to one place that wanted a deposit for a reservation.

It's their busy season because of all the people going north for the fall foliage. Well, talk about money down the drain, right when I have to get the damned truck fixed!"

"Baby, I've been looking forward to that trip as much as you have. I just didn't let myself think about it much until after I passed that state exam. I'm sorry to postpone it, but how can I turn this down? This is just the kind of break I've been hoping for since I started those classes."

Ed turned around, his face a study in incredulity. "What? Have you thought this through? You'd have to—no, *we'd* have to—move to Indy! Geez, is that stupid license burning that big a hole in your pocket?"

"Is that such a terrible thing, moving a hundred miles away?" Rick walked to the window to lay a hand on Ed's arm, but Ed moved away from him.

"I think it's pretty terrible considering all the people who depend on us to be here for them. What about my family? What about Claire and the kids? What about *Mrs. Penfield*? After all she's done for us, fixing up this apartment and counting on us to be here for her, you're gonna just say thanks and move out?"

Rick didn't seem to have an answer for that, so Ed went on, his voice getting louder.

"Didn't you consider that at all?"

"Well," Rick said, looking rather ashamed, "I guess I hadn't thought it through quite that far."

"I guess not. And what about my clients? My business? What the hell am I supposed to do in Indy while you're busy becoming a real estate tycoon? Keep house for you? For that matter," he went on sarcastically, "where would we live, with your parents?"

"Hardly," Rick snorted.

"I knew it," Ed shouted. "This is all about your parents, isn't it? You want so bad to prove them wrong you'll do anything to go into real estate, even tear apart our life here just to make a point."

"This isn't about them." Rick looked distinctly uncomfortable, though, robbing his words of any real impact.

"It goes back to that phone call on my birthday, doesn't it? I tried to get you to tell me what they said, and you wouldn't. You kept changing the subject. So what did they really say? You might as well tell me now."

"Oh, all right, I'll tell you if it's so goddamned important."

Rick began to pace back and forth through the living room and the kitchen. Jett, who'd obviously heard enough, stiffly climbed down from his chair and hobbled down the hall, no doubt en route to his hiding place under the bed.

"My parents, my wonderful parents, so badly want me to give up the idea of real estate as a career that they tried to bribe me. They said if I was so interested in a career in business they'd pay for me to go back to college and finish my degree, and if I didn't want the liberal arts degree I started all those years ago, I could switch to a business degree and prepare for what my dad called 'a less risky, stable job with an appropriately liberal company.' Can you believe that?"

"Well, yes," Ed said with a shrug. He could believe it. It sounded exactly like the kind of thing John would suggest.

"Oh, so I suppose you think it's a good idea, too!"

"I didn't say that. I just meant that I'm not surprised your dad said it."

"Yeah, but you do think it's a good idea, don't you?"

"Oh, for Christ's sake," Ed groaned. "I fell in love with a mailman. I love you just the way you are. You don't have to prove anything to me."

"So I'm supposed to deliver mail for the rest of my life to make you happy? Here I've been busting my ass to make a better life for us, and you don't really give a shit about it, do you?"

"Well, who asked you to?" Ed hollered. "Geez, all I wanted was for us to settle down and enjoy being married for a while, but oh, no, Mr. Big Plans had to keep pushing, pushing—had to make everything happen at once, made yourself exhausted from the studying and the worry. What did any of it have to do with me? Seems like from the very beginning it's all been about trying to piss off your parents. You wouldn't have even gotten this big idea about real estate if you hadn't been mad at them clear last spring."

"It is not about them," Rick hollered back. "It's about trying to make us independent so we don't have to worry about what people—*and* my parents— think about us. It's about having money and security so we can thumb our noses at people like Ruth Dorsey. Who held your fuckin' hand after she went off on you, huh? You spent that whole Cedar Point trip worrying about what she'd do, no matter how hard I tried to get you to stop worrying. You said yourself that day that you're happier when we're away from Porterfield. Maybe this job offer is the kick in the ass we need to realize we need to get out of this town and build a good life around people like us."

"'People like us.' Oh, that's just great, coming from you," Ed said in disgust. "Do you know how many times I've heard you rip apart all the gay men you knew in Indy? How *refreshing* it is for you to be away from that crap? Well, I got news for you, buddy. If you want to sell houses to those guys you always call a bunch of snotty queens and cockhounds, you're gonna have to put up with their shit, and plenty of it!"

Rick shrugged impatiently. "Yeah, well, nothing's perfect. I know that, and I thought you knew it, too."

"Yeah, I know it. I know something else, too. I'm not about to rip my life apart and move to Indy just so you can sweet talk a bunch of house-hunting faggots into making you money, *and* prove a point to your mommy and daddy. I have commitments and responsibilities here. Geez, after this I'll certainly never call you a responsibility freak again!"

Rick glared at him. "I thought I had a responsibility to us."

"Us? Where's the 'us' in all of this? You said this was the break *you'd* been waiting for."

"Yes, trying to hold up my end of the deal in making a better life for us. And what about you? I've talked myself blue in the face trying to encourage you to spend time in your workshop doing the things you really like to do. So what happens? You do one project and then stop the minute you find someone who can help you. You were too busy, you said. I wasn't too busy to hold down a full-time job and take those classes!"

"For your information," Ed said through clenched teeth, "I had every intention of spending this afternoon, my first free workday afternoon in weeks, at Clyde's. But no, I had to spend it taking your niece to the dentist because *you* were too busy planning *your* future!"

Rick opened his mouth, paused for a moment, and then closed it with a shake of his head. He walked to the hallway, his back to Ed, and leaned against the wall.

"Okay, okay," he said in a quieter tone of voice. "Whether I take this job or not, I was excited that someone, actually two real estate professionals, thought enough of me and my potential to offer me this opportunity. I thought you'd be excited about it, too."

"Well, I'm not, 'cause you didn't even stop to really think about me and everyone else, and—"

"Okay," Rick said gently, "I got carried away like I do, and—"

"I'll say," Ed shouted. "That's what you're famous for, huh? Getting carried away and leaving everyone else behind."

And then something seemed to snap in Ed, and he found himself practically screaming at Rick.

"Is that what you want? Do you want to put on that goddamned business suit and move to Indy and leave me the hell here? Well, go right ahead. I sure the fuck ain't goin' with you. I'm just the stupid handyman, the loser who watches dumb TV and doesn't need to set the world on fire. I don't have to fucking prove anything to anybody. I'm the one you just have to drag along, right? You make the decisions and then tell me what's right for me! Well, not anymore."

Rick looked shocked. "Baby, do you really think I—"

"And I'm not your baby! I'm a grown man who's capable of making his own decisions and running his own life. And I *thought* I was your husband.

Well, I guess the joke was on me."

Rick's face crumpled. He took a deep breath that turned into a shudder that racked his whole body. "I—I'm sorry, I—"

"You're sorry all right," Ed said, moving for the door.

He grabbed his jacket and turned to make one last comment before he stormed out, but the look on Rick's face stopped him. The absolute pain and bewilderment in Rick's expression twisted into Ed's heart like a knife. Ed stared in horror as one tear slid down Rick's cheek. Ed suddenly comprehended the things he had said and knew how deeply he had hurt the man he loved.

And realizing that, Ed felt tears of his own begin to form. He managed to fumble his way out of the door, slam it shut, and get all the way downstairs before he doubled over, his body heaving with sobs.

# Chapter Twenty-two

Ed reluctantly bit into the P & J cheeseburger. He managed to chew and swallow, then forced himself to take another bite. He was eating only because he knew he had to.

He was sitting in his truck, which was parked at the little picnic area on Stratton Creek where he had taken Josh one day back in July. It was kind of funny, now that he thought about it; he and Rick had been arguing then, too.

There were no stars visible through the heavy cloud cover, and a nippy breeze blew through the dry leaves of the oak trees surrounding the picnic area. Although Ed assumed very few people visited the little roadside rest during autumn evenings, he hoped the weather would keep away any possible nighttime hikers or dog walkers. He wanted to be alone with his thoughts.

Earlier that evening, when Ed had finished crying in a dark corner of the workshop, he fled to his truck. He drove aimlessly through the streets of Porterfield rehashing the fight, angry with Rick but much angrier with himself.

He drove past Gordy's apartment, but Gordy's car was gone. Sure enough, when he drove by his house he saw the Grand Prix in the driveway. The house appeared alien to him. The happy times with Rick within its walls seemed to have happened in another lifetime. He found himself smiling bitterly. He hoped Gordy and Doug were enjoying themselves, for if things did work out for them, surely the day would come when one or both of them would be as miserable as Ed was now.

He drove by his mother's house but didn't even think of stopping. He remembered all too well her words the day after he and Rick had made their commitment: *I want you to know, here and now, that when you're ready to walk out on him, don't think you can come running home to Mother. I'll just march you right back here, telling you to find a way to make it work. That's what my mother* did. *You've made a commitment to this, and I expect you to see it through.* Ed wasn't ready to go marching back to Rick. He needed to make sense of what had happened and, yes, figure out a way to make it work.

When he realized hunger was churning in his stomach along with the anxiety, anger, and regret, he swung by the P & J. Mindful of the truck's transmission, he didn't pull under the drive-in canopy but idled the truck in the takeout lane at the side of the building. He mumbled his order to the carhop, face averted, hoping she wouldn't notice how red and swollen his eyes were. Once he had his food, he drove to Stratton Creek.

Now, realizing he had eaten as much as he could, he jumped from the truck and threw the half-eaten cheeseburger and the untouched fries into a trash barrel. Back in the truck he sipped from the Pepsi he had bought earlier from a vending machine outside of the downtown Sunoco gas station.

Shivering a bit, he started the engine to get the heater going. The radio came on softly, and when he recognized the song he turned up the volume. Bobby Caldwell was singing about how some people went around the world and still never found the love they had dreamed about in "What You Won't Do for Love."

Ed had found his dream of love in Rick. However, as Norma had so recently pointed out, he'd been a little too busy dreaming to see the complete reality of the man he loved. Rick's ambitions were stronger than Ed's, and his ability to accept change was a good deal more flexible than Ed's as well.

As Bobby sang the chorus of the song, Ed puzzled over the lyrics and the idea of doing something you wouldn't do for love.

Well, if that were true for Ed, wouldn't he be willing to move to Indianapolis for Rick's career? He turned that question over in his mind. Yes, he cautiously admitted. He had said many times that he would be willing to leave Porterfield if it were the best thing for both of them. At this time, though, Ed wasn't sure it was the best thing. The thought of leaving Mrs. Penfield when she was counting on them so much brought about a feeling of guilt in Ed almost as bad as the guilt he felt over the terrible things he had said to Rick earlier.

When Ed relived the argument in his mind, he realized that Rick had begun to see for himself how difficult the move would be for those who depended upon them and was ready to discuss the matter sensibly. But Ed's anger had gotten the best of him, and any chance of a reasonable solution had been shattered by his hateful words.

"What You Won't Do for Love" faded out and was followed by a raucous old Motown stomper. Ed flipped the radio from AM to FM and paused, his hand on the volume knob, as haunting music he'd never heard before began to flow through the speakers. Eventually a familiar voice began to sing, and

Ed quickly identified the vocalist, Lou Gramm of Foreigner, who was singing "Waiting for a Girl Like You."

As Ed listened for the first time to what would become one of the most popular songs on the radio that fall, he thought back to the time when he had admitted to himself he wanted a man and not a woman to share his life. From that moment until a year earlier, he had waited for a man like Rick. Rick had been and still was his Dream Man. Ed was learning, though, that the reality of his flesh-and-blood dream come true was less than perfection.

Did he expect Rick to be perfect? *No, of course not,* he thought. But when he recalled the fantasies he had spun, first of some imaginary guy, then of Rick, he realized, wincing, that those fantasies had a way of being endlessly calm and peaceful, occasionally exciting, and always, always, included an argument-free happy ending.

He had been so taken with Rick, so amazed by their mutual love and desire, that he transferred his fantasies to their day-to-day life. Oh, for the most part it was great; Ed couldn't help but smile when he thought of the daily tender kisses, the Sunday breakfasts Rick cooked for him, and how comfortable so many of their evenings were, the two of them sprawled on the sofa, legs entwined, quietly reading or watching television.

But he was still irritated by that five a.m. alarm that startled him out of sleep almost every day. When Rick had a touch of hay fever in August, Ed had really noticed for the first time the loud way Rick blew his nose and his consistently noisy throat clearings. Rick, as Norma had pointed out months ago, occasionally could be bossy, usually asking or bluntly telling Ed to do things Ed had planned to do but hadn't gotten around to yet. Yep, he thought, the reality was that his Dream Man was a real guy with the same annoying faults and quirks everyone had, including Ed. He snorted, wondering what little things he did drove Rick right up the wall as well.

Ed realized he had learned to live with all of those things. This latest issue, though, was a bit harder to swallow. He now understood that he and Rick had different approaches to their future goals, and unless they found a middle ground—some kind of compromise—it could create trouble for them over and over again. Unless, of course, Ed decided Rick and their marriage weren't worth the bother. He could always go back to being alone, drifting through life entertained by his always-sunny fantasies.

He rubbed the ring on his left hand. No, he wasn't going to do that. He had made a commitment to Rick, to the man he loved, and his parents had taught him to honor his commitments and see them through. He was going to find a way to work this out with Rick; that is, if Rick wanted to as well.

Shame swept through Ed as he once again recalled the words he had unthinkingly hurled at Rick. *I'm not your baby,* he had screamed. He couldn't imagine anything worse he could have said to the man whose love and devotion had filled Ed's life with so much joy and happiness. *Baby* may have been a pretty common endearment, but the nickname was Rick's way of telling Ed, even in the most banal of conversations, how much he loved him.

*How do you apologize for something like that,* Ed wondered as the radio station went into a commercial break. He turned down the radio volume, thinking of the movie all the girls in high school had wept over, *Love Story*. "Love means never having to say you're sorry" had been the catchphrase from that movie, and now, as he did when he first heard it, Ed rolled his eyes.

"What bullshit," he mumbled.

He needed to tell Rick he was sorry, needed to know if there was some way Rick could forgive him. His fear, though, that Rick couldn't or wouldn't forgive him kept him motionless by the creek, listening to the radio and the wind blowing acorns into the truck bed.

Unwilling to go home but suddenly too restless to stay where he was, Ed put the truck in gear and was relieved when it obediently moved forward. He drove north, skirting the town limits and, on an impulse, turned west, then south.

He slowly entered the little cemetery west of Porterfield where some of his ancestors were buried. As he drove to the older section in the rear, he remembered the cold, windy autumn day he had first brought Rick here and the bitterly cold January night they had stood near the century-old graves, watching the stars and making decisions about their future.

He slipped the truck into neutral by the huge spreading pine tree and hopped out, walking to the spot where they had stood almost nine months earlier. There were no stars or moon on this night; the timeworn tombstones and the dead leaves skittering by them in the wind spoke only of the past, not a potentially bright future for two people in love.

Ed shuffled his work boots through the leaves, remembering that winter night and the words Rick had said.

*I guess I've always known my home would be wherever my heart is. Right now, and forever I think, it's with you.*

Did Ed feel the same way? Yes, he did. If he hadn't known it before, he did now, standing in the place where Rick had declared his desire to be with Ed for the rest of his life.

And the answer became clear at last. It had been a bad day for Ed. He had taken his stress and frustration out on the person he loved the most. Now he needed to apologize and go about seeing if he could make up for the awful words he had thrown at his husband. Then, with some calm, practical discussion, they could go about making a plan for their future that was agreeable to both of them. Because Ed knew, beyond any minor or major irritation Rick might cause him, his heart was with Rick, and therefore his home was, too.

He jumped back in the truck and drove toward Porterfield, anxiety replacing the calm he had achieved in the cemetery. Would Rick be ready to talk to him? Would he accept Ed's apology? The questions tumbled through Ed's mind as he entered the town and drove to the big old house on the corner of Spruce and Race streets.

Still mindful of his dead reverse gear, Ed parked the truck on Spruce Street. He ran along the side of the house and anxiously approached the carriage house. He stopped to peer inside the garage doors and gasped.

Rick's car was gone.

*Oh, no,* Ed thought, his stomach twisting into one more painful knot.

He stood there, his nose pressed against the window glass, wondering when and if he'd see his Dream Man again.

◆

"Ed? Ed! Wake up. What on earth are you doing here?"

Ed's eyes flew open, and his head thumped against the pillow on the parlor sofa in surprise as he recognized Mrs. Penfield's anxious face above him.

"Ohhhh," he moaned, sitting up, a quilt fashioned by Mrs. Penfield's late mother-in-law clinging to his sweatshirt and jeans. "What time is it?"

"It's just a little after seven. Ed, why in heaven's name were you sleeping in the front parlor? Surely you were not worried about me. I'm doing quite well these days."

The night before, Ed had remained near the garage doors for several hours, waiting for Rick to come home. When the cool breeze reduced him to shivering inside his jean jacket, he had given up, assuming Rick would not return. Unable to face the carriage-house apartment or their bed alone, he had snuck into the main house and collapsed in the parlor. After tossing and turning for many hours, he had finally fallen into a troubled sleep.

"Well," he now mumbled to Mrs. Penfield, "Rick and I had a fight, and I ended up here."

"Oh, dear." Mrs. Penfield sighed, her gaze steady upon the sight of her rumpled and careworn young friend.

"Well, come along to the kitchen with me. You might as well tell me what happened."

Ed followed her to the back of the house, and while she made coffee for herself and tea for Ed, he recounted the whole ugly scene from the past evening and his moment of reckoning in the cemetery.

"So when I got home last night, he was gone," he said as he sipped his tea.

Mrs. Penfield nodded. "I see. Well, he was certainly home this morning. I heard him get into his car and leave for work as usual around six. I had a rather restless night myself," she said with a knowing grin. "Perhaps I was somehow aware of the discord on the property."

Ed's heart lifted a bit. "He was here? Really?"

Mrs. Penfield nodded again. "So you see, Ed, your responsibility freak is still quite responsible."

"Well, there's hope, then."

"Of course there is hope," she said gently but adamantly. "All couples have arguments, and most of them are easily resolved."

"But the awful things I said . . ."

Mrs. Penfield set her coffee cup aside to lay a hand on Ed's. "Ed, that's simply human nature. I don't claim to understand it, but I know it's true. When George Junior was reported as killed in action, George and I exchanged many terrible words. In our mutual and individual grief, we lashed out at each other on several occasions. Why, I remember one scene so terrible that George stormed from the house, as you did last evening, and spent the night in his office downtown."

Ed remembered making up with Rick after their argument that hot day in July. At that time he had asked Rick why people in love hurt each other. He asked Mrs. Penfield the same question now.

"I don't have a confident answer for that, Ed," she responded. "I do suspect, though, that perhaps we take our negative emotions out on those closest to us because we know they will eventually forgive us. It seems to be a part of the commitment of love we share with our spouses, families, and friends. By declaring our love, we seem to say, I'll accept you even at your worst, and you can rid yourself of your anger with me, because my love allows me to understand and forgive."

"But what if you push someone too far? What if you cross a line and say or do something unforgivable?"

"Well, I suppose that is why we have divorce courts," Mrs. Penfield sighed. "Again, Ed, I don't claim to have all the answers. A good teacher would never make such a claim. All I can do is share my experience and acquired wisdom with you and do my best to point you to where you may find your answers. In this case, I believe both Rick and your future with him will eventually provide that knowledge."

"If I have a future with him," he muttered.

"Of course you do," she said confidently. "This is merely the first time you and Rick have come to loggerheads over a serious issue. I have the utmost faith that you will work it out and hopefully acquire some wisdom of your own for the next time it happens."

"Oh," Ed groaned. "I don't want to think about a next time."

"Nor should you at the moment."

Mrs. Penfield frowned and looked away, apparently lost in thought. "Ed," she finally said, "do you remember that little sermon I gave you last fall about strength and adversity?"

"Of course. You gave it to Rick, too, and we're always referring to it."

She smiled. "Well, I'm glad to see my words had such an impact on the two of you. I suspect, though, that you both use it more in reference to the possible disapproval you might face from the narrow-minded, but as I recall, I meant much more than that."

Mrs. Penfield poured more coffee for herself as she continued. "I seem to recall telling you that adversity tests our love for one another the most. It's true. It's quite easy to love in the good times, but it's the bad times that prove our love for one another. George and I discovered that after George Junior's death. Since you and Rick care deeply for each other, I believe this current test of your love will only bring you closer together, as happened for George and me. Being strong enough to apologize and accept responsibility for your actions will make you an even stronger man, Ed. The same holds true for Rick. Therefore, the strength you acquire now will help you achieve an even greater strength for the next adverse situation, whether it be the disapproval of one of Porterfield's citizens or merely another disagreement between Rick and yourself.

"Your love has been tested, and mightily so," she gently concluded. "But this is one exam I know you will both pass."

As always, Ed was comforted by her words. His smile of gratitude was the only thanks he needed to express.

Mrs. Penfield rose from the table. She patted Ed on the shoulder and said, "Now, keep your resolutions close to you throughout the day. I've no doubt Rick will return this evening as usual, and by then you will be ready to repair this situation, as you are always ready to repair with your handyman skills the things in need of fixing."

Ed grinned, thinking of James Taylor's song "Handy Man." James claimed he could fix broken hearts in that song. Ed didn't know if his own handyman skills were quite that advanced, but he now knew he had the confidence to try.

He returned to the carriage house. Once inside, he cautiously looked around for any evidence that Rick planned to leave on a more permanent basis. The kitchen was in order, and he noticed that Jett had been fed. The 45 of "Don't Give It Up" he had bought the day before had been placed on the stereo. Ed sighed, thinking of Robbie Patton's vocal plea to his girlfriend to take another chance on their relationship. He hoped Rick was as ready as he was to do just that.

In the bedroom he saw the bed was neatly made, and a tentative glance into Rick's side of the closet revealed his luggage in its usual place. He shrugged. Apparently there was nothing to do now but wait.

So he made a breakfast he was actually hungry for, went through his usual morning routine in the bathroom, and avoiding the truck with the faulty transmission, walked to Mrs. Ilinski's house, where he spent the day cleaning her carpets with a rug shampooer she had rented from the hardware store.

He was on his way home by four o'clock. The heavy clouds from the night before had broken up somewhat, and occasional shafts of sunlight highlighted the brilliant colors beginning to appear in the trees. He nostalgically thought back a year in time to the day he was raking leaves in his yard, waiting anxiously to see the new mailman. He was just as anxious to see him today and could only hope the feeling was mutual.

Once home, he settled on the sofa to mentally prepare what he wanted to say to Rick. Jett climbed onto the sofa next to him and, with his purring machine at full blast, commenced to wash his face. Jett, it seemed, had forgiven him, giving Ed hope that Rick would do the same.

As the clock moved past five, Ed's confidence began to waver and the nervousness he had been able to keep at bay most of the day returned. On an impulse he ran down the hall and began to dig through the bottom drawer of the chest he shared with Rick. He pulled out the Wexler's jewelry box he had hidden there three months earlier. He had held off giving Rick the gold chain he had purchased that muggy day in July until the time was right. Suddenly Ed knew the time had come.

Ed's nervousness increased when he heard Rick's car enter the driveway. He hid the jewelry box in the record cabinet, slid the door closed, and returned to the sofa as he heard Rick's steps on the stairs. The door slowly opened, and Rick hesitantly entered the apartment.

Ed looked at Rick, really looked at his tall Dream Man. He saw the postal uniform perfectly fitting his broad shoulders, noticed the neatly trimmed, dark brown beard he loved to caress, and most important he looked into the deep brown eyes that had shone with love for Ed for so long. With just one look Ed could tell that love was still there.

Rick blinked when he saw Ed on the sofa. "Hi," he said.

"Hi." Ed stood up. "Your baby is sure glad you're home."

Rick blinked again. A shaky version of his warm and tender special came to his face as he began to laugh, then cry.

Ed walked across the room and took Rick in his arms. Rick began to cry harder but managed to choke out, "Oh, baby, I'm so sorry."

As tears came to his own eyes, Ed forgot the speech he had prepared. "Darlin', I'm sorry, too. So sorry. Can you ever forgive me?"

"Yeah, I forgive you," Rick whispered as he clung tightly to Ed. "Do you forgive me?"

"Yes."

Apparently no more needed to be said. They stood, holding each other close, until the tears ceased for both of them. Then with one brief look between them, a gentle kiss seemed to seal the deal.

They settled on the sofa next to Jett, who began once again to purr in earnest.

"I think he's glad his dads have stopped yelling at each other," Ed remarked.

Rick chuckled. "Yeah? Well, me, too. Baby, I know we have a lot to talk about, but most importantly, I need you to know how much I love you . . . still love you."

"I love you, too." Ed sighed with relief. "So where were you last night? I ended up on the couch in the front parlor."

Rick shook his head, still chuckling. "I ended up on the couch at Claire's. I just couldn't face sleeping in that bed without you. I snuck into her house and out again this morning before the kids even knew I was there. I saw the truck parked out front when I came home this morning. I can't tell you how relieved I was to see it. How's the transmission? I was so full of my stupid-ass self last night I never even asked what's wrong with it."

"The reverse gear is shot. I drove around and around last night, making sure I never had to go in reverse, worrying the whole damned thing would crap out and leave me stranded somewhere. I was afraid to come home, though. I couldn't until I knew I had the courage to face you and apologize for the things I said."

"Apology accepted," Rick said softly. "Even as hurt as I was, I think I knew you didn't really mean any of it. As for the truck, well, if it'll still run for a few more days, how 'bout we drop it off at Wagner's on our way to Michigan so they can fix it while we're gone?"

Ed looked closely at Rick. "You really want to go?"

Rick nodded. "Very much. I called Walt Granger when I was at Claire's this afternoon watching the kids. I told him I was unavailable this weekend but that after *we* had talked it over, maybe *we* could come down in a week or so and meet with him."

"I'd like that, darlin'."

"Really?"

"Really. I went to the cemetery last night. Remember the stuff we talked about there last winter? Well, what you said goes for me. My home and my heart are with you, and whether we're in Porterfield or Indy, I don't care, as long as we're together."

Rick pulled Ed close to him for a wonderfully tight squeeze. "Whatever you say. After you left last night I really thought about it, and I realized how right you were, how awful it would be for us to leave Mrs. Penfield after she's been so good to us. Thing is, I think she above anyone else would understand, but I don't know if I could go through with it."

"I know, but you're right, too. She would understand, and maybe there's some way we could work it out. I don't know. We really do need to talk about it, but then we've got that long car ride to Mackinac and back for that, right?"

"Right. I don't know if moving away would be a good thing. At the moment I was offered the job it seemed like the perfect solution, and as you saw last night I lost my head and my good sense about the whole thing, but now I'm not so sure. We'll both think about it, then discuss it like rational married people, okay?"

Ed giggled. "Okay."

Rick sighed deeply. "Oh, baby, I am so beat. I hardly slept at all. Do you realize last night was the first night we've spent apart since we were married?"

"I know. I barely slept, too. Hopefully we'll sleep tonight. I sure feel a lot better."

"Me, too. And just think, in three days we leave for that wonderful vacation you planned for us. I'm really looking forward to sharing that with you, and celebrating our anniversary."

"Yeah. It was almost a year ago that I got Glen to send that certified letter so you'd have to talk to me, remember?"

Rick's warm and tender special was glowing. "Oh, boy, do I remember. It's been one hell of a year, hasn't it?"

"Hell yes, as Gordy would say. But we're together, darlin'. Still. That's the best part."

"It sure is." Rick kissed Ed, and Ed could feel in Rick's kiss the promise of many more years to come.

"Oh," Ed exclaimed, pulling away from Rick. "I almost forgot."

He got up and went to the record cabinet. He retrieved the box he had hidden, and with a smile, held it out to Rick.

Rick looked bewildered. "What's this?"

"A little something I picked up for you. Actually, I got it right after our Cedar Point trip, and I was going to give it to you in Michigan, but I decided I didn't want to wait."

Rick opened the box and gasped. "Oh, baby," he whispered, gingerly lifting the gold chain. "It's beautiful. I never . . . well, when I said I'd like something like this . . . still, I thought maybe on our tenth anniversary or something . . . damn!"

Ed grinned, enjoying Rick's stumble to find the right words. "You told me to buy it when I knew the time was right. So I did. For some reason it wasn't the right time to give it to you, though. I've thought about it a lot, and almost gave it to you lots of times, but I know now what I was waiting for."

Rick, still admiring the chain, looked up. "What was that?"

"Well, when I was at the cemetery last night I realized that the most important thing in my life was you, and the commitment we made to each other."

Ed took the chain from Rick and laid it across the ring on his left hand. He then placed Rick's hand on top of his own.

"See, darlin', you gave me this ring as a symbol of your commitment to me, and after last night I knew I wanted you to know just how committed I am to you. Laurie told me once that people just say those wedding vows and hope for the best. Maybe she's right, but I want you to know, right now, how much I mean them, and when you're wearing this chain you'll remember how much I mean them."

Rick shook his head, smiling. "I am not going to cry again," he murmured.

"Nah, don't cry, darlin'. I think we've cried enough already. How 'bout I just put the chain around your neck?"

"Okay."

Rick turned his back to Ed, and Ed carefully laid the chain against Rick's skin, fumbling a bit with the clasp. Once it was secure, he took Rick's hand and led him to the bedroom so Rick could see it in the mirror.

Rick's warm and tender special was at full glow as he saw the chain sparkling at his throat. "Thank you," he said simply.

"You're welcome."

"You're something else, you know that, baby?"

"Yeah? You are too, darlin'."

Rick pulled Ed to the bed, where they collapsed in a heap with their arms around each other. As Rick nestled his head into Ed's neck, Ed let out a long sigh of both relief and contentment. The reality of his marriage to his Dream Man wasn't anything like the pretty fantasies he had spun when he had been alone, but it was okay. No, it was better than that. Even in the bad times they had already experienced, and thinking about the bad times that might be ahead of them, Ed realized the opportunity to share his life with Rick Benton was the best thing that had ever happened to him. And for that he was truly grateful.

Annette Owens Photography

## About the Author

Nick Poff, a native Hoosier, currently lives in Fort Wayne, Indiana. In addition to writing, he also works in the radio industry and admits to beginning that career in the days when disc jockeys actually spun records. *The Handyman's Reality* is his second novel. For more information on this book, the music included in the story, and his first novel, *The Handyman's Dream*, visit www.nickpoff.com and www.writermen.com.